We Begin at the End

We Begin at the End

Chris Whitaker

Henry Holt and Company
New York

Henry Holt and Company
Publishers since 1866
120 Broadway
New York, New York 10271
www.henryholt.com

Henry Holt® and 🄷® are registered trademarks of Macmillan Publishing
Group, LLC.

Originally published in the United Kingdom in 2020 by Zaffre,
an imprint of Bonnier Books UK.

Library of Congress Cataloging-in-Publication Data

Names: Whitaker, Chris, author.
Title: We begin at the end / Chris Whitaker.
Description: First U.S. Edition. | New York : Henry Holt and Company, 2021.
Identifiers: LCCN 2020010399 (print) | LCCN 2020010400 (ebook) |
ISBN 9781250759665 (hardcover) | ISBN 9781250759672 (ebook) |
ISBN 9781250793768 (Canadian edition)
Subjects: GSAFD: Suspense fiction.
Classification: LCC PR6123.H556 W4 2021 (print) |
LCC PR6123.H556 (ebook) | DDC 823/.92—dc23
LC record available at https://lccn.loc.gov/2020010399
LC ebook record available at https://lccn.loc.gov/2020010400

Our books may be purchased in bulk for promotional, educational, or business
use. Please contact your local bookseller or the Macmillan Corporate and
Premium Sales Department at (800) 221-7945, extension 5442, or by e-mail at
MacmillanSpecialMarkets@macmillan.com.

First U.S. Edition 2021

Designed by Meryl Sussman Levavi

Printed in the United States of America

1 3 5 7 9 10 8 6 4 2

For my own little outlaw

We Begin at the End

You see something and you raise your hand.

Doesn't matter if it's a cigarette paper or a soda can.

You see something and you raise your hand.

Don't touch it, neither.

Just raise your hand.

The townspeople readied, their feet in the ford. Movement in line, twenty paces between, a hundred eyes down, but still, they held together, the choreography of the damned.

Behind, the town emptied, the echo of a long, pristine summer had been smothered by the news.

She was Sissy Radley. Seven years old. Blond hair. Known to most, Chief Dubois did not need to hand out photographs.

Walk held the farthest side. Fifteen and fearless, his knees shook with each step.

They marched the woodland like an army, cops led, flashlights swept, through the trees was the ocean, a long way down but the girl could not swim.

Beside Walk was Martha May. They had dated three months, confined to first base, her father was minister at Little Brook Episcopal.

She glanced over. "Still want to be a cop?"

Walk stared at Dubois, head down, last hope on his shoulders.

"I saw Star," Martha said. "At the front with her father. She was crying."

Star Radley, the missing girl's sister. Martha's best friend. They were a tight group. Only one was absent.

"Where's Vincent?" she asked.

"He might be on the other side."

Walk and Vincent were close like brothers. At nine they'd cut palms, pressed them together, and sworn oaths of classless loyalty.

They said nothing more, just watched the ground, past Sunset Road, past the wishing tree, Chuck Taylors parting leaves. Walk focused so hard but still, he almost missed it.

Ten steps from Cabrillo, State Route 1, six hundred miles of California coast. He stopped dead, then looked up and saw the line move on without him.

He crouched.

The shoe was small. Red and white leather. Gold-tone buckle.

A car on the highway slowed as it came, headlights traced the curve till they found him.

And then he saw her.

He took a breath and raised his hand.

PART ONE

•

The Outlaw

1

W alk stood at the edge of a feverish crowd, some he'd known
     since his birth, some since theirs.

Vacationers with cameras, sunburn and easy smiles, not knowing the
water was stripping more than timber.

Local news set up, a reporter from KCNR. "Can we get a word, Chief
Walker?"

He smiled, shoved his hands deep in his pockets, and looked to thread
his way through when the people gasped.

Fragmented noise as the roof caved and crashed to the water below.
Piece by piece, the foundation lay crude and skeletal, like the home was
no more than a house. It had been the Fairlawn place since Walk could
remember, a half acre from the ocean when he was a kid. Taped off a
year back, the cliff was eroding, now and then the people from California
Wild came and measured and estimated.

The stir of cameras and indecent excitement as slates rained and the
front porch clung. Milton, the butcher, dropped to one knee and fired off
a money shot as the flagpole leaned and the banner hung in the breeze.

The younger Tallow boy got too close. His mother pulled his collar
so hard he tumbled back onto his ass.

Behind, the sun fell with the building, dissecting the water with cuts of orange and purple and shades without name. The reporter got her piece, seeing off a patch of history so slight it barely counted.

Walk glanced around and saw Dickie Darke, who looked on, impassive. He stood like a giant, close to seven feet tall. A man into real estate, he owned several houses in Cape Haven and a club on Cabrillo, the kind of den where iniquity cost ten bucks and a small chunk of virtue.

They stood another hour, Walk's legs tired as the porch finally gave up. Onlookers resisted the urge to applaud, then turned and made their way back, to barbeque and beer and firepits that waved flame light on Walk's evening patrol. They drifted across flagstone, a line of gray wall, dry laid but holding strong. Behind was the wishing tree, a major oak so wide splints held its limbs. The old Cape Haven did all it could to remain.

Walk had once climbed that tree with Vincent King, in a time so far from now it would barely count. He rested a shaking hand on his gun, the other on his belt. He wore a tie, his collar stiff, his shoes shined. His acceptance of place was admired by some, pitied by others. Walker, captain of a ship that did not ever leave port.

He caught sight of the girl, moving against the crowd, her brother's hand in hers as he struggled to match her pace.

Duchess and Robin, the Radley children.

He met them at a half run because he knew all there was to know about them.

The boy was five and cried silent tears, the girl had just turned thirteen and did not ever cry.

"Your mother," he said, not a question but a statement of such tragic fact the girl did not even nod, just turned and led.

They moved through dusk streets, the lull of picket fences and fairy lights. Above the moon rose, guided and mocked, as it had for thirty years. Past grand houses, glass and steel that fought nature, a vista of such terrible beauty.

Down Genesee, where Walk still lived in his parents' old house. Onto Ivy Ranch Road, where the Radley home came into view. Peeling shutters, an upturned bike, the wheel lying beside. In Cape Haven a shade beneath perfect might as well have been black.

Walk broke from the children and ran up the path, no lights from inside but the flutter of television. Behind, he saw Robin still crying and Duchess still looking on, hard and unforgiving.

He found Star on the couch, a bottle beside, no pills this time, one shoe on and the other foot bare, small toes, painted nails.

"Star." He knelt and patted her cheek. "Star, wake up now." He spoke calmly because the children were at the door, Duchess, an arm on her brother as he leaned so heavy into her, like he no longer held bones in his small body.

He told the girl to dial 911.

"I already have."

He thumbed open Star's eyes and saw nothing but white.

"Will she be alright?" The boy's voice.

Walk glanced over, hoping for sirens, squinting at fired sky.

"Could you go look out for them?"

Duchess read him and took Robin outside.

Star shook then, puked a little and shook, like God or Death had hold of her soul and was wrenching it free. Walk had given it time, three decades had passed since Sissy Radley and Vincent King but still Star slurred about eternalism, the past and the present colliding, the force spinning the future off, never to be righted.

Duchess would ride with her mother. Walk would bring Robin.

She looked on as the medic worked. He did not try a smile and for that she was grateful. He was balding and sweating and maybe tiring of saving those so determined to die.

For a while they stayed in front of the house, the door open to Walk, there like always, his hand on Robin's shoulder. Robin needed that, the comfort of an adult, the perception of safety.

Across the street drapes moved as shadows passed silent judgment. And then, at the end of the road, she saw kids from her school, pedaling hard, faces red. News moved so fast in a town where zoning often made front pages.

The two boys stopped near the cruiser and let their bikes fall. The taller, breathless, a sweep of hair plastered down as he walked slow toward the ambulance.

"Is she dead?"

Duchess lifted her chin, met his eye and held it. "Fuck off."

The engine rumbled as the door swung closed. Smoked glass made matte of the world.

Cars snaked the turns till they tipped from the hill, the Pacific behind, rocks broke the surface like heads of the drowning.

She watched her street till the end, till trees reached over and met on Pensacola, branches like hands, linked in prayer for the girl and her brother, and the unfurling tragedy that had begun long before either was born.

Night met others just like it, each swallowing Duchess so totally she knew she would not see day again, not the way other kids saw it. The hospital was Vancour Hill and Duchess knew it too well. When they took her mother, she stood on the polished floor, light mirrored up, her eye on the door as Walk brought Robin inside. She walked over and took her brother's hand, then led him toward the elevator where she rode to the second floor. The family room, lights dimmed, she pushed two chairs together. Across was a supply room, and Duchess helped herself to soft blankets and then made the chairs into a cot. Robin stood awkward, the tired dragging him, haunting dark circled his eyes.

"You need to pee?"

A nod.

She led him into the bathroom, waited a few minutes then saw he washed his hands well. She found toothpaste, squeezed a little onto her finger and ran it around his teeth and gums. He spit, she dabbed his mouth.

She helped him out of his shoes and over the arms of the chairs, where he settled like a kind of small animal as she covered him over.

His eyes peered out. "Don't leave me."

"Never."

"Will Mom be okay?"

"Yes."

She cut the television, the room dark, emergency lighting left them in red, soft enough that he slept by the time she reached the door.

She stood in clinical light, her back to the door; she would not let anyone inside, there was another family room on three. An hour and Walk appeared again and yawned like there was cause. Duchess knew of his days, he drove Cabrillo Highway, those perfect miles from Cape Haven to beyond, each blink a still of such paradise people crossed the country to find them, buy their homes and leave them empty ten months of the year.

"Is he asleep?"

She nodded once.

"I went to check on your mother, she'll be alright."

She nodded again.

"You can go and grab something, a soda, there's a machine next to—"

"I know."

A look back into the room saw her brother sleeping soundly, he would not move until she stirred him.

Walk held out a dollar bill, she took it reluctantly.

She walked the corridors, bought the soda and didn't drink it. She would keep it for Robin when he woke. She saw into cubicles, sounds of birth and tears and life. She saw shells of people, so empty she knew they would not recover. Cops led bad men with tattooed arms and bloodied faces. She smelled the drunks, the bleach, the vomit and shit.

She passed a nurse, a smile because most of them had seen her before, just one of those kids dealt a losing hand.

When she returned she found Walk had set two chairs by the door. She checked on her brother then sat.

Walk offered her gum and she shook her head.

She could tell that he wanted to talk, to bullshit about change, a slick on the long road, how it would all be different.

"You didn't call."

He watched her.

"Social. You didn't call."

"I should." He said it sad, like he was letting down her or the badge, she did not know which.

"But you won't."

"I won't."

He had a stomach that strained his tan shirt. The chubby, reddened cheeks of a boy whose indulgent parents never told him no. And a face so open she could not imagine he carried a single secret. Star said he was all good, like that was a thing.

"You should get some sleep."

They sat like that till stars leaned to first light, the moon forgot its place and held like a smear on new day, a reminder of what had gone. Opposite was a window. Duchess stood at the glass and pressed her head to the trees and the falling wild. Birdsong. A long way and she saw water, specks that were trawlers crawling the waves.

Walk cleared his throat. "Your mother . . . was there a man—"

"There's always a man. Whenever anything fucked up happens in the world, there's always a man."

"Darke?"

She held straight.

"You can't tell me?" he asked.

"I'm an outlaw."

"Right."

She wore a bow in her hair and fussed with it often. She was too thin, too pale, too beautiful like her mother.

"There's a baby just been born down there." Walk changed it up.

"What did they call it?"

"I don't know."

"Fifty bucks says it's not Duchess."

He laughed gently. "Exotic by rarity. You know you were going to be Emily."

"Sore must be the storm."

"Right."

"She still reads that one to Robin." Duchess sat, crossed her leg, rubbed the muscle, her sneaker loose and worn. "Is this my storm, Walk?"

He sipped coffee, like he was searching for an answer to an impossible question. "I like Duchess."

"You try it awhile. If I was a boy I might've been Sue." She lay her head back and watched the strips blink. "She wants to die."

"She doesn't. You mustn't think that."

"I can't decide if suicide is the most selfish or selfless act."

At six a nurse led her.

Star lay, a shadow of a person, even less of a mother.

"The Duchess of Cape Haven." Star, her smile there but weak. "It's alright."

Duchess watched her, then Star cried and Duchess crossed the room, pressed her cheek to her mother's chest and wondered how her heart still beat.

Together they lay in amid the dawn, a fresh day but no light of promise because Duchess knew promise was a falsity.

"I love you. I'm sorry."

There was much Duchess could say, but for the moment she could find nothing more than "I love you. I know."

2

At the crest of the hill the land fell away.

Sun climbed cerulean sky as Duchess, riding in the back with her brother beside, took his small hand in hers.

Walk eased the cruiser down their street, pulled up out front of the old house, then followed them in. He tried to fix breakfast but found the cupboards so bare he left them and ran to Rosie's Diner, then returned with pancakes and smiled as Robin ate three.

After she'd washed Robin's face and laid out his clothes, Duchess went out front and found Walk sitting on the step. She watched the Cape begin its modest wake, the mailman passed, Brandon Rock from the house beside came out and hosed down his lawn. That they did not give a second look to the cruiser parked outside the Radley home made Duchess sad and glad.

"Can I give you a ride in?"

"No." She settled beside him and tied her lace.

"I can collect your mom."

"She said she'd call Darke."

Duchess did not know the true nature of her mother's friendship with Chief Walker, though she guessed he wanted to fuck her, like the other men in town.

She looked out at their tired yard. The last summer she'd set about planting with her mother. Robin had brought a small watering can and softened the dirt, his cheeks colored as he made trip after trip. Blue-eyes, Indian mallow, and mountain lilac.

They died of neglect.

"Did she say what it was?" Walk said it gently. "Last night, you know why?"

It was the kind of cruel question she was not used to from him, because, mostly, there wasn't any kind of reason. But this time she knew why he asked, she knew about Vincent King, about her aunt Sissy who was buried in the cemetery by the edge of the bluff. Everyone knew her grave, behind the sun-bleached picket, with the babies that hadn't made it, the children cut down by the same god their parents prayed to.

"She didn't say nothing."

Behind they heard Robin. Duchess stood and fixed his hair, wiped toothpaste from his cheek with her spit, and then checked his schoolbag, that he had his reading book and journal, his water bottle.

She slid the straps over his shoulders, and he smiled and she smiled back.

They stood side by side and watched the cruiser pare the long street, and then Duchess slipped an arm around her brother and they began to walk.

The neighbor cut the hose and walked over to the edge of his yard, slight limp he tried hard to correct. Brandon Rock. Broad, tan. A stud in one ear, feathered hair, silk robe. Sometimes he benched with the garage door up and metal blaring out.

"Your mother again? Someone should call social services." Voice like his nose had been broken but never fixed. He carried a dumbbell in one hand and curled it now and then. His right arm noticeably bigger than the left.

Duchess turned to him.

Breeze blew. His robe parted.

She wrinkled her nose. "Flashing a kid. I should call the cops."

Brandon stared as Robin led her away.

"Did you see Walk's hands shaking?" Robin said.

"Always worse in the morning."

"Why?"

She shrugged but knew. Walk and her mother, their shared troubles and the way they dealt with them.

"Did Mom say anything, last night, when I was in my room?" She'd been doing her homework, her project on her family tree, when Robin hammered at the door and said Mom was sick again.

"She had her photos out. The old ones, with Sissy and Grandpa." Robin had taken to the idea of having a grandpa the first time he'd seen the tall man in their mother's photographs. That he'd never met him, that Star said next to nothing about him, did not seem to matter. Robin needed people, the cushion of barren names that would keep him from feeling so vulnerable. He longed for cousins and uncles and Sunday football and barbeque, like the other kids in his class.

"Do you know about Vincent King?"

Duchess took his hand as they crossed onto Fisher. "Why, what do you know about him?"

"That he killed Aunt Sissy. Thirty years ago. In the seventies, when men had mustaches and Mom wore her hair funny."

"Sissy wasn't our aunt, not really."

"She was," he said, simply. "She looked like you and Mom. The same."

Duchess had got the bones of the story over the years, from Star when she slurred it, from the archives at the library in Salinas. The same library where she'd spent the past spring working on their family tree. She'd traced Radley roots back far, then dropped the book to the floor when she'd made the link to a wanted outlaw named Billy Blue Radley. It was the kind of find she'd been proud of, something more when she stood up front and presented to the class. There was still a whole load of nothing on her father's side, just the kind of question mark that drew an angry exchange with her mother. Not once but twice Star had been with a stranger, got herself pregnant, left two children with a lifetime of wondering just whose blood pumped their veins. *Slut*, she'd whispered beneath her breath. It saw her grounded for a month.

"You know he's coming out of prison today?" Robin kept his tone hushed like it was a grave secret.

"Who told you that?"

"Ricky Tallow."

Ricky Tallow's mother worked dispatch at Cape Haven PD.

"What else did Ricky say?"

Robin looked away.

"Robin?"

He folded quick. "That he should've fried for it. But then Miss Dolores yelled at him."

"Should've fried. You know what that means?"

"No."

Duchess took his hand crossing onto Virginia Avenue, the lots a little bigger. The town of Cape Haven tumbled its way toward the water, land value inverse to the hills; Duchess knew her place, their home on the farthest street from the ocean.

They fell in with a group of kids. Duchess heard talk about the Angels and the draft.

When they got to the gate she fussed with his hair once more and made sure his shirt was buttoned right.

Kindergarten stood beside Hilltop Middle. Duchess would spend her break at the fence, looking over at her brother. He'd wave and smile, and she'd eat her sandwich and watch him.

"You be good."

"Yeah."

"Don't say nothing about Mom."

She hugged him, kissed his cheek, and sent him in, watching till Miss Dolores took over. Then she moved on, the sidewalk thick with kids.

Duchess kept her head down as she passed the steps where a group gathered, Nate Dorman and his friends.

Nate, collar flicked up, sleeves rolled over skinny biceps. "Heard your mom got fucked up again."

Laughter chorused.

She squared to him straight off.

He stared back. "What?"

She met his eye.

"I am the outlaw, Duchess Day Radley, and you are the coward, Nate Dorman."

"You're crazy."

She took a step forward and watched him swallow.

"Talk about my family again and I'll behead you, motherfucker."

He tried a laugh but didn't quite manage it. There were rumors about her; despite the pretty face and slight frame, she could turn, lose it so bad not even his friends would step in.

She pushed past, heard him exhale heavily as she walked on, into school, eyes burning from another tortured night.

3

The eroding cliffs ran a twisting mile before the road swept the bay and vanished into the tall oaks of Clearwater Cove. Walk followed the line, never edging past thirty.

He'd left Duchess and Robin then driven to the King house, bagged leaves from the path and picked litter from the yard. He'd tended it weekly for thirty years, part of his staid routine.

At the station he checked in with Leah Tallow on the front desk, just the two of them, Walk on call every day of his life. From the window he watched seasons change and vacationers come and go. Picnic baskets were left. Wine and cheese and chocolate that saw him punch another hole in his belt each year.

They had an auxiliary, Valeria, she came in when they needed her, parades, shows, or times when she was just plain bored of tending to her yard.

"You all set for today, return of the King?"

"I've been ready thirty years." He tried to keep his smile in check. "I'm heading out, I'll pick up pastries on the way back."

He strolled up Main, same every morning, the practiced walk, the cop stride he'd seen on TV. He'd tried a mustache, like Magnum, made notes when watching *Forensic Files*, and once even bought a beige rain-coat. If a real case ever came in, he'd be ready.

Flags hung from streetlamps, shiny SUVs parked nose to tail, and green awnings cast shade over a spotless sidewalk. He saw the Pattersons' Mercedes double-parked, wouldn't write it up, maybe just offer a friendly warning when he next saw Curtis. He quickened by the butcher's, but Milton came out fast, then stood on the stoop, whites splashed red, a cloth in his hand like he could rid the stains from his palms.

"Morning, Walk." Milton was hairy. Thick swirls sprouted from every inch of him, the kind of man who had to shave to his eyeline three times a day in case a passing zookeeper shot him with a tranquilizer dart.

Strung deer in the window, so fresh a day back it had been roaming the Mendocino. Milton hunted, during the season he'd close up and don his deerstalker, load the Comanche with rifles and sheets and a cooler of beer. Walk had gone with him one time, couldn't find an excuse that lasted long enough.

"Did you talk to Brandon Rock yet?" Milton spit the name, every word labored, like he'd run clean out of breath during a decent conversation.

"On my list."

Brandon Rock had a Mustang that misfired so bad half the street called it in the first time it happened. It was becoming a nuisance.

"I heard about her. Star. Again." Milton dabbed sweat from his head with the bloody cloth. Rumor had it he ate nothing but meat, and it was taking a toll.

"She's alright. Sick, this time she was just sick."

"I saw it all. Damn shame . . . with those children." Milton lived directly across from Star. He took the kind of interest in her and the kids that spoke more of a lonely life than the dwindling Neighborhood Watch group the man commanded.

"You always see it all, Milton. Maybe you should've been a cop."

Milton waved a hand. "I got enough on with the Watch. Ten fifty-one the other night."

"Wrecker needed."

Milton used police codes liberally, and badly.

"She's lucky she's got you looking out for her." Milton pulled a toothpick from his pocket and got to work on a piece of flesh lodged between his two front teeth. "I was thinking of Vincent King. Is it today? People said it's today."

"It is." Walk bent, picked up a soda can and dropped it into the trash, the sun warm on his neck.

Milton whistled. "Thirty years, Walk."

It would've been ten, worst case ten, but for a fight inside. Walk didn't ever get the full report, just knew his childhood friend had two deaths on his hands. Ten years became thirty, manslaughter became murder, a boy became a man.

"I still think about that day. Us walking the woodland. So, he is coming back to the Cape?"

"Far as I know."

"You can send him here, if he needs anything. Actually, tell you what, Walk. How about I put a couple trotters aside for him. How does that sound?"

Walk searched for the words.

"So." Milton cleared his throat and looked down at the ground. "The sky tonight . . . supermoon. It'll be a sight, and I just got myself a new Celestron. I mean, I need to set things up, but if you wanted to stop by—"

"I've got something on. Another time?"

"Sure. But come here after your shift, I can give you the neck." Milton nodded toward the deer.

"Please, God, no." Walk backed away, then patted his stomach. "I need to lose—"

"Don't worry, it's lean. If you stew it right it's a decent cut. I'd offer up the heart but once I get a sear on it that flavor just sings."

Walk closed his eyes, the nausea creeping up. His hands shook. Milton noticed, looked like he wanted to say something more so Walk moved on fast.

He saw no one around so he popped a couple of pills.

He was acutely and painfully aware of his dependency.

He moved past cafés and storefronts, said hello to a few, helped Mrs. Astor load grocery bags into her car, listened as Felix Coke bent his ear about the traffic on Fullerton.

He stopped by Brant's Delicatessen, rows of pastries and cheeses filled the window.

"Hey, Chief Walker."

Alice Owen, hair pulled back and a full face of makeup despite the workout clothes. She carried some kind of miniature cross so skinny Walk counted off its ribs as it trembled. He reached forward to pet it and watched the teeth bare.

"Would you mind holding on to Lady while I pick something up? I'll just be a second."

"Sure." He reached for the leash.

"Oh, you can't put her down. She's just been clipped and her nails are tender."

"The claws?"

Alice thrust the dog into his arms and headed inside.

He watched through the window as she placed an order then stopped and talked with another vacationer. Ten minutes passed, the dog panting into his face.

When Alice finally made it back she was laden with bags so he carried the dog over to her SUV and waited while she loaded it. She thanked him, then reached into a paper bag and handed him a cannoli. He made a fuss of trying not to take it, then waited till he was clear of Main before eating it down in two bites.

He walked along Cassidy then cut through onto Ivy Ranch Road. At Star's place he stood on the porch awhile, listening to the music play inside.

Star opened the door before he could knock, met him with the kind of smile that kept him from giving up on her. Hollowed out but beautiful, beaten down but her eyes still shone. She wore a pink apron like she'd been baking. Walk knew the cupboards were bare.

"Good afternoon, Chief Walker."

In spite of himself he couldn't help the smile.

There was a fan moving slow, drywall bare in spots, drapes pulled from their rings like Star couldn't close out the day quick enough. The radio played loud, Skynyrd sang about Alabama as Star danced her way through the kitchen, loading a garbage sack with empty beer bottles and packs of Lucky Strike. She grinned at him, looking like a kid as she did. She still had that way, vulnerable, troubled and trouble.

She spun once, then tossed a foil ashtray into the sack. Above the fireplace was a photo, the two of them, fourteen, ready and waiting for the future to come at them.

"How's your head?"

"Never better. I'm thinking clear now, Walk. Thanks and all . . . last night. But I think maybe I needed it, you know. One last time. Now I'm seeing right." She tapped her head, then moved on, still dancing. "The kids, they didn't see nothing, right?"

"Are we going to talk about it, today?"

As the music faded out she finally stopped moving, wiped the sweat from her head, and tied her hair back. "It'll come and it'll go. Does Duchess know?"

Star asking him about her own daughter.

"The whole town knows."

"You think he's changed?"

"We all have."

"Not you, Walk." She aimed for admiration but all he heard was disdain.

He hadn't seen Vincent in five years, though he'd tried often. The visits were close at first, he'd ride with Gracie King in the old Regal. It had been cold and hard, the judge sending a fifteen-year-old boy to a men's prison. Star's father took the stand, told of Sissy, of the kind of girl she was becoming. They showed photos of the scene, little legs, blood on a small hand. They called in Principal Hutch, and he told about the kind of boy Vincent was. Trouble.

And then it was Walk's turn, and his father had looked on, brown shirt, honest face. He was foreman at Tallow Construction, they had a factory that smoked away dreams two towns over. That same summer Walk had gone with him, for orientation. He'd stood in coveralls and watched, all the grays, the pipes and scaffold so intricate like bowels, a cathedral of metals.

In that courtroom Walk met his father's proud gaze and offered up the kind of unabridged truth that sealed his friend's fate.

"I don't need to be looking back anymore," Star said.

He made coffee. They took it out to the deck, birds on the swing set flapping lazy and high when Walk settled into an old chair.

She fanned her face. "You going to get him?"

"He said not to. I wrote him."

"But you'll go anyway."

"I will."

"Don't tell him . . . about me and all." Her knee bounced, she tapped the chair with her finger. All energy before the real purge came.

"He'll ask."

"I don't want him here. I don't think I can, in my house."

"Okay."

She lit a cigarette and closed her eyes.

"So, there's a program, a new one, over in—"

"Save it." She held up a hand. "I told you. It's behind me now."

They'd tried counseling, Walk had driven her to Blair Peak each month for a lifetime. The shrink seemed to get through, progress had been good. Walk would drop her, leave her, and head to a diner to wait. Three hours, sometimes more, before she called. Some days the kids would ride the hours with them, silent in the back, looking on as their innocence trailed the cruiser, slipping further behind.

"It can't . . . this can't go on."

"Still popping pills, Walk?"

He wanted to tell her it was different, but then he wondered how. They were the afflicted. Plain and simple.

She reached over and squeezed his hand, no harm meant.

"I think you've got cream on your shirt."

He glanced down and she laughed.

"Look at us. You know, sometimes I still feel it."

"What?"

"Fifteen, baby."

"We're getting old."

She blew a perfect smoke ring. "Not me, Walk. You're getting older and me, I'm just getting started."

He laughed hard, and then she laughed too. And that was them, Walk and Star, thirty years unwinding till all that was left was a couple of kids talking shit and making jokes.

They passed another hour in easy silence, neither saying it but both knowing there was only one thing on their minds. Vincent King was coming home.

4

Walk drove with an eye on the water, on folding golds and roaring surf.

A hundred miles east to Fairmont County Correctional Facility.

Thunderheads formed like gathered mistakes, the men in the yard stopped and looked skyward.

He pulled into a sprawling lot and killed the engine. The sound of buzzers, men hollering, the lonely wave of caged souls rolling out toward miles of godless plains.

It was not a place for a fifteen-year-old boy, no matter the detail. The judge had sat stone-faced as he made that dazzling call to corrective, the harsh truth of reformation more than a world from that courthouse in Las Lomas. Walk sometimes wondered about the damage done that night, immeasurable, the spiderweb of hurt that shadowed so many lives, replacing the new with the old, the fresh with decay. He saw it in Star and had seen it in her father, but none more so than Duchess, who carried that night long before she was born.

A rap on the trunk, he got out and smiled at the warden, Cuddy, tall and lean and grinning. Forget the hardened silhouette, the man ground down and ruthless by the forced company, Cuddy had always been friendly and kind.

"Vincent King," Cuddy said with a smile. "You look after your own in Cape Haven, right? How is it over there, still a shade of heaven?"

"It is."

"Got to say, I wish I had a hundred more like Vincent. Most days the boys say they forget he's there." Cuddy moved and Walk fell into step with him.

They passed a gate, then another, then into a low, squat building painted a shade of green that Cuddy said they brightened every season. "Most restful color for the human eye. Speaks of forgiveness and personal transformation."

Walk watched a couple of guys with brushes, trailing the baseboard with care, mouths tight in concentration.

Cuddy placed a hand on Walk's shoulder. "Listen. Vincent King has served his time, but getting him to realize that won't be easy. You need anything, you call me."

Walk stood in the waiting room and watched the wide views and the men that did circuits, heads high like Cuddy had taught them the sin of shame. If it wasn't for the wire that carved the landscape with such brutality it might have been a scene that stopped breath, *Our Good Earth*, men in jumpsuits nothing but the lost children they once were.

It had been five years since Vincent stopped receiving visitors, so, if not for the eyes, still blue enough, Walk might have had trouble recognizing him. Tall, thin, close to gaunt, sallow cheeks, a long way from the cocksure fifteen-year-old that had walked in.

But then Vincent saw him, and he smiled. It was a smile that had got him into and out of more trouble than Walk could remember. He was still in there, no matter the warnings, the way people said it changed you, his friend was still in there.

Walk took a step forward, thought of opening his arms but then extended his hand slowly.

Vincent looked at the hand like he'd forgotten it could hold a greeting and nothing more. He shook it lightly.

"I told you not to come." He spoke in a flat, quiet tone. "But thank you." There was something reverential in the way he moved.

"It's good to see you, Vin."

Vincent filled out the paperwork, a guard close and watching; a man freed after thirty years was not a sight that drew comment. Another day in the state of California.

A half hour later and they were at the last gate, both turned when Cuddy came out.

"It'll be tough out there, Vincent." He hugged him, quick and tight, something passing between them, maybe thirty years of decorous routine finally broken.

"More than half." Cuddy kept hold of Vincent for a moment. "That's how many come back to me. Make sure you're not one of them."

Walk wondered how many times Cuddy had spoken that weighted line over the years.

They walked side by side, and at the cruiser Vincent lay a hand on the hood and looked at Walk.

"I never saw you in your uniform. I got the photo, passing out, but here, in the flesh, you're a cop."

Walk smiled. "I am."

"Not sure I can be friends with a cop, man."

Walk laughed, the relief almost flooring him.

He drove slow at first, Vincent with an eye on just about everything, window low and the breeze on them. Walk wanted to talk but they crawled those first miles in something like a dream.

"I was thinking, that time we stowed on the *Saint Rose*," Walk said, trying to sound casual, like he hadn't practiced conversation starters on the way up.

Vincent looked up, a half smile at the memory.

They'd met up early, ten years old and first day of summer. They'd pedaled down to the water, hid their bikes, and crept onto the trawler, breathing heavy beneath the tarp as the sun rose and light passed through to them. Walk still remembered it, the throb of the engine as Skip Douglas and his men aimed her at the endless ocean. He hadn't even been pissed when they crawled out, instead radioed back and said he'd keep them the day. Walk hadn't ever worked harder hours, scrubbed the wood and boxes, the smell of fish blood no match for the feeling, a taste of life beyond the borders.

"You know Skip still works, guy named Andrew Wheeler runs a charter. Skip must be eighty now."

"My mother tore me a new one that day." Vincent cleared his throat. "Thanks. The funeral, doing all that."

Walk dropped the visor to the sun.

"You gonna tell me about her then? Vincent shifted in his seat, legs hunched, pants an inch long at the ankle.

Walk slowed at a railroad, a freight crossed them, boxes of steel, rust red and whining.

They rolled over the track and into the kind of town that had run when the mines had, and then Walk finally spoke. "She's alright."

"She's got kids now."

"Duchess and Robin. You remember that first time we saw Star?"

"Yeah."

"You'll head right back there when you see Duchess."

Vincent, lost then, Walk knew where his mind was. That first day Star's father rolled his Riviera into the Cape. Vincent and Walk rode up, saw a life packed into the trunk, clothes and cases and boxes pressed the glass. Side by side, hands on their Stelbers, sun hot on their necks. The man got out first, he was big and broad and he'd eyed them like he knew their kind. They were kids, though, that's what Walk remembered, concerns limited to finding the Willie Mays Pro card because Vincent's Magic 8-Ball told them they were due some luck. Then he scooped out a little girl, still sleeping, her head on his shoulder as he looked up and down his new street. Sissy Radley. They were about to turn, to head back to Walk's yard and the treehouse they'd been working on, when the rear door opened to the longest legs Walk ever saw. Vincent had cursed, mouth open, eyes fixed on the girl, their age and Julie Newmar beautiful. She got out, chewing gum as she glanced at them. *Holy shit*, Vincent said again. And then her father ushered her into the Kleinmans' old place, but not before she turned and cocked her head at them, no smile, just a look that burned its way into Vincent's soul.

"I missed you. I would've come, you know. If you'd let me. I would've come and visited every weekend."

Vincent's eyes never left the scenes, the interest of a man that had lived life through a television set.

On the Central Valley Highway they stopped at a diner by Hanford and ate burgers. Vincent finished half, his eyes fixed on the window as he watched a mother and her child, an old man that stooped like he was carrying each of his years on his back. Walk wondered what he saw. Cars he did not know the names of, stores he had only ever seen on screen. From 1975 through the turn of the millennium, 2005 had once looked like flying cars and robot maids, now here they were.

"The house—"

"I check on it. It needs work, the roof, the porch, half the boards are rotten."

"Alright."

"There's a developer, Dickie Darke, he crawls over it each month before summer. If you did ever want to sell—"

"I don't."

"Alright." Walk had said his piece. If Vincent wanted money he could sell the place, the last home on the front line, Sunset Road.

"You ready to go home?"

"I just left home, Walk."

"No, Vin, you didn't."

There was no fanfare when they arrived back in Cape Haven, no friendly faces or party or fuss. Walk noticed the other man take a breath as they crested the Pacific, the endless water coming at them, the tops of pines and grand houses on the Cape and beyond.

"They've built," Vincent said.

"They have."

There'd been resistance at first, just not enough because the promise of money was more than kept. Business owners like Milton held the floor and said they were tiring of the struggle. Ed Tallow said his construction company was struggling to keep the lights on.

Cape Haven was carved into the cliffs, tranquil and preserved, a town lifted from Anaheim. Walk felt it, each new brick laid right on top of his childhood, on the memories he so desperately needed to hold on to.

Walk stole a look at his friend's hands, at the legion of deep scars that crossed his knuckles. He'd always been tough. Finally, they rolled the slope onto Sunset Road, where the King house stood like an unwelcome shadow on the brightest day.

"The neighbors are gone."

"They fell. The cliffs are breaking, like Point Dume. Last one yesterday. Fairlawn. Your place is far enough back, and they put in the breakwater a couple of years ago."

Vincent looked at the scene, taped off like the crime it was. There were homes behind, near enough to keep the street from isolation, but far enough for the King house to command the most spectacular view.

Vincent got out and stood before it, an eye on the rotting gables and fallen shutters.

"I cut the grass."

"Thank you."

He followed Vincent up the winding path, the steps, and then into the cool, dark hallway. Papered walls with flowers recalling the seventies and a million velvet memories.

"I laid sheets."

"Thank you."

"And stocked the refrigerator. There's chicken and some—"

"Thank you."

"You don't have to keep saying that."

Above the fireplace was a mirror and Vincent passed it without looking. Walk thought he moved differently now, each step a cautionary tale about placement and better judgment. He knew the first years had been rough, and not rough in a cry-and-can't-sleep way, rough in the handsome-boy-among-the-darkest-kind-of-men way. They'd written letters, Walk and Gracie King, to the judge and the supreme court and even the house on Pennsylvania Avenue. They'd asked for segregation at least. They'd got nothing.

"You want me to stick around?"

"You get back, do what you do now."

"I'll check in later."

Vincent walked him to the door and offered a hand.

Walk pulled him into a hug, his friend, back now. He tried not to feel the flinch, the way Vincent tensed up.

They both turned when they heard the engine. Walk watched the Escalade. Dickie Darke.

Darke climbed out. He wore his size like an ill-fitting suit. Shoulders slumped, eyes down. He dressed in black each day, jacket, shirt, pants. Distracted, affected.

"Vincent King." His voice was deep, serious. "I'm Dickie Darke." No smile. Never a smile.

"I got your letters," Vincent said.

"The town must look different now."

"It does. The wishing tree is about the only thing I still recognize. You remember we used to stash cigarettes in the hole under there, Walk?"

Walk laughed. "And a sixer of Sam Adams."

Darke finally looked up and met Walk's eye with the kind of stare that chilled him. Then Darke eyed the house. "The last of the front line. You own the land behind as well."

Vincent looked at Walk.

"I'll pay a million. Current value is eight-fifty, the state it's in. And the market is turning."

"It's not for sale."

"You'll have a price."

Walk smiled. "Come on, Darke. The man just got home."

Darke stared a little longer. And then he turned and left them, strolling, unhurried, so big his shadow cast far.

Vincent watched him, his eyes locked on Darke like he could see something Walk could not.

• • •

Duchess had an arrangement with the kindergarten teacher, Miss Dolores; she would let Robin stick around for three long hours till Duchess finished class each day, mainly because Walk had stepped in and asked, and also because Robin was not even the slightest bother.

When Robin saw her he tidied his things, picked up his bag, and ran over. Duchess knelt and hugged him, then waved to Miss Dolores and they turned.

She helped Robin slip the straps over his shoulders and then checked he had his storybook inside, and his water bottle.

"You didn't eat your sandwich." She glared.

"Sorry."

The school bus passed, parents in SUVs, teachers out on the grass and chatting as kids tossed a football beside.

"You need to eat, Robin."

"It's just . . ."

"What?"

"You didn't put anything inside," he said, reluctantly.

"Bullshit."

He looked down at his shoes.

Duchess unzipped his pack and took out the sandwich. "Fuck."

"It's alright."

"It's not." She put a hand on his shoulder. "I'll fix hotdogs when we get in."

He smiled at that.

They kicked a stone together, kept it going till they got to the end of East Harney and Robin sent it into a drain.

"Did the kids say things, about Mom?" he said as she took his hand and they crossed the street.

"No."

"Ricky Tallow did, he said his mom told him about our mom."

"What did she say?"

They ducked beneath the limbs of a willow and cut down the track between Fordham and Dupont.

"She said he couldn't come to our house because Mom wouldn't watch us right."

"You could go there."

"His mom and dad are always yelling at each other."

She mussed his hair. "You want me to talk to her, see if I can sort something?"

"Yes."

Duchess knew Leah Tallow. Cape Haven PD, just her and Walk and an auxiliary named Valeria, who was old as shit. Duchess couldn't imagine any of them working a real crime.

"Ricky said he'll move into his brother's room when he leaves for college. He said his brother has an aquarium. Can we get one?"

"You've got a mask. Go look at fish in the sea."

When they got to Main they saw a group of girls outside Rosie's Diner, same group, always, drinking shakes and taking over two tables in the sun. Whispers and laughter as the two passed. They went into the grocery store, Mrs. Adams at the counter.

Duchess found a pack of frankfurters and Robin fetched the buns. She took out her purse and counted out three dollars in bills, all she had.

Robin looked up. "Can we get French's?"

"No."

"We need ketchup at least. It'll be dry."

Duchess took the pack and the buns up.

"How's your mother doing?" Mrs. Adams looked down over her glasses.

"Fine."

"That's not what I heard."

"Why the fuck did you ask then?"

Robin tugged her hand. Mrs. Adams might've told her to leave but Duchess tossed three dollar bills onto the counter before she could.

"Don't curse like that," Robin said as they walked up Main.

"How's your mother today?"

Duchess turned and saw Milton, out front of his butcher shop. He wiped his hands down his apron, blood smeared.

Robin walked up to the glass and looked at the rabbits, hooked at the throat.

"She's fine," Duchess said.

Milton took a step nearer, that smell so strong it got in her throat. Blood and death.

"You look an awful lot like her, you know that."

"Yeah, you told me that before."

She noticed small bits of flesh embedded in the thick hair on his arms. He stared at her awhile, like he'd forgotten his place, then snapped back when he saw her grocery bag and what was inside.

He tutted. "That's not even sausage. They grow that in a lab. Wait there."

She watched him head in, wheezing with each step.

A couple of minutes and Milton returned, brown paper bag folded over, sealed with a bloody print. "Morcilla. You tell your mother where these came from. Send her over if she wants to know how to cook them right."

"Don't you just fry it?" Robin said.

"Maybe in prison. If you want those flavors dancing you need to get acquainted with a Dutch oven. You see, it's all about the pressure and the—"

Duchess snatched the bag, grabbed Robin's hand, and felt Milton's eyes on her as she hurried away.

At Rosie's Diner, Duchess took a breath and led Robin in, shutting out the girls and their looks. Busy inside, vacationers filled tables, the smell of coffee rose thick. Loud talk, second homes, plans for the summer.

Duchess stood by the counter and saw the jar, the packets of ketchup inside, free if you bought something. A quick look over at Rosie, busy, tending the register.

Duchess collected a single ketchup packet for Robin and was about to turn.

"Don't you have to buy something to take the ketchup?"

She looked up. Cassidy Evans, from her class. Robin looked on, nervous, shifting from foot to foot.

Cassidy smirked, lip gloss pout, shiny hair, resting bitch face.

"It was only one packet."

"Miss Rosie, don't you have to buy something to take a ketchup?" Cassidy said it loud, innocence dripped from her voice.

Talk died, strangers' eyes so hot Duchess felt the burn.

Rosie set down a cup and came to the counter. Duchess shoved the packet back in the jar, then flinched as it fell to the floor and the glass shattered.

She snatched Robin's hand and led him through, Cassidy on her heels, Rosie calling out.

They walked in silence down quiet streets.

"We don't even need the sauce," Robin said. "It'll still be nice."

Along Sunset Road they saw a couple of kids tossing a ball on the sand below. Robin watched them intently. Duchess played with him often, toys, soldiers, cars, a stick he thought looked like a wand. Sometimes he'd holler for Star to come out, but most days she'd be lying in the dark living room, television muted. Duchess heard talk of bipolar, anxiety, dependence.

"What's going on?" Robin said.

Ahead they saw kids, three boys running back toward them, sprinting fast as they passed them by.

"It's the King house," Duchess said, and they stopped across the street and looked on. The front window blown, a jagged hole in it the size of a small rock.

"Should we tell?"

She watched the house, saw a shadow move inside, and shook her head. She took Robin's hand and led him away.

5

Walk sat in the back row of the bleachers and watched the football spiral its way fifty yards into the end zone, where the receiver fumbled it. The quarterback raised a hand and the kid smiled then shook it off. They'd run it again.

Walk had followed the Cougars his whole life. Vincent once played, wide receiver. Natural talent, talk of all-state. They hadn't won much since, never more than a couple of games on the bounce. Still, Walk took his place on a Friday night between clusters of teenage girls with painted faces, screaming themselves raw. After a win they'd pack Rosie's Diner, players and cheerleaders and the kind of feeling that made Walk smile.

"He's got an arm," Vincent said.

"He has."

Walk had picked up a sixer of Rolling Rock but Vincent hadn't touched a drop of his. He'd called by after his shift and found Vincent working on the house, despite the fading light. He'd already sanded most of the rear deck, hands blistered and face tight with the exertion.

"He'll turn pro." Vincent watched as the kid loaded up another. This time the receiver caught it and whooped.

"Like you could've."

"You want to ask me about it?"

"What?"

"Everything."

Walk sipped his beer. "I can't imagine what it was like."

"You can, you just don't want to. And that's cool. Whatever it was, I had it coming."

"You didn't. Not the way it went."

"I went to her grave. I didn't . . . I didn't leave flowers or nothing. I didn't know if I should."

Beneath the lights pass after pass landed. Way down, in the farthest corner, Walk saw the shape of Brandon Rock, ball cap backward. Walk saw him at every game.

Vincent followed his eye. "Is that Brandon?"

"Yeah."

"Now I thought he'd make it. I mean, back then he was good, right."

"Knee. It popped out and never back in, not properly. He works for Tallow Construction, something in sales. He limps, should probably use a cane but you know what Brandon is like."

"Not anymore."

"He's still got his father's Mustang."

"I remember the day his old man got it. Half the street gathered."

"You wanted to steal it."

Vincent laughed. "Borrow it, Walk. Just borrow it."

"He loves that car. I think he sees it, you know. A better time in his life. The hair, the clothes, the guy still lives in '78. You see, he hasn't changed, Vin. None of us have, not really."

Vincent stripped the label from his beer but still did not drink. "And Martha May? Has she changed much?"

Walk stalled at the mention of her name, just for a second. "She's a lawyer over in Bitterwater. She handles breakups and family stuff mostly."

"I always thought she was it for you. I know we were young, but the way you looked at her."

"Kind of like the way you looked at Star."

The receiver fumbled and the ball bounced its way toward the stands.

Brandon was up quick and moved fast considering the limp. He scooped up the ball but instead of passing it to the receiver he sent it forty yards to the quarterback, who plucked it out of the air.

"He's still got the arm," Walk said.

"Makes it worse, I guess."

"Will you go and see Star?"

"She told you she didn't want me there."

Walk frowned and Vincent smiled. "I can always read you, Walk. When you said you think she needs a little time . . . Shit, hasn't it been long enough? But then I was thinking she's right. Sometimes there's just too much history there. But you and Martha."

"She . . . we don't speak anymore."

"You want to tell me?"

Walk opened another beer. "That night, after the verdict. We were together. She fell pregnant."

Vincent stared at the field.

"And her father. What with him being a minister and all."

"Shit, Walk."

"Yeah."

"And she wanted to be a minister too, follow in his sacred steps."

Walk cleared his throat. "He made her . . . abortion. I mean, it was for the . . . we were kids. But you can't come back from something like that. And it wasn't just the way he looked at me, it was the way she did. Like she saw a mistake."

"And you looked at her and saw—"

"Everything. I saw it all. Like my parents, they were together fifty-three years. House and kid and life."

"Did she marry?"

Walk shrugged, like he hadn't wondered the same thing a hundred times over the years.

"It's not too late to fix things."

"I could say the same to you."

Vincent stood. "I'm thirty years too late to fix things."

• • •

The bar was in San Luis, which wasn't more than a wide stretch of highway that carved fallow fields and sloped its way toward the Altanon Valley.

Star had borrowed the old Comanche from Milton across the street. The AC didn't work so Duchess and Robin leaned their heads out the window like a pair of dogs, both tired, but this was how it went at least once every month.

Duchess had brought her project with her, and she clutched the papers tight as Star led them across the lot, squeezing between two pick-ups and through a back door. Star carried a beat-up guitar case, wore denim cutoffs high on her ass and a top cut low on her chest.

"You shouldn't dress like that."

"Yeah, well, the tips are better."

Duchess cursed under her breath and Star turned. "Please. Just lay off tonight, watch your brother and don't get in any trouble."

Duchess led Robin to a booth at the back, slid him in first, then sat beside, fencing him off from a place he had no business being in. Star fetched them a soda each as Duchess set out her report, and then some plain paper for her brother. She took out his pencil case and laid his pens out.

"Will she sing about the bridge?" Robin said.

"Always."

"I love that one. Will you sing it with her?"

"No."

"Good. I hate it when she cries up there."

Smoke drifted from spilling ashtrays. Dark wood, flags above the bar, the light dim enough. Duchess heard laughter, her mother sinking shots with two men, she needed them before she went on.

Robin reached for the bowl of nuts on the table, Duchess pushed his hand away. "Full of piss."

She stared at the page, the space for her father, the long empty branches of her family tree. The day before, Cassidy Evans had stood up front and told of her lineage, then showed off a crooked, noble line that ran from her to the du Ponts, so vivid was her telling that Duchess could almost smell the gunpowder.

"I drawed you."

"Drew."

He pushed the paper across and Duchess smiled. "My teeth that big?" She pinched his side till he laughed so much Star looked over and motioned them quiet.

"Tell me again about Billy Blue Radley," Robin said.

"The way I read it he was fearless. He held up a bank then led the sheriff for a thousand miles."

"He sounds bad."

"He was looking out for his own. His men, like family." She put a hand on his chest. "That's our blood right there. We're outlaws."

"Maybe you are."

"We're the same."

"But my daddy and yours, they're not the same—"

"Hey," she gripped his face lightly, "Radley blood, we're the same. Just because our fathers were no good at all . . . we're the same. Tell me."

"We're the same."

When it was time the light dropped a little and Star sat up front on a stool and played a set of covers, a couple of her own. One of the men she drank with whistled and hollered and catcalled after each number.

"Assholes," Duchess said.

"Assholes," Robin agreed.

"Don't say that word."

And then the man stood, gestured toward Star and grabbed his crotch. He said something else, like there was history there. Called her a cocktease. Said maybe she was a dyke.

Duchess got to her feet, picked up her soda, and launched the glass across the bar. It fell short and smashed by his foot. He stared at her open-mouthed, she stared back, arms out wide, telling him to bring whatever he could, that she wouldn't turn away.

"Sit down." Robin tugged her hand. "Please."

She blinked down at him, saw the fear there, then turned to her mother, who mouthed the same words.

The man glared. Duchess flipped him off and sat.

Robin finished his soda as Star called for her daughter. "Duchess, come up here. My baby can sing better than her momma."

Duchess sank into the bench, stared at her mother, and shook her head no matter how many turned and beckoned and clapped. There was a time when she would sing, when she was smaller, before she knew about the world. She would sing at home, in the shower, in the yard.

Star declared her daughter no fun at all and moved on to the last song, the song that saw Robin set his pens down and watch their mother like she was the last of the blessed. "I love this one."

"I know."

When Star was done she slipped from the stage, collected her money and stuffed the envelope in her purse, maybe fifty bucks. And then the man was back, and this time he grabbed a handful of her ass.

Duchess was on her feet before Robin could plead no. She moved fast, across the floor. She knelt and picked up a shard of the glass.

Star pushed the man back but he reared, clenched a fist till he caught the eyes, not on him but beyond. He turned, and there she stood small and ready. She held it high, the jagged edge aimed at his throat.

"I am the outlaw, Duchess Day Radley. And you are the barstool pussy, and I'll cut your head clean off."

She heard the faint cries of her brother. Star grabbed her wrist and shook it hard till she dropped the glass. Other men came, stepped between them and made things calm. Drinks were poured without charge.

Star shoved her out the door, scooped up Robin and followed.

The lot was dark as they climbed into the truck.

Star laid into her, yelled and told her she was dumb, that the man could've hurt her, that she knew what she was doing and didn't need a thirteen-year-old looking out for her. Duchess sat still, waiting for it to end.

When it did Star moved to start the engine.

"You shouldn't drive now."

"I'm straight." Star looked in the mirror and fixed her hair.

"You don't drive my brother when you're like this."

"I said I'm straight now."

"Straight like Vincent King was?"

Duchess saw the hand coming, didn't turn from it, just took the slap to her cheek like it was nothing.

In the back Robin cried.

Duchess leaned over, took the key from the ignition, and crawled back there with him. She smoothed his hair and tears and helped him change into his pajamas.

Duchess slept an hour, then climbed up front and handed Star the keys. They left the lot and drove toward home, mother and daughter side by side.

"You know it's his birthday this weekend," Duchess said, quiet.

A beat before Star answered.

"Course I know. He's my prince."

It made Duchess's stomach hurt. She had no money of her own. She worked a paper route, she pedaled and sweated each weekend, but it did not pay well.

"If you can give me some money I'll take care of it."

"I'll sort it."

"But—"

"Shit, Duchess, I said I'll sort it. Have a little faith."

She might've said she lost her faith each time her own birthday passed by without mention.

The car bumped along till they turned onto the highway.

"You hungry?" Star said.

"I fixed hotdogs."

"Did you pick up any sauce? You know Robin likes it."

Duchess looked at her mother with tired eyes. Star reached across and stroked her cheek. "You should've come up there tonight."

"Singing for a bunch of drunks. I'll leave that to the professionals."

Star pulled a cigarette from her bag and gripped it between her teeth while she fumbled with her lighter. "If I put the radio on will you sing something for me?"

"Robin is sleeping."

Star slipped a hand around Duchess's shoulder and pulled her close. She kissed her head as they crawled along the freeway. "There was a guy there tonight, he's got a studio in the valley. He gave me his card and told me to call. This could be it."

Duchess yawned, her eyes growing heavy, the streetlights beginning to blur.

"The Duchess of Cape Haven. You know I always dreamed about having a daughter. Pretty bow in her hair."

Duchess knew that.

"Do you know about Billy Blue Radley?"

Star smiled. "Your grandfather used to tell me about him. I thought he was making it up."

"He was real. Radley blood, Mom." She thought about asking after her father again but let it slide because she was too beat to get into it.

"You know I love you, right?"

"Sure."

"Serious, Duchess. Everything I do . . . all I got, it's all for the two of you."

Duchess stared out at the night. "I just wish . . ."

"What?"

"I just wish there was a middle, you know. Because that's where people live. It doesn't have to be all or nothing . . . sink or swim like that. Most people just tread water, and that's enough. Because when you're sinking, you're pulling us down with you."

Star wiped her eyes. "I'm trying. I'll be better. I said my affirmations again this morning. I'll say them every day. I want to do it for you."

"Do what?"

"I want to be selfless. Selfless acts, Duchess. They're what make you a good person."

It was almost midnight when they drove through town, Duchess dying a little when she saw Darke's Escalade in the driveway.

They drew up, the gate open, Darke would be in the yard, on the porch, waiting, staring out into nothing in that way that scared her, like he could see something in the shadows. She didn't like him. He was too quiet, too fucking big, stared too fucking much. She'd seen him outside of school, by the fence, just sitting in his car and watching her.

"I thought you were pulling the midnight shift tonight?" Duchess said.

Star had been cleaning offices over in Bitterwater.

"They . . . I didn't show last night so they told me not to come back. Don't worry about it. I can tend bar at Darke's place, that's probably why he's over."

"I don't like you working there."

Star smiled, then held up the business card again like it was proof of something. "Our luck is turning."

Duchess scooped up her brother. He was light, thin legs and arms, his hair getting long but she could not afford to take him to Joe Rogers on Main, where the other boys went. She was glad he was too small to notice, the other kids too. It would change soon enough, she worried about that.

Their shared bedroom, posters she'd hung, science and planets, he would be the smart one. One book on the shelf, Max all hungry and wild, but the end, that's what Robin loved, because the supper showed Max was cared for. She borrowed it from the small library in Salinas, renewed it every other week, two miles each way on her bicycle.

Outside she heard talk. Darke owned the house, Star could not afford the rent. Duchess was old enough to know what that meant, young enough to keep from understanding it.

Her mind ran to her schoolwork, the shit she'd be in if she didn't complete it. She couldn't get detention, there'd be no one to collect Robin. Star could not be trusted.

She made the decision to doze till sunrise and get on it early. She parted the drapes. The street slept. Across was Milton's house, the porch light burned all night, moths gathered and fluttered. She saw a fox, graceful as it left light for the shadows. And then, by Brandon Rock's house, she saw a man, and he was watching her window. He could not see her, the way she stood, back just enough. He was tall, not like Darke, but still tall. Cropped hair, stooped shoulders, like pride had slid right from him.

She lay back in her spot.

And then, as her eyes grew heavy, she heard a scream.

Her mother's scream.

She moved from the room with practiced care, a girl used to the terrors of night, to a mother who courted the worst of men. Behind her she closed the door, he would sleep, even if he got up he would not remember. He never remembered.

She heard Darke's voice, steady, like always.

"Calm down."

She watched through the door, the edge, the room cut into a slice of hell, the lamp on its side, throwing shade over her mother, who lay on the rug. Darke watched her intently, like she was a wild creature he'd just sedated. He was too big, too big for the chair and the small house and too big to take down.

Duchess knew what to do, which boards made noise, and she moved along the hallway to the kitchen. She would not call 911, there would be a record. As she dialed Walk's cell she heard the noise and turned too late, and then Darke took the receiver from her.

She dug her nails into his hand and clawed until she felt him bleed. He guided her from the kitchen, his hand firm on her shoulder. She scrabbled, knocked the side table down, a photo of Robin coming to rest by her eyes, his first day of kindergarten..

Above her Darke stood. "I won't hurt you, so don't call the cops on me." Voice so deep it was almost inhuman. She had heard stories about him, just snippets, that a man cut in front of him on Pensacola and Darke pulled him out of his car and stamped his face to mush. And that he did it with a calm that held bystanders mesmerized.

He watched her, like he always did. He studied her face, hair, eyes, mouth. Taking in the detail, making her shiver.

She glared up at him, fierce, small nose twisted into a snarl. "I am the outlaw, Duchess Day Radley, and you are the woman beater, Dickie Darke."

She scooted back, her head to the door. Above the streetlight fell through the glass, bathing her in orange as she watched her mother scream and yell and run at Darke.

She wouldn't rise and help, she knew not to do that. Instead she stood when she saw the shape through the glass.

Behind, her mother swung fists. Darke gripped her hands and tried to keep them level.

Duchess made her decision quickly; whatever was outside could be no worse than what was within. She unlatched the door and looked up into the man's face. She moved aside and he passed, grabbed hold of Darke and they struggled. He landed one punch, caught Darke hard in the side of the head.

Darke did not flinch, saw who it was and stopped dead, stared, calm enough as he weighed options. He was much bigger, broader, but the other man looked like he burned with it, that need to fight.

Darke fished keys from his pocket, unhurried, and walked from the house. The man followed him out, Duchess behind.

She watched the Escalade till the lights faded from view. The man turned and looked at her. And then past her, where Star stood behind, on the old porch, breathless.

"Come on, Duchess."

Duchess said nothing, just followed her mother back into the house, looking back once, where the man stayed, like he'd been sent there to guard her.

In the melee his shirt had been torn, and it was as the moon caught him she saw it. The crisscross of scars that covered him, raised and angry and fresh.

6

The tiredness ran over her, uncontended, she let it, labored steps and breaths and burning eyes, ears full of smothered sounds at times so distant she did not react.

She felt the small tug on her hand, the face of her brother, earnest, his night was spent in dreams.

"Are you alright?" He worried.

Duchess carried his bag and hers. A bruise on her forearm, where she'd fallen. In her bag was her paper, half done, her family tree. Her grades were middling, she knew to keep them that way. She did not cut anymore, tried not to get in shit, she could not risk any kind of involvement from Star. Parents' evenings she would make the excuse, *My mother has work, you know how it is.* She ate alone, scared in case the other kids saw what she'd made. Sometimes just buttered bread, so stale it could be snapped. Some had it worse, she knew that, just did not wish to join them.

"I slept on your bed, you kept kicking me in the night," Duchess said.

"Sorry. I thought I heard noises. Maybe I was dreaming."

She watched him run ahead a little into the neighbor's front yard, where he found a long stick and brought it back, like a dog. He held it out and used it as a cane, pretending he was an old man till she laughed.

And then the front door opened. Brandon Rock, he tended his Mustang with the kind of attention Star said he'd have been better showing
his ex-wife.

He wore a letterman jacket, so faded and tight the sleeves stopped
midforearm. He glared at Robin. "You stay away from the car."

"He didn't go near it."

Brandon crossed the grass and stood close to her. "You know what's
under that cover?" He motioned toward the car, the blue tarp wrapped
it tight. Each night she watched Brandon put it to bed like a firstborn.

"My mother said it's a penis extension."

She saw his cheeks flush.

"It's a '67 Mustang."

"Sixty-seven, same year that jacket was made."

"That's my number. Ask your mother about me. All-state. Used to
call me the bull rush."

"The ball rash?"

Robin walked back over and grabbed her hand. She felt Brandon
watching her the whole way up the street.

"What's he so mad about? I didn't go near the Mustang."

"He's just pissed because he wanted to date Mom and she blew him
off."

"Did Darke stop by last night?"

Ahead there was sunlight, shutters up and shopkeepers readying. "I
didn't hear."

Duchess preferred Cape Haven in winter, where honesty stripped
away the veneer and left a town like the rest. She suffered the summer,
long and beautiful and ugly.

She saw Cassidy Evans and her friends sitting outside Rosie's, short
skirts and tanned legs, aiming pouts at each other.

"Let's go down Vermont," Robin said, and she let him lead her, away
from Main and the girls that would laugh. "What'll we do this summer?"

"Same thing we always do. Hang out, go to the beach."

"Oh."

He kept his eyes down. "Noah is going to Disney. And Mason, he's going to Hawaii."

She put a hand on his shoulder and gave it a squeeze. "I'll find something for us."

Robin ran over to the trees by Fordham. She watched him part the willow and move beneath, he would try to climb the low branch.

"Morning."

Duchess turned, she had been too tired to hear the cruiser, drifted too far to notice Walk pull up beside.

She stopped a minute and he killed the engine, took off his sunglasses and watched her too close.

"Everything alright?"

"Sure." She blinked away Darke's hand, her mother's scream.

Walk let it hang there, fiddled with his radio and drummed the door. "Last night, all okay?"

He always fucking knew. "I just said, didn't I."

He smiled then. He never rode her about anything at all. He watched out, but Duchess knew sometimes adults thought watching out meant doing shit that'd lead to the kind of consequences that rippled far beyond them.

"Alright," he said.

His hand shook, thumb and index finger meeting over and over.

He clocked her noticing and pulled it into the cruiser. She wondered how much he drank.

"You know you can talk to me, Duchess."

She felt too tired for it, his fat, kind face and loaded eyes. He was soft, jelly, pudding. Soft smile, soft body, soft way of looking at her world. She had no use for soft.

When they got to school she saw Robin into kindergarten and then waved to Miss Dolores and turned. Last days of school, she needed to keep low, but the paper was a problem, her family tree would get her into shit. She didn't miss assignments. Her stomach hurt and she placed a hand there, feeling the knot all tight like something bad was coming. She couldn't stand before the class and say she didn't know who her father was. She could not do that.

In the halls she found her locker, tried to smile at the girl beside but got nothing back. It had been like that a long time, like the other kids knew, all she was, spent, responsibility and consequence, no time for what they wanted in a friend.

In class she took her seat, in the middle, by the window with a view out over the field. A cluster of birds tilled the dirt.

She thought of Robin, who'd collect him if she got detention. There was no one. No one. She swallowed a lump, her eyes hot. She did not cry.

The door opened, and it wasn't Mr. Lewis. An old lady shuffled in, holding a Styrofoam cup, steam lines, coffee, glasses hung from string. A substitute teacher.

Duchess slumped on the desk when the lady told them to get out their textbooks and have a little quiet time.

• • •

Walk found him on the lot, vacant now, the Fairlawn house little more than rubble. Men were clearing the site, making it safe, diggers moved wood and slate and loaded trucks ready to cart the memory away.

Darke watched them, his presence alone enough for them to pick up the pace. When he saw Walk he straightened up a little, and Walk couldn't help but take a step back.

"Nice day out here. Leah said you called the station. Trouble at the club again?"

"No."

No small talk, no matter how hard Walk tried. It was not possible to get the man to say more than absolutely, painfully, necessary.

Walk tucked a shaking hand into his pocket. "So?"

Darke pointed to the house behind. "I own that place."

The small home behind, peeling shutters and rotting porch, an effort to keep it up but it looked about ready to be pulled down and replaced.

"That's Dee Lane's place." Walk saw her standing by the window. He waved a hand but she stared straight past him, the water now there, the million-dollar view opening up in a callous breath of nature.

"She rents it. She won't leave. I served the papers in time."

"I'll talk with her. You know she's lived there a long time."

Nothing.

"And she has the girls."

Darke turned away, toward the sky, maybe something finally landing.

Walk took the opportunity to appraise him. Black suit. Simple watch wrapped around a wrist as thick as Walk's ankle. Walk wondered what he benched, guessed maybe a family car.

"What will you do with it now, the house?"

"Build."

"You applied for a permit?" Walk monitored applications, objected to the change each and every time. "I heard there was a little trouble last night. The Radley house."

Darke just stared.

Walk smiled. "Small town."

"Not for much longer. Did you speak to Vincent King again?"

"He said . . . I mean he's just got out, so at the current time . . ."

"You can say it."

Walk coughed. "He said to tell you to go fuck yourself."

Darke, his face a mask of sadness or maybe just disappointment. He cracked his knuckles, the sound like gunshot. Walk could only imagine the damage he could do with his size eighteen boots.

Walk moved on, up the site, broken ground, men at their machines, cigarettes hanging and eyes squinting toward the sun.

"Chief Walker."

Walk turned back.

"Miss Lane can take another week. I have a storage place. If she's got anything tell her to leave it out front, I'll have it collected and kept. No charge."

"That's good of you."

In Dee's yard was a small deck and the kind of neat border of flowers that spoke of pride of place, no matter how small that place was. He'd known her twenty years, each of them she'd spent in the home on Fortuna Avenue. She'd been married, till her husband fucked around and left her with the bills and two kids to bring up.

Dee met him at the screen door. "I should fucking murder him." She was small, maybe five-one, attractive in a hard way, like the past years had gunned down the person she had once been. Her against Darke, mismatch didn't come close.

"I can find you someplace to—"

"Fuck off, Walk."

"Is Darke right? Is it today?"

"It's today, doesn't make him right though. Three years I rented this place from him, after he took on the mortgage . . . dealt with the bank. Then the Fairlawn house fell, opened up my view, and I get this in the mail." She fished through a stack of papers and thrust the letter at him.

He read it carefully. "I'm real sorry. Can you talk to someone?"

"I'm talking to you."

"I don't think, legally . . ."

"He told me I could stay here."

Walk read the letter again, then the notice papers. "I can help you box things. The girls, do they know?"

Dee closed her eyes, opened them to tears and shook her head. Olivia and Molly, sixteen and eight.

"Darke said you can take another week."

Dee took a breath then. "You know we dated once . . . after Jack."

Walk knew.

"I thought . . . I mean Darke, he's nice-looking, but he's a fucking freak, Walk. There's something missing. I'm not even sure what it is, there's just a coldness to that man. Like a robot. And he wouldn't touch me."

Walk frowned.

"You know what that means."

He felt his cheeks burn.

"I'm not desperate or nothing, but you date five or six times and it's natural. But not with him. There's nothing natural about Dickie Darke."

Seeing boxes in the front yard, he moved to fetch them in but she told him to leave them. "It's all trash. I started boxing up my life this morning. And you know what I realized?" She cried, no noise or sobbing, just the steady fall of tears. "I failed them, Walk."

He went to speak but she held up her hand, so close to breaking. "I failed my girls. I've got no home for them now. I've got nothing."

· · ·

That night when Robin and her mother were sleeping she climbed from her bedroom window and wheeled her bicycle from the house.

Dusk, blue day broke down, trash cans out, the smell of barbeque. Duchess was hungry, never quite enough to fill her. She made sure Robin ate all he could.

She turned onto Mayer, the low hill falling away, letting the bike coast, streamers on one side. She wore shorts and no helmet, her top zipped and sandals on her feet.

She slowed at the turn for Sunset Road.

The King house had always been her favorite, the way it stood, part ruin, flipping off the surround.

She saw him straight off.

The garage door was up, the man on a ladder, gently removing slate. He'd stripped half, a roll of tar paper lay, tools like hammers and picks and a wheelbarrow full of dry and dusty rock. He had a lamp and it shed just enough light.

She'd seen photos of Sissy, they were the same kind of girl, light hair and eyes and freckles atop small noses.

She crossed slowly, legs out, the saddle hurting, balancing this way and that, one foot pushing.

"You were at my house."

He turned. "I'm Vincent."

"I know that."

"I once knew your mother."

"I know that too."

He smiled then, not real, maybe like it was called for, like he was learning to be something again. She did not smile back.

"Is your mother alright?"

"She's always alright."

"How about you?"

"You don't need to ask that. I'm an outlaw."

"Should I be worried? Outlaws are bad, right?"

"Wild Bill Hickok killed two men before he became sheriff. Maybe I'll straighten out one day, maybe I won't."

She wheeled a little closer. He was sweaty, his T-shirt dark at the chest and beneath the arms. Above the garage was an old hoop, the net gone, she wondered if he remembered playing, if he remembered anything about before.

"Freedom," she said. "Is it the worst thing to take? Worse than anything. Maybe it is."

He climbed down the ladder.

"You have a scar on your arm."

He looked down at his forearm, the scar ran the length, not angry, just there.

"And you have scars all over your body. Did you get beaten in there?"

"You look like your mother."

"Don't let that fool you."

She scooted back a little, fussed with the small bow in her hair as he watched. "Subterfuge. People see a girl and nothing else."

She rolled the bicycle back and forth.

He found a screwdriver and walked over slowly. "The brake is sticking, that's why it's hard to pedal."

She watched him carefully.

He knelt by her leg, careful not to touch her skin, and fiddled with the brake then stood and moved back.

She rocked again, felt the wheel move easy, turned as the moon fell, starred sky behind him and the old home.

"Don't come by our house again. We don't need anyone."

"Alright."

"I don't want to have to hurt you."

"I don't want that either."

"That boy that broke your window, his name is Nate Dorman."

"Good to know."

She turned and slowly rode back, away from him, toward home.

When she reached her street she saw the car, the hood so long it jutted from their driveway. Darke was back again.

She pedaled hard and dropped her bike to the grass, frantic, she should not have gone. She moved down the side of the house and then into the door by the kitchen, quiet, sweat rolling down her spine. She took the phone from the cradle on the wall. And then she heard it, laughing, her mother's laugh.

She watched from shadows they could not see. A bottle on the coffee table, half gone, a cluster of red flowers, the kind they sold at the gas station on Pensacola.

She left them and stepped out into the yard, climbed back through the window and checked their bedroom door was still locked. She peeled off her shorts, kissed Robin's head, then opened the drapes and lay at the foot of his bed. She would not sleep till the giant man was gone.

7

"Tell me about the girl," Vincent said.

They sat at the back of the old church. Through the window was the cemetery and beyond that the ocean, each given stained colors. They'd stopped by Sissy's grave, Walk leaving his friend alone for a while. Vincent had brought flowers, dropped to his knees and read the stone. He stayed there an hour, till Walk came and gently rested a hand on his shoulder.

"Duchess, she's older than she should be, you know." Walk guessed he knew better than most.

"And Robin?"

"She looks out for him. Duchess does what her mother should."

"The father?"

Walk looked at the old benches, painted white, droplets had made it to the stone floor. The roof was high and arched and intricately knotted, the kind of beautiful that impelled vacationers to take photographs and pack the place out every Sunday.

"Nothing in it, both times. She was seeing a couple guys back then, she was out a lot. I'd see her come back in the morning."

"Walk of shame."

"There wasn't shame in it. You ever know Star to care?"

"I'm not sure I know Star at all."

"You do. She's the same girl you took to junior prom."

"I wrote Hal. Her father."

"Did he write back?"

"He did."

Ten minutes passed, Walk wondering but not wanting to know. Star's father was hard. He had acres in Montana, the Cape too painful even to visit. He had not met his grandchildren.

"At first he told me to kill myself."

Walk looked at the sainted wall, the depictions of judgment and forgiveness.

"I might've done it. Then he changed his mind. Death was too good. He sent me a photo of her." Vincent swallowed. "Sissy."

Walk closed his eyes as the sun cut through and found the pulpit.

"You been into town yet?"

"I don't know this place anymore."

"You will know it again."

"I had to go into Jennings to pick up some paint. I saw Ernie owns the place now."

"Did he give you a hard time? I can talk to him." Ernie had been one of the walkers that night. He'd been the first to see Walk raise his hand, the first to run back over then stop dead at the scene, double over and retch at the sight of the little girl.

They stood together and walked out, through the green grass and over the leaning gravestones. At the cliff edge they watched water break over jagged rock one hundred feet below.

Walk felt dizzy at the sight. "I think about it often. How we were. I see the Cape Haven kids, like Duchess, and I think of me and you and Star and Martha. Star said to me some days she still feels fifteen. We can get together, the three of us. In time, we can get things back. It was simpler, right. It was—"

"Listen, Walk. What you think you know, or might know, about what happened over the years. Whatever I was, I'm not now."

"How come you didn't let me visit, after your mother?"

Vincent kept his eyes on the scene, like he hadn't heard. "He wrote me, Hal. Every year. On Sissy's birthday."

"You shouldn't—"

"Sometimes it was short, to remind me, like I needed it. Other times he went on for ten pages. It wasn't all anger, some was on change, what I could do, how I could let others live their lives and not pull them down."

Walk got it then; it was not self-preservation of any kind, the way he'd reasoned it.

"If you can't right a wrong, if you can't ever do that . . ."

Together they watched a trawler, *The Sun Drift*. Walk knew it, blue paint and rust, curved lines of steel and wire. It moved silent from where they were, no waves just the carve of its hull.

"Some things just are, right. There's a reason, always, but talk won't change any of it."

There was much Walk wanted to ask about the last thirty years of his friend's life, but the scars on Vincent's wrists told him that time might well be worse than he could ever have imagined. They walked back toward town in silence, Vincent keeping to the side streets, head down, always. "Star," he said. "She saw a lot of guys then?"

Walk shrugged, and, for a moment, thought he had heard the slightest note of jealousy in Vincent's voice.

He watched his friend walk away, back toward Sunset, to patch up the old, empty house.

After lunch Walk made the drive to Vancour Hill Hospital. He rode the elevator to the fourth floor, took his place in the waiting room, and read a glossy, pages of stark homes as minimalist as their keepers, reflected light, all sanitary stucco. He kept his head low, though the other person was a young woman as determined as he was there in betraying body, mind displaced. His name called, he moved fast, no outward sign, no matter the aches and pains, that only a few hours earlier he could barely stand.

"The pills aren't working," he said, as he sat. The office was uniform, the only personal touch a framed photo that faced away. The doctor was Kendrick.

"Your hand again?" Kendrick said.

"Everything. A half hour to get up each day."

"But you haven't slowed down, in other ways? Walking? Smiling?"

He smiled despite himself. She returned it.

"Just the hands, the arms. Stiffness. Nothing more, I know it'll come."

"And you haven't told anyone. Still?"

"They chalk me as a boozehound."

"And you're okay with that?"

"My line of work, it's a good fit, right?"

"You know you'll have to tell someone."

"And then what? I won't sit behind a desk."

"You could try something else."

"I tell you, you ever see me wasting my days on some fishing boat, you just come down and shoot me. Being a policeman is . . . I like my place. I like my life. I want to keep both."

Kendrick smiled a sad smile. "Anything else?"

He stared out, the window more than a view then, a way to leave himself while he detailed what needed saying. A little trouble pissing, a little trouble shitting. And more than a little trouble sleeping. Kendrick said it was normal, made suggestions, lose a little weight, diet, therapy, changing dose, levodopa. Nothing he did not know. He was not someone who walked blindly into medicating. He spent his free time in the library, reading up, six stages, Braak's hypothesis, even back to James Parkinson.

"Fuck," he said, then raised a hand. "I'm sorry for cursing. I don't do that."

"Fuck," Kendrick agreed.

"I can't lose my job. I just can't. The people need me." He wondered if that was true. "It's only the right side," he lied.

"There's a group."

He made to stand.

"Please," she said, and he took the pamphlet.

...

Duchess sat on the sand. She hugged her knees as she watched Robin, ankle-deep and hunting shells. He had a collection, mostly fragments, his pockets fit to burst.

Off to the left was a group of kids from her school, the girls in bathing suits and the boys tossing a ball. The noise floated on, right through her. She had that ability, to feel totally alone on a beach full of people, in a class full of kids. She got that from her mother, but she fought it with everything she had. Robin needed stability, not a pissy teenage sister who bitched her way through her shitty life.

"Another," Robin called.

She stood and walked over, the water cold for a moment, lines of rugged coast stretched far in either direction. She fixed Robin's sun hat and felt his forearms, warm, they could not afford lotion. "Don't burn."

"I know."

She helped him search, fished a perfect sand dollar from the clearest of water and watched him smile.

Robin saw Ricky Tallow and ran at him, the two greeting each other with hugs that made her smile.

"Hi, Duchess." Leah Tallow. She was plain, the kind of even features that Duchess sometimes wished her own mother had. Just a mom, not a singer in a bar with her ass and tits out, not the kind of woman men stared at when they walked along the beach.

"We have to go soon." Robin's face fell but he didn't say anything.

"We can run him back if you want to get on. Where is it you live?"

"Ivy Ranch Road." Ricky's father, head of gray hair long before he should've, bags beneath his eyes that seemed to get heavier every time Duchess saw the man.

Leah shot her husband a look.

He looked away, emptied out a bag full of beach toys. Robin eyed them, keeping his mouth straight. He wouldn't ask her, she hated that, loved him for it but still hated that.

She weighed it awhile. "You sure?"

"Of course. Ricky's brother is joining us later. He can show the boys how to toss a ball."

Robin looked up at Duchess, wide eyes.

"We'll drop him back before dinner."

Duchess took Robin aside, knelt in the sand, and cupped his face tight. "You know to be good."

"Yeah." He glanced over his shoulder, where Ricky was beginning to dig out a channel. "Yes, I'll be good. I swear."

"Don't leave them, don't run off, be polite. Don't say nothing about Mom."

Robin nodded, his most serious face, and then she kissed his head, waved to Leah Tallow and crossed the hot sand to grab her bicycle.

She was sweating by the time she reached Sunset Road, got off and pushed the last fifty. Outside the King house she stopped.

On the porch Vincent sanded, his back bent as sweat dripped from his chin. She watched awhile. He had muscles, low and tight on his arms, not the bulging kind she saw on the beach. She crossed the street and stood at the end of his driveway.

"You want to help?" Vincent had stopped, sitting now, a block and sandpaper in hand, he offered out another.

"Why the fuck would I want to do that?"

He went back to work. She propped her bike against the fence and moved nearer.

"You want a drink or something?"

"You're a stranger."

She noticed he had a tattoo that showed when he stretched, peeking from beneath the arm of his T-shirt. He worked on for another ten minutes.

She moved nearer still.

He stopped, sat again. "That man . . . the other night, you know him?"

"He looks at me like he knows me."

"Does he stop by often?"

"More and more lately." She wiped sweat from her head with the back of her arm.

"You want me to tell Walk?"

"I don't want anything from you."

"You got anyone else you can call?"

"I'm an outlaw, it says so in the records."

"You want to call me if it happens again?"

"Dallas Stoudenmire killed three men in five seconds. I think I can handle one." She shifted her weight and leaned on one hip, then moved nearer and sat on the bottom step, five down from him.

He turned and bent and began to sand again, sweeping his hand, even, firm. She reached out, took the other block, and got to work on her step.

"How come you don't sell this shitty house?"

He knelt like he was praying before the old place.

"People say . . . I mean, I heard them in Rosie's and they were saying you could get a million bucks or something crazy. And you want to stay here."

He looked behind at the house, for so long it was like he could see something she could not. "My great-grandfather built this house. This town, Cape Haven, when Walk drove me in I was glad I still knew parts of it. It's not just the vacationers that have changed, it's . . ." He paused like he did not know what to say. "I didn't think I was all bad, back then. When I see it, when I look back that far I see someone that wasn't all bad."

"And now?"

"Prison has a way of turning the light out. And this house, it's . . . a small flame maybe, but it's still burning. If I let it go, if I let that last light go, then it's all dark, and I won't be able to see it anymore."

"See what?"

"You ever think people look at you but don't really see you?"

She let that sit. Fussed with her bow, tucked her lace into her sneaker. "What happened to Sissy?"

He stopped again, this time sat back, one arm in the sun, eyes squinting at her. "Your mother didn't tell you?"

"I want you to tell me."

"I took my brother's car out."

"Where was he?"

"He went to war. You know about Vietnam?"

"Yes."

"I wanted to impress a girl so I took her out in the car." She knew who the girl was.

"After I dropped her home I drove Cabrillo—you know the bend by the town sign?"

"Yes."

He spoke quiet. "I didn't know I'd hit her. I didn't even slow."

"Why was she out?"

"She was looking for her sister. Your grandfather, he worked nights sometimes, that factory, Tallow Construction. That still there?"

She shrugged. "Just about."

"So he slept the days off. Star was in charge of her."

"But Star wasn't there."

"I called her. We had a couple beers. Us, and Walk and Martha May. You know her?"

"No."

"I lost track of time. She'd left Sissy in front of the television set." His voice had no depth. The rote recital that made her wonder what was left of him.

"How did they find you?"

"I think Walk was a cop even back then. He came to my place that same night. Saw the car, the damage."

They worked on in silence. She grit her teeth and smoothed the wood, so hard her shoulder pained.

"You need to look out for yourself," he said. "I know that kind. Darke. I saw men like that, something in the eyes, not right."

"I'm not scared. I'm tough."

"I know."

"You don't."

"You have a brother to look out for. It's a lot of responsibility."

"I lock our bedroom door so he doesn't see nothing. And anything he hears he chalks up to bad dreams."

"You lock him inside, is that safe?"

"Safer than what's outside."

She watched him then, his mind far, like he was weighing something heavy.

A while before he finally met her eye. "You're an outlaw?"

"I am."

"Then give me a minute. I've got something for you."

She watched him go into the house, and she wondered about absolution. She knew reprieve was a temporary notion, so fleeting that when she saw him return it was like watching a dead man walking.

8

Sometimes I think she hates me."

Walk glanced at Star but she did not look back. There was a calm to her that morning, he knew it would not last.

"She's a teenager."

"You really believe that's all it is, Walk? I don't need bullshit, not from you."

As they passed Brandon Rock's place Walk saw the drapes move, and then Brandon was out. He fought the limp, mouth tight as he crossed the yard. Walk stalled a little and Star sighed.

"Morning." Brandon smiled at Star.

"You woke half the street again, Brandon. You best fix that engine or Duchess will come out and do it for you."

"That's a 1967—"

"I know what car it is. Your father's car, same car you've been working on for the past twenty years. I even saw you talking about the fucking thing in the local newspaper."

The spread had been crude, a local lives spot buried near the classifieds. Brandon talked pistons for half a page then a photo showed him lying across the hood, hair feathered, pouting lips. Duchess had defaced their copy with a marker then taped it to Brandon's front gate.

"It'll be fixed up in time for July 4th. So I was wondering if you wanted to head up to Clearwater Cove. I could make us a picnic. Twinkies, right. You like Twinkies. Pineapple chicken. I even got a fondue pot." He carried his dumbbell, curling, the veins in his right arm popping.

"I don't want to date you, Brandon. You've been asking me out since high school and it's getting tired."

"You know one of these days I'll just give up on you, Star."

"Can I have that in writing?"

She took Walk's arm, strolled on.

"He still thinks we're in high school," Star said.

"And he's still sore about losing you to Vincent."

When they reached the end of Ivy Ranch Road he looked back and saw Brandon Rock still standing there, staring after them.

They walked, a weekly ritual that had gone on near a decade. Walk stopped by on a Monday morning and made sure Star got out of the house and talked. It wasn't much, but sometimes he thought that routine was good for her. If she wouldn't talk to a shrink, she could talk to him.

"So, how is he?"

"He's alright."

She squinted. "What the fuck does that mean, Walk? Alright. Give me something."

"I heard. About what happened the other night."

"My hero, right. I had it under control. I don't need Vincent fucking King showing up to fight my battles."

"He used to fight all of our battles. Remember when the Johnson boy thought I stole his bike?

Star laughed. "Like you'd steal anything."

"He was big."

"Not big enough to take Vincent. I liked that about him. He was tough, but only we saw beneath it. Sissy used to love him. We'd be on the couch and she'd come and jam in between us. He spent time with her, you know. Took her drawings home and kept them."

"I remember."

"You remember everything, Walk."

"Why'd you let him round? Darke. He's not right."

"It's nothing, not what you think. I got pissed with him. I started it. It's forgotten. I'm pulling a shift at the club tonight."

At the corner of Sunset he stalled a little, her eyes past him, at the King house. He let her lead, and she led them away and down toward the beach. Cars passed, then an SUV.

He saw it was Ed Tallow, raised a hand but Ed's eyes didn't stray from Star as he passed.

Walk loosened his tie as Star kicked off her sandals and stepped onto the hot sand. He followed, his shoes filling as she raced toward the water, heels kicking up as they burned. She stopped ankle-deep and laughed as he plodded his way to her.

They strolled the shoreline.

"I know I'm failing, Walk."

"You're not—"

"I know I'm fucking up the one thing I'm supposed to be good at."

"Duchess loves you. She's a handful, but I see the way she looks out for you. And Robin—"

"Robin's easy. He's all . . . he's the best of me. He's a prince."

They sat in the sand.

"Thirty years, Walk. And then bam, just back into the town you left behind. I thought about him, too much I thought about him over the years. And I know you liked that, you wanted to talk about him like we're all the same people."

He felt the heat then, the sweat across his back. "You do this, get drunk or high and nearly die, and then we walk and talk and nothing much changes."

"You were cursed with pathological honesty, Walk. You carry weight you don't even see. It's not me who Duchess looks up to, it's you."

"No, it's not—"

"You remind her of everything good. You are the man in her life, the person that doesn't lie or cheat or fuck people over. She doesn't say it, but she needs you. And you can't ever let her down, because that'd be like turning out the light."

"You'll be alright. You can be that person for her."

She tilled the sand, scooped it and let it run through her fingers. "What do I do? How do I stop being me?"

"See him."

"Forgive him?"

"That's not what I'm saying."

"Every time I slipped or fell, it was him I was thinking about. I'm not strong enough to deal with it. What it all means, what having him back in my life means. And it's not just my life."

"He's better than Dickie Darke."

"Fuck, Walk. You're like a kid. Better and worse. Bad and good. None of us are any one thing. We're just a collection of the best and worst things we've done. Vincent King is a murderer. He killed my sister." Her voice wavered. "I should've moved. I should've moved like Martha did, left the Cape behind."

"I've watched out for you, and the children."

She gripped his hand. "And I love you for it. You're the best friend I ever had. There's a grand plan, Walk. There's cosmic forces, cause and effect."

"You really believe that?"

"The universe finds a way to balance the good and the bad." She stood and dusted the sand from her. "When he asks, you tell him I was done with him a long time ago. And don't mention him again, Walk. And as for Duchess and Robin, they're all that matters. And I'll do all I can to prove that to them."

He watched her leave, and then turned back to the ocean. They were words he had heard many times before, and words he prayed that this time she meant.

• • •

Midnight and a low rumble, headlights swept across the room, the closet without doors, the dresser with the broken drawer.

No posters of her own, artwork, hints at her thirteen years. A carpet worn thin, nylon threading to bare boards, and a small bed beside her brother's, where she slept tormented hours.

She checked Robin, sound asleep, out of his sheets, air so warm his hair was slick. She closed the door tight, then went to the street door and opened it on the chain.

Star lay on dead grass.

Duchess went cautiously.

Up the street, the coruscation of brake lights as the Escalade made the turn away.

Duchess rolled her mother over, skirt hitched, indecent.

"Star."

A mark by her eye, her lip fuller, the skin just about damming the blood.

"Star, wake up."

Across the street she saw drapes move, the silhouette of the butcher, always watching. And then beside, the hard glow of Brandon Rock's security light as it cast over the covered Mustang.

"Come on." She slapped her mother's cheek.

Ten long minutes to get her up, another ten and into the house. Star puked in the hallway, a kind of hard retching like she was bringing up her charcoal soul.

Duchess got her to the bed and lay her on her stomach, like she knew, pulled free her heels, cracked her window to the cigarette smoke, sweet alcohol, and perfume. Sometimes her mother woke her late when she stumbled in from a shift tending bar at Darke's place. But this was the first time she had been beaten.

She went to the kitchen and filled a bucket. She cleaned the vomit so her brother would not see, then washed up and pulled on her jeans and sneakers.

In their bedroom she found her brother sitting up, a vacant look as she laid him back to sleep. She pushed the button, locked their door, lifted the window and climbed out.

Cape Haven slept, Duchess rode streets with care, away from Main and Sunset, where Walk sometimes sat and watched out. She thought of her mother and Walk, and the draw of alcohol and drugs that lessened the world.

A mile out, along Cabrillo, a half hour and her thighs burned.

The club came into view, The Eight, Duchess knew it because all the kids knew it. There was light pressure to close it every few years, when the primaries opened and the mayor-elect chased wholesome votes.

Monday night, late enough for the lot to sit empty, the place lost in dark, dead neon and empties in the gravel.

Across Cabrillo Duchess saw the bluff, rocks of no shape, a cluster of trees waved her way, culling the breeze. The water at night, so far and dark it might well have been the edge of her world. Not a boat or a passing car, just her, and she dropped her bike and crossed the lot, tried the big wood doors but knew they'd be locked up. The windows were blackened, peeling at one edge. A sign promised happy hour from two till seven, Duchess wondered what kind of man visited when sun lit the sin.

Above, piped neon, a profile of ass and legs but dulled now. At the side she found a rock and hurled it at a pane, saw it crack and tried again. Breathless when it broke, for just a moment deafening, then nothing at all. A beat till the alarm called out, so loud she finally did hurry. In her bag was a book of matches and she stepped through the jagged shape, not crying out when her arm caught and sliced. She moved with aim, found herself in a dimly lit backroom, mirrors of light, stools and makeup and the kind of costumes she did not know. A smell, sweat but sanitized.

There were lockers, too many, each carried a photo. She looked at faces and pouts and swept-back hair. Beside them were names that promised innocence and purity. She moved along and ran a hand through feathers and corsets.

In the bar glasses lined in front of a mirrored wall. She took a bottle of Courvoisier and emptied it over a leather booth. She took the matches from her bag, lit the book, and dropped it, watching the flames crawl blue and hypnotic.

She stood and stared for so long she did not notice when the heat reddened her cheeks, when her chest grew tight and she began to cough. She stumbled back as the fire crawled and gathered. She clutched her arm, blood on her fingers, as flames ran up and out, along to the lights and tables.

Almost out and she remembered.

She ran back through thick smoke, hooked her T-shirt over her nose as she opened door after door till she found the office. Mahogany desk topped with green leather, another, smaller bar, crystal glass and a box of cigars. She found a bank of screens beside and opened the cabinet beneath, popped the security tape from the machine, and shoved it into her bag.

She moved fast, head down as the flames ran for her.

In the night air she panted and grabbed her bicycle. On her T-shirt were stars and a half moon with a face that smiled out. Behind her she heard it, crackling and carnage. And then, finally, the call of the alarm being answered.

She rode hard, Cabrillo sweeping down and then climbing. She passed a car, kept her head bent then followed the trees away from the road and into Cape Haven. She cut down Sunset then onto Fortuna, where she drew up by a pile of junk, an old side table, boxes and trash bags spilling and ready to be hauled away by a truck. She dropped her bike, ran across and stuffed the tape into a garbage bag

She'd covered her tracks. She was smart enough.

Her street and her yard, she moved as quiet as she could, left her bike propped and climbed back through the window. The house still slept. In the bathroom she stripped off her clothes, paid no mind to the cut, crept naked to the washer and got to work.

When she was done she got into the tub, ran water from the shower head, and soaped and cleaned. And then, in the mirror, she pulled a half-inch piece of glass from her arm and watched blood pour out as it went.

She looked at the red, at the history there, her outlaw ancestry steeling her.

They were not a family that had a medicine cabinet, or a first-aid box, but Duchess found a pack of children's Band-Aids she'd picked up a year back, selected the biggest, stuck it down hard and watched it color.

She lay at the foot of her brother's bed, curled like a cat, waiting for sleep that did not find her.

First light, the hot night behind, she wondered what would come.

It would be bad.

She cursed herself fully.

9

Walk found him at the edge of the cliff.

The rear fence pulled down, Vincent stood with his toes free of the rock, where the slightest wind would carry him a hundred feet down. He wore jeans and an old T-shirt, his eyes cloaked with tired. Walk knew how he felt. He'd been woken a little after one, the call about Darke's club. He'd pulled on his uniform and driven the mile, the sky lit red, Fourth of July all over again. He'd followed the heat, noise, and lights, left the cruiser across two lanes, a little traffic building but most having the sense to double back.

Darke had stood apart from the onlookers as smoke rose and grayed the sky. No emotion.

"You want to take a step back from the edge, Vin? You're kind of making me nervous here."

Together they walked back up to the shade of the house.

"Were you praying or something, standing there like that? I worried you were going to jump."

"Is there a difference between a prayer and a wish?"

Walk took his hat off. "You wish for what you want and pray for what you need."

"Pretty sure mine are one and the same."

They sat together on the steps of the rear deck. New panels leaned beside them, not yet stained. It would take a lifetime to restore the place.

"You know that guy, Dickie Darke?"

"I don't really know anyone, Walk."

Walk waited, did not press.

"The Radley girl, and Star. He was giving them shit so I stepped in. No one else seems to."

Walk took it. "Star says they're friends. She won't press charges."

"Friends."

Walk heard it again, that softest note of jealousy. Vincent still cared.

"His place, it burned last night."

Vincent did not speak.

"He owns a club on Cabrillo, money in the jar. Darke mentioned your name, so I had to—"

"It's alright, Walk, don't even worry about it."

Walk ran his hand along the leaning rail. "So, you were home last night."

"I imagine a man like that has a fair few people pissed at him."

"I've got a fairly good idea who I need to talk to."

Vincent looked over.

"We had a call, driver, saw a kid on a bicycle."

"Can you just, I mean, could you just leave it? I know what I'm saying, I don't have a right to get involved, but she's a kid. Star's kid."

"She is. Anyway, whoever did it had the good sense to take the security tape, so long as they keep quiet . . ."

"Right."

And that was it, Vincent said nothing else and Walk left him to it. He logged the conversation, he was doing his job, he would always do his job.

He left Vincent, then found the girl and the boy on Sayer, the long route, away from Main. They walked, Robin out in front, crossing yards, every now and then checking back that he wasn't alone. And Duchess, that careful way she carried herself, like she was listening out, expecting trouble at all times. She turned as he drew up and regarded him with that same equanimity he saw in Vincent.

Walk killed the engine, got out and stood, the sun creeping above a clad house. That morning his hands did not shake, the dopamine, the new dose. Respite would not last long.

"Morning, Duchess."

She had those tired eyes too. She carried her bag and her brother's. She wore jeans and old sneakers and a T-shirt that had a small hole beneath one arm. Her hair was tousled, blond like her mother's, the bow there, like always. She was pretty enough that the boys would have lined up, if they didn't know, if everyone didn't know.

"Do you know about Darke's place?"

He looked for a tell, she had none at all. He was glad of that. He willed her to play it right, to give the answers he needed.

"It burned last night. Someone saw a kid on a bicycle, around that time, you know?"

"I don't."

"It wasn't you?"

"I was home all night. You can check with my mother."

He rested his hands on his bulging stomach. "I buried a lot over the years. Each time I questioned myself. The times you got caught stealing—"

"Food," she said, sad. "It was just food."

"This is different. A lot of money, if someone was in there they could've died. Some things I can't protect you from."

They stood together as a car passed, a neighbor, old and looking on, a quick glance at them and then away. Star's girl, not a hint of surprise.

"I know about Darke and what he's like."

She palmed her eyes, too tired, her muscles all tight. "You don't know shit, Walk." She said it quiet but he took it hard. "Why don't you go stroll up Main and help the vacationers with their dogs."

He looked for something to say, but instead he dropped his eyes to the grass and thumbed his badge, redundancy fit him like a second skin.

She turned and walked on, not looking back. He knew if it wasn't for Robin keeping her straight, his hands would be full.

At the school gate she saw the car, the Escalade, black with windows that shaded out the world. It sat idle, the unknowing passed by. Yellow buses lined up like flowers.

She knew it would come; Star always talked about balance, cause and effect. She waved off her brother and watched him into the red doors.

In the air was still fire, floating embers that charred her arms and clung to her nose. She wondered who'd seen her at that hour, that night hour when the socially concerned should've been home and sleeping off the perfect day. Bad luck, that was all. A part of her was glad, because fuck Dickie Darke.

She crossed the street and walked up to the car window. She was outside her school, where she was safe, with teachers and people who promised to notice strangers.

The window dropped. Darke's eyes, swollen, bloated like he'd been dredged from the water, except instead of the ocean it was money and greed that filled him.

She stood still, her knees shaking beneath her jeans, but she fixed him with a hard look.

"Get in." Not angry, not loud.

"Fuck you."

A group of kids from her class passed and did not see her, all excitement, last week of school. Sometimes she wondered what it would be like, a little more ordinary, a little more nothing.

"Kill the engine and take the key out."

He did.

She walked around. "I'll leave the door open."

He gripped the wheel, thick fingers, huge knuckles.

"We both know."

She watched the sky. "We do."

"Do you know about the principle of causation?" He looked so sad, so fucking big and tough and sad. A creature not of this world.

"Come at me."

"You don't know what you did."

On the mat was a single spent butt, just stubbed and burned in. The brand her mother smoked.

"You're not like your mother," he said.

Duchess watched a bird hold still and perfect in the air.

Darke rubbed a hand along the wheel. "She's got a way out. She owes rent. I need a favor."

"She's not a whore."

"Do I look like a pimp to you?"

"You look like a cunt to me."

The word sat there awhile.

"That's okay. So long as I don't look like the man I really am." He spoke with a flatness that chilled her.

"You took something last night."

"You've got enough."

"Who decides what enough looks like?"

She stared.

"Your mother can make this go away. You need to ask her. That would level things a little."

"Fuck you, Darke."

"The tape, Duchess. I need the security tape."

"Why?"

"Trenton Seven. You know what that is?"

"The insurance place. I see the billboards."

"They won't pay the money because the tape is missing and they think I had something to do with the fire."

"You did."

He took a long, deep breath.

She grit her teeth.

"I won't forget."

She met his eye. "You shouldn't."

"I really don't want to have to come for you." Something in his voice made her believe him.

"But you will."

"I will."

He reached across her, into the glove compartment, took out his sunglasses, not before she saw it, sitting there, the barrel facing her.

"I'll give you the day. You tell your mother what you did. She can fix it, or I'll have to. And you get the tape back."

"You'll give it to Walk."

"No."

"The insurance guys will get the cops involved."

"Maybe. But you got to ask yourself something, Duchess."

"And what's that, Dick?" Maybe he caught the tremor then.

"Would you rather have the cops come looking for you? Or me?"

"I heard you stamped a guy to death."

"He didn't die."

"Why did you do it?"

"Business."

"The tape. Maybe I'll hold on to it."

He stared at her, those eyes that bore deep.

"You stay away from my mother and maybe one day I'll give it back to you."

She climbed from the car, then turned. He watched her, studied her, taking in every feature, committing her to memory.

She wondered what he saw as she walked into the school building, beside other kids, their lives so light they dazzled her. The day crawled. She checked the clock often, her eye on the window, the teacher's words not reaching her ear. She ate lunch alone, watched Robin from the fence and felt what little control she once had slip from her grasp. Darke could do immeasurable damage. She needed the tape. She believed he wouldn't take it to Walk. She reasoned there were two types of people in the world, the kind that called the cops and the kind that did not.

When the bell sounded she watched the other kids file in, kids playing ball tried for one last play, Cassidy Evans led her group. Duchess slipped down the side of the main building, then ran across to the parking lot and drifted through Fords and Volvos and Nissans. She would get caught, no doubt about it, but she'd tell her mother she was feeling sick, time of the month, something the school would not press.

She walked fast, feeling the eyes of everyone she passed. She skirted Main in case Walk was looking out of the station. It was hot, so fucking hot she could barely breathe. Sweat all over her, T-shirt damp.

When she made it to Fortuna she found the old house, for once glad she had fucked up, that she hadn't made time to destroy the tape.

But then she stared at the yard, all the junk cleared, the garbage truck had already come.

The tape was gone.

She looked up and down, breathing hard, like her last hope had deserted her.

She spent the afternoon on the beach, sitting on the sand and watching the water. She clutched her stomach, the pain was hard and constant and followed her all the way back to collect Robin.

He talked the whole way home, about his birthday, about being six and what came with that. He asked for a house key, she smiled and stroked his hair, her mind someplace she hoped he'd never follow. In the empty house she fixed scrambled eggs and they ate together in front of the TV. And, when the sun fell, she got him into bed and read to him.

"Can we have green eggs one time?"

"Sure."

"And ham?"

She kissed his head and cut off his light, closed her eyes for a moment, then woke to darkness. She walked through the house, turned on a lamp and heard music from outside.

Duchess found Star on the deck, the old bench needed painting. The moon lit her mother as she strummed the old guitar. Their song. She closed her eyes, the words cut her.

She needed to tell her mother what she had done, that she had taken a match and burned the very bridge that kept them out of troubled water. They were in the shallows now, but the deep would come for them, it would sink them down till not even moonlight made it through.

Duchess took steps, feet bare, she did not notice the splinters.

The strum of soft chords. "Sing with me."

"No."

Duchess slid along till her head came to rest on her mother's shoulder. No matter what she had done, no matter that she was tough and she was an outlaw, she needed her mother.

"Why do you cry when you sing?" Duchess asked.

"Sorry."

"Don't be sorry."

"I called that guy, the music guy from the bar. He wanted to meet for a drink."

"Did you go?"

Star nodded slowly. "Men."

"What happened last night?" She did not ask often, but this time she needed clarity.

"Some people just can't hold their liquor." Star shot a look at the neighboring house.

"Brandon Rock. He hit you?"

"It was an accident."

"He couldn't take no for an answer."

Star shook her head.

Duchess watched the tall trees sway against night sky. "So Darke didn't do nothing this time."

"Last thing I remember was him helping me into the car."

Realization was cold, and for a while Duchess could not speak. And then she thought of Darke, his hands on her. She grit her teeth, steeled herself. Bad things happened to bad men.

"You know it's Robin's birthday in the morning."

Star looked sad then, not broken but close, her lip still a little swollen, her eye still dark. The kind of look that made the pain worse. There was no gift for her brother. Her mother had not remembered.

"I did something bad, Mom."

"We all do bad things."

"I don't think I can fix it."

Star closed her eyes, still she played and sang as her daughter gently leaned on her.

Duchess wanted so desperately to join in but her voice began to break.

"I'll protect you. That's what mothers do."

Duchess did not cry, but right then she came close.

10

Walk suffered the indignity of the fall alone.

Small blessing. One minute he was walking, the next he was on his back looking toward the sky. His left leg, just gone from under him.

He sat in the cruiser, in the lot at Vancour Hill. He did not go in. Kendrick said he might have problems with balance, still, that loss of control, it was frightening.

The radio was low, static and talk, 2-11 in Bronson, 11-54 in San Luis. A coffee cup from Rosie's Diner, a burger wrapper on the mat. His stomach pressed his shirt and he rested his hands there. Slow shift. He'd driven by Vincent's, the house was coming along, the shutters removed and stripped, ready for painting.

He searched for the polestar, dwelled on the disease and felt it in his bones, his blood, his mind. Synapses firing slow, the correspondence not lost but delayed.

A little before midnight the radio jolted him from a light sleep.

Ivy Ranch Road.

He licked the dry from his lips.

And then the call again.

He reached for the radio and started the engine, ran the lights and lit the street as he headed back toward Cape Haven. The caller gave no detail, just that they needed to come. He prayed it was nothing, maybe Star was drunk again.

Past Addison. The quiet side of Main, no lights at all.

He slowed on Ivy Ranch Road, saw nothing but sleeping houses and breathed again.

Up to the curb outside her house. Calm till he saw the street door open, and then that feeling came, sharp in his gut, no air in his lungs. He climbed out and reached for his gun, which he hadn't done in as long as he could remember.

A glance at the Rock house, then across at Milton's, no sign of life at all. A calling owl, a garbage can fell a way off, maybe raccoons. He took the porch in one step and pushed the door.

The hallway, a side table with phone book. Sneakers in a messy line. Pictures on the wall, art that Robin had made, tacked in place by Duchess.

In the mirror was a crack, Walk met his own eyes, wide and fearful. He gripped the gun tight, flipped the safety off, thought about calling out but stayed quiet.

He made his way down the hallway, two bedrooms, doors open to clothes strewn, a dressing table knocked over.

The bathroom. The faucet ran slowly, the basin filled and spilling. He shut it off, his shoes in the puddle.

Into the kitchen, nothing but the steady hand of the clock cut the quiet. He scanned slow, the mess that was always there, a butter knife, dishes in the sink; Duchess would get to them, she always did.

He didn't notice the man at first. Sitting at the small table, palms up and open, like he meant no harm at all.

"You need to go into the living room," Vincent said.

Walk noticed the sweat on his head, realized his gun was trained on his childhood friend but he would not lower it. Adrenaline carried him.

"What did you do?"

"You're too late to change things, Walk. But you need to go and make your calls. I'll be here. I won't move at all."

The gun shook.

"You should cuff me. That's what is expected. You need to do this correctly. If you toss them over here I'll do it myself."

Walk, his mouth so dry he could barely speak. "I don't—"

"Pass me the cuffs, Chief Walker."

Chief. He was a cop. Walk reached for the cuffs on his belt and tossed them onto the table.

He moved into the living room. Sweat bled into his eyes.

The scene came at him.

"Shit, Star." He crossed fast and knelt. "Oh Jesus, Star."

She lay on her back. For a minute he thought she'd chased with something bad, which had happened before. But when he noticed he fell back and cursed again.

Blood, all over, so much of it he fumbled for his radio, his fingers slick as he called it.

"Jesus." He pawed at her clothes, tried to make sense of it before he found the wound, the hole, torn flesh, above her heart.

He smoothed hair from her face, pale and gone. He tried for a pulse, found nothing but started CPR. He looked around as he worked, a lamp lying, a picture on the carpet, a small bookcase upended.

Specks of blood climbed the wall.

"Duchess," he called.

He worked on, sweating, muscles burning.

Cops and medics arrived and gently pushed him off. It was clear enough she was dead.

He heard yelling from the kitchen, Vincent on the ground, then led out.

Walk stood, dazed, the world spinning the wrong way as he headed into the street, the neighbors gathering. He saw in reds and blues as he sat on the porch and gulped air. He rubbed his head, his eyes, hit his own chest a few times to make sure it was all real.

They took Vincent before he could reach the car, he jogged a little but panted and dropped to his knees, each year of his life unraveled.

A team ran control, swept it from him, taped the area and moved people far enough back. News vans, lights and reporters. A tech van cut in and up onto the curb. It was a scene and they controlled it well, that was until Walk heard noise inside.

He stood, still dazed, made his way through and ducked the tape, and in the house he saw Boyd from state and two cops from Sutler County.

"What is it?"

A cop turned, eyes loaded with anger. "The kid . . . the boy."

Walk stepped back, hit the wall and felt his legs weaken, braced for what would come as his vision tunneled.

Boyd waved them back a little.

And then Walk saw him, squinting up, a blanket around his shoulders.

"He's alright?" Walk said.

Boyd checked him carefully. "The bedroom door was locked. I think he was sleeping."

Walk knelt by the boy, who looked anywhere but at him. "Robin, where's your sister?"

• • •

Duchess pedaled three miles, traversed dark roads that led from her town. She held her breath as cars came at her, dipped their beams or flashed or sounded their horns. She could have taken the pretty streets, a mile added, she was tired enough.

The Chevron on Pensacola, blue sign on gray pillars. She leaned her bicycle against a coalbin and made her way across the lot. An old sedan parked bad, the owner stretching the pump.

Robin would wake six years old, she would not let him wake to nothing.

Eleven bucks, taken from Star's purse. Duchess hated her, mostly, loved her now and then, needed her totally.

In the gas station was a cop standing at the coffee machine, dark tie and slacks, neat mustache, shield on his chest. He eyed her and she ignored him, then his radio crackled and he threw a couple of dollars at the counter and headed out.

She walked aisles, passed towering refrigerators, signs that called BEER and SODA and ENERGY.

No birthday cakes, just a pack of Entenmann's cupcakes, the kind with pink frosting. Robin would be pissed about that, inside at least, but he wouldn't say anything that might be deemed ungrateful. She picked up a pack and found some candles. Six bucks left.

Behind the counter was a kid, nineteen, maybe, acne cheeks, too many piercings.

"Do you have toys?"

He pointed to a rack that had the sorriest collection of plastic Duchess had ever seen. She carefully studied a magic set, a stuffed rabbit, a pack of colorful hairbands, and a figure that bore a libelous resemblance to Captain America. She clutched it tight, it was a find. It was also seven bucks.

She took it with her back to the cakes, saw she had the only pack that could pass as something special, and cursed her mother once again. She stood beneath yellow striplight, so dim it drained the fight right from her. She thought of lifting the candles but saw the kid behind the counter watching on, like he could read the tortured turns of her mind. She squeezed the cake box, just enough to dent it.

At the counter she argued it, showed the kid the damaged cake, asked him to take a buck off. At first he refused, then the line started to grow and he took her money with a scowl. She hitched her bag over the handlebars and set off toward home, pedaling slow as another cop car passed her, lights on and siren harsh against the warm night.

Later, when she knew, she'd look back at that last ride and wish she'd felt it, the last night of anything at all. She'd wish she'd taken the long route, along the coast, noticed the endless water and night songs, the perfect glow of each lamp on Main. She'd wish she'd breathed it deep and held it, the last moment of her normal, because if it was bad before, and it mostly was, it was something altogether different when she made it back to her street and watched the neighbors part for her bicycle, like she'd commanded them, like she was all-powerful.

When she saw the cop cars her first instinct was to turn. An hour earlier, when she'd picked up her bicycle and wheeled it down the side of the house, she'd made a stop outside Brandon Rock's place. She'd found a stone, sharp enough, walked up his driveway, lifted the cover from the Mustang, and dragged the rock down the door and fender, so hard and deep she could see the silver beneath. He hit her mother. Fuck him.

But this was too many cars, too much noise, more than Walk and that look he gave her.

She dropped her bike, dropped her bag, kicked out at a cop when he tried to move in front of her. He backed off, she knew that wasn't normal.

She ran at the house, ducked the tape and another cop, cursed at all of them. All the bad words she knew.

She found her brother and calmed, with Walk looking on, his mouth set straight but his eyes telling everything, all of it. They wouldn't let her in the living room, no matter the way she flailed her arms at Walk, the way she caught him by the eye, the words she used, the feral way her brother cried.

Walk half carried her out into the yard, where the people could not see her. He set her down in the dirt and she called him a motherfucker, and beside them Robin sobbed like tomorrow would no longer happen.

Strangers all over, men in uniform, men in suits.

When they thought she'd calmed she broke and ran and ducked them. She was fast enough to make it through. At the door and inside, through a home reduced to a single scene.

She saw her.

Her mother.

She did not fight when the arm closed around her, no longer kicked out and cursed, just let Walk carry her like the child she was.

"You and Robin can stay with me tonight."

To Walk's cruiser, Robin holding her hand tight. Neighbors stared on, a TV camera lit them up. Duchess did not have the strength to glare.

She saw Milton at his window, met his eye before he turned and moved back into the shadow.

She'd picked up the bag from the yard, inside she saw the cakes, the doll, and the candles.

They sat there a long time, till the hours lay so heavy on Robin he fell into a troubled sleep beside her, moaning out and calling as she stroked his hair.

Walk drove slow out of their street, Duchess watching the bright light that was her home, the dimming scene that was her life.

PART TWO

•

Big Sky

11

Walk drove with an arm in the sun as endless plains rose and fell from prairie to steppe and grasslands beyond. East was the river that slithered through four states before emptying into the Pacific.

He left the radio off. Miles of nothing but the call of crickets and the occasional passing of beaten trucks with bare-chested drivers. Some dipped their heads, others locked tight ahead like they had plenty to hide. Walk kept his speed low, he had not slept in a long time. They'd spent a night in a motel, their rooms joined by a door Walk left cracked all night. He'd offered to fly with them, but the boy was afraid. Walk was glad, he'd never liked flying.

They sat in the back, each staring out, watching the land like it was something all foreign. Robin had not told anything of that night, not to Walk or his sister, or the special cops that came down. Armed with compassion, they'd settled him into a room of pastel colors and murals and animals with smiling faces. They gave him pens and paper, talked around him with looks of finality, like he was fragile pieces so far from one whole. His sister watched on, unimpressed, arms folded, nose wrinkled like she didn't much care for the bullshit they were peddling.

"You alright back there?"

He got nothing.

They passed towns, water towers, rusting scaffolds. For fifty miles the railroad accompanied them, brown weed grown over burnt slats like the last train had left the station a lifetime before.

He slowed by a Methodist chapel, white boards and lightest green slate, the steeple an arrow that pointed to more.

"You hungry?" He knew they would not answer. It was a long trip, a thousand miles. The scorched stretch of Nevada, Route 80 without end, the dirt as dry as the air. It took an age for the world to change, orange to green, Idaho upon them, Yellowstone and Wyoming just beyond. Duchess took an interest for a while.

At the Twin River Mills they stopped at a diner.

In a torn booth Walk ordered hamburgers and milkshakes and they watched a gas station across the way. A young family, U-Haul, moving between shells, the little girl a sticky mess of chocolate and her mother fussing after her with a wet wipe and a smile.

Robin stopped eating and watched. Walk placed a hand on his shoulder and the boy stared back down into his shake.

"It'll be alright."

"How'd you figure that?" Duchess fired back, quick like she'd been expecting something.

"I remember your grandfather, when I was small. He's a good man. I heard he's got a hundred acres, maybe you'll like it. Clear air and all that." He didn't know what he was saying, just that he wished he could stop. "Fertile soil." He'd worsened it.

Duchess rolled her eyes.

"You talked to Vincent King?" She did not look up.

Walk dabbed his lips with a napkin. "I'm . . . I'll assist the state police."

They'd bumped Walk from the case the morning after, left him to arrange the safeguarding of the scene till they were done. Two days, tech vans and busy people, Walk liaised with locals, closed half the road. They moved on to the King house. Again, Walk was left to safeguard the scene. They deemed him too small-town, Cape Haven PD too small to cope. He had not argued.

"They'll put him to death."

Robin looked over at his sister, his eyes tired but intense, the last flares of a dying fire.

"Duchess—"

"It's what they'll do. A man like that, there's no coming back. Shooting a woman, unarmed. You believe in an eye for an eye, Walk?"

"I don't know."

Duchess fished a fry in her ketchup and shook her head like she was disappointed in him. She spoke of Vincent often, the man that shot her mother dead and left her small family in ruins.

"Eat your burger," Duchess said to Robin, and he ate. "And the green."

"But—"

She stared.

He picked up a piece of lettuce and nibbled the corner.

Another hour and Walk saw the sign for Dearman. Razor wire ran a quarter mile, keeping people in and out of fractious lives.

A guard in a tower, eyes beneath a wide-brim hat and one hand on a rifle. In the mirror Walk was tailed by dust, like he'd stirred the calm.

Robin slept in his seat, face tight like his dreams were keeping pace with his days.

"That's a prison," Duchess said.

"It is."

"Like the kind they got Vincent King in."

"Yes."

"Will he get beaten in there?"

"Prison's not nice."

"Maybe he'll get all raped."

"You shouldn't talk like that."

"Fuck off, Walk."

He more than understood the hate, but he worried what it would do to her, those cinders, the lightest breeze and they'd flare.

"I hope he gets beaten so bad. I see it, you know, when I'm lying down at night. I see his face. I hope he gets beaten till there's nothing left."

He pushed back in his seat, aching bones, tremoring hands. That morning he'd lain so helpless he worried it wouldn't pass, that the girl would have to fetch help. He thought back to the start, a pain in his shoulder, just a pain in his shoulder.

"I worry I won't remember Cape Haven." She spoke to the views they passed.

"I can write you. I can send photos."

"It's not home now. Where we're going, that's not home either. He took it all."

"It'll be . . ." He stopped himself, the words catching.

She turned and watched Dearman till it smoked to nothing, then closed her eyes to Walk and the changing world.

An hour off the hottest part of the day, heat rose in calling waves while both children slept. Duchess, her eyes sunken, swollen from the strain because she didn't cry. She wore shorts. He saw grazed knees and pale thighs.

For a hundred miles the land had pitched and fallen, the arid now lush, the thirst quenched by westerlies that blew relief from the water. Montana arrived with little fanfare, just a sign, a blue, red, and yellow welcome. Walk rubbed his neck and yawned, then itched at the stubble on his cheeks. He had not eaten much since. He had dropped five pounds.

Another hour and he turned by the Missouri River. Helena behind, the sky a canvas so big, not even God's work could distract him from the blues that afternoon. The roads and a track, the farm appeared like it belonged, painted into the landscape with delicate strokes, mud red barns white topped, three in total, and two silos that nested with cedars. The house was wide, the porch wrapped it with seats and a swing and timber that was gnarled and beautiful. Walk saw her watching now, wanting to ask but keeping her mouth tight.

"That's it," he offered.

"Is there people anywhere?"

"Copper Falls, only a few miles. They have a movie theater." He'd checked it all the night before.

Gum trees tangled from both sides and shaded them, white picket needed painting. He followed the curve and saw Hal, standing still and watching, no smile or wave or anything at all.

Duchess craned her head over Walk's shoulder as she slipped her belt off.

When they stopped Walk climbed out and Duchess did not.

"Hal," he said, walked over and extended a hand.

Hal shook it firmly, his hand tough and calloused. He had blue eyes that shone with more than age but no smile, not till his granddaughter emerged from the cruiser and stood just as still, a vision of her mother.

Walk watched the two, eyeing each other, exchanging judgment. He tried to beckon her but Hal shook his head once. She'd come when she's ready.

"Long drive. Robin is sleeping, I didn't know whether to wake him."

"He'll be up early enough tomorrow. The farm has its hours."

Walk followed Hal up to the house.

The old man was tall, muscled, unforgiveness in every step. He walked with his head high, chin up a little; this is my land. Behind, Duchess wandered, looking at the long stretch of world, a new life already growing old. She bent and touched the grass, made her way to a barn and peered into cool dark. The smell was strong, animals and shit but she did not turn away.

Hal brought beer so cold Walk didn't turn it down. He wore his uniform and they settled onto hard wooden chairs.

"It's been a long time," Walk said.

"It has."

Montana, portrait to landscape, the kind of open that was almost too much to breathe in.

"What a mess," Hal said. He wore a plaid shirt, sleeves rolled over muscled forearms.

Mess was the wrong word, but as close a fit as any.

"Did she see?"

Walk looked at Hal but the old man kept his gaze on the acres. "I think so. After. She ran at the cops and made it into the living room."

Hal cracked a knuckle, scarred hands, grizzled voice. "The boy?"

"No. Maybe he heard something, screams, gunshot, he won't speak about it. He was locked in his bedroom. He's seen someone a couple times, a doctor. He'll have to see someone here, I can put you in touch, he needs it. Maybe he'll remember, maybe it's best he doesn't."

Hal drank, half the bottle in one sip. He wore a simple watch on a thick wrist, tan from years working beneath the open sky. "I haven't seen them, Duchess . . . she was a baby, when I last saw my daughter. And then Robin . . ." He trailed away.

"They're both good kids." The words sounded trite, empty when they were not, like there was another kind of child in the world.

"I wanted to come, for the burial. But I made a promise." Hal offered no further explanation.

"It happened fast. As soon as they released the . . . as soon as they released Star. Small service at Little Brook. Beside her sister." Duchess had held her brother's hand. She did not cry, just watched the coffin like the great equalizer it was.

They watched as Duchess came out of the barn, a chicken trailed her. She glanced back, as if it were following her.

"She looks like her mother."

"Yes."

"I made up a room. They'll share. The boy, he like baseball?"

Walk smiled but did not know.

"I bought a ball and glove."

They saw Duchess peer into the cruiser, check on Robin and then head back toward the barn, still eyeing the chicken.

Hal cleared his throat. "Vincent King. I haven't said that name in a long time. I hoped I'd never have to again."

"He hasn't spoken a word yet. I found him there, in the kitchen, he was the one that called it in. I have my doubts." Walk said it with a conviction he wondered if Hal could see through, that he was so far out of his depth that the state cops would barely keep him in the loop.

"They're holding him."

"No official charge yet. They've got him on a bail condition. Broken curfew."

"But, Vincent King."

"I don't know. What Vincent did, and what this is."

"I go to church but I don't believe in God. He goes to prison but is not a criminal."

Hal's face, etched lines so deep they told a story that had begun thirty years before.

Hal cracked his knuckles again. "The minister said we begin at the end. It would have made for easier years if I thought for one second Sissy was somewhere better than a small wooden box. I try though, every Sunday I try."

"Sorry."

"It wasn't your—"

"Not just Sissy. Your wife. I never got to say it, after."

It made the local news. The first time any of them saw Star's mother was the first day of the trial. Maggie Day rolled into the courtroom. She had the hair and the eyes and drew looks, but an air of fallen glamour chased the beauty from her.

"She was sad for Vincent. Said watching a child draw a man's sentence just about broke her all over again." Hal drained the last of his beer. "When Star found her, that night. We had a painting, a print, *Temeraire*, you know it?"

"The boat."

"She was sitting beneath it, head tipped back. All that haunted sky, like she was part of it."

"I'm sorry."

"She wanted to be with Sissy." He said it simply, like there could be anything simple about the suicide of a wife and mother. "Vincent King is the cancer of my family."

Walk held the cold bottle to his forehead. "Listen, Hal. There was a man, Dickie Darke. He was . . . him and Star. He was rough with her." He watched the old man, his mouth tight. "And I don't know what happened with Duchess, but someone burned his place down. Strip joint."

Hal looked out at his granddaughter, standing small on the endless acres.

"I don't think he'll try and find you, not after all that's happened."

"He might come here?"

"I don't think so, but Duchess thinks he will."

"She said that?"

"She doesn't really say anything. She just asked if Darke could find them up here. She won't say exactly why. I can't rule it out, that he had something to do with Star."

"And if he did?"

Walk took a breath as he watched the car, where the boy slept. Maybe the only witness.

"He won't find us here. I'm not listed, and the land . . . there's a lien. I had some bad years. I can keep her safe. And the boy. That's the one thing I'm sure I can do."

Walk followed the line of the house, then down to the picket. There was water, too big for a pond and too small for a lake. He saw mirrors, sky and trees and the ripples of his own drawn face.

"I don't want to stay here."

He turned to Duchess.

"That man is old. I don't even know who the fuck he is."

"There's nowhere else. It's here or Social, that's . . . can you do it for Robin?"

He wanted to reach out and take her hand and tell her soft lies.

"Don't call here, Walk. You can write, maybe. Robin, that shrink said he needs to forget. Maybe just for a while. It's too bad for him. Too much for a child."

He wanted to tell her she was a child too.

After, he knelt in the dirt, ruffled Robin's hair and met his frightened eyes. Robin looked past, at Hal and the old house. And then Walk stood, faced Duchess and searched for words.

"I'm an outlaw," she said.

He took a breath, sadness washed over him.

"And you're a lawman."

He nodded. "I am."

"So fuck off now."

He climbed into the cruiser and edged from them.

The sun died, he slowed by the water, beneath the gum trees, he watched her, a hand on her brother's shoulder as they walked toward the old man, slowly, cautiously.

12

Duchess did not eat that first night on the farm.

Instead she watched Robin and made sure he finished his bowl. It was some kind of stew, and he looked at her with those eyes that told her he wanted to cry. She fed him the last mouthfuls herself.

Hal stood awkward, watched awhile then moved to the sink and looked out over the land. He was big to Duchess, broad and powerful and imposing. To Robin he must have looked like a giant.

Duchess took their bowls over.

"You need to eat," he said.

"You don't know what I need."

She dumped her food into the trash, then led her brother from the kitchen and out onto the porch.

Sunset. Burnt haze that washed the rolling acres and cannoned from the water. Animals gathered far out, a cluster of elk that faced the falling light.

"Go run around." She gave him a push.

Robin left her, walked the low hill, found a stick and dragged it in the dirt. In his other hand he clutched Captain America.

He had not let it from his sight since he'd woken that morning at Walk's house.

She'd already asked him, when it was late and Walk slept, she asked about that night and told him it was alright to tell if he'd heard something. He told her nothing at all, the place where the memory might have been lay in total darkness.

She had yet to process the death of her mother, the funeral, the new grave that stood beside Sissy's on the Little Brook cliff. She wanted to cry, though knew if she did the grief would settle right there in her chest, not let her breathe when she needed strength most. She would be there for her brother. It was the two of them. The outlaw and her brother.

"I have a ball for him."

She did not turn and did not acknowledge Hal. To think of him as family, his blood to hers. Not there when he was needed, which was too often. She spit in the dirt.

"I know it's been difficult."

"You don't know shit." She let it hang long in the dusk air, the dark sprinting at them so fast it was as if she had blinked away the color.

"I don't like cursing in my house."

"My house. Walk said it was our home."

He looked pained then. She was glad.

"Tomorrow will be different in all kinds of ways. Some you might like and some you might not."

"You don't know what I like and what I don't. Same for my brother."

Hal sat on the swing seat, motioned for her to join him but she would not. The chains pulled on the cedar like they might wrench the soul from the old farmhouse. Her mother had told her about souls, vegetative to rational. She wondered what could be rational about the most base form of life.

He smoked a cigar and it carried to her, she wanted to move but wouldn't, her sandals rooted. Her instinct was to ask him about her mother, about her aunt and Vincent King. About where the fuck they were in the world, the land so different and the sky too vast. She got that he would enjoy that, to talk to his granddaughter like a bond would form. She spit in the dirt again.

At an hour far from bedtime Hal sent them up. Duchess struggled with their case. She would not let him help.

She changed Robin into his pajamas and then brushed his teeth in the small bathroom that led from their sparse bedroom.

"I want to go home," Robin said.

"I know."

"I'm scared."

"You're a prince."

Duchess dragged the nightstand across the scarred wood floor then heaved and pushed until the beds were joined.

"You'll say your prayers now," he said from the door.

"The fuck we will," she fired back. She watched him take it, hoped to see him flinch but he did not. He stood there, mouth perfectly straight. She traced his face for a sign of herself, her brother, her mother. Maybe she saw a little of all of them or maybe he was just an old stranger.

A few minutes till Robin moved fully into her bed. He pulled her arm around himself till he slept.

In a breath a steady buzz made its way into her dreams. She reached over and slammed the alarm clock, then sat up quickly and for a few, cruel moments she thought of calling out to her mother.

Robin slept on beside her, she reached across and covered him and then heard Hal below, the whistle of the kettle and the heavy step of boots.

She lay back, tried to sleep but saw the light of the hallway tip into the room as Hal climbed the stairs and opened the door.

"Robin." Her brother stirred to the old man's voice. "The animals need their breakfast, would you like to come help?"

Duchess watched her brother, the thought pattern easy to place. She had seen how curiously he had eyed the barns and the chickens, the big cows and the horses. He climbed from the bed, turned to her till she went and fetched his toothbrush.

Below were bowls of porridge. Duchess emptied hers into the trash. She found sugar and spooned some into Robin's bowl. He ate quietly.

Hal appeared at the door, behind him light mist steamed like a fire burned beneath the land.

"Ready to work." Not a question.

Robin finished his juice and hopped down from the chair. Hal reached out a hand and Robin took it. Duchess watched from the window as they walked toward the barn, the old man speaking words that did not carry, Robin staring up like the last six years no longer counted.

She pulled on her coat, laced her sneakers, and headed out into dawn air.

Behind, mountain sun crept, the promise of something new lay heavy on her chest.

. . .

Walk had driven through the night, the states and the scenes all much of the same in the darkness, just signs counting miles, telling him to take a break, tiredness kills. When he'd got home he'd unplugged the telephone, pulled his drapes and lay, not sleeping, just thinking of Star and Duchess and Robin.

Breakfast was two Advils and a glass of water. A shower but no shave.

At eight he arrived to a reporter standing in the lot, Kip Daniels from the *Sutler County Tribune*. Beside Kip were a couple of vacationers and locals. Walk had heard it on the short ride in, that the state of California was preparing to charge Vincent King with the murder of Star Radley. He didn't buy it, just stations trying to make news.

"Nothing new to tell you, I'm afraid."

"Anything on the weapon?" Kip called.

"Nothing."

"Charges?"

"Don't believe everything you hear."

Vincent was back at Fairmont. That he wouldn't speak, that he was at the scene, it made for a simple puzzle. There was no one else in the frame. State cops occupied the back office, Boyd and his men, pulling in locals and making noise. It was winding down already.

Inside the station he found Leah Tallow on the front desk, lights on the phone blinked frantically. "Crazy in here this morning. You hear the news?"

Walk watched her pick up another call and make no comment.

They'd called in Valeria Reyes, a decade older than Walk. She sat behind her desk and ate nuts, a neat collection of shells by the telephone, mute to the furor.

"Morning, Walk. Busy in here. Got the butcher in."

Walk stopped and scratched the stubble on his cheek. "Where?"

"Interview room."

"What have they got him in for?"

"Think they tell me anything?" Valeria ate another nut, choked a little, and washed it down with coffee. "You need to get some sleep, Walk. And maybe a shave."

He looked around, the appearance of normal. Leah's sister owned the florist on Main and dropped an arrangement in each week. Blue hydrangea, alstroemeria, and eucalyptus. Sometimes he thought the station resembled a set, maybe a daytime TV cop show, they played their parts, background extras, nothing more.

"Where's Boyd?"

She shrugged. "He said not to talk to the butcher till he gets back."

He found Milton in the small room at the back of the station that they might've used for interviews, had they ever had to take a statement. Milton clutched his chest, massaging it like he needed to get his heart firing again. Although the butcher was stripped of his apron, Walk still smelled blood, as if it were matted to every hair that carpeted Milton's body.

Walk shoved his hands deep into his pockets. He found himself doing that more now, the drugs again, nothing helping.

Milton stood. "I don't know why they told me to hang around. I have to get on. I came to them, after all."

"With what?"

Milton looked at his shoes, loosened his collar, and fired his cuffs. He'd dressed for the occasion. "Remembered something."

"And?"

"I like to look out, right. Watch the water, the sky, got my Celestron, computerized now. You should come over one time and we could—"

Walk held up a hand, too tired for it.

"That night, before the shot. I think I heard yelling. Had my window open, I was broiling a little rabbit, you know, soften the bones."

"Think you heard?"

Milton looked to the lights above. "I heard yelling. An argument."

"And this has only come to you now?"

"I could be in shock still. Maybe it's wearing off."

Walk stared at him. "You see Darke that night?"

A moment before he shook his head. Maybe a couple of seconds but Walk caught it. There had been mention of Dickie Darke's name in connection, but that mention had come from Walk himself. Duchess wouldn't say anything about the man. Walk wondered if she was scared.

"Brandon Rock." Milton puffed out his chest. "The car . . . this morning. I get up early, and that guy comes home at all hours. I need my sleep, Walk."

"I'll talk to him."

"You know we had another person drop out of the Watch. It's like they don't care about the neighborhood anymore."

"How many you down to now?"

Milton sniffed. "Just me and Etta Constance. But she can't watch all that much with the one eye. Peripheral." He waved a hand around for effect.

"I sleep better knowing the two of you are looking out."

"I document it all. Big suitcase under my bed."

Walk could only imagine the kind of notes the man kept.

"I was watching a show and the cop took a civilian on a ride along. You ever thought about that, Walk? I could bring a little cotechino . . . spice up the cabin. And then after we could—"

Walk heard noise outside and turned as Boyd filled the doorway. Broad, buzzcut, soldier to cop.

Walk followed him out.

Boyd led him to his own office and then sat heavily in his chair.

"You want to tell me what's going on?" Walk said.

Boyd leaned back and stretched, his shoulders big as he steepled fingers behind his neck. "I just got back from the DA's office. We're going to charge Vincent King with the murder of Star Radley."

Walk knew it would come, but hearing it straight from Boyd still rocked him.

"The butcher told us he saw Vincent King get into it with Dickie Darke a few nights prior. Said it looked like Vincent was warning him off. Jealous. Right outside the Radley house."

"And what does Darke say about this?"

"Corroborates. He came in with his lawyer. Big fucker, right. Sounds like he was seeing the victim, though he says they were just friends."

"Milton, the butcher. He's called a lot over the years, likes to watch the town, you know. He gets . . . excited. He sees things that maybe aren't there."

Boyd licked his teeth and pursed his lips. He was always moving, like holding still would see his middle fill out and his hairline race back. Strong smell of cologne. Walk eyed the window and wanted to pop it open.

"We've got Vincent at the scene, prints. His DNA on her. She had three broken ribs, his left hand was swollen. He won't deny it, won't say anything. It's easy, Walker."

"No residue," Walk said. "The gun. No residue and no gun."

Boyd rubbed his chin. "You said the faucet was running. He washed his hands. The gun. We've had people out, everywhere, but we'll find it. He kills her, loses the gun, returns and calls it in."

"Doesn't make sense."

"We've had the ballistics report back. The bullet they pulled was .357 Magnum, hell of a kick. We ran the address and it turns out Vincent King's father had a gun registered in the midseventies."

Walk watched the man, not liking where he was going. Walk

remembered it, a couple of threats were made toward the Kings, serious enough for Vincent's father to keep a gun.

"See if you can guess the caliber, Walker."

Walk stayed even, despite the way his stomach flipped.

"The DA wanted more. Now we've got the motive and access to the murder weapon. We'll go for the death penalty."

Walk shook his head. "There's still people we need to talk to. I want to go over Dickie Darke's alibi again, and then there's Milton and I'm not sure—"

"Leave it alone, Walker. It's open and shut. I want to hand it over to the DA by the end of the week. We've got enough on. Then we'll be out of your hair."

"But I really think—"

"Listen. It's alright, what you've got going on here. I've got a cousin that works in Alson Cove and he loves it, the pace is slow, the work is easy. There's nothing wrong with that. But when was the last time you worked a real case, I mean something more than a misdemeanor?"

Walk had not worked more than an infraction.

Boyd reached over and gripped his shoulder tight. "Don't fuck this up for us."

Walk swallowed, the wheels turning frantic. "If he pleads. If I can get him to plead?"

Boyd met his eye, didn't say it but didn't have to.

Vincent King would die for this.

13

Clouds cascaded down the mountain behind, framing the farmhouse like it belonged in a print.

She worked, legs heavy, the skin on her hands torn beneath her gloves.

Whatever job he gave her, mucking, cutting back the long vines by the house, shifting branches from the winding driveway, she did with quiet hatred. Hal playing grandfather now her mother was deep in the ground.

The funeral had been shamefully quiet. Walk had fished out an old necktie for Robin, the same he'd worn when his own mother passed. Robin had held her hand through it, the minister trying to lead them away from their broken lives, talk of God's need for another angel like he knew nothing of the tortured soul that had been taken.

"We'll break for lunch now." The old man snapped her from the memory.

"I'm not hungry."

"You have to eat."

She turned her back on him, reached for her brush and swept dirt from the cracked driveway with hard strokes.

Ten minutes then Duchess dropped her brush and walked back, slow.

At the house she stepped up onto the porch and looked through the window. Hal with his back to her, her brother eating a sandwich, coming up a head over the table. He had a cup of milk.

She walked through the back door and into the kitchen, cheeks burning hot. At the table she picked up Robin's cup and emptied the milk into the sink, rinsed it, and pulled a carton of juice from the refrigerator.

"I can drink milk at lunch, I don't even mind," Robin said.

"No, you can't. You drink juice, like you did at—"

"Duchess," Hal said.

"You shut up." She turned to him. "You don't say my name, you don't fucking say it. You don't know anything about me or my brother."

Robin began to cry.

"Enough now," Hal said, gentle.

"You don't tell me 'enough.'" She was breathless, shaking, the anger coming up so hot she could barely control it.

"I said—"

"*Fuck you.*"

He stood then, raised a hand and brought it down hard on the table, sending his plate to the floor. It smashed on the stone and Duchess flinched, and then she turned and ran. Past the water and the driveway, arms pumping, across the long grass and into the rough and toward the trees.

She didn't stop till she had to, till she took a knee and swallowed mouths of warm, heavy air. She cursed him out, kicked a thick oak and felt pain shoot back through her. She screamed at the trees, so loud birds lifted and speckled the clouds.

She thought of her home. The day after the funeral, what little they owned outright was boxed by Walk. Nothing in the checking account, thirty bucks in her mother's purse, nothing passed down.

She walked a mile before the Douglas fir thinned. She was mucky and sweaty, her hair damp and knotted. She slowed a little and walked the center line of a road, counting off broken lines.

Beside was grass and wood, edging out, a river in the distance and moving on, the sky all blue forgiveness. Sometimes she expected more, a clue, something wilting or graying or not carrying on, something that told her the world was a different place now her mother was dead.

A sign announced the town. Copper Falls, Montana. A line of stores, orange brick too new for the scene, flat roofs and fading awning, flags that fell limp. Bleached signs long forgotten, Bush and Kerry, stars and stripes. A diner, HUNTERS WELCOME, convenience, pharmacy, Laundromat. A bakery that made her mouth water. She stood and looked in, saw old couples at each table, eating pastry and drinking coffee. Outside a man sat and read a newspaper. She passed a barber, the old kind with the glass pole and the offer of a shave. Beside it a beauty salon, women in chairs, heat reaching out the open door.

At the end of the street was a mountain that held the horizon, so towering like a challenge or reminder, there was plenty bigger out there.

She passed a small, skinny black boy. He stood on the sidewalk, coat over his arm despite the eighty degrees, watching her intently. He wore slacks and a bow tie, suspenders pulled the pants high enough to highlight white socks.

He would not turn, no matter how hard she glared.

"What the fuck are you looking at?"

"Some kind of angel."

She took in the bow tie with a shake of her head.

"I'm Thomas Noble."

He continued to look, mouth a little open.

"Stop staring, you freak." She pushed him and he fell back onto his ass.

He looked up at her through thick lenses. "That was worth it, just to feel your touch."

"Ugh. Is everyone in this town fucked in the head?"

She felt his eyes on her all the way to the top of the street.

She took a seat on a bench and watched the pace, so slow her eyes weighed heavy.

A lady stopped beside, maybe sixty, so much glamour Duchess stole glances. Towering heels, lipstick and stinking of perfume, her hair falling in waves like she'd just stepped from the salon.

She set her bag down, Chanel, and jammed in beside.

"This summer."

A kind of accent Duchess didn't know.

"I keep telling my Bill to fix the air conditioner but you reckon he has?"

"I reckon I don't give a shit. And maybe Bill doesn't either."

She laughed at that, slipped a cigarette into a holder and lit it. "Sounds like you know him, or maybe you've got a daddy like him. Start a job and lose interest quick. That's men for you, sweetheart."

Duchess exhaled, hoping to ward her off with attitude alone.

The lady reached into her shopping bag and pulled out a smaller paper bag. She took out a donut, then offered one to Duchess.

Duchess tried to ignore her but the lady shook the bag a little, like she was enticing a wary animal. "You ever had one of Cherry's donuts?" she persisted, shook the bag until Duchess took a donut, sugar falling onto her jeans as she bit into it carefully.

"Best donut you've ever had?"

"Average."

The lady laughed like she'd made a joke. "I could eat a dozen maybe. You ever tried to eat one without licking your lips?"

"Why the fuck would I do that?"

"Let's give it a go then. Harder than it sounds."

"Maybe for an old lady."

"Only as old as the man you feel."

"How old is Bill?"

"Seventy-five." Heavy laugh.

Duchess ate, felt the sugar on her lips but didn't lick them. She watched the lady do it too, for a while fighting it, like an itch, and then she licked her lips and Duchess pointed and the lady laughed so raucous Duchess fought a smile.

"I'm Dolly, by the way. Like Parton, only without the chest."

Duchess said nothing for a while, just letting it hang there, feeling Dolly look over once, then away.

"I'm an outlaw. You probably shouldn't be seen conversing with me."

"You've got swagger. Not enough do in this world."

"Clay Allison's gravestone read, 'He never killed a man that did not need killing.' That's swagger."

"So does the outlaw have a name?"

"Duchess Day Radley."

A look, not pity, but close. "I know your grandfather. I'm real sorry about your mother."

Duchess felt it in her chest then, a tightening, like she couldn't breathe. She looked down at the street, locked on her sneakers, eyes too hot.

Dolly stubbed out her cigarette, didn't even take a single drag.

"You didn't smoke it."

Dolly smiled, neat, blinding white teeth. "Smoking is bad for you. Ask my Bill."

"So why then?"

"My daddy caught me smoking once. Beat me something awful. But I kept it up, on the sly. I didn't even like the taste. You must think I'm a mad old bat."

"Yes."

Duchess felt a hand on her shoulder. He stood, smiling wide, curls matted with sweat, dirt beneath his nails.

"I'm Robin."

"Pleased to meet you, Robin. I'm Dolly."

"Like Parton?"

"But without the tits," Duchess added.

"Mom liked Dolly Parton. She used to sing it, that song about working nine to five."

"Ironic, seeing as she never could hold down a job."

Dolly shook his hand and told him he was just about the most handsome boy she'd ever seen.

Duchess saw Hal across the street, leaning on the hood of the old truck.

"I'll see you soon, I hope." Dolly handed Robin a donut, left them and headed back down the street, nodding at Hal as she passed.

"Grandpa was scared. Please don't make trouble."

"I'm an outlaw, kid. Trouble finds me."

He stared up with sad eyes.

"Try and eat that donut without licking your lips."

He looked at the donut. "Too easy."

"Go on then."

He took a bite and licked his lips right off.

"You just licked them."

"Did not."

They walked back down the sidewalk, the sky covering over, those rolling clouds chasing the day so fast.

"I miss her."

She squeezed his hand. She still hadn't decided if she felt the same.

• • •

Thirty years in the same room, steel toilet and basin, walls dug out and scrawled. A door that slid open and closed at set times each day.

Walk stood outside Fairmont County Correctional Facility and took in the sun, high and merciless no matter the month. He glanced up at the camera, watched men in the yard, the chain links turning them into puzzle pieces that did not fit anywhere at all.

"I can never get used to the colors. Everything looks washed-out."

Cuddy laughed. "Missing your blue, Walk."

Cuddy lit a cigarette, offered Walk one but he waved him off.

"You ever smoke?"

"Never even tried it."

They watched men shoot hoops, bare chests, sweating.

A man fell, got up, and squared off but caught sight of Cuddy and squashed it quick. The game went on, the ferocity, life or death and no room for the between.

"It got to me, this one," Cuddy said.

Walk turned but Cuddy kept his eyes on the game.

"But then I used to think some people weren't meant for this place. When I started out, working the floor, I'd see them bring in a white-collar, lawyer or banker or something, and I'd think they don't belong here. But then maybe there aren't degrees of bad. Maybe it doesn't matter by how much you cross the line."

"Most people get near. At least once in their life."

"Not you, Walk."

"There's still time."

"Vincent crossed when he was fifteen. My father worked that night they brought him in. News crews were here. I remember the jury called it late."

Walk remembered too.

"My father said it, worst night of his life. And you can only imagine the things he saw. Booking in a kid. Watching the men, arms through bars, calling. A couple were alright, supportive even. But most, you know. Keep the noise up, welcome him that way."

Walk clutched the fence, fingers through the diamonds, the air beyond just as hard to breathe.

"I was nineteen my first day here." Cuddy stubbed out his cigarette and kept hold of the butt. "Four years older than Vincent. I worked his unit, on three. Shit, I used to look at him and see a kid, same as everyone. Maybe a kid from my school, maybe a little brother, whatever. I liked him right off."

Walk smiled.

"I thought about him, at home, when I was on vacation, when I caught a movie with a girl I liked."

"Yeah?"

"His life and mine. They aren't all that different, save for a single mistake. And it was that. Child's life . . . Jesus. Two children if you count

Vincent. If he's back here, if he came to nothing, it's more tragic, right. More of a waste."

Walk had tried out those same ideas.

"I was happy when you came and got him. End one chapter, too long, start a new one. He had the time, Walk. We're not all that old, you know."

"I know." Walk thought of the disease, how it was twisting him into someone he was not ready to be.

"Sometimes people complained I favored him, said I gave him more time in the yard and shit. I did. I did all I could to give him it. Life . . . partial life, whatever. We're not supposed to question guilt, we do our jobs, right?"

"We do."

"I never ask this question. I never asked it, not once in thirty years here."

"He didn't do it, Cuddy."

Cuddy breathed heavily, like he'd been holding that question a long time. And then he turned and opened the gate.

"I got you a room."

"Thank you." Walk had been dreading talking through the phones, easier to stay distant with Plexiglas between them.

Cuddy led him to an office, empty of everything but a metal table and two chairs. The place for lawyer and client, lines fed, appeal and hope and which circuit to exhaust next.

Vincent filed in, Cuddy uncuffed him, looked over at Walk then left them.

"What the hell are you doing?" Walk said.

Vincent took the seat opposite and crossed his legs. "You've lost weight, Walk."

Another two pounds. He ate breakfast and nothing more, just drank coffee. He had a pain in his stomach, not sharp, just heavy and constant, like his body was turning on him again. His new pills were doing their job, helping him stay steady, helping him stand and walk and almost take both of those things for granted.

"You want to tell me what's going on?"

"I sent you a letter."

"I got it. *I'm sorry.*"

"I meant it."

"And everything else in there."

"I meant that too."

"I won't put the house up. Maybe after the trial, once we know the future."

Vincent looked pained, like he'd called on a favor and found Walk all out. He'd been clear, the letter, his writing so graceful Walk read it twice. Sell the house. Take the offer, the million bucks from Dickie Darke.

"I already have the check. I just need you to take care of the paperwork."

Walk shook his head. "Just wait and we'll—"

"You look like shit," Vincent said.

"I'm fine."

They settled back to silence.

"Duchess and Ro . . . and the boy. The little boy." He said the names quietly, like he wasn't worthy of speaking them.

"You need something, Vincent. We can talk about it, we can sort something out, but I think you need to take some time on it."

"That's something I do have."

Walk took a stick of gum from his pocket and offered one over.

"Contraband," Vincent said.

"Right."

Walk stared at him, looking for something he couldn't see. Not guilt, not remorse. He'd toyed with the idea that Vincent missed it, institutionalized. He didn't buy it, it didn't fit at all. Vincent looked away, all the time, never meeting his eye for longer than a blink.

"I know, Vin."

"What do you know?"

"That you didn't do it."

"Guilt is decided long before the act is committed. People just don't realize it. They think they have a choice. They look back, play it different, sliding doors, but they never really did."

"You won't speak because you know I'll tie you up. You can't keep a consistent lie."

"That's not—"

"If you did it where's the gun?"

Vincent swallowed. "I do need you to instruct a lawyer for me."

Walk breathed out, smiled, and tapped the table with the flat of his hand. "Yes, good. I know a couple of guys, good trial lawyers."

"I want Martha May."

Walk stopped tapping. "Excuse me?"

"Martha May. I want her and no one else."

"She works family law."

"She's the only lawyer I want."

Walk let it settle awhile. "What's your angle here?"

Vincent kept his eyes down.

"What the hell is wrong with you? Thirty years I've been waiting for you." Walk slammed the table with his hand. "Come on, Vincent. You weren't . . . your life, it wasn't the only one on hold."

"You think our lives have been close to the same?"

"That's not what I meant. It was hard on all of us. Star."

Vincent stood.

"Wait."

"What is it, Walk? What do you need to say?"

"Boyd and the DA. They're going for death."

The word hung there.

"You tell Martha to come see me. I'll sign papers."

"It'll be a capital case. Jesus, Vincent. Think about what you're doing."

Vincent knocked the door and signaled the guard. "I'll see you, Walk."

That half smile again, the smile that took him back thirty years and kept Walk from giving up on his friend.

14

They slept till eight that first Sunday.

Duchess woke first, her brother pressed close to her, his face washed gold. He caught the sun quick.

She stepped from the bed into the bathroom and caught the shape of her face in the mirror. She'd lost weight, skinny to start, her cheeks now hollowed, collarbones proud. Each day she looked more like her mother, so much that Robin told her that she should eat something.

As she walked out and into the hallway she saw it. A dress. Flowers on it, maybe daisies. Beside was a hanger and on it a smart cotton shirt and dark slacks, the tags still on, size 4–5.

She took the stairs slow, still learning the noises of the old house. At the kitchen door she stood and watched him. Shoes shined, tie, stiff collar. Though she was certain she made no sound he turned.

"I left you a dress out. We go to church on a Sunday. Canyon View, we don't miss it."

"Don't say 'we' like you mean me and my brother."

"The kids like it at the church. They have cake after. I already told Robin and he was alright."

Robin, Judas, would do anything for cake.

"You go to church. We'll stay here."

"I can't leave you alone."

"You have for thirteen years."

He took it.

"You didn't even buy the right size. Robin is six. You bought four to five, you don't even know how old your own grandson is."

Hal swallowed. "I'm sorry."

She walked over and poured herself coffee. "What makes you think there's a God anyway?"

He pointed in the direction of the window. She turned and looked out.

"I don't see nothing at all."

"You do, Duchess. You see it all. I know you do."

"I know what I do see."

He looked up, tensed a little, like he was more than ready for it.

"I see the shell of a man who's made a decent mess of his own life, who's got no friends and no family and no one to give a shit when he drops dead." She smiled, innocent. "Probably happen in his field, his special fucking land painted in God's color. He'll lay there till his skin is green, till the oil tank comes and the delivery guy sees the crows, a hundred crows among the wheat. The animals will have torn him up by then. But it won't matter because they'll stick him straight in the ground. No one to mourn."

She saw a slight tremble in his hand as he picked up his coffee. She wanted to go on, maybe she'd talk of her aunt, her darling, beautiful aunt whose grave would've gone untended because her mother couldn't face it and Hal had left her so totally alone. If it wasn't for her, riding the hill, picking the wildflowers, Sissy would have just rotted alone. But then she looked up and saw her brother at the door.

Robin climbed up onto the chair opposite Hal. "I dreamed about cake."

Hal watched Duchess.

"You'll come to church, won't you?" Robin stared at her, and she saw it in his eyes, that need for her. "Please, Duchess. Not for God, just for the cake."

She climbed the stairs and snatched the dress down from where it hung above the bedroom door, swinging on the frame. In the bathroom she opened the cabinet, fished through Band-Aids and soap and shampoo, found a pair of scissors, and got to work.

She cut it short, the daisies stopping high on her pale thighs. A couple of random slashes, showing her back, the top of her stomach. She didn't run a brush through her hair, just tousled it till it was wild. She dug her old sneakers out from beneath the bed and kicked the new sandals across the floor. She had a cut on her knee, grazes from crops that stood as tall as her, and a scar on her arm that she knew would not heal. If she'd had a bust she'd have cut the dress low in front. They were outside when she came down. Hal had washed the truck the day before, Robin helped him, the two of them soaping it up beneath falling sun, rinsing it off and wiping it down with a worn chamois.

"Oh, Jesus," Robin said when he saw her.

Hal stopped, stared, took it, then climbed into the truck.

They passed another farm, a line of transmission towers, white rusted brown, the steady hum of the lines lost beneath the rattle of the engine. East a pipe rose from the land like a worm feeling the first drum of rain, it carried five hundred yards then buried.

Ten minutes and they passed a lone sign hammered into the dirt, THE TREASURE STATE.

"Did that say 'treasure'?"

She patted Robin's knee. She read with him nightly, ten minutes. He was smart, already she could see that, too smart for her and Star. She worried he'd slip behind, old life tugging him back like vines around his feet.

"Minerals." Hal kept a hand on the wheel but turned once and raised his eyebrows at Robin. "*Oro y plata*. Gold and silver."

Robin tried a whistle but never could get much of a sound.

West was the Flathead, so far Duchess could not make out the buffalo. She could see prairies, hundreds of something, cattle maybe.

"And the headwaters. That water that flows through the rest of the country starts out here."

Robin did not whistle at that.

They turned. A sign told them it was Canyon View Baptist. The only view she could see was more browns.

The church, vernacular, wood and white, the gable front splintering and the bell tower low enough to throw stones at.

"You couldn't find a shittier church?"

There were cars and trucks in the small lot. Duchess climbed out into sunlight and stared around. Fifty miles out wind turbines spun.

An old lady wandered over, smiled wide, liver spots and hanging skin, like the earth was calling the flesh to be buried but her brain was too stubborn to cede it.

"Morning, Agnes," Hal said. "This is Duchess and Robin." Agnes extended a skeletal hand. Robin shook it with great care, like he worried it might come free and he'd be tasked with fixing the mess.

"Oh my, that's a pretty dress," Agnes said.

"This old rag. I thought it was a little short, but Hal said the minister would enjoy it greatly."

Agnes kept her smile though confusion tried hard to replace it.

Duchess led Robin off toward the church. There was a cluster of kids by the side window, neat hair, every one of them smiling.

"I'm getting cult vibes," Duchess said.

"Can we go play with them?"

"No. They'll try and steal your soul."

Robin looked up at her, trying to search for a smile. She held firm.

"How will they steal it?"

"They'll distract you with unrealistic ideals."

She fussed with his hair and pushed him toward the others, nodding when he turned back.

"Your sister's dress is gross," a little girl said.

Duchess walked over, the kids all watching her careful. The girl looked past her and waved at a large lady wearing purple eye shadow.

"Is that your mom?" The barb took form.

The girl nodded.

Robin looked up at her, pleading in his eyes.

"We have to go inside now," Duchess said, swallowing it down.

Robin breathed again.

They sat on a bench at the back of the church.

Dolly strutted in, towering heels and a wave of perfume. She winked at Duchess.

Robin sat between them and asked Hal questions about God that could not be answered by the living.

The minister led them, spoke of places far away, war and famine and the desecration of kindness. Duchess let it roll over her till he mentioned death and new beginning, the climax of a plan so vast we should not try to understand or question it. She watched Robin, rapt, knowing for certain where his mind was.

When they bowed their heads in prayer she found Star's face behind her eyes, so clear and untroubled she wanted to cry out. She felt tears well so kept them locked tight. And when the old minister spoke again she stayed bowed, stayed locked to the gateway for fear she would lose that last image she was not yet ready to.

She felt a hand on her, a big hand, reaching over her brother and trying to offer her comfort when she needed it least.

"Fuck you," she whispered. "Fuck all of you."

She stood and ran from the church, so fast and so far she could scarcely hear the call of damnation, pressing her into the dirt.

She sat in the long grass and tried to breathe herself calm. She did not notice Dolly until she came to sit beside her.

"Nice dress."

Duchess ripped up a handful of grass and tossed it into the light breeze.

"I won't ask if you're alright."

"Good."

Duchess stole a glance at her, bright lips and smoked eyes, hair curled. She wore a cream skirt, navy top cut low, and silk scarf. So much a woman Duchess felt even more a girl.

"That's a lot of tit for church."

"I take my bra off and they'd roll down the aisle."

Duchess did not laugh. "It's all bullshit. In there."

Dolly lit her cigarette, the smoke just about covering the perfume. "I see you, Duchess."

"What do you see?"

"I used to hate like that. The flames get too hot sometimes, right." The cigarette flared a little in the breeze.

Duchess went back to tearing at the grass. "You don't know shit about me."

"I know you're still young enough. I didn't work it out till I was old."

"Work out what?"

"That I wasn't alone in the world."

Duchess climbed to her feet. "I know I'm not alone. I've got my brother. And I don't need anyone else. Not Hal, not you, and not God."

•••

Bitterwater was a sprawl of concrete and steel. Storefronts papered with fliers for bars and bands and cheap liquor. Twenty miles inland from the Cape, the kind of place where something critical went wrong during planning meetings.

Walk passed rows of industrial units, shipping containers stacked, self-storage and trade supplies, before he found the place.

The law office of Martha May, part of a strip mall on the edge of town, was sandwiched between a dry cleaner and a Mexican place that advertised eighty-nine-cent tacos.

Walk left the cruiser in a spot and crossed the lot.

Bitterwater Dental, Spirit Electronics, Red Dairy. A salon where a masked Asian woman sprayed the nails of a tired-looking mother, who rocked a stroller with her foot.

Above the sky grayed and beside the neon blinked. TACOS. He pushed the door and was met by wall-to-wall people. All women, all with kids and the kind of eyes that told similar, sorry stories. There was a desk, a secretary pushing seventy, blue hair and pink frames. She smacked gum as she typed, cradled a phone between her ear and shoulder, and winked at a little girl who was screaming the place down.

Walk stepped out again.

He sat in the car till six, counted off the leavers and watched the secretary climb into a rusting Bronco and spend a good minute firing the engine. When she was gone he crossed the lot. The Mexican place was warming up with weary office workers sipping beer in the window.

He tried the shop door but found it locked, so he knocked a couple of times.

He heard her on the other side of the frosted glass. "We're closed. You'll have to come back tomorrow. Sorry."

"Martha. It's Walk."

A minute till he heard the lock snap. And then there she was.

They eyed each other for a moment. Martha May, brown hair framed an elfin face. She wore a gray suit. Walk almost smiled when he saw the Chuck Taylors she paired with it.

He thought of moving for a hug but she turned, no smile. She led him to her office, which was nicer than he was expecting. Oak desk, potted plant and wall-to-wall law books. She sat, then motioned for him to follow.

"It's been a long time, Walk."

"It has."

"I'd offer you coffee but I'm too beat."

"It's nice to see you, Martha."

Finally a smile, and it got him the way it always had.

"I'm so sorry about Star. I wanted to come, but I had a court date and couldn't move it."

"I got the flowers."

"Those kids. Jesus."

There were files on her desk, stacked neatly but towering high. They talked awhile, about Star, the shock of it and the way Boyd had taken over. He made it sound like he was on the case too. There was something strained there, the only way it could be when two people who've seen each other naked reconvene.

"And Vincent?"

"He didn't do it."

She walked over to the window and looked out at a view of the highway behind. He heard the passing cars, the occasional horn, the roar of a motorcycle.

"You've done well here, Martha."

She tilted her head a little. "Why, thank you, Walk. Your approval means so much to me."

"I didn't mean—"

"I'm too tired for small talk. You want to tell me what you want?"

His mouth dried. He didn't want to be there, calling on the kind of favor he had no way of repaying.

"Vincent wants you."

She turned. "Wants me how?"

"Wants you as his lawyer. I know how that sounds."

She laughed. "Do you, Walk? Because the way I hear it you don't have a goddam clue." She took a breath and calmed. There was a plaque on the wall, Southwestern, and a corkboard beside, with cards and photos of smiling mothers and their kids.

"I'm not a criminal lawyer."

"I know that. I told him."

"No. That's my answer."

"Alright. I asked."

She smiled. "Still doing Vincent King's bidding."

"I'd do anything to stop an innocent man being put to death."

"It's a capital case?"

"Yes."

She slumped in her chair, kicked her sneakers up onto the desk. "I can recommend someone."

"I already tried that."

She fished a candy from a bowl, peanut M&Ms. "Why the hell does he want me?"

"Thirty years in there, it's easy to forget, you and me are all he's got now."

"I don't even know him. And I don't even know you anymore, Walk."

"I haven't changed all that much."

"That's what I'm afraid of."

He laughed. "You want to grab something to eat and catch up?" He spoke quietly, his cheeks beginning to redden. "If you've got eighty-nine cents I know a great taco place."

"Can I be honest, Walk?"

"Sure."

"I've spent a long time leaving Cape Haven behind. I don't want to head back there."

He stood, smiled, and walked out the door.

15

Walk watched the slow wake of Main.

Milton stood bloodied, laying out cuts with an eye for the artistry, brisket and prime and short. Walk bought his steak there, at a price the vacationers wouldn't get near.

He'd just got off the phone with Hal. He checked in weekly, asked about Robin, maybe the only one who might have heard something that night. Hal said they'd found a doctor, a shrink, a lady that worked out of her home twenty miles from the Radley farm. They mentioned no names, no towns. Walk was overly cautious.

"You want coffee?" Leah said from the door.

Walk shook his head. "You alright, Leah?"

"Tired."

Some days it was clear she'd been crying, red eyes swollen. Walk guessed it was Ed, he'd always had an eye. Walk reasoned men were just wired different, flawed design, fucking idiots.

"I need to get on those files soon. The state of that back room."

She'd been riding him about it for years, a change of system, new forms. It was no secret Walk liked things the way they were. Every time an application was put through to pull down an old house and replace it he lodged an objection.

The state cops had gone, left a trail of hamburger wrappers and coffee cups with Boyd promising to keep him updated.

"You reckon I could pick up some extra shifts? I mean, I know I'm doing the days, but I wondered if you needed me to hang around later."

"Everything alright, Leah?"

"You know how it is. Got one heading off to college, and Ricky wants some video game."

"Sure. I'll sort something out." They had a limited budget but he'd make it stretch for her. Ed owned Tallow Construction and she used to work admin there, but then the market turned on them. Still, he wondered if that was all it was. She seemed to be at the station more, at the beach, anywhere but home with her husband.

He had the file open, Star staring back. The reports were in now.

Beside that he had Vincent's file. He'd spent the previous night looking back thirty years. He read transcripts, the first, looking into the death of Sissy Radley. And then he'd looked at the second, the prison brawl that got out of hand. The dead man's name was Baxter Logan, and the way Walk read it he was the kind of person the world was well shot of. He was already serving life for the abduction and murder of a young realtor named Annie Clavers. Walk read the interview, Vincent's voice clear in his mind.

I did it. We got into it, I hit him and he went down and didn't get up again. I don't remember much else. I don't know what more to tell you, Cuddy. You give me something to sign and I'll sign it.

Three more pages and Cuddy had explained the facts, tried to coax and lead in that subtle way Walk saw so clear. Let us call it self-defense, because everyone knew that's what it was. *It wasn't self-defense. Just a fight. Doesn't matter who started it.* The state went in heavy again, settled on second-degree murder. Vincent settled on twenty years tacked on.

He picked up the phone and called Cuddy, got him after five minutes.

"I'm looking through the Vincent King file."

Cuddy sniffed like he was fighting a cold. "I thought Boyd was done with that."

"He is."

"Right."

"The report I got, Vincent King and Baxter Logan. There's not much detail in the autopsy."

"That's all we've got, I'm afraid. Logan died when he hit the stone floor. Twenty-four years ago, Walk. Reports weren't as detailed."

"How is Vincent doing?"

He heard the big man lean back in his chair, the leather stretching. "He doesn't speak. Not even to me."

"Did he see himself on the news?" The locals were ramping up the pressure on the DA to finally bring the charges.

"He doesn't have a TV."

Walk frowned. "But I thought—"

"Oh he could have one. I've offered, many times."

"So what does he do in there?"

Silence, a long time. "Cuddy?"

"He's got a picture of the girl. Sissy Radley. He's got it on the wall, and that's the only thing in that cell."

Walk closed his eyes as Cuddy told him to stay in touch. He checked the report. The autopsy was carried out by David Yuto, MD. It gave an address and phone number. He called it, got an answering machine and left a message. Twenty-four years, he doubted the man was still there. And if he was, Walk wondered what the hell he'd ask him. He was trying to be a cop, to work a case as best he could. Despite Boyd's warning, he'd push on. He just didn't know which direction to head in.

Valeria Reyes came in, sat down opposite, not talking, just watching the window, like always.

Walk flipped a page and stared at Star, her hair fanned behind, arm bent at an angle like she was reaching out for someone to help her.

"You need to tidy this office." Valeria looked at the stacked papers, the mess all over.

"I want to talk to Darke myself."

"Because you'll do better than the state cops? You're tough like that?"

"I've known Darke since—"

"Nothing, Walk. That's what that means. Nothing. Look at Vincent King, and I see you looking his way, like you expect him to still be the kid that left here thirty years back. He's gone, though, whatever you knew about him, it left him the day he stepped into Fairmont."

"You're wrong."

"Serious, Walk. I know you didn't change. But everyone else did."

Out the window Walk saw the colors too bright, blues and white, polished glass and bleached flags.

"So what else is there?" she said.

"Burglary. The place was trashed."

"But nothing missing. More like a fight that got out of hand."

"Milton's lying."

"No good reason for that."

"Let's go burglary. Could be Star disturbed them," he said, again reaching, so far he almost stumbled over his words.

"All of this, what you're saying, you have to discount the fact that we found a man, sitting in the house, her blood on his shirt, his prints all over everything, possible motive."

"No way," he fired back quick.

"And yet here we are. On a hunch."

"Vincent won't say a word. He won't say why, he won't say how he got in, what time it happened. Shit, he called it in himself. From their phone."

"He was vicious. Star . . . how many ribs did he break? You've got the photos in front of you."

He looked at them again, the marks angry across her chest, blue to purple, streaks upon broken bones. There was feeling involved, a kind of hatred so hot Walk could feel it searing.

"And the swelling by her eye."

"He's there, however he got in, no sign of a break-in. She invites him in, something happens. He beats her. Shoots her dead. Runs, hides the weapon, returns and sits down in the kitchen, calls it in. And waits for us. The kid, Robin, he's locked in his bedroom, mercifully, but there's a chance he heard something."

Walk stood and opened the window to the call of another perfect morning. An hour or two at his desk, that's all he could ever take.

"I need to talk to Darke," he said again. "There's history with Star. He's violent."

"Alibi is tight."

"That's why I've called her in."

"Boyd said to leave it alone. Don't fuck with a state case."

Walk took a deep breath, everything swimming, nothing clear at all, other than the fact he knew Vincent. No matter what Valeria said. He knew Vincent King. Fuck the thirty years, he knew his friend.

"You need to shave, Walk."

"So do you."

She laughed at that. And then Leah called through and told him Dee Lane was waiting.

He found her at the desk, then led her through to the compact office in the back. A small table, four chairs and a wide vase bursting with Vendela roses. View out over Main, more grandmother's guesthouse than interrogation room.

Dee looked better than the last time he'd seen her. She wore a simple yellow summer dress and her hair was styled. A little makeup, just enough to push the soft in front of the hard. She carried a paper bag and handed it over to him.

"Peach galettes," she said by way of greeting. "I know how much you like them."

"Thank you."

He had no tape recorder, no pad or pen.

"I already spoke to the officers from state police."

"I'm just running over things. You want a coffee?"

She dropped her shoulders a little. "Sure, Walk."

He left her, found Leah and asked her to put a pot on. When he returned Dee was standing by the window.

"It looks different out there," she said. "Main. The new stores and the new faces. I mean, it was gradual, right. You know about the application for new homes?"

"It won't pass."

She turned, sat again and crossed her legs. "You think I'm weak . . . with Darke."

"Just trying to understand it."

"He showed up, brought me flowers and told me he was sorry. One thing led to another."

"Tell me how it started with him."

"He came into the bank, opened a checking account. I thought he was . . . cute isn't the right word to describe the guy. He was quiet but tough.—Shit, Walk, I don't know what to say. He came in a few more times, always got in my line. I asked him out. He said yeah. That's how it goes, right?"

"Before, you said there was nothing natural about him."

"I was pissed, the house. I was lashing out. I tell you one thing about him."

"What?"

"He was good with my girls. Attentive. He used to watch them, push them on the swings, you know. Just be with them. One time I came in from the yard and found him with Molly on his lap. Watching a Disney movie. There's not many guys that would take to another man's kids."

Leah brought the coffee and left them. His hand shook as he took his cup, so bad he set it down again.

"You alright, Walk? You look tired. And maybe you need a shave. I mean, no offense or nothing."

"So he stayed all night, Darke?"

"I kicked him out early, before the girls got up."

He slumped back in his chair, the tired washing over him, eyes dry and muscles aching.

"I know you don't want to see it, Walk. Vincent and Star and all that.

But Darke, the guy can be an asshole, but he's not what you think he is. Or maybe what you want him to be."

"What do I want him to be?"

"The guy that makes Vincent King innocent."

· · ·

When she was done with the corral she moved on to the stable, the smell of shit not so bad anymore. Two horses, a black and a smaller gray. They had no names, that's what Hal said when Robin asked. He'd been puzzled by that: *Everyone needs a name.*

Mucking out, scooping damp straw and shit and bagging it. Fetching a small packed bale from the store and forking it out and over. She knew to leave the wet spots, to let them dry before she covered them over. She filled their water, gave grain twice a day, same exact time, the gray could get colic. She led them to their place and closed the gate, sometimes watching them run hard then kick and thrash like they were about to be roped. Duchess liked horses, as every outlaw should.

Gunshot.

It shook the calm from Duchess with such force she fell to her knees. The elk, one foot raised, heads tilted. And then they scattered and ran, so fast they were gone by the time she stood.

She sprinted for the house, heart hammering as her mind ran to Darke.

She calmed a little when she saw Hal on the porch, but his face was drawn with worry.

"He's upstairs, in the closet."

She took the stairs fast, into their room, and saw him on the floor, the blanket over his head.

"Robin."

She didn't touch him just yet, instead scooted herself under till she was close.

"Robin," she spoke softly. "It's alright."

"I heard it." So quiet she leaned in.

"What did you hear?"

"The gun. I heard it. I heard it again."

• • •

That afternoon Hal led them down to the red barn and told them to wait out in the sun. Duchess walked over to the door, peeked through the crack and saw Hal roll the mat back.

"Grandpa said to wait here."

She hushed her brother.

Hal pulled up a door in the floor and stepped down. He returned with a gun. He held it loose in his hand, by his side, a small tin box in his other hand.

Duchess stood close to her brother.

"This is a Springfield 1911. It's a handgun, light and accurate. Every farmer needs a gun. What you heard before was just hunters, it's important you get used to the sound. I don't want you to be afraid." He knelt and held the gun out to them. Robin took a step behind Duchess's leg.

"It's not loaded and the safety is on."

After a minute Duchess reached out and took it, colder than she thought, heavy when he said it was light.

She studied it with care, then Robin stepped out and looked. He ran a finger over the handle.

"You want to try shooting, Duchess?"

Duchess looked down at the gun, her mind on her mother. The hole torn in her chest. She thought of Vincent King.

"Yes."

Out to the green field, crops no higher than Duchess's ankle. Beyond they came to the first of the cedars, tall, ladders to the sky.

On a trunk wider than them both was a smattering of marks, pocks, neat and ordered. Leaves long dead and settled, green moss crept to fallen sticks and puddles that shone with the canopies above them.

Hal led them back fifty paces, removed four bullets, and showed them the chamber as he loaded. He ran through the safety and sight, the correct two-hands and how to breathe nice and even. And then he handed each a pair of ear protectors.

The first time Hal fired, Robin jumped clear back and Duchess held him. The second he did it again. The third and fourth a little less.

Duchess loaded next, Hal instructing. She handled the bullets with care like he said but her heart still quickened, the memories fluid, carrying her back totally. Walk and the other cops, her brother. The tape and the news vans and the noise.

She missed six in a row, each time yanking her hand back from the kick instead of planting her feet. Robin grew bolder, still clutching Hal's hand but not turning his head.

She loaded again, this time only the forest noise with her, Hal watching close but letting her figure it out.

The first time she hit the tree she took a chunk from the edge.

Then she put two in the center, Robin whooping and clapping.

"You can shoot," Hal said.

She turned back before he could see the small smile.

She worked her way through the box, till she could sink them into the middle of the cedar, or a little higher or lower. And then Hal moved her back twenty paces and she learned all over again. Correcting the angle, shooting as she knelt, then from her stomach. Devoid of emotion, adrenaline, the human traits that ruined finesse.

As they walked back toward the farmhouse Robin ran on ahead to check on his birds. The chickens. He collected the eggs each morning, his job alone and he lived for it.

Duchess watched the land as the sun began its drop, not low enough to splinter the colors but she felt the heat dying. Summer was breathing its last, Hal said fall was spectacular.

She drew up by the gray, who came to her. Duchess stroked her gently.

"She doesn't come for me," Hal said. "She likes you, and she doesn't like many people."

Duchess said nothing, not wanting to fall into conversation, not wanting to lose that fire that kept her moving through each day.

That night she ate dinner alone on the porch, stomach tight as she listened as Hal laughed at something Robin said. It was moments like those it came for her and dragged her back to the Cape. The old man laughing, smiling, after what his grandchildren had been through. A bond was forming.

She walked back into the kitchen, opened the cabinet, and pulled a bottle of Jim Beam from the top shelf.

She took it down to the lake, unscrewed the cap, and drank. She did not flinch at the burn. She thought of Vincent King, drank some more, then Darke, and drank again. She drank and drank till the pain eased, her muscles unwound, and the world began to spin. Problems melted, edges softened. She lay flat on her back and closed her eyes, feeling her mother.

An hour till she puked.

Another till Hal found her.

Through the haze she saw his eyes, those watery blue eyes as he gently scooped her up.

"I hate you," she said in a whisper.

He kissed her head as she pressed her cheek to his chest and let the dark find her.

16

If houses had souls Star's place was black as a December night.

Walk figured Darke would've got on as soon as they released it, maybe freshen it up for a new tenant, or just pull the place down and start over. But it stood untouched, the street door replaced with plywood, a window popped out and boarded up. The grass was long and yellowed.

"I know you miss her, Walk. I do too. And the kids." Walk didn't need to turn, he smelled the blood right off. "Any news on Vincent King? I thought they would have charged him by now. Newspapers say he'll be put to death when they find him guilty."

Walk tensed a little. Last he'd heard the DA had asked Boyd to have another look for the murder weapon. With the parole violation Vincent wasn't going anywhere, time was on their side.

"I like the beard by the way. Nice. Real nice. It's coming in thick. I could grow one, you know. We could both have beards. That'd be funny, right, Walk?"

"Sure, Milton."

Milton wore sweats and an undershirt, the thick hair swirled from his shoulders down to the backs of his hands.

"This place, what happened here. It's frightening, right. Blood and all.

It's alright when it's an animal. I mean, vegans see it different, but then they'll eat the white meat, so long as it's sliced thin enough."

Walk scratched his head at that.

"But Star, when I think of her lying there." Milton clutched his stomach. "Don't worry, I've been watching the place. If I see kids or anything, I'll call it in. Ten fifty-four."

"Livestock on highway."

Milton turned and headed back across the street, shuffling feet, that metallic smell trailing him.

Walk headed up the path and banged on Brandon Rock's garage door.

It opened to a blaze of light, Van Halen playing loud, the strong smell of sweat and cologne. Brandon wore Lycra pants, a muscle top cropped just below his chest.

"Walk. That you talking to Sasquatch just now?"

"You fixed that engine yet?"

"Was he bitching again? You know I applied to do a little work on the house. I wanted to open the back, put a dojo above the garage. Guess who lodged an objection?"

Brandon opened a bottle of water and dumped half the contents over his head. "Cool down. I earned it."

"Fix the car, Brandon."

"You remember him at school, Walk? I was dating Julia Martin at the time, and she said Milton used to follow her home. Fucking creeped her out."

"That was thirty years ago."

Brandon stepped out and stared at the old Radley house. "I wish I'd been here that night. Maybe I could've done something, I don't know."

Walk had read the interview, brief as it was. They'd gone door-to-door. "So you were away that night."

"Just like I told the lady from state. Ed Tallow had me out with clients, looking to build on the edge of town. You heard? Japanese, you know how they like to party."

"Right."

Brandon worked his right arm. "Keeping it strong. When I get surgery on the knee I'll be tossing again."

Walk didn't touch that one.

Brandon punched his arm gently, then headed back into the garage. He closed the door, cutting the light and muffling the noise.

Walk stepped across into Star's front yard, steeling himself as that night came back to him. He felt the tremor in his body, put it down to the memories and nothing more, and then walked down the side of the house.

He opened the side gate, never locked, not in the Cape, and then he stopped still when he heard the noise within. He pressed close, peered in the window and saw the flashlight.

Up onto the porch, he drew his gun and was about to move through.

Walk took a step back, the man towered over him.

"Darke."

The stare, no words.

"You scared me." Walk holstered the gun as Darke sat on the bench.

Walk joined him, sat beside without an invite. "What are you doing here?"

"It's my house."

"Right."

Walk was more than accustomed to the heat but still wiped sweat from his head. "I heard you spoke with the state cops. I read the report but I wanted to talk to you myself. I was going to call but now you've saved me the trouble."

"The kids. How they doing?"

"They're . . ." He searched for the words.

"I wanted to talk to the girl."

Walk stared at him then, his body stiffening. "Why?"

"Tell her I'm sorry."

"For what, exactly?"

"She lost a parent. She's tough, right?" He spoke slow, like each word was chosen with great care.

"She's a child."

Moonlight found them through the trees.

"Where'd they go?"

"A long way from here."

Giant hands rested on giant thighs. Walk thought about moving through life like that, crowds parting, people staring.

"Tell me about her."

"Duchess?"

Darke nodded. "She's thirteen, yes?"

Walk cleared his throat. "We got a couple calls over the years. Hilltop Middle. People said they saw a car sitting by the school fence. Black car. No one ever took the plates."

"I've got a black car, Chief Walker."

"I know."

"You ever think about the things you've done?"

"Sure."

"And the things you know you'll have to do?"

"I'm not sure I know what you mean."

Darke looked to the moon.

"You know there's rumors about you, Dickie."

"Yes."

"People say you're violent."

"I am violent. You tell them that."

Walk felt his throat dry as the big man kept his eyes skyward.

"I see you at the church," Darke said.

"I don't see you."

"I don't go inside. What do you pray for?"

Walk rested a hand on his gun. "A fit and just end."

"Hope is secular. And life is fragile. And sometimes we hold on too tight, even though we know it'll break." Darke got to his feet, casting Walk into shadow.

"If you speak to the girl you tell her I've been thinking about her."

"I've still got questions."

"I told those state cops everything. You call my lawyer if you need anything else."

"And Vincent? You know about the house? He's thinking about selling. Any idea why he changed his mind?"

"Maybe he found his price. Tragedy brings clarity of thought. I'm talking to the bank. I'll get the money."

He turned and left. Walk stood and pressed close to the glass and reached for his flashlight.

The kitchen, every unit pulled down. Ceiling panels popped, drywall punched through in spots. Whatever else Darke had been doing there, one thing was certain. He'd been searching for something.

• • •

Summer bled from Montana faster than it had in the Cape, first in small drips, then the deluge of shaded mornings, brooding dusk.

Duchess received a postcard from Walk, just a photo taken from the Cabrillo Highway. He wrote on the back in blue pen, his scrawl in a shaking hand, so bad she almost could not read it.

> I think of you both.
> Walk.

She tacked it to the wall behind her bed.

She still did not speak to the old man, instead muttering to the gray horse. It became an exercise, she'd talk about the things she did not want to, Darke and Vincent, the time she fished vomit from her mother's mouth with her fingers, the time she and Robin practiced the recovery position beneath the okame cherry at Little Brook.

Some nights she sat on the stairs and listened as Hal spoke to Walk on the telephone.

Robin's coming along, loves the animals. He sleeps well. He eats well. That shrink, she said he's doing better. Half hour each week, he doesn't complain.

And then the change, the swing reaching its high and coming back down, middling the gains. *She's . . . she's still here, Walk. She does her jobs and she doesn't complain. Some days I lose her to the land, she crosses the barley and she's just gone. I panicked, at first I ran down the lines, crossed the dirt and drove the truck around. I found her on her knees, there's a spot by the wheat, away from the water and hidden. It's hollowed out, a space I made for a barn but never needed. And she was there on her knees and I couldn't see her face but I think she was praying.*

She made sure not to go back to that place. She'd already scoped out a new one, a clearing in forest so thick she knew Hal would not find her again.

She looked back at the night when her mother had died, and she thought maybe she had been in shock each day since. But the grief came now, slowly, each hour, little by little, catching her out when she needed to be strong.

Some days she screamed.

When she was deep, half hour from the farmhouse, from her brother and his ruddy cheeks as he helped dig the soil, she'd tilt her head back and scream to the clouds. The kind of scream that saw the gray straighten, head up in her field, long neck so graceful. When she was done she'd raise a hand to the horse, tell her go on, eat the grass.

At night, in the dark, they talked.

"Those cops," Robin said.

"Yeah."

"They thought I was lying to them."

"That's just the way cops look."

"Walk doesn't look like that."

She didn't argue. But whatever he was, the guy that had come and filled their refrigerator and driven them to the movie theater, he was still a cop.

"How did it go today?" she said, same each week.

"She's nice. She let me call her Clara. She's got four cats and two dogs, imagine that."

"Hasn't found the right man. Did you talk about that night?"

"I couldn't. It's just . . . I try, but there's nothing there at all. I just remember you reading to me, then sleep, then I think maybe I woke in Walk's car."

She leaned up on her elbow as he rolled to the flat of his back. "If you ever do remember hearing something, you should tell me first. I'll decide what we do about it. You can't trust these cops now. Or Hal. We've only got each other."

Each afternoon she fired the gun. Hal took her to the spot with the wide tree, Robin leading them now, unafraid. She still spoke only when she had to, and when she did she aimed for the gut, something about God or abandonment, but Hal took it different now, the barbs did not grip, the hook slipped harmlessly from his skin. She let him know she did not love him and never would, would never call him anything but his sanitary given name, and would think nothing about taking Robin and leaving him to die alone the second she was old enough.

His response was to teach her to drive.

The old truck bumping along wildly, the flattest acres saw her speed climb and Hal's hands tighten on the seat. Behind them Robin sat in his booster, watching them, wearing his bicycle helmet and elbow pads because Hal worried she'd roll it. She got the hang of the stick, not grinding out the gears so much, feeling the bite like he told her. Some days she got to sixty before he scolded her, when his eyes were on the sky like there was too much of the day now, waiting on first rain. A week in and she could bring the truck to a stop without Hal slamming hard into the dash, cursing for forgetting to belt himself in.

After, they'd walk back toward the house, Duchess holding Robin's left hand, Hal, his right. Hal would tell her she did good and she would tell him he was a lousy teacher. He would say she handled the runs smoothly and she would say his truck was a piece of shit. He would promise to take her out the next day and she would say nothing to that, because, well, she liked to drive.

Some mornings she'd catch the old man watching Robin eat or watching him with the chickens or climbing on the harrow, and he'd get this look in his eyes that was part love and part regret. And those times she'd fight to hate him, a fight she'd won with ease when they'd arrived, but now a fight she was having to put more and more into.

She still kept her clothes in a case, folded neat. Sometimes he'd do the laundry and she'd yell at him to leave their shit alone. She'd find their clothes hung in the closet and she'd take them down and return them to the case. He'd buy the wrong kind of toothpaste for Robin and she'd yell at him, the wrong kind of shampoo, the wrong brand of breakfast cereal. She'd yell so much her throat hurt. Through it, Robin watched. Sometimes he'd ask for quiet and she'd give it. She'd walk the acres and curse at the dropping sun like a fucking mad girl.

She gave less thought to Vincent King, to Dickie Darke, they were turned pages in the darkest chapters of her life. She knew they would appear again, the twists, the sting in her tale.

Most of all she felt tired. Not from the work or the sleep, just from the wretched hatred that lived deep inside her.

17

I need to carry a gun to school."

"No." Hal was anxious that first morning.

Robin was anxious too, he had questions about the school, about where he'd meet her and what would happen if she didn't show. There was no bus that ran out as far as their land so Hal said he would drive them and collect them. He groused about it eating into his day, till Duchess told him they'd hitch a ride with a rapist trucker instead, or maybe she'd sell her body to raise cash for a taxi.

"Will the other kids like me?"

"You're a prince."

"Of course," Hal said. "And if they don't then they'll deal with your sister."

"And yet you still won't let me pack." She finished her cereal, then checked Robin's schoolbag, made sure he had his pencil case and his water bottle.

Hal let her drive the truck, just to the point where the gum trees folded over the sky. She left it idling as she climbed from her seat and Hal climbed from his. They crossed at the trunk, Hal nodding once and Duchess nodding a return.

"You watch out for each other," he said, eyes on the road.

"In case the big kids take our lunch money?" Robin said, perking up and wide-eyed.

"They can try. I'm the outlaw Duchess Day Radley and I'll put a bullet between their eyes."

"You need to learn to ride the gray if you want to be an outlaw," Hal said.

"You know nothing. I can ride, it's in my blood."

"I did some reading on Billy Blue Radley once."

Duchess looked over, the scowl replaced by interest.

"If you want I could tell you about him sometime."

"Okay." It was not a truce or offering.

Robin tensed when they moved into the turn, the bus and the parents, noise and SUVs. She saw a Ford with muddied wheels and a Mercedes too shiny. She thought of Darke, his Escalade, his fading promise.

"You want me to walk you in?" Hal drew the truck up to the curb.

"No. People might think you're our father. The bullying would be merciless."

She took Robin's bag and his hand and they emptied into the street.

"I'll be here at three," Hal said from the window.

"We don't get out till three-fifteen," Robin said.

"I'll still be here."

They moved between groups of kids, tanned from the summer and catching up with loud, exaggerated stories. She caught pieces that made a similar whole, vacations and beaches and theme parks. They drew looks and she gave them back.

She led Robin to his classroom and took him inside, a cluster of mothers knelt and kissed and fussed over their children. A little boy was crying.

"He'll be the wuss, don't hang around with him," Duchess said.

The teacher was young, smiling as she made rounds, kneeling and shaking small hands. Duchess led Robin to the pegs and found his name and his animal picture above.

"What animal is it?"

Duchess squinted. "Rat."

"That's a mouse," the teacher said, appearing beside.

Duchess shrugged. "Vermin is vermin."

The teacher knelt by them, took Robin's hand and shook it lightly. "I'm Miss Child, and you must be Robin. I've been so looking forward to meeting you."

Duchess nudged him.

"Thank you kindly," he said.

"And you must be Duchess."

"I am the outlaw Duchess Day Radley." Duchess pumped the teacher's hand so hard she left it white.

"Well, I hope you have a lovely day, Miss Duchess," Miss Child said, affecting a sweet drawl. "Your brother and I are going to have lots of fun today, right, Robin?"

"Yes."

Miss Child left them and went back to the crying boy.

Duchess bent to her brother and met his eye, cupped his face till he stayed locked onto her. "Any shit at all, you come find me. You just go into the hall and you scream my name. I'll be close."

"Okay."

"Okay?"

"Yeah," he said, a little firmer. "Okay." She stood.

"Duchess."

She turned to him.

"I wish Mom was here."

Outside in the halls, thinning with stragglers, boys carried a football, red-faced and sweaty. She found her classroom and took a seat by the window, far enough back to keep from being called up.

"You're in my seat."

He was tall, odd angles, his shirt coming up small and his shorts high.

"You borrow your sister's shorts? Keep walking, motherfucker."

He blushed, turned, and went to a seat on the other side of the room. Beside her was a black boy, so thin she guessed he carried worms or some other parasite. He had a hand twisted into something that no longer looked like a hand. He caught her noticing and stuffed it into his pocket.

He smiled.

She looked away.

"I'm Thomas Noble. You remember me?" The teacher came in.

"What's your name?"

"Quiet now, I'm here to learn."

"That's a funny name."

She silently willed him to burst into flames.

"I saw you that time in town. You're the angel with the golden hair."

"If you knew anything at all, you'd know I'm about as far from an angel as you can get. Now shut the fuck up and face forward."

···

Walk sat in the parking lot, window open to the smell of Mexican food.

It was late, floods and moonlight replaced the sun as the sky purpled over the Bitterwater sprawl.

He'd been to see Vincent again, three hours in the airless waiting room with nothing but CNN and a busted fan for company. And then he'd sat with him for fourteen minutes. And for each of those he'd begged and pleaded with the man to retain counsel, a criminal lawyer who would at least stand a chance of finding the truth. Vincent had said it was Martha May or no one. And though Walk said it, that she wanted no part of either of them, or Cape Haven and the memories it stirred, Vincent had said nothing more. And then he'd called the guard, and Walk had watched him leave.

The light still burned in Martha's office, despite the late hour, despite her secretary having left a couple hours ago. Walk had tried to get out of the car, felt dizzy enough to sit back and close his eyes for a while. He'd tried to call Kendrick, left a message then checked the leaflet that came with his medication. The side-effects were long enough to fill out two pages.

When he saw her emerge from the office he climbed out and walked slowly across the lot. It was emptying, last cars leaving, a couple of old beat-up sedans outside the Mexican and then Martha's car, a gray Prius with a WWF bumper sticker. Walk remembered she liked animals. On her fifteenth birthday they'd cut school with Vincent and Star and gone to the petting zoo at Clearwater Cove. It was full of little kids, but Martha had smiled the whole day.

"Martha," he called.

She saw him, tossed her case into the trunk, and then stood and waited as he walked over, hand on her hip, like she was more than ready.

"I don't see you in years and now it's twice in a month."

"I want to buy you dinner." He said it with a confidence that surprised him, and maybe her, because, slowly, she smiled.

Yellow walls and green arches, small tables with checkered cloths. A fan spun slow, moving the smell of chili around the tired bar behind. They took a table in the corner, by the window with a view of the parking lot. Martha ordered for them, tacos and beer. She hadn't lost her girl-next-door smile, and when she aimed it, the waiter hurried.

Walk sipped the cold beer and felt his muscles unwind, that tightness across his shoulders ease a little as he sank into the chair. Music played quietly, something soft and Latino.

They drank in silence, Martha draining her beer then signaling for another. "I'll take a cab home."

"I didn't say anything."

"Jeez, I'm drinking with a cop."

He laughed. The waiter brought over the food and they ate. It was good, better than Walk had hoped for but still he pushed his food around, barely eating.

Martha dumped half a bottle of hot sauce on her food. "Zing me, baby. You want in on this, Chief?"

"Not unless you want to continue this conversation in the restroom."

"Hmm, have you seen the restroom?"

"I'm sure I will later."

"I like the beard."

He rolled his eyes.

"I'm sorry," she said. "The other night, it had been a long day. And I wasn't expecting you."

"I should be apologizing to you."

"You totally should."

He laughed.

"So, you want to get it over with now or you want to wait till I've had another beer?"

"I'll wait."

This time she laughed, and it was the sweetest sound Walk had heard in a while.

He took a breath and told her. Everything, from Vincent's release to Star, to Dickie Darke and Duchess and Robin. He told her about the state cops and how they had cut him out. And he told her details of the case that hadn't been released. Broken ribs, swollen eye, no murder weapon, Vincent unwilling to speak. She wiped tears from her eyes, reached across and took Walk's hand when he told her about the funeral.

"Shit," she said, when he was done. "What a mess. Star, the way her life turned out. Back then I thought we'd be friends forever."

"I don't blame you for not looking back."

"Is that what you think?"

"I'm sorry. I didn't mean—"

"I looked back plenty. I just couldn't go back."

"Right."

"And Vincent still says he only wants me?"

"He trusts you. The only other lawyer that worked for him was Felix Coke. And look how that turned out."

"You know the kind of cases I handle, Walk? Battered wives. Adoption. A little divorce work. I do whatever I can to pay the bills each month, and after that I pick and choose who needs me the most. I have a line of women whose sole purpose in life is to get their children back."

"Vincent needs you."

"Vincent needs a criminal attorney."

He moved to pick up his beer, felt the shake in his hands and set it down again.

"Everything alright, Walk?"

"Tired. I haven't been sleeping much."

"It's a lot to take."

"Please do this, Martha. I know how it looks. I can see it, me showing up and asking for a favor. Believe me it hurts."

"I believe you."

"I can't give up on him. Just come to the arraignment, stand by him at the hearing. And then we can sort something out, we'll make him see sense. I just . . . I know he didn't do it. And I know how that sounds, like the words of a desperate man, but that doesn't make me wrong. I need to figure things out. I need time to look into everything.

"I've thought about you over the years. Every day, I think about you and us and everything that went on back then. I know I can't fix things, or roll back the clock, but I can help Vincent now. But I can't do it without you." He slumped back, exhausted, spent.

"The arraignment. When is it?"

"Tomorrow."

"Jesus, Walk."

18

The courtroom in Las Lomas was busier than usual.

A Tuesday in September, the air-conditioning busted, Judge Rhodes fanned himself with a file and loosened his collar.

Walk sat near the front, just as he had thirty years before.

"There's no hope of bail, not for a capital case," Martha said.

She'd met him outside early, and they'd crossed the street and grabbed a coffee. She was smart, suit and heels, light makeup, enough to make Walk feel dumb for ever thinking he might've had a shot at keeping her.

He looked around, lawyers and their clients, navy suits against orange suits, pleas and deals and deficient promises. Judge Rhodes fought a yawn.

The courtroom hushed when he was led in. The people seeking Death, a case with profile.

Judge Rhodes sat up a little straighter, rebuttoned his collar. Reporters at the back, no cameras, just pens and pads. Martha left Walk and went up to the bench, where Vincent settled beside her.

The DA, Elise Deschamps, straight, stern, took to the front and ran through the charges. Walk tried to read his friend, but from where he sat he could not clearly see his face.

When Elise was done, Vincent stood. Walk felt the lean, edge of seats, eyes locked on the man that had killed a child, then came back thirty years later for her sister.

Vincent stated his name.

Judge Rhodes detailed the charges again, then added the state would settle for life with no parole in exchange for a guilty plea.

Walk breathed again. The deal had been offered.

When Judge Rhodes asked for his plea, Vincent turned and met Walk's eye.

"Not guilty."

Now there were murmurs, talk till Rhodes quieted them. Martha looked at the judge, something desperate in her eyes led to a call to approach. "Mr. King. Your lawyer is worried you don't understand the charge and the offer," Rhodes said.

"I understand."

Vincent did not look back as the guard led him from the room.

Walk stepped out and into the morning sun. Las Lomas, the pretty square with the towering statue, a kneeling woman, her head bowed by the hallowed court.

The trial was set for the following spring.

The drive back, Walk's body breaking into cold sweats, the quaking so bad it tired out his mind. He caught his eyes in the rearview mirror but could not rub the blood from them. The beard was long, he'd made a new notch on his belt. His uniform was big now, the shoulders fell over onto the tops of his biceps.

He pulled into a liquor store by Bitterwater and bought a six-pack.

Martha lived in a small house on Billington Road, far enough out of town. A white gate led to a path bordered by neat lines of flowers, the grass beside green and lush. Baskets hung from ornate hooks, the kind of house that would've made him smile on another day.

Inside was cluttered with papers, every inch of the house spoke of work, of defending those less able.

He found his way onto the privacy of the porch and was two beers down by the time Martha came out with a bowl of corn chips. He ate one and she laughed as the flavor seared his taste buds.

"You're an animal."

"Some like it hot."

They sat close, side by side as they drank.

It was not until the day fell away that Walk calmed. Two beers, that's all he'd allowed himself. He wanted to get drunk, to scream and curse and shake sense into Vincent King.

Martha sipped wine. "You have to get him to plea."

Walk rubbed the tension from his neck, always there now.

"Vincent's case is not winnable, you do know that," she said.

"I know that."

"Which means only one thing."

Walk looked up.

"Vincent King wants to die."

"So what do I do?"

"You sit here and drink with me while we lament the sorriest state of affairs."

"Tempting. Or?"

"You work the case."

"I am."

Martha sighed. "Knocking doors and praying someone saw something isn't working a case. You have to get out there and find your angle. And if it can't be found you make it yourself. Balls, Chief. It's all about balls now."

Wind blew across the highway and smoked dust from the ground. Early evening, only a couple of pickups but Walk heard music before he reached the door. He stopped for a moment, looked at the wide strip of San Luis and thought of Star there, dragging the kids behind her.

Inside was dull light, the strong smell of tobacco and stale beer. The booths were empty, just a couple of guys at the bar and a small cluster around a stage built from painted wooden crates. The singer was old, bluegrass, a long way from home, but the men tapped their thighs as they drank.

He had a description of the guy from Duchess, given over when he'd sat her down and they'd slowly gone through the kind of months and years that saw his head heavy by the time they were done. The girl had spoken with an evenness that wrenched his soul, like she knew nothing of childhood at all. He found him straight off, cropped hair and thick beard, strong arms that hinted at field work. Bud Morris. Walk sidled up as Bud rolled his eyes like trouble with the law was a consequence of his way.

"Could I speak with you?"

Bud looked him up and down, then laughed.

Walk drank club soda. He was not a man who enjoyed confrontation, despite the training, the badge and what it meant. Words rang loud in his ears. Leave it to state. He gripped his glass hard. Martha's words rang louder.

Bud went to the restroom. Walk stood and followed him in, took a deep breath and drew his gun as the man was pissing.

He pressed it to the back of Bud's head.

Adrenaline coursed, his hands shook, his knees shook.

"Fuck." Bud pissed on his jeans.

Walk pressed harder. Sweat ran down his nose.

"Jesus, alright. What the hell is wrong with you?"

Walk lowered the gun. "Now I could have done that at the bar, in front of your friends, made you piss your pants for an audience."

Bud glared, then dropped his eyes, defeat coming at him fast. Outside they heard hollers as the old guy moved on to "Man of Constant Sorrow."

"Star Radley," Walk said.

Bud looked confused, then it hit him and he sobered right up.

"I heard you got into it with her, and her daughter. She was playing, you couldn't keep your hands to yourself."

Bud shook his head. "Nothing in that."

Walk felt wired. He wondered about his sanity, pulling a gun on a man in a restroom. Looking for his angle.

"I took her out a couple times."

"And?"

"It didn't work out, that was all."

Walk reached for the gun again, till Bud stepped back. "I swear it. Nothing happened."

"You got rough with her?"

"No. Never. Nothing like that. I treated her nice. Shit, I even took her to that place on Bleaker. Twenty-dollar steak. I booked a motel . . . a nice one."

"She said no."

Bud looked at his feet, his pissy jeans, the gun. "Not just no. I'm not a man that can't take no. Shit, there's women, ask around. I do alright. But Star, she gave the illusion of it. Being into me. But it wasn't just no, not now. It was never. That's what she said. Never. What the fuck is that? Never. It was like she was trying hard to be someone she wasn't. An act, maybe. All of it an act."

"An act?"

"I reckon she did the same with other men. The neighbor. I picked her up one time and he came over, told me not to waste my time."

"Which neighbor?"

"Right next door. Seventies-looking dude."

"Where were you June 14th?"

Bud smiled when it came to him. "I know when it was. We had Elvis Cudmore playing. I was right here, ask anyone."

Walk left him there, cut through the small crowd and headed out into night air, heart still pounding.

He crossed the lot, squatted by a Dumpster and puked.

19

She ate her lunch beneath an oak tree, eyes fixed on her brother.

The first week had passed quietly, she did not speak to anyone. Thomas Noble made overtures, she dismissed him curtly.

Robin was in K2, they had their own area sectioned off by a low fence. Each day he played with the same girl and boy. They stood at the mud kitchen, Robin and the girl short-order cooks, the other boy fetching and delivering to oblivious others.

She didn't notice she was not alone until shadow cut the light, shade falling over her as she looked up.

"I thought I might enjoy your tree." Thomas Noble carried his lunch, a bulging sack, in his good hand.

She sighed.

He sat and cleared his throat. "I've been watching you."

"Well, that's not creepy at all." She shuffled further from him.

"I was thinking. Would you like to—"

"Never."

"My father said my mother turned him down the first time. But her eyes said yes so he persisted."

"Spoken like a true rapist."

Beside her he spread out a large, thick cloth napkin. Then he laid out a bag of potato chips, a Twinkie, Reese's Peanut Butter Cups, a bag of marshmallows, and a can of soda. "It's a wonder more people don't know about this spot."

"It's a wonder you haven't contracted diabetes."

He ate quietly, each bite muted as he pushed thick frames up his nose. He kept his bad hand holstered in his pocket. Watching him open the marshmallows with his teeth was painful.

"You can use the weak hand," she said, finally. "Don't hide it on my account."

"Symbrachydactyly. It's when—"

"I do not care."

He ate a marshmallow.

Robin ran up to the fence and showed her a purple plate with a clump of dirt on it. He mouthed "hotdog" and she smiled.

"He's a cutie," Thomas Noble said.

"You some kind of pervert?"

"No . . . of course not, I just . . ." He left it there.

Behind was woodland, out of bounds, long timbers stacked to make fencing, bleached back to bone.

"I heard you're from the Golden State. Beautiful this time of year. I think I have a cousin in Sequoia."

"The national park."

He went back to eating.

"Say, do you like movies?"

"No."

"How about ice skating? I'm actually quite good at—"

"No."

He shrugged off his jacket. "I like your bow. There's a photo of me with a bow in my hair when I was a baby."

"Do you have an inner monologue?"

"My mother liked to pretend I was the daughter she always wanted."

"But then all that testosterone kicked in and shat on her dreams."

He offered her a peanut butter cup.

She pretended not to notice.

They watched a group of boys pass. One of them said something and they laughed. Thomas Noble shoved his hand even deeper into his pocket.

She straightened a little when she saw a boy snatch the plate from Robin. Robin went to grab it back but the other boy, taller, held it from his reach, then threw it to the ground. As Robin bent to pick it up he was pushed over.

Duchess, up on her feet and moving, eyes locked tight on the kid as Robin began to cry. She watched other girls laughing, talking in clusters and twirling their hair, a different species altogether. She hopped the fence. There was no teacher, no lunch lady watching out. She helped Robin up, dusted his shorts down, and palmed his tears.

"Alright?"

"I want to go home." He sniffed.

She pulled him close and held him till he calmed. "I'll get us home. I promise it. I've got it figured, when I'm done here I'll get a job and a place and we can go home, right?"

"I mean home to Grandpa."

His friends stood beside, the girl and the boy. The girl came over, plaited hair, dungarees with a flower on the pocket. She patted Robin's back.

"Don't worry about Tyler, he's just mean to everyone," she said.

"Yeah," the boy agreed.

"You want to go fix more hotdogs for the diner?"

Duchess smiled and he left her. She watched him go play, nothing more to do about it, all forgotten.

She turned and found Tyler by the fence, going at it with a stick.

"Kid."

He turned and she knew the look. "What?"

She knelt in the dirt, rough on her knees, the sun behind. She grabbed his shirt and pulled him close.

"You touch my brother again and I'll behead you, expletive," Principal Duke said, fingers steepled over his stomach, his face tight with concern.

Duchess straightened. "I never said 'expletive.'"

Hal smiled. "Well, that's something. What did you say?"

"Motherfucker."

Principal Duke flinched like the word cut him deep. "Now this does give us a problem."

Duchess could smell the coffee on his breath, the cologne splashed onto his polyester tie just about masking the body odor beneath.

"I don't see why." Hal, hands red, skin cracked. He smelled of the acres, outside and forest. Radley land.

"It's the nature of the threat. I mean, beheading like that."

"The girl's an outlaw."

Duchess almost smiled.

"I don't think you're taking this as seriously as you should."

Hal stood. "I'll take her out now, the rest of the day out of school. I'll talk to her, it won't happen again. Right?"

She might've fought it then, made trouble because the bedrock was laid. She thought of Robin, already making a couple of friends here.

"If he touches Robin then I can't promise—"

Hal cleared his throat loud.

"I won't use those words again."

Principal Duke looked like he had more to say as she stood and followed Hal from the office.

They drove out in silence. Duchess rode up front. Instead of making a left Hal headed east, the road opening up beneath a sky that flashed silver as the sun hid. A dairy farm, steel barns the color of mint, then a town nothing more than Main and the small streets that fed it. Down backwater roads before they met pines like skyscrapers. A river beside them shone like mica as it fed the gorge, the mountain that loomed frosted white at the peaks, lazy tracks winding their way up. They climbed, Duchess craning to see back as they cleared the trees and the waterway snaked its own path. They slowed for another truck, passing opposite, a cowboy who dipped his hat.

They parked by a bluff, rock sand and dust, the pines picking up again, growing out and wide on the side of the mountain.

Hal got out and she followed.

He threaded the trees and she kept pace, the faintest of gaps but Hal navigated like he knew the trail and where each of its branches would carry.

Montana unfolded in front, a thousand miles of natural shades, water and land. She caught pine scent, watched men in waders fishing the clearest water a mile up. Beside her Hal lit a cigar.

"Trout streams." He pointed toward breaks, the fishermen like dots on a mighty canvas. "There's a canyon fifty miles in, so deep people say it doesn't bottom out till red rock. Take any trail, the backcountry, you won't see another person again. A million acres free."

"Is that why you ran here? Hide from the world?" She kicked a rock and watched it fall.

"You want to call a truce?"

"Not even a little."

He smiled at that.

"Your brother tells me you like to sing."

"There's nothing I like."

Ash fell to the dirt.

"The natives called this the backbone of the world. There's water a shade of teal you've never seen. It's so cold . . . the glacial melt and silt, nothing can grow beneath. It just stays clear for all time, no clouding, nothing hiding. There's something special about that, don't you think?"

She stayed silent.

"And that reflection, so true it's like the world is nothing but sky, flipped on its head. I'll take Robin out when he's a little older, on the Jammer, maybe a boat trip if he wants to fish. I'd like you to come along too."

"Don't do that."

"What?"

"Talk about tomorrow like it's real, like you'll be here and we'll be here." She did not want to scream again, to shake up the still.

On the side were flat leaves, berries the darkest purple. He picked one and ate it.

"Huckleberries." He held one out. She did not take it, instead pulling her own free. It was good, sweeter than she thought. She ate a handful, then filled her pockets for Robin.

"Bears like them too." Hal bent to pick them and she saw he carried the gun, the same one she'd shot with.

She took a breath. "You didn't come back."

He stopped then, straightened up, and turned to her.

"You didn't come back. You knew my mother. You knew what she was like and what life might've been like for us. You knew she could barely look out for herself. You're bigger than me. You're tall and tough and we needed—"

She broke off, fiddled with her bow, kept her voice even because she would not show him how deep the pain ran.

"So when you point it out, all this beauty, all this that you see and you think I see too. You should know it pales beside what I saw before. This purple"—she waved a hand at the huckleberries beside—"makes me think of her ribs, beat dark like that. The blue water, that's her eyes, clear enough to see there's no soul behind them anymore. You breathe the air and you think it's fresh, but I can't even take a breath without feeling that stab." She beat her chest hard. "I am alone. I will look after my brother and you will leave us because you don't really care. And you can say what you like, what you think will make me feel better. But fuck you, Hal. Fuck Montana, and the acres and the animals and the . . ." Her voice shook so she stopped it there.

The moment stretched between them and out over the pines. It swept the sky and the clouds, buried the promise of new totally. It reduced them to the nothing they were, so small against a backdrop endless in its beauty. He held his cigar but did not smoke, held the berries but did not eat them. She hoped to God she had shattered all the certainty he saw for them.

She turned and closed her eyes tight to the tears, forcing them back. She would not cry.

20

Walk felt the grace slip from Cape Haven as the summer finally began to dim.

It had begun the morning after Star, when reporters blocked Ivy Ranch Road and police tape streaked alien across the Radley home. He felt it then, the streets a degree cooler, the vista a shade off bright. Mothers ushering their kids, shutting big gates, smothering warmth from within. He shouldered it as best he could, offers rescinded, the cop that was friends with the killer. He spent lazy summer evenings walking every street in the Cape, from the pillared mansions on Calen Place to the small clapboard homes on the highest roads. He knocked on doors, hat in hand, beard there but trimmed a little neater, and he offered a tight smile as the desperation seeped from him. He asked, implored, leaned and probed, and led memories places they never had been. No one saw anything that night. No cars or trucks or anything out of the pristine normality of their summer.

He watched security tapes from every store on Main. The quality was shitty so he could not skip forward. Instead he viewed the video in real time, ten hours, sundown to sunup, his eyes propped open only by the torment that fell when he closed them.

He looked at Darke, tentative, no interview could be called without raising the interest of Darke's lawyer, and, in turn, Boyd and the state cops. He made a couple of calls, spoke with a Sutler cop and ran FasTrak tolls, hoping to catch an easy lie. He got nothing.

Martha had still not agreed to formally represent Vincent, though Walk picked up the phone most evenings and filled her in on what he'd got, which was mostly nothing. One Sunday morning he drove her to Fairmont, and the two sat with Vincent and reminisced about old times. When talk turned to mounting a defense Vincent signaled the guard.

The two passed the hundred miles back in heavy silence. She invited him in and again they sat on her porch and sipped beer. She cooked, some kind of stew so spicy his cheeks burned, she laughed and he stuck his tongue into his beer.

They talked a little about the past years, how she'd set up where she was needed most. Bitterwater had a low median income and a high crime rate. She spoke of her work with the kind of pride that made him smile. She showed photos of families she had brought back together, and letters from kids she had saved from abusive parents.

It was left unsaid, the exact time from their past when they'd been torn from each other. They skirted religion, he did not know her feelings anymore, after what had transpired between them, her parents, their faith. That was alright, they had a job to do and Walk didn't ever let that slip from his mind. Not when he leaned in to kiss her cheek, or when she brushed his leg with hers. Sometimes she noticed the way his hands tremored, or the way he shook his head lightly when trying to recall something, and then she watched him like she knew. And when she did that he told her good night and drove back to the Cape, his place, his town.

At dusk he strolled to Ivy Ranch Road, the fundamentals of his job very much in the way of the bigger picture.

Brandon met him at the door, no top, just sweatpants. Behind was his old football jersey, framed on the wall. Beside that a pool table, an arcade machine, the staples of a bachelor finding his feet after a decade of perceived servitude.

"Is this about that freak across the street again?" Brandon looked past

Walk and stared at Milton's place. "You know what I found in my yard, Walk? A fucking head."

"A head?"

"A fucking sheep or something. Deer, whatever. Hollowed out like a warning."

"I'll talk to him. But you know, Brandon, I hear that car fire up from my place." Walk noticed the guy was standing on his toes, looking for an extra inch.

"Tell you what," Brandon said. "It is quieter without Star rolling in late. I mean, it's tragic and all, but maybe Milton will sleep easier now he's not waiting up for her."

"How's that?"

Brandon leaned on the door frame. Tattoo on his chest, some kind of trite Japanese symbol. "Sometimes I got in late and I saw him at the window."

"He watches the stars."

Laughter. "Yeah, one in particular. You ask him about that, Walk."

"He said you pissed in his yard."

"Bullshit."

"Whatever. I really don't give a damn. I just don't want either of you on me."

"You look tired, Walk. Are you hydrating?"

"Listen, Brandon. I'll go over and have the same talk with Milton, but do you think you could just calm things down? I've got a lot on, and I could do without having to come over and see you over some bullshit dispute."

"You need to exercise, man. Stress relief. Stop by one night and we'll drop some circuits. Rock Hard. You know I tried to patent that, for my fitness—"

Walk left him talking and headed across the street. He knocked on the door.

"Walk." Milton wore a smile so wide Walk almost felt bad for him.

"Can I come in?"

"Into my place?"

Walk tried not to sigh.

"Yes. I mean, sure, yes. Please." Milton stepped to the side and Walk headed into the house.

"You want something to eat?"

"No, thanks."

"You on a diet, Walk? You look thinner. How about a beer?"

"Sure, Milton."

Milton smiled, a little too eager, then disappeared into the kitchen while Walk took in the living room. The place was stacked, Milton the kind of hoarder that kept and piled even old *TV Guides*. He stepped over a cluster of coasters bearing the names of states he well knew Milton had never visited. He ordered them in, from all over, the kind of crap that portrayed a full life, travel and friends. He had a photo frame on the television set, a picture of a blacktail, dead eyes.

"Got that one in Cottrell. Nice, right?"

"Sure, Milton."

"I didn't have beer, just the coffee liqueur. I couldn't find a date on it, maybe it's been there a while. But liqueur doesn't go bad, right, Walk?"

Walk took the glass, set it down, cleared a space to sit and motioned for Milton to join him.

"I wanted to talk to you about that night."

Milton shifted, made to cross his legs but couldn't quite manage it. Walk sipped his coffee liqueur, tried not to bring it back up.

"The way I hear it you've been talking to everyone in town about that night. But I already told the real cop everything."

Walk took the blow, certain Milton didn't mean it. "Now, you said you heard fighting."

"That's right."

"You also said you saw Vincent and Darke getting into it a few nights before Star was murdered."

He flinched at her name. Star used to tell how he'd take her trash cans out if she forgot. Small things, she needed them.

"Why'd they fight?"

"I think maybe Vincent King was jealous. I remember them, Walk. Back at school. They were like, they'd get married or something, have kids. I thought maybe Vincent had been dwelling on that inside, dreaming up a future based on the past."

A glance around the room, wood-paneled wall, shag beneath his feet. Boulder rocks around the fire, suburban ranch throwing back to the seventies. Air sweetly freshened, cans all over but still, it was there, the blood beneath.

Milton cleared his throat. "You can't do what isn't right. You can't just skip a piece of the past, highlight the good. You know?"

"You called us before, lot of times, seemed like every time Star had a man stop by. Even when it was Darke, right? Said you were worried."

Milton bit his lower lip. "It's part of the Watch. But maybe I was mistaken those times. Darke's a good man. It's the way he looks, that's why people talk. I know. I know how it feels. You don't think I hear the kids? Brillo. Wookiee. Furby. Meat packer. Joke's on them because I don't even pack the meat."

The clock chimed, sunburst, ten minutes slow. Milton turned his head, Walk saw sweat pool beneath his arms.

"Hey, Walk. You want to head up the Mendocino again?"

Walk smiled. "I enjoyed it, but I think I'm more of a fisherman than a hunter. Get me out on the waves and I'm happy."

"Not me. Never did learn to swim. I had the lessons, but I used to open my mouth all the time, try and swallow it all down. I like the chlorine."

Walk didn't know what to do with that.

"Doesn't matter, I got other friends into it." Milton looked like he was desperate to share.

"Yeah?" Walk took the bait.

"I went hunting with him."

"Who?"

Milton grinned. "Darke. He took me in his Escalade. You seen it? I tell you, that man can shoot. Brought back two blacktail."

"That right?"

"You've got him wrong, Walk. He's . . ."

"Different?"

"A good friend." He said it firm, eyes locked on Walk. "He said he'd come here for the next shower. Not till February but still. I think he'll actually show."

The barb was there, but Walk didn't have the energy to feel any guilt.

"I asked him to come away in the spring. A week, the hunt. I bought him a veil, gaiters, the wax kind."

Walk looked at the spilling shelves beside, so many books, most on hunting. "You don't know him. You should be careful, Milton."

"So should you, Walk. You look sick."

"I also wanted to let you know that I talked to Brandon again. Leah said you called in."

Milton stiffened at that. "Well, it didn't do any good. He does it because he knows I have to be up early. Last night I went to the window and he was just sitting there revving the engine. And when he saw me he smiled. I'm not a kid now, Walk. This isn't like school. You know he used to bully me. Flushed my head down the toilet. I don't have to put up with it. I should—"

"Leave a sheep's head in his yard?"

Milton stared, wild eyes, hair spilling from the top of his shirt. "I don't know nothing about that."

"You said he urinated in your yard."

"Yes, sir."

"How'd you know it was him."

"Caught in the act. I opened the drapes and came eye to eye with it."

"Jesus."

"I filed a report. Ten ninety-eight."

"Jail break."

"And you know he's got a boat, fixed it up nice. He keeps it at Harbor Bay. I figured maybe he'd sell the car and spend his time on the water."

"He said he's willing to try if you are. He said you're a decent neighbor and he feels bad about it."

"He said that?"

Walk knew Milton could not read him at all. "So you'll knock all this shit on the head."

"It was never on me, Walk."

Walk stared, pleading in his eyes.

"Maybe one day I'll send him over a cut or something. Nothing too special, not at first. Chuck. How does that sound?"

"Thank you, Milton."

Milton followed him to the door.

On the porch Walk stopped and looked over, across the street.

"I miss her," Milton said. "I'm real sorry I . . ."

"What?"

"I'm just sorry she's not there anymore."

"We owe it to her and the children to arrest the man that did this."

"You already did, Walk."

Milton would not meet his eye, instead letting his wander to the night sky. He stood there, hands deep in his pockets, lost to Walk and the town and the blood that had been spilled.

21

They sat in the yard as the Santa Ana warmed them.

Walk had been trying to sleep, despite the early hour, but instead found himself staring up at the ceiling when he heard the knock at the door.

"I can't believe you still live at home, Walk. That's so uncool," Martha said.

She'd brought dinner, chili she warmed on the old stove that Walk used to store take out menus.

"I feel like I should line my mouth with wax before I try this."

"Relax, Walk. I went easy. Barely blips on the Scoville. Chili for pussies."

He touched the fork to his tongue and immediately felt the lava. "Seriously? It's like an illness. You are actually ill."

She laughed. "Just eat the cornbread. You look like you could use it. I hope you're taking care of yourself, Walk."

He smiled. "You ever miss the Cape?"

"Every day."

"I told Leah I'd been seeing you again."

"Seeing me?"

"I didn't—"

She laughed. He blushed.

"Leah Tallow. She still married to Ed?"

"She is."

"Wow, she must've put up with a lot over the years. I remember him at school, used to chase after Star."

"Everyone did."

"Tallow Construction. I see their signs up sometimes. I had a client a while back, husband was laid off by Tallow, he turned to the bottle."

"The market is tough. It'll turn."

"Especially if they start building all those new homes."

He stood and topped up her wine. "I went to see Milton again."

"The butcher. I remember him at school. Does he still smell of blood?"

"He does. He's certain he heard arguing, and he'll testify he saw Vincent and Darke get into it outside Star's place. And he'll speculate it was over Star."

The agreement was there, uneasy at first, but Martha was settling into it. Walk would work the King case, and anything he found he would bring to her, and she would unravel it and repackage it and tell Walk if it was worth more than a damn in a court of law. She was clear enough, though; under no circumstances would she go to trial. They'd build the case as best they could and then pass it over to a trial lawyer. And if Vincent wouldn't retain one then at least she'd tried.

"Did you have a chance to look at the papers?"

"Sure, what else would I be doing? It's not like I need sleep or anything."

He smiled as she left him, went out the side gate to her car, then returned with her briefcase. Walk cleared the dishes away while Martha spread papers out over the table. Citronella burned, five candles battled the night sky and gave them just enough light.

Tax returns, statements, company filings, going back twenty years. All Walk could pull on Dickie Darke.

"The records are straight and ordered, Walk. Darke earns decent money. Maybe two fifty a year. Nothing really raises any red flags. I went back far, when he bought a small home on Lavenham Avenue, Portland."

"Oregon," Walk said to himself.

"I guess that's where he's from. He remodeled and sold it on for a thirty-thousand-dollar profit, which he declared in full. Modest expenses. Then another a block away, made forty-five. And then nothing."

"Nothing?"

"Must have found another income. Four years of nothing. And then he stepped it up massively, seemed to move from town to town, working his way along the coast, wherever he could make a buck. Just like that."

"Always real estate?"

"Mostly. A place in Eugene, another in Gold Beach. In the summer of '95 he arrived in the Cape, bought the old bar on Cabrillo and spent a year trying to get a license."

Walk remembered the night it opened; again, no fuss or launch party, just light in the darkness.

"The first year it grossed half a million dollars." Martha sipped her wine. "The second year it doubled. It was a gold mine, Walk. And that's just what he declared, place like that, it's all cash, right? It might be all he had, but it was all he needed."

"So he leverages that to buy the King house. At least he would have."

"There were payments, though, eye-watering payments."

"To who?"

"My guess would be whoever invested with him. Not a bank."

"Loan shark?"

"Could be. His credit history is sketchy, a lot of moving around, would've made it hard to borrow from a regular bank. And then he bought the house on Fortuna Avenue."

"Dee Lane's place."

"And the house on Ivy Ranch Road."

"The Radley house."

"Small houses, just rentals. And an investment in a development called Cedar Heights."

Walk had seen the advertisements in the local newspaper.

"Sorry, Walk. Nothing strange at all in this."

Walk sighed.

"That club he owned. It's called The Eight, right?" Martha said.

"Yeah."

"I had a girl from there come in. She had problems with a boyfriend. I think she mentioned Darke once."

"Can I talk to her?"

"Maybe. I'll ask."

"We need to know about those payments."

"All I've got is an account number."

"Could be something."

"Or nothing. I know the case file now. What you've got is a whole load of nothing. And what you need is a smoking gun. Nothing short of that."

He stood when his cell rang, saw it was Milton. The man sounded breathless, out for his evening walk, burning off some of the meat. He spoke for a minute.

Martha gathered the papers. "Everything alright?"

"Milton runs Neighborhood Watch."

Martha raised an eyebrow.

"He's the only member since Etta passed. He said there's a ten ninety-one on Sunset. I'd better head over."

"Ten ninety-one?"

Walk sighed. "Stray horse."

He drove to Sunset, didn't even think of running the lights.

A sedan outside the King house, so nondescript Walk figured them for cops.

He pulled the cruiser up right behind, flashed his lights once then got out and walked up to the window.

Two men, neither moved to roll down a window. Walk watched the empty street, the empty lots, the moonlit waters of the Cape. A strange car stood out. He tapped the glass gently. Slowly the driver turned, maybe fifty, head of dark hair and handsome.

"Can I help you with something?" Walk smiled.

The man looked at his friend, older, maybe sixty-five, beard and glasses. "Did we do something?"

"Not that I know of."

"So fuck off then."

Walk swallowed and felt the adrenaline kick a little. "And if I don't?"

A smile came back, just small, like Walk should have known something he did not, and could still be punished for it.

"We're looking for Richard Darke."

"Darke doesn't live here." Walk didn't draw but kept a hand there to show his intent.

"Any ideas where we can find him?"

Walk thought of Darke, the payments, the kind of men he was most likely in business with. "I don't know where he lives."

"You see him, tell him we're not going away," the older guy said, not looking at Walk.

The driver started the engine.

"I need you to step out of the vehicle."

The driver looked up at Walk, then at the King house behind. "Darke's good at spinning plates, till one drops."

"I said I need you—"

The driver closed the window and pulled into the street.

Walk considered giving chase, radioing, instead he watched them coast down Sunset, his hand still on his gun.

•••

She took Robin's hand as they opened the gate and walked over toward the two horses, grazing side by side.

"Can you eat with us one time?"

Duchess muzzled the black gently, patting his nose with the flat of her hand. "No."

Then she muzzled the smaller gray, tried to pet her but she moved her face away. Duchess liked her.

She roped the muzzles and led them gently, Robin keeping far to the side. He ran the last steps then closed the gate behind, like she'd shown him.

When she was done she told them good night, then found Robin on a patch of grass by the water. He knew not to go too close, though he could swim well, she had ridden three buses with him to the lido in Oakmont each Saturday for close to a year because they taught kids for free.

When she got close he scooted away.

"You're pissed at me."

"Yes." He balled a fist and kept it in his lap. He wore shorts, thin legs, knees grazed. "You shouldn't have said that to Tyler."

"He shouldn't have pushed you down."

Hollow night fell as quick as dusk began, the warmth lifting till nothing but cool remained.

"Alright."

"It's not alright." He hit the grass with his fist. "I like it here. I like Grandpa and I like the animals. I like Miss Child and the new school. I don't need . . ."

"What?" she said it quiet but the challenge was there. A month back he would have stayed silent.

"You. I've got Grandpa and he's an adult. He can care for us. I don't want you to fix my food."

He cried quietly. She watched him huddled, chin to chest, knees up and arms around them. She knew about the things that shaped people, memories and events that print your soul. She needed Robin to be alright, more than anything she needed that. He saw the shrink each week, though no longer told her what was discussed. *I don't have to tell. It's private.*

"I know you're an outlaw, but I'm not. I just want to be a kid."

She scooted nearer, her jeans in the dirt. "You're a prince, remember. Mom said that and she was right."

"Just leave me alone."

She made to ruffle his hair but he moved from her hand, stood and then ran for the house. For a moment she thought she might cry too, just let the past months and years rot her into the dirt, wash her skin from her bones and her blood to the water.

She heard the rumble of a truck, tensed for a moment, then saw it was Dolly. Dolly left the high beams cutting a sweep of light over the water.

"Mind if I sit awhile?" Dolly stopped by now and then. She wore a cream dress, heels with red soles, the kind of woman that did not own work clothes.

"I didn't see you at church last week," Duchess said.

"Bill's been sick." Her cigarette glowed as she held it away.

"Oh."

"He's been sick a long time. Some days are better than others."

"Right."

"I missed seeing that dress."

Duchess had cut a new swath to show off her belly button.

"You can come by, you know. If you ever want some female company. I don't have siblings, no mother, grew up fending for myself."

"And you're alright."

"I'm good at fronting, Duchess. I'm a fucking master. Anyway, Hal knows where to find me if you want to stop by."

"I try not to talk to Hal all that much."

"And why's that?"

"Would I have met him . . . I mean, if my mother . . ."

The water slopped gently. "He made the drive."

Duchess turned.

"To Cape Haven." Dolly spoke quietly, as if betraying a trust. "I just, I thought you should know."

"When?"

"Every year. Same day. June second."

"My birthday."

A smile, small though it was. "He'd take a gift. He used to ask me to help him pick out something you'd like. And then, when Robin was born, he'd make that drive twice each year. And this is a man that never takes a day off, can't afford to."

Duchess looked back at the old farmhouse. "How'd he know? Star said she never spoke to him."

"Oh, she didn't. Stubborn one, your mother. Sounds like someone else I know."

"Save it."

"He still had someone there. Called him now and then. A policeman."

Duchess closed her eyes. Walk. "I never got them."

"Oh, I know. He'd come back with them. Same each time. Didn't stop him trying, though. He wouldn't see you without your mother's blessing."

"She blamed him. For everything."

Dolly laid a hand on her shoulder.

Duchess knew about her grandmother, her spirit so free Duchess still carried the Day before Radley. Star had been seventeen. She'd tried college, came home early and saw the note right off.

I love you. I'm sorry. Call your father and don't go into the kitchen.

Star never was one to follow rules.

Dolly stood. "I brought a pie for Robin. Two-mile-high mud. I reckon he'll be disappointed it's not real mud."

Duchess followed her to the truck and took the pie from her.

"Your grandfather is old."

"I know."

"You ever made a mistake, Duchess?"

Duchess thought of the Cape, the fire, the fights, scratching Brandon's Mustang. "Never."

Dolly grabbed her then, held her. She smelled of sweet perfume. Duchess tried to break it but Dolly held her tight. "Don't lose yourself, Duchess."

After, she watched the truck fade.

First rain fell on her shoulders.

It turned on her fast, so heavy it kicked up the mud around and splashed her legs. She stood there and tilted her head toward the sky, the opening heaven not enough to cleanse her. She found Hal on the porch. He held a towel. She let him wrap her and walked to the seat, took the cocoa he handed her, the mug steaming away her protest. The rain fell so loud it drowned the scream of that voice that told her to kick and kick.

"Robin is sleeping. He didn't mean what he said." Hal sat beside her, far enough up the bench.

"He did."

"I saw you in the field. Big Sky is beautiful, even in the rain."

"Dolly brought a pie." Duchess handed him the dish by her foot.

Inside the phone rang. It did not ring often. She watched the old man head in and speak a few words that did not carry.

"Who was it?"

"Walker."

"Did he mention Darke?"

"He was just checking in."

"Darke will come."

"There's no way of knowing that."

"You don't get it."

"Tell me."

"He promised he'd come for me."

"Why?"

She said nothing.

They sat and drank and breathed the earthy rain.

"I dream more here. I don't want to."

He turned to her.

"And my dreams are fucked up."

He did not flinch at the curse. "Tell me."

"No."

"Tell the gray. She can hear you from here. Just talk, that's all, Duchess."

"That's all," she said quietly.

He closed his eyes to the rain. She saw him then, a life of paid mistake, the lure of second chance, the plaintive ask of redemption.

"I rise above the farmhouse and see slates and green, the gutter of leaves that remind me of fall and seasons that change no matter who dies. I am high in the sky and Montana is a footnote, patchwork fields stitched by tractors like ants, people that bob like they are drowning in ordinary.

"The ocean is endless but I see its end. I see the earth, the curves are tomorrow but it won't turn. I see clouds that hold sky, a sunset in the desert and a rise over metals. Before long I am darkness and stars and their moons. The world is a nothing, so small I raise a finger and hide it. I am the God I don't believe in. I am big enough to stop the bad men."

She would not cry.

Hal watched her carefully. "If he comes I will stop him."

"Why?"

"To protect you and Robin."

"I can protect us."

"You're still a child."

"I'm not a child. I am an outlaw."

He placed an arm around her and she melted into the warmth, hating herself as she did.

22

The apartment was above a five-and-dime, one window punched out and replaced with a board, the others grimy enough Walk couldn't imagine much light made it through. Beside the door was a vent, the smell of Chinese food pumped out, despite the early hour.

The girl's name was Julieta Fuentes and she'd worked at various clubs as a dancer. Martha had left several messages on her cell but gave Walk the address when the girl didn't get back to her. It wasn't on Walk, he didn't press, but Julieta had trouble with an ex and Martha was worried about her.

He found the door open and climbed the narrow staircase. Mold crept its way from the mottled ceiling.

He knocked on the door, waited a little then hammered it.

Julieta was small, dark hair, wide hips, the kind of beautiful that almost drove him to take a step back.

She glared. He flashed his badge and she glared some more.

"My son is sleeping inside."

"Sorry. I got your details from Martha May."

Julieta softened then, just enough to take a step out into the narrow hallway and pull the door to behind her.

She pressed close to Walk. He tried to move back, dropped down a step but found his eyes level with her bust. He coughed once, turned a shade of red that saw her glare return.

"Get it over with, whatever you want to know."

"You worked at The Eight."

"I took my clothes off for money, is that a crime?"

Walk wanted to loosen his collar, felt it constricting the blood, sending even more to his cheeks. "I just wanted to ask you a couple of questions about Dickie Darke."

No change in the glare.

He cleared his throat. "Martha said you had some trouble with a guy. Is it the father of—"

"I don't sleep around, officer. Not all girls that dance are whores, you know."

Walk glanced around, half hoping to see backup arrive. "I'm sorry. I just, I'm trying to find out about Dickie Darke."

"He didn't do it."

"What?"

"Whatever you think he did."

"That the party line?"

She tightened her robe, opened the door a little and listened out. "My son sleeps late. Up all night."

"Like his mother."

The first hint of a smile. "Listen, people look at Darke and see the size of him, guess he's some kind of tough guy. I mean, don't get me wrong, he can handle himself. I've seen him. This guy tried to grab me once, and Darke just picked him up by his throat. I mean clean off the floor. Like something out of a movie."

"But he's not violent."

Julieta hit his arm, hard enough. "You're thinking like an asshole cop."

"How should I be thinking?"

She thought on that. "Maybe like a father looking out for his girl."

"That's what Darke was like?"

She sighed like she was dealing with an asshole cop. "He didn't watch us. Dancing. He never watched, never tried to date us, never asked for a blow job. And believe me, that's not usual. If we had trouble, came up short, he'd see us right. You talk to any girl from The Eight, you won't hear nothing bad about the man."

"This guy, father of your son, did Darke sort that too?"

She didn't speak, but her eyes told him what he wanted to know.

"Anything at all you can tell me? He might be in trouble."

"What kind of trouble?"

"There's men looking for him. Two guys, one had a beard and glasses."

He could tell by the look on her face she knew them.

"I'm just trying to get answers here. Please."

"I know those men, they stopped by each month, second Friday, left with a fat envelope. Not unusual, the kind of clubs I worked in, there's always guys collecting."

"He always paid."

She laughed. "You don't have a choice with guys like that. You pay or they make you pay. Darke knows that."

"And the fact they're looking for him now . . ."

"You think they give a shit The Eight burned? Not their problem. They want their money."

"I don't think he can pay them."

A flash of concern then. "He should run."

"I'm sure Darke can take care of himself."

"You don't understand him. Beneath it all . . ."

"Tell me."

"There was a dancer there, Amber, now that one was a whore. She thought Darke had money, so she made her move. And he told her he wasn't interested."

"Did he say why?"

"He said he didn't look at her that way. Said he had a girl. That was all. We never saw her."

"So he was seeing someone. Anything else, even if you think it doesn't matter."

"Jesus. You cops keep pushing, right."

"Please, it's important. Anything."

"You're looking to bust the man but all I can tell you is he looked out for us, for me. Me and another girl, we were his favorites."

"Why?"

"We had kids. He was protective, soft even. One night I didn't show for work and he turned up here. He saw me, my face that night. He was worried."

"And the other girl?"

"Layla. He was the same with her. He even took them out, Six Flags. I mean, even I was jealous. He's a decent guy."

"Can I talk to Layla?"

"She's gone, somewhere out west. Her and her little girl."

"She had a daughter."

"Yeah, used to have a picture on her locker. Beautiful girl."

Walk heard noise from inside. The kid calling out.

"We done here?"

"Sure."

"Happy hunting, officer."

An hour to Darke's place. On the drive he called Martha. Julieta's ex-boyfriend was Max Cortinez, and he had been beaten half to death outside a bar in Bitterwater two months prior. Walk got Martha to read the report.

Max was stamped on, so hard and so many times he'd lost all but one of his teeth. Big boots. Max, the kind of guy Bitterwater PD didn't waste any hours on. Walk tried to call him direct, got told to fuck off when the guy finally answered his cell.

Walk caught his own eyes in the rearview mirror, beard a little longer, face a little thinner, slow slide toward someplace darker. Not just his body betraying him; he no longer questioned breaking the kind of rules he'd based a life on. It would lead somewhere bad, it couldn't not.

Cedar Heights, a half-finished estate, wide lots, grand and soulless. A gatehouse, the brick too new, even the woodland surrounding had an air of manufactured. Darke had put money into the place.

He drew up by the barrier. A man stepped out, straggly beard, smart polo, strong smell of weed. The kind of eyes that told Walk he existed in a permanent state of confusion.

"Morning, officer."

"I'm here to see Dickie Darke."

The man looked toward the sky, scratched the beard, and tapped the side of his head like he was working loose an answer. "I don't think he's home. I haven't seen him."

"He's expecting me."

A minute passed while the guy made a call. "He's not picking up."

"I'll go and knock."

Another beard scratch.

Walk leaned an arm out while the man weighed things. "What's your name?"

"Moses Dupris."

A silent flinch.

Beside was a water fountain, dry and green, mosaic tiles were missing in spots.

"I'll say I steamrolled you, Moses. How's that sound? Threatened to make a scene, knock his neighbors' doors."

"Well, to be honest there's not a lot of neighbors."

"Which house?"

Moses pointed. "Darke . . . Mr. Darke, he stays in the model home at the moment. You can pull up right on the driveway."

Inside the gate was a single road that curved its way around a dozen homes. A couple were finished, most were boarded, scaffold stood, half painted, a pile of rubble towered. The model home sat by woodland, pretty enough, white stucco, pillars and sash windows. Walk hated the place, the sterile feel. He thought of Cape Haven and the will to make it some-place like this. People were buying parcels of coast, hoping one day they'd get approval to build. He hoped he'd be long dead before the green tide rolled in.

Up close the house had already aged, a deep crack crept its way to broken guttering that hung loose. Grass grew long, weeds poked their way through beds.

The door was large, Walk couldn't find a bell so he hammered the way cops did on television. Heavy, urgent thumps. He stood there awhile, birds singing at him.

He walked along the front of the house, the drapes pulled, no gaps at all. At the side was a gate, wrought iron, black and heavy but opening when he tried it.

A pool, barbeque area built up and out, TV screen by the chairs. Walk stopped still when he saw the back door, open.

"Darke," he called.

He stepped inside. His heart beat quick. Thought of drawing but found his hands not cooperating. That's how it was now.

A fan spun above. He saw neat order, opened a cabinet to canned food, labels front, perfectly so.

He moved through, sweating now. Past the dining room, an office, the living room, television on, the sound muted, ESPN, Karl Ravech in front of a wall of books, talking Bautista and Braves.

The whole place was dressed, every item carefully chosen to project an ideal. He saw plastic fruit in a bowl, plastic flowers on a side table, and photo frames filled with a model family sporting plastic smiles.

He imagined Darke living there alone, big and awkward and trying not to make a mess.

Walk climbed the stairs, wood, carpet runner, cream and thick. He passed a mirror and saw himself reflected, hand still on his gun, a kid playing cowboys, hunting down Vincent and his plastic tomahawk.

He tried guest rooms, three before he found the master. Everything immaculate.

"What are you doing here?"

He spun, his heart hammered away.

Darke stood at the top of the stairs, shorts and vest and earphones in. The stare was cold and hard.

"I came to check on you."

Just the stare, nothing more.

"There were people asking about you. Didn't look like the kind of guys you want paying you a visit."

Walk followed him down the stairs and into a plush den.

"You want to get this over with?"

Walk took a seat on the soft leather couch. Darke stayed standing, the gulf between them grew.

"Julieta Fuentes," Walk said, and then watched.

Sweat coated Darke, down muscled arms and legs.

"You remember Julieta?"

"I remember everyone that works for me."

"You remember her boyfriend, Max Cortinez?"

Nothing.

Walk stood and moved over to the window. The yard was small but landscaped, trees and borders, some kind of sculpture carved out of a log. "I don't blame you. What you did to Max. It was one-sided, him and Julieta, you evened things up."

Darke just stared, but for a moment something else crept in. Sadness, maybe regret.

"It's noble. You did her a favor. You showed heart."

"Julieta earned more than the others."

And then the fit. He was protecting his asset. Dickie Darke, his sole purpose the pursuit of money.

Walk's throat dried as he strayed deeper. "You lost it, though. Beat him too badly. He could've died. Is that what happened with Star?"

Darke's face, the disappointment plain enough. "You're asking the wrong questions to the wrong person."

Walk moved closer, adrenaline firing again. "I don't think so."

"Vincent King, you don't want to see the man he is, only the boy he was."

Walk took another step.

Darke straightened up. "You're out of your depth. You're losing yourself. I know how that feels."

"How does it feel?"

"Sometimes we just want to get on. People get in the way of that."

"How did Star get in the way?"

"How's her girl doing? You told her I was thinking about her."

Walk tensed at that, gritted his teeth. Another day and he might have squared off with the bigger man, another day or maybe another life. His breathing grew so labored the room started to dim. "I better get on."

He walked out and into the kitchen. Darke followed.

Walk slowed a little as he felt the blood rush from his head. He held out a hand to steady himself. The medication, the fucking disease making him weak.

By the street door he noticed it, the small case in the corner. "You taking a trip, Darke?"

"Business."

"Anywhere nice?" Walk turned to face him.

"Somewhere I was hoping I wouldn't have to visit."

The moment passed between them, and then Walk turned and left, climbed into the cruiser and headed back to the Cape. It wasn't till he crossed the town line that he pulled over, and dialed Montana.

23

It rained so long Duchess took to sitting on the window seat, sky watching, just like the old man. She noticed him watching her close, and watching the drive, like he was waiting on a visitor.

Robin got sick, a flu that saw him take to his bed for a week. Duchess brought him hot drinks and fussed, though it sat there between them, like a weight on her chest, a kind of divide she would break down absolutely.

On the third night his fever spiked, he cried out for their mother, up in bed, slick hair and wild eyes. He screamed and wrenched sounds from deep, a kind of pain she knew well herself. Hal was panicked, asking Duchess if he should call a doctor or an ambulance. She ignored him, wet a cloth and stripped Robin naked.

She sat with him all night, Hal by the door. Not speaking, just there.

The next morning it broke and he ate a little soup. Hal carried him down and settled him on the porch swing so he could watch the rain and breathe the mist.

"I like how it drums the lake," Robin said.

"Yes."

"I'm sorry. What I said before."

She turned and knelt on the rough wood, her pants already torn at the knee from working her jobs. "You don't ever need to say that to me."

Hal had a VCR. They watched Rita Hayworth one lazy Sunday. Duchess did not know a woman could be so exquisite. And then, in the attic, she discovered a bag full of Westerns, sat beside the old man and watched them through the night till Robin was all better. For a day she lost her name and chased a band of Mexicans through sapping wheat, Hal watching on from the porch, shaking his head like he'd taken in a loon. She called him Tuco and told him he was the ugly and she was the bad. The good clapped his hands, his curls rain plastered, his yellow mac dripping wet.

On the days she practiced, she marched a hundred yards back, hit the tree bang center and called herself Sundance.

The first time she rode the gray she felt closer to Butch than she ever had. Close to her blood, a little less foreign, a root taking hold in Montana earth. She laid a hand on the gray and felt the heat from her, patted gently and told the horse she wouldn't ever kick her and, in return, maybe she could agree not to throw a cowgirl to the dirt. She gripped the horn tight and shook rain from her hair as Hal led her around the paddock, just a gentle trot that left her fighting the widest smile when she was done. Another week and she watched the endless carbon sky begin to crack and the rain ease, the blue edge its way in, and sunlight bless the ground for the first time in a month.

As she looked out across the land she saw Hal by the harrow and Robin by the coop, both of them turning skyward and smiling. Hal raised a hand, Robin too. And then, slowly, with great effort, Duchess raised her own to them both. In math she learned the triangle was the strongest shape.

There was a gradualism to Montana days, fall sweeping them along with leaves a thousand kinds of brown.

One Saturday Hal drove them to Glacier. They hiked to Running Eagle Falls, the aspens catching the light and stopping her breath. They walked on a carpet of leaves, some so big they came to Robin's shoulder when he drew them up. He tried to collect them, got so many he could barely see over them. Hal brought them to a clearing and they watched the stark yellow cottonwoods wave like fool's gold.

"Beautiful," Hal said.

"Beautiful," Robin echoed.

Duchess just stared. Some days, mean and tough was hard to locate.

They stopped at rocks, water cascading loud. They stood beside a family of four, so symmetrical Duchess looked away from the mother and father like they'd committed a modern-day sin. She reasoned they'd divorce soon enough, harden their little angels till all that was left were slammed doors and angry tears. She did smile at that.

Duchess still wore her dress each Sunday to Canyon View Baptist. Each time Hal still frowned and the other kids still stared, but the old people, the couples that stopped and bowed, widowed ladies that carried themselves with earned decency, they all took to her. None more so than Dolly, who sought her out most weekends and sat beside her.

Fall shadows, the candles and lanterns needed. Robin sat across with three other kids, brothers all older but they let him trail them. Their mother hushed them now and then. Robin watched them in quiet awe, bigger boys, there was nothing that compared.

"He will come."

"Who?" Hal said.

"Darke. You should know that he will come."

"He won't."

"I'm Josey Wales and he's a Union soldier. The bounty is my blood. He will come."

"You still haven't told me why you think he's coming."

"He thinks I wronged him."

"Did you?"

"Yes."

The old minister called communion and she watched the line form, so hungry for purgation they'd share cheap wine and spit.

"You want to go up?" Hal said, same every week.

"Do I want to contract herpes, Hal?"

He looked away and Duchess took that as a small victory. Robin lined up with the bigger boys. He wore an old bolo tie they found in the attic and a panama hat at least seven sizes too big.

As they passed, Robin turned to them. "John, Ralph, and Danny are going up to take communion. I want to stay with them but I don't want to contract herpes."

Hal frowned at Duchess.

They stayed for cake. Duchess ate a slice of chocolate and a slice of lemon, made eyes at a slice of pear and date but an old lady took it before she committed. She had gained a little weight, enough to edge off the severity.

When they arrived back at the farmhouse Duchess saw the bicycle, old and shitty, lying in the dirt by the porch.

"It's Thomas Noble," Robin said, his face at the glass.

Thomas Noble stood at the bottom step, bad hand tucked into the pocket of green corduroys. He wore a smart green shirt and green jacket.

"Jesus. He looks like a fucking booger."

They climbed from the car.

Duchess stood, hand on hip and scowling. "What are you doing here, Thomas Noble?"

He swallowed, looked at her dress then swallowed again.

"I hope you're not checking me out. Hal will shoot you. Right, Hal?"

"Yes," Hal said. Then he ushered Robin into the house, made a promise to let him drive the riding mower after he changed out of his church clothes.

"I . . . the math paper. I needed someone to—"

"Don't even try that bullshit."

"I just thought maybe we could hang out. Being as I live just over there." He pointed with his good hand.

"I know Radley land, there's no neighbor close. How long did you ride?"

Thomas Noble scratched his head. "Four miles. Maybe. Mom said I could do with the exercise."

"You're skinny to the point of malnourishment. She'd do better advising a change of diet."

He smiled a simple smile.

"I'm not fixing you any lunch or even a drink. This isn't the 1950s."

"I know."

"Well, I'm going to pull the weeds by the water. Work doesn't stop just because you don't have the good sense to call ahead."

She went into the house, changed into her old jeans and shirt, then found him still there, standing dumb and looking down at his sneakers.

"I suppose you can make yourself useful and help me."

"Yes," he said quick.

He trailed her down to the lake edge, knelt beside, and pulled weeds she pointed at. She took a cigar from her pocket, stolen from Hal's dresser.

"You can't smoke that. You'll catch the cancer."

She flipped him off, then bit the top off the cigar and spit it into the dirt. "Jesse John Raymond held a smoke in his mouth when he slaughtered the coward, Pat Buchanan." She gripped the cigar in her teeth. "You got a light?"

"Do I look like the kind of boy that has a light?"

"Fair point. I could just chew it, like Billy Ross Clanton."

"I think that's a different type of tobacco."

"You know nothing, Thomas Noble." Duchess bit a large chunk off the cigar, chewed and tried mightily not to vomit.

Thomas Noble cleared his throat, then squinted up at her. "So . . . the reason I came. There's this dance. The winter formal. It's not for a while but—"

"I hope you're not working up the courage to ask me. Now of all times. When I've got a mouth full of tobacco."

He shook his head quickly, then went back to the task. "You should know that I don't intend to marry. And I especially wouldn't marry you . . . with the hand."

"It's not hereditary. I was an anomaly. Doctor Ramirez—"

"You can send me his findings but I won't have time to look over them this year."

He worked on in silence, then stopped to squint up at her again. "I'll do your math homework for a month."

"Alright."

"Alright yes?"

"No. I still won't go with you. But I'll permit you to do my math."

"Is it because I'm black?"

"No, it's because you're a weakling asshole. I'm looking for bravery in a man."

"But—"

"I'm a fucking outlaw. When will you realize that? I don't dress up nice and date boys. I've got bigger things on."

"Like what?"

"There's a man after me," she said, and he watched her carefully. "A man named Dickie Darke and he drives a black Escalade and he wants to kill me. So, you want to do something useful, you'll keep an eye out for him."

"Why does he want to kill you?"

"He thinks I wronged him."

"Tell the cops. Or your grandfather."

"I can't tell anyone. If they find out what I did I'll get in shit. They might take me away from Robin."

"I'll look out."

"You ever done anything brave in your whole life?"

Another head scratch. "The tire swing by Cally Creek."

"That's not brave."

"You try it with one hand."

She almost smiled.

"My mother birthed me without pain relief. Bravery is passed down, right?"

"Shit, Thomas Noble. You must've weighed a couple ounces when you were born. Probably shot out when she sneezed."

He went back to pulling, squinting the whole time.

"Where are your glasses?"

"I don't even need them."

"You're pulling the fucking bluebells. I happen to like bluebells."

He gingerly laid the bluebell carcasses back on the bank. "It's not always easy to be brave, you know. I'm not like you. You see the kids laughing at me. They're in a group, a head taller, bigger, they've got muscles."

"It's not about how big you are. It's the way you sell it."

He thought on that. "So I act like I can fight?"

"And then you don't have to."

"This man looking for you. Will it work on him?"

"No. You see him and you tell me right away."

"Alright. But maybe you should be more worried about that kid you threatened. Tyler. He has an older brother and he's looking for you."

She waved a hand. "Fuck him and his family. Now pull that big weed and then be on your way. It'll be dark by the time you make it home. And you can ill afford to get hit by a truck and lose use of another limb."

He stood with reluctance.

She watched him walk, pick up his bicycle, and set off toward the gate. She waited till he was out of sight before she spit out a mouthful of tobacco, shuddered, and scraped her tongue with her fingers.

24

The Iver County Parade.

Main bustled. A boy roping straw-bale calves, cursing as he missed. Girls tossing beanbags into hoops. There was a stall selling hot-dogs, a ramp for skateboards nothing more than plywood resting on an upturned plant pot. Hal took Robin to get his face painted. Duchess sat on the sidewalk and watched the floats. Mount Call Insurance, Trailwest Bank. Little girls with tiaras, waving to the flash of a couple of cameras.

She saw Thomas Noble and his mother. Mrs. Noble. She was tall and striking, heads turned as she strolled. Beside was an old man, short and thin and white.

Thomas headed over.

"Your mother doing charity? Help the aged or something."

Thomas Noble followed her eye. "That's my father."

She frowned. "Jeez, what's the attraction there, financial or fetishistic?"

He tugged her arm. "I've got something to tell you. It's urgent."

She stood with reluctance as he led her from the crowds. Duchess could only guess at what Thomas Noble deemed urgent, and her guesses ranged from him believing his mother was fooling around with the mailman, to feeling certain his withered hand was getting stronger, and that he'd soon be able to crush cans with it. He had a thing about crushing cans.

"This better not be about your mother fucking the mailman." Her relationship with Thomas Noble had blossomed into the kind of one-sided friendship where he confided in her and she used his secrets against him, without mercy.

He wore a sunhat, took it off and fanned himself with it as they moved beneath the shade of a maple tree. "That kid, Tyler. His brother is here and he's looking for you."

"You thought that was urgent?"

"You don't understand. He's big. I think you should head home."

"Where is he?"

Thomas Noble swallowed.

"Don't be a pussy all your life, Thomas Noble. Take me to the big boy so I can hand his ass to him."

He led her, shaking his head, wiping sweat with a trembling hand. Word spread, kids clustered in the alleyway behind Cherry's Bakery.

"That's him."

Duchess looked at the kid, Tyler, the boy that had pushed Robin over. And then she looked to the kid beside him, taller, fatter, uglier. He wore shorts that stopped at his calves, pale legs like trunks, Converse worn and faded. Dark hair, bowl cut, a little acne on each cheek.

Tyler pointed her way and the bigger kid came toward her.

"Who the fuck are you?" Duchess said, fixing the bow in her hair.

"Gaylon."

"Shit. I guess you had to grow up tough."

"You messed with my family." He stepped forward.

She rolled her eyes.

"You threatened to hurt my brother."

"Actually I threatened to behead that motherfucker."

A dozen kids now, blood in the water.

"You apologize to him."

"Shut the fuck up, fat boy."

Collective gasps as kids backed up a little, Thomas Noble no longer beside her.

Gaylon took another step, clenched a fat fist.

And then she heard it. Part war cry, part girlish scream. The crowd parted for Thomas Noble as he sprinted through. He'd loosened his shirt and, for reasons Duchess did not dare contemplate, tucked his pant legs into his socks.

Thomas Noble moved fast, boxed shadows and switched feet, circling Gaylon as he bobbed his head back and forth.

Duchess brought a hand to her face and watched through her fingers as Gaylon laid him out with a single punch.

And then the back door opened. Cherry taking out a trash bag. The crowd moved fast, Tyler and his brother disappeared.

Duchess walked over and assessed the damage.

"Did I win?" Thomas Noble said as she helped him to his feet.

"It's the taking part that counts."

He touched his eye gingerly. "I'll have a black eye."

"It's already black," she reasoned.

"Maybe a blue eye then."

"Come on, I'll get you some ice." She took his good hand in hers. Despite the pain, he managed a wide smile.

"That was brave, right?"

"More stupid than brave."

It was as she turned onto Main that she saw it.

Black Escalade.

Her blood drained.

Darke had found them.

She let go of his hand and moved along trucks. Bumper stickers, SWAN MOUNTAIN and MONTANA ELK, DISTRICT NINE. She thought of Darke, trying to blend in, his soulless eyes giving him away.

Duchess saw Hal's truck, the windows rolled down. She popped the door and slipped into the passenger seat. Thomas Noble looked on as she opened the glove compartment and slid the Smith & Wesson from its place inside.

She tucked the gun into her jeans.

Thomas Noble, the fight left him before it even arrived.

They moved back to the sidewalk. The sun cast a hand over the street, lighting the kids and their parents, smiles of the unknowing. The pair walked up, outside Cherry's, past the barbershop. They hugged storefronts, Duchess scanning, hand on her belt.

The gun, no longer cold but burning hot, waiting on her.

Across the street was the Escalade. She imagined Darke inside, watching her in that way he did.

She stepped into the road, fear keeping pace, but she forced it down behind a smile. She'd let Darke see it, she was glad he had come because she wanted it done now. She would kill for Robin, she didn't even need asking.

"What are you doing?" Thomas Noble tugged her arm but she shook him off, turned and glared.

"Stay there."

"You can't just go up to him."

Thomas Noble looked like he could cry, like he wanted to turn and bolt, but the emerging man inside was jostling for place with the frightened kid.

She circled to the back of the Escalade.

The sidewalk now, beside the car, she trailed a hand along the paint, the shine deep enough to mirror her.

"Duchess, please," he called, but she didn't turn.

She slipped the gun from her jeans, kept it between herself and the car as she reached for the handle and pulled hard.

It was locked.

She pressed her face close to the glass and saw it empty.

She spun around. The parade rolled on, drums, ribbons. Kids marched in the band while girls twirled and beamed.

Duchess pushed her way through a group and heard kids curse her.

Thomas Noble stayed beside. She saw Darke in everyone, warm smiles and cold eyes. She knew what men could do, all of them, capability was enough.

She was about to turn, and then she saw him.

She ran now, flat out. She knocked Coke from a kid's hand, sent an old lady sprawling as people yelled. When she reached him he turned, and he looked up and smiled.

She knelt and took Robin into her arms.

"What is it?" Hal said.

And then a lady noticed what she held in her hand.

"GUN."

Hal pulled her close as panic broke out around them.

• • •

The call came after dinner. Hal filled him in. By the time the panic had died the Escalade was gone. Duchess did not get the plates. It could have been anyone. The reminder kept them all focused.

As he cut the line it rang again.

"You're popular," Martha said.

He'd promised to cook for her, lost track of the day so ended up ordering in. Martha had laughed, said she was relieved she'd at least get something palatable. He'd left her in the house, working through more papers.

"Cuddy," Walk said into the phone. He hadn't checked in with Cuddy in a while so was relieved to hear the big man's voice on the other end. "How's he holding up?"

"I got him back in his old cell, had to move a runner on, bitched something awful but Vincent seems more settled in there."

"Thank you."

"Any news on the case? I tried asking Vincent about it but he wouldn't say anything. Not like the others, always crying innocence and injustice. I swear, you'd think we'd locked up a bunch of choirboys."

Walk laughed. "So he hasn't spoken to anyone?"

"No. I tell you, it's like he never left here. Straight back into the old routine. Starting to think he missed the place."

They made small talk awhile, and then Walk heard Martha call.

He stood, left his beer on the deck, and made his way into the living room.

Martha didn't say anything at first, just straightened slightly, then leaned closer to the stack of files, put her glasses on and focused. She'd been the one that made the break, that traced Darke to a company registered in Portland.

"You get something?"

"Maybe. Go bring me some snacks. I need some thinking peppers. You got any habanero?"

He shook his head.

"Malagueta?"

"I don't know what that is."

"Shit, Walk. Some fucking poblano. I need heat. Jesus. Prepare for me next time."

Suitably chastised he made his way into the small kitchen, brewed coffee, and watched the street. They'd been at it four hours, from dinner to late, both yawning and red-eyed but both knowing they would sooner work than lie restless in their beds. The case was getting to her now, more because of the way Walk looked, like he was being ravaged by the detail.

He handed her the coffee and a pepper mill.

She fought a smile, then flipped him off.

He watched her pace, in her hand was a corporate tax filing, a statement of registration. The trail was the kind of complex that had already seen her call in favors from a taxation lawyer she knew.

"Fortuna Avenue," she said.

"The second line homes."

"All but a couple are owned by the same holding company. When did the report come in, the first one? The eroding cliffs. California Wild." Martha chewed the cap of her pen.

Walk fished through a heavy stack of papers. "May 1995."

Martha smiled, then held up her paper. "This company bought the first house in September 1995. And they've bought another almost every year since. Eight homes, rolling finance, each mortgaged to pay for the next. That worked for the first six, till the rate hikes."

"And then?"

Martha paced again, walked over to the cabinet, topped off her coffee with whisky and did the same to Walk's. "So this company bought every house on the second line. California Wild gauged it at ten years, right?"

"Give or take. Then they built the breakwater. The King house is safe."

"The second line, they're not worth all that much. Small family homes. Got them cheap, doesn't look like they increased much over the years."

"Until?"

"Until the front line started to fall, and the vacationers started to come. One by one they went down. So all that stood between the company and what . . ."

"Five million dollars. At least."

"And all that blocked it was Vincent King and his family home. The land around. It can't be built on. No one would get a permit while the King house stands."

"This company, what's it called."

"The MAD Trust."

"What kind of name is that?"

"The name, it doesn't matter. But guess who the sole director is."

She handed Walk the paper and he held it tight, trying to steady it.

And there it was, at the top, bold print.

Richard Darke.

25

That night Duchess woke in a cold sweat.

She saw shapes, the closet taking Darke's soulless form.

When she calmed she checked Robin, then slipped from the room and down the stairs. She wore a soft robe. Hal had left it out for her. It was something they had fallen into. She would still take nothing from him directly. No food or drink, no help with the horses even when she had homework due and the day was draining fast. Instead he left things for her and she took them when he was not around. She marveled at his patience.

She drank water straight from the faucet.

As she turned to head back up she heard it.

Movement on the porch. Maybe the swing of the seat, the chains loud no matter how much Hal oiled them. She ducked low, her heart again racing away from her.

She fumbled for the drawer, found a decent length knife and gripped it tight. She crept to the door, saw it open a little as moonlight fell onto her bare feet.

"Can't sleep?"

"Shit. I was about ready to kill you."

"That's a bread knife," Hal said.

He sat on the swing, reduced to the glow of his cigar, though as she neared she saw the shotgun by his feet.

"You believed me then," she said.

"Maybe I'm just waiting on a bear."

"I should've got the plates. I picked up the gun and forgot everything else. Fucking rookie." She spit the words, mouth tight.

"You were protecting your family, not many people brave enough to do that."

She shook her head. "Does Dolly know?"

After Hal had gently taken the gun from her, Dolly had appeared and led her into the safety of the diner beside.

"She's tough. Thought it'd do good to have another set of eyes out there. She asks after you, every time I see her. I think maybe you remind her a little of her younger self."

"Why?"

"Dolly's about the toughest lady you'll ever meet. She had it rough, she doesn't tell any of it. Her Bill, though, I was drinking with him one time. Dolly's father, he was mean. He caught her smoking once."

"And gave her a hiding."

"No. He burned her with it. She's still got the scars on her arms. He told her she'd never have the guts to light one up again."

Duchess swallowed. "What happened to him?"

"She got older and he put his hands . . . He went to prison."

"Oh."

Hal coughed. "She dressed different back then, I saw photos. She wore boys' clothes, shapeless, baggy, but he still came."

"Some people are all dark."

"They are."

"James Reyes, paid assassin and gunslinger. He went to church regular, didn't drink or smoke. But rumor was he killed fifty. A mob lynched him. You know what his last words were?"

"Tell me."

"Let 'er rip."

"The mob got it right then. If the good stand by idle, are they still good?"

It was starry enough for snow. Hal said winter had not touched them yet, that when it did they'd know it so well they'd forget the colors of fall.

He scooted over.

She did not sit.

They stayed in silence for a long time. When he finished his cigar he lit another.

"The cancer will get you."

"It might."

"Not that I care."

"Of course not."

Darkness hid his eyes. He watched out, trees and water and the nothing that was slowly becoming something to her.

He stood and walked into the kitchen and she heard the whistle of the kettle.

She took a seat at the far end of the bench and eyed the shotgun.

He returned with cocoa and set a cup down on the porch beside her. Soft light from the kitchen showed marshmallow in hers.

He sipped whisky, a small measure. "There was a storm once. Bad one. I sat right here and watched lightning cross our land. I thought about the devil, I saw his face in the sky, serpent tongue lashing out like that. The barn burned."

She had seen an acre out where nothing grew, just the soot shape of what had once stood.

"The gray. Her mother was in there."

Duchess looked over at him, grateful for the dark so that he could not see the panic in her eyes.

"I couldn't get her out."

She breathed in that moment, knew well about the haunt of memory.

"We had storms sometimes," she said. "Back home."

"I think of Cape Haven often. I prayed for your mother, for you and Robin."

"You don't believe in God."

"Neither do you, but I know you go to the clearing and you kneel."

"Just a place to think."

"Everyone needs one. The storeroom, the guns, that's where I go to mull things. I sit down there and I shut out the world and I focus on what matters." He glanced over. "I wrote to him."

"Who?"

"Vincent King. Over the years I wrote him letter after letter. And I'm not a writer."

"Why?"

He blew smoke toward the moon. "That's a big question."

She rubbed her eyes.

"You should go to bed."

"My sleep patterns are none of your concern."

He set his glass down. "At first I wasn't going to send them. Just, after Sissy, and then all that happened with your mother and your grandmother. I wanted an outlet, maybe. But then I thought why shouldn't he know. Maybe he thought he'd ruined his life. I wanted him to know about ours. Maybe he had a vision of me, retired here, sitting on beautiful acres. I told him about the work, about the debt, the bills and living under that kind of weight."

"Did he write back?"

"He did. At first it was all sorrow. I know it was an accident . . . I do know that. But that doesn't really mean anything."

She picked up her cocoa and spooned the marshmallow into her mouth. It was too sweet then, catching her out, like she'd forgotten the good things.

"I went there, to his parole hearings. I went to each one. He could've served less. He would have got out with his best years still ahead."

"So how come he didn't? Walk never told me. I just figured he got in shit, in that place, he did bad things."

"He didn't. Cuddy, the warden, he spoke up each time. But Vincent declined a lawyer. Walk was there too, same every time. And we both saw each other but I never said anything to him. Because that was Walk's friend up there, close like brothers. I remember that back then. Thick as thieves, of course Vincent did the thieving but Walk always backed him."

Duchess tried to see Walk as a boy, as Vincent King's best friend. Instead she saw Walk in his uniform, never out of it, not since she remembered. He was all cop, and Vincent was all bad.

"Toward the end of the hearing they'd always ask that same question. If you get out, are you likely to break the law again?"

"What did Vincent say?"

"He'd meet my eye, and he'd say yes, he would. He was a danger to the people."

Maybe he thought it was something noble, to serve the whole term, penance like that, small recompense but intent was everything. But now, knowing what she did, he was telling it straight. Vincent was a danger.

"That pain. Losing your mother, losing my daughter, my wife, all that was ever good for me. I know it all. I didn't think I'd get through it."

"So how did you?"

"I came here. I took it back to breathing. Montana is good for that. You might see that one day."

"Star said there's correlation between suffering and sin."

He smiled, like he could hear the words direct from his daughter's mouth.

"What was Sissy like?"

He stubbed his cigar. "Death has a way of making saints out of mortals. But with children . . . there is no bad. She was small and beautiful and perfect. Like your mother was. Like Robin is."

He knew better than to mention her.

"She liked to paint. She cried during Fourth of July fireworks. She ate carrots but nothing green. She doted on your mother."

"I look like her. I saw the photo. Me and Star and Sissy."

"You do. Beautiful like that."

She swallowed. "Star said you were hard. She said there was nothing

soft about you, not after. She said you were a drunk. She said you didn't
go to my grandmother's funeral."

"We begin at the end, Duchess."

"If you thought that you'd be alright. You're full of shit." She spoke
quietly and without malice. "Are all the things she told me true?"

"I am a constant disappointment to myself."

"I know there's more. Why you didn't come back, why she wouldn't
let you see us. What did you do?"

He swallowed. "A few years after. I mean . . . I heard talk of parole
after five. For what he did. My Sissy."

She heard the hurt there, a lifetime later and it was still so present.

"Maybe I did drink too much. Someone came. He had a brother in
there, Fairmont County, with Vincent. He made an offer. He could make
it go away, right the wrong. It wasn't even a lot of money. I . . . if I could
have my time over, would I have been stronger and told him no?"

"The man Vincent killed in Fairmont. It was self-defense."

"It was."

She took a long breath, his words so weighted she could not form a
response.

"Your mother found out. And that was it. All and everything. A single
act on a distant night and here we are because of it."

She drank her cocoa and thought of her mother. She searched for a
memory that might warm the night but found nothing but the white of
Star's eyes.

"Is that why you go to church?"

"Understanding for what we have done and might do."

When she was done she stood. She felt tired, thought of Darke coming and looked at the old man and the shotgun.

At the door she turned. "Vincent. At the parole hearings. Why do
you think he did that?"

Hal looked up at her and she saw Robin in his eyes.

"They'd lead him off, and Walk would look at Cuddy like they
couldn't make sense of it. But he wrote me. He tried to tell me."

She stared at him.

"After that night, after what he did, he knew none of us would find freedom again."

• • •

They stood outside the old Radley house. From the moonlight that fell Walk could just about make out Martha, the shape of her face, small nose, hair just past her shoulders. He smelled her perfume, something light. They held flashlights and both flicked them on.

Walk had the record, the time Vincent made the call and the coroner's estimate of time of death. They could be accurate, Duchess had ridden her bicycle to the gas station on Pensacola, Walk knew she stuck to the main roads, despite the risk, so it took her forty-five minutes. That gave Vincent around fifteen minutes to lose the gun. They had to work the assumption he was the killer, and that assumption had kept Walk awake the night before.

"We'll head every direction he could have gone."

Martha had a stopwatch. They'd allow for the fact he could've run, sprinted there and back, though Walk didn't recall if the man appeared out of breath, or sweating, but then Walk couldn't recall much of the detail of that night, aside from the sight of Star's face, which he knew he'd carry for the rest of his life. The memory loss, it was creeping on him. He'd taken to making notes, pretending he was writing up when really he was just keeping check. The order of his day, the time he took pills, he noted it all now.

They started out into Star's backyard, stepped over the broken fence, which had been there as long as Walk could remember. Into light woodland, just a copse that separated Ivy Ranch from Newton Avenue. They were methodical, every walkway, every tree and bush and cluster of flowers. They checked drains; they knew Boyd and his men and dogs had already run the same routes but Walk was hoping for something more, something only a local would notice. He closed his eyes and put himself into Vincent's shoes.

They walked seven routes, some slight deviations from the last. They got nowhere at all.

"He didn't have it. If he had we would've found it, or more likely Boyd would have."

"It's a hole in their case. A big one," Martha said. "The DA will be pissed."

They found their way back to the Radley house and stood on the sidewalk. She reached out and grasped his hand. He was close to breaking. Every way he turned he couldn't figure it. He'd lost Darke, tried his cell over and over and left so many messages he'd filled up the mailbox.

He felt it. Darke had killed Star and pinned the blame on Vincent King in order to get his hands on the house that would save his empire and make his fortune. It was flawed, but that's all he had to work on. As for the girl, he took comfort in the fact that Hal was a ghost, Radley land was buried, the kids were safe up there.

At the end of Newton she led him down the neighbor's driveway and then hopped a low fence, hidden by thick barberry.

"You still know all the shortcuts," Walk said.

"Star showed me that one."

Twenty minutes and they were by the old wishing tree, stars over the ocean, the tower at Little Brook like an abandoned lighthouse.

"I can't believe it's still here. You remember we used to make out under this tree."

He laughed. "I remember everything."

"You never could unhook my bra."

"One time I did."

"No. I unhooked it before, let you have your moment."

She sat down, then reached up and pulled him down beside her. Together they leaned back against the wide oak and looked up at the stars.

"I never said I was sorry," she said.

"For what?"

"Leaving you."

"It was a long time ago. We were kids."

"We weren't, Walk. Not according to the judge. Do you think about it?"

"What?"

"Me. Pregnant. A baby."

"Every day."

"He didn't get over it, my father. He wasn't all bad. It's just . . . he thought he was doing right by me."

"But wrong by God."

She said nothing for a while. The lights of a boat drifted, moving with the tide.

"You didn't marry," she said.

"Of course not."

She laughed gently. "We were fifteen."

"But I knew it."

"That's what I loved about you. That pure belief, in good and bad and love. You never said anything, about my father, about what he did. You never told anyone. Even though I left you behind, and Star went to another school, and it was just you, and this thing. This giant fucking sickening thing that Vincent did."

Walk swallowed. "I just wanted you all to be happy."

That laugh again, nothing about it was pitying.

"I did see you," he said. "Maybe a year after. At the mall in Clearwater Cove. I was with my mother, and you were standing in line outside the movie theater."

She was quiet before it came to her. "David Rowen. Just a boy. It didn't mean anything."

"Oh, I know that. I didn't mean because of that. I just . . . you looked happy, Martha. And I thought about that boy, and he didn't know, right. He didn't know what we all went through, and I thought that must've been alright. You could just, it wasn't there between you. You didn't have to share that thing. You could just . . . be."

She cried.

He held her hand.

26

As winter arrived the Radley land froze and the sky whitened with light snows.

Robin lay flat on his back and watched it so long Duchess had to drag him in when his fingers turned white. The field work eased but the animals still needed tending. The gray and the black wore coats as they grazed. Duchess began to take the gray out each morning alone, saddling her at first light and following tracks she began to learn well. She took enjoyment from the Montana quiet, so thick it was as if God had laid down a blanket over the woodland and smothered all but the loudest chickadees.

They watched out for Darke, Hal sitting till late each night, a deerstalker and blanket and the shotgun by his feet. Some nights Duchess woke and went to the window, saw him down there then promptly fell back into deep sleep. Other nights she went down and he fixed cocoa. They would sit, mostly in silence, but sometimes she allowed him to tell her stories of Billy Blue, so dazzling and detailed she wondered if the old man made them up himself. One night she fell asleep on his shoulder, then woke in her bed, the cover pulled up tight.

She spent weekends with Thomas Noble and Robin, tramping white woods, giving them a head start then tracking their boot prints. The cold was crisp and fresh and brought clarity to her wandering mind. She thought less about Cape Haven and its unchanging seasons, and more about Montana and, occasionally, the future. She chose memories of her mother with great care, seeking only the diamonds among a mountain of coal.

Her grades improved, she sat at the back and got on with her schoolwork, drafting Indians and settlers and making them live through her writing. She sent Walk a photo of Radley land, taken from the window in her bedroom the day they woke to thick snow. She went with Hal into town each Saturday morning, they did the grocery shopping then headed to Cherry's to drink cocoa and eat donuts. Most days Dolly was there and they sat and talked with her. Bill's health had worsened, and beneath Dolly's faultless face Duchess saw cracks beginning to snake in a show of prescient mourning that left her fretful after. They drove up to Hamby Lake, the water so deep it might've been an ocean. Hal rented a boat, cutting crystal water as they drifted and fished, the sun stealing the cold away for an afternoon as close to perfect as Duchess could allow herself to imagine. Robin pulled out a decent rainbow trout, then cried till Hal threw it back.

Thomas Noble spoke of the winter dance often. Some days she merely told him to fuck off, others she accused him of plotting to spike the punch then do wicked things once she had passed out cold. She called him a sexual predator and he scratched his head and pushed his frames up his nose.

The first day of December he brought her a bunch of bluebells he'd been saving. Long dead, a sorry sight, but the sentiment was there. He biked the four miles through icy roads and up their carpeted driveway. By the time he arrived mild frostbite had set in and he was seeing stars. Hal sat him in front of the fire till he thawed.

"I won't dance with you," she said as they watched the flames. "I won't kiss you or hug you. I won't hold your good hand. I won't dress pretty and I may not even speak to you for most of the night."

"Okay," he said, a slight chatter in his teeth.

From the doorway she saw Hal and Robin smiling and she flipped them off.

The next Sunday, after church, Hal drove them to the strip mall in

Briarstown. Ten stores in a neat row, from Subway to Cash Advance. She found women's clothing in a place called Cally's. She riffled rails of polyester, held a sequined gown to the light and saw it bald in at least five places. "It's like being in Paris."

Hal pointed to a yellow dress and she asked him what the fuck he knew about fashion. She pointed to his boots and faded jeans, his plaid shirt and wide hat, and declared him a scarecrow. They circled the store three times. Robin brought over gaudy finds, beaming as he held them against her then running off when she asked him if he wanted his sister to dress like an eighties streetwalker.

Cally herself came out, read the mood and retreated to the counter. She wore a beehive and platforms and hid twenty surplus pounds beneath a wide belt. Hal smiled at her and she returned a smile in sympathy.

Duchess found it at the back, stopped still and stared. Then, slowly, she reached out and picked it up. She placed the hat on her head and felt her stomach flip, her mind on Billy Blue, her blood. Her place.

It was a thing of beauty, leather studs, brim just right, the kind of hat an outlaw would kill for.

Hal appeared behind. "Suits you."

She took it off and checked the tag. "Jesus."

"Stetson," Hal said, like that explained the eye-watering price.

She would not ask for it. It was too fancy, but still, she glanced back longingly as she walked back to the dresses.

"It'll have to be this piece of shit then." She snatched the yellow dress from the rail.

Hal made to speak, to tell her that was the very dress he'd picked out near an hour ago. She glared and he thought better of it.

• • •

Cuddy set up the meet. A burger joint just south of Bitterwater, Bill's, all fading red paint and the air of going out of business, handwritten signs told of three-dollar specials. It was empty, Walk rolled down the window as he headed to the drive-thru.

The guy was old, Hispanic, hairnet and apron and furrowed brow, the kind of old man that took shit from punk kids then picked up their trash like a tip. Walk checked the name tag, "Luis."

Luis clocked Walk, then pointed to the lot.

Walk drove over and parked, got out and sat on the hood. Ten minutes till he came, stooped walk, shuffling feet.

"I only got five minutes' break," Luis said.

"Thank you for meeting me."

"Any friend of Cuddy."

Luis had occupied the cell beside Vincent's for eight years. Armed robbery, the last in a long line of crimes. Tattoos on his arm spoke of affiliation, Walk guessed he was long past all that now.

"You ask and I answer. And then I get on. The boss man, he doesn't like cops around his joint."

"Fair enough. Tell me about Vincent King."

Luis lit a cigarette, kept his back to the windows, and fanned the smoke as he blew it. "The only guy I ever met who didn't say he was set up."

Walk laughed.

"Serious. He didn't say much of anything."

"He didn't have friends in there."

"No. Not Vincent. He didn't even take his yard time, man. And the pudding cups."

"Excuse me?"

"Pudding. The food is dog shit, the pudding isn't. I seen a man get stabbed for his pudding cup. Vincent gave me his every day."

Walk wondered what to do with that one.

"You don't get it, cop. He ate just enough. He said just enough. Shit, he breathed just enough."

"Enough to what?"

"Stay alive. No existence beyond the fundamental. He stayed alive to serve his time. And he made fucking sure it was the worst time he could serve. No TV, radio. No nothing. Would've spent his time in solitary if Cuddy had let him."

Luis held the smoke deep.

"He had trouble in there," Walk said.

"Everyone does at some point. He had a girl, right? Outside. Others talked about her, maybe that was his weakness. Maybe thinking of her with someone else. Jealousy, I tell you, inside it'll drive a man crazy. He dealt with it well enough, made sure others let him be after."

"But they still came for him. I've seen the scars."

"The only enemy that guy had was himself."

"How do you mean?"

"He asked me to get him a blade. No big deal. I figured he wanted to settle up with someone."

"He didn't?"

"Same day I gave it to him I heard the guards hollering. Ain't unusual, but this was Vincent's cell so I went up to see."

"And?"

Walk watched his color drain.

"Messy, man. Cut himself to ribbons. Deep, serious cuts. He didn't hit the arteries. He didn't want to die, just to suffer."

Walk let that sit awhile, found himself unable to speak, throat tight like he could barely breathe.

"We done?"

"I need a character reference for him."

"You won't find no one. Because no one knows Vincent." Luis dropped his cigarette, stubbed it out, then bent and picked up the butt. He winked at Walk, extended a hand and tutted when Walk went to shake it.

Finally, Walk pulled out a twenty and Luis took it.

27

Dolly showed at their door, laden with a big box. She was there to collect Robin, he would spend the night at her place as Hal said he'd keep free in case Mrs. Noble couldn't collect them after the dance. Always looking out, worrying.

She led Duchess up to the bedroom and opened the box to a startling array of makeup and perfumes.

"Don't make me look like a whore."

"I can't make any promises, sweetheart."

Duchess smiled at that.

An hour later she walked down the stairs, her hair expertly curled and her lips shining pink. She wore a new bow and new shoes that Cally had helped pick out. She'd gained a little more weight, no longer so skeletal, her muscles tight from the work.

She saw Hal wearing something like pride on his face so she told him to shut the fuck up before he could say a word.

"Beautiful," Robin marveled. "You look just like Mom."

...

They tailed Dolly and Robin till they turned off at Avoca. Snow fell lightly but the roads were salted. Dolly's place was big, fancy and lit with warm window light. She'd asked after Bill. Dolly said he didn't have the good sense to give up.

They passed a sign blinking DRIVE SLOW.

"You nervous?" Hal said.

"About getting pregnant tonight? Nah, what will be will be."

They turned onto Carlton.

"I'm worried about Robin," she said.

He glanced over.

"What he knows about that night. It's . . . it's not back but, I don't know. He dreams about it. I think maybe he heard it all."

"Then we'll deal with it."

"Just like that?"

"Yes. That sound alright?"

She nodded.

They made the turn onto Highwood Drive.

"Shit."

"What?" And then he saw, and he tried not to smile but lost the battle fully.

The path to the Noble house, swept of snow but lined with rose petals.

"Fucking shoot me now."

At the window she saw him, face pressed to the glass like Robin waiting on Christmas.

"He's wearing a fucking bow tie. He looks like a magician." Hal brought the truck to a stop. The street door opened and Mrs. Noble stood there, camera in hand. Behind her was Mr. Noble, and he held a video camera, so big it mounted on his shoulder and threw out a blinding spotlight.

"Turn back. No way I'm walking into that freak show."

"It's alright. Maybe do it for them, just once."

"A selfless act."

"I'll be waiting up. You call me if there's a problem."

She took a deep breath, then reached for the mirror and fussed with her bow.

"You have a good time tonight."

"I won't."

She opened the door and the cold met her. "My dress is plain. Not like the other girls'."

"Since when do you want to be like them? You're an outlaw."

"I'm an outlaw." She stepped into the snow.

He fired the engine and as she moved to shut the door she called, "Hal."

"Yes, Duchess."

She met his eye, he looked old then, capable but she knew the toll and its cost. She thought of her mother, of Sissy.

"I'm not sorry for everything I've said to you." She swallowed. "I just . . ."

"It's alright."

"It's not. But I think one day it might be."

"You go on now. Try and have fun. Smile for the cameras. Both of them."

She flipped him off but added a smile to it.

The glitter ball spun and Duchess watched light shards over the crowd. The theme was Wonderland and she stared at the cotton snow and frosted flowers. Above them balloons hung in white and blue, painted stars and cardboard trees circled a dance floor made to look like ice.

She fiddled with her corsage. "It itches. Did you find it in a Dumpster?"

"My mother picked it up."

They hung at the back. She saw girls in fancy dresses and heels, teetering. She said a silent prayer they would fall.

Thomas Noble wore a dinner suit, a size too big so his bad hand withdrew into the cuff. Draped behind was a silk cape, so fantastically bizarre she could not tear her eyes from it.

"My father said a gentleman always sports a cape to a formal event."

"Your father is a hundred and fifty years old."

"He's still got moves. I have to go in the backyard when they make love because the noise is deafening."

She stared at him, suitably horrified.

The music started up and Duchess watched a group of girls run at the dance floor.

Thomas Noble fetched them a juice and they found seats at a table by a heart-shaped stage and a photographer.

"Thanks for coming with me."

"You already said that eighteen times."

"You want cake?"

"No."

"How about some potato chips?"

"No."

They played something fast. Jacob Liston cleared a space and broke out his best moves while the girl he was with clapped awkwardly.

Duchess frowned. "I think he might be having a fit."

The song switched to something slow, the floor thinned. "You want to—"

"Don't make me say it again."

"Nice suit, Thomas Noble." Billy Ryle and Chuck Sullivan. "At least it hides his cripple hand." Laughter.

Thomas Noble sipped his juice and kept his eyes on the dance floor.

She reached over and took his bad hand. "Dance with me."

As they passed she leaned over and said something to Billy.

He moved away quick.

"Keep your hands away from my ass," she said as they reached the floor.

"What did you say to Billy?"

"I told him you had a ten-inch cock."

He shrugged. "That's a quarter truth."

She laughed, so much and so hard she'd forgotten how good it felt.

She held him. "Shit, Thomas Noble. I can feel every rib."

"And that's in clothes. You wouldn't want to see me topless."

"I can imagine. I once saw a documentary about famine."

"I'm glad you came here."

"You wore me down with relentless pressure. Your father would be proud."

They bumped into Jacob Liston and his date. Jacob was wriggling like he needed to piss. Duchess shot his date a compassionate smile.

"I mean here. Montana. I'm glad you came to stay."

"Why?"

"I just—" He stopped moving and for a wretched moment she thought he might try and kiss her. "I just never met an outlaw before."

She stepped a little closer and moved with him.

• • •

Walk sat in his office, blinds drawn but town lights cut the dark. He cradled the phone on his shoulder, made notes as he spoke to Hal. He rested his feet on a stack of papers, saw his tray fit to burst. He'd get to it all, the mess bothered everyone but him.

He checked in each week, same time on a Friday night. It was usually quick, a catch-up about how the boy was doing alright, still seeing the shrink. And then on to the girl. Sometimes they'd speak five minutes, just long enough for Hal to tell of something bad she'd done, and how he'd had to check his laughter till he was done being pissed. Walk knew that act well.

"It's slow," Hal said. "With Duchess it's slow, but she's getting better. It's getting better."

"That's good."

"Tonight she's at the school dance."

"Wait a minute. Duchess is at a dance?"

"It's the winter formal. They go all out. The whole of Evergreen Middle is lit up, you can see the spotlight from Cold Creek."

Walk allowed himself a smile. The girl was doing alright. Against the odds, and they were stacked, she was living a life.

"And Robin. I think he's starting to remember."

Walk dropped his feet down again and pressed the receiver so tight he could hear the old man breathing.

"Nothing concrete."

"Did he mention any names? Darke?"

Hal must have heard the desperation there because he spoke the next lines softly. "Nothing concrete, Walk. I think he's slowly opening himself to the fact that he might have been there when his mother was murdered. The shrink is good, she doesn't ask or pry or try and guide him anyplace at all."

"Part of me hopes he doesn't remember."

"I said that to her. She told me there was a decent chance he never would."

"I think about all of you up there."

"I watch out for him. This Darke. When she saw the car I thought he might've come, like she always said."

"And now?"

"I'm still waiting. Shoot first ask questions later."

Walk smiled a tired smile. Sleepless nights had taken their toll, wrestling his thoughts to the ground and pounding them clean out of his head. Some days he found himself on a stretch of highway and clean forgot where he was supposed to be heading.

"Good night, Hal. You take care."

He replaced the receiver and yawned. Normally he was so beat he'd head right home, drink a sole beer and watch ESPN till sleep found him. But right then he got the overwhelming urge to see Martha, not even to talk, just not sit the night alone.

He picked up the phone, started to dial then killed it. He was fully aware of what he was doing, gradually sliding into a life he had no right to interfere with. It was cold, no matter how he felt, it was a cold and cruel thing to do. When she saw him she remembered the darkest part of her life, and she always would.

He walked down the hallway slowly, the station in darkness.

"Leah, I didn't know you were still here."

She looked up, tired, not even a smile. "Overtime, right. Someone's got to sort the filing system out. It'll take me the next month, even working through the night."

"You need a hand?"

"No, you get on. Doesn't matter if I'm here all night, Ed wouldn't even notice."

He went to say something, wasn't sure what, but then she turned her back and went back to work.

He headed out, thinking of Duchess Day Radley at a school dance, and smiling his way into the warm evening.

. . .

The snow, like the talk, worsened as they drove. Mrs. Noble asked Thomas about the dance. He told her it was the best night of his life.

Duchess watched snow build on the farmland beside, usually lost to the dark she could see a mile out to mountains.

When they reached Radley land Mrs. Noble went to turn but the driveway was deep now. Hal couldn't keep on top of it, it was too long and the snow fell too fast.

"I can walk it from here."

"You sure, honey? I'd take a run at it but I think we might get stuck the night."

"Hal will be on the porch. He'll see your lights and start walking down. You get on."

She climbed out quick and set off up the driveway, before Mrs. Noble or Thomas could get out and try to follow.

Halfway, she turned and waved and watched them trail light into the distance.

She trudged the snow, lifting her new shoes high at each step. The gum trees stood, branches weighed under snow, an arc of white like she was walking through a wedding arch. Free, she faced the sky, the turning snowflakes, the beauty almost too much to take. She thought of Robin and how they would spend their weekend, fanned-out angels and snow-men as tall as their grandfather.

When she cleared the reaching trees, moonlight graced the old farm-house and she smiled without knowing why. In the distance light burned in the kitchen.

She took another step and then stopped dead.

Prints in the snow, almost covered but still they remained.

Footprints.

Big prints.

The first time that night she felt the cold, the real, true bite of Mon-tana cold.

"Hal," she said, quiet.

She picked up her pace a little, her heart beginning to race. Some-thing was wrong. She could feel it.

And then she saw him. And she calmed.

He was sat on the bench, the gun by his feet.

When she reached the porch she waved, smiled wide, then climbed the steps. She'd tell him about her night, just how bad it was.

But then she looked at his face, pale, tight, sweat by his head. Labored breaths, but still, he tried to smile for her.

She approached slow, and then, with great care, she pulled the blan-ket from him.

And that's when she saw the blood.

"Oh fuck, Hal," she whispered.

He kept a hand pressed to his stomach but the blood drained fast and steady.

"I got him," Hal said.

He offered one hand to her as his life emptied. She took it, his blood to her like some fatal disease.

She let go and ran for the phone in the kitchen. Iver County PD on speed dial, she told all she could.

She left prints of Hal's blood on the receiver. She fetched whisky from the cabinet and ran back out.

"Fuck." She put the bottle to his lips.

He coughed, the blood there now.

"I got him, Duchess. He ran but I got him."

"Don't talk. People are coming, people who know what to do."

He watched her. "You're an outlaw."

"I am," she said, her voice breaking.

"You make me proud."

She clutched his hand tight, pressed her head to his, closed her eyes and held her tears back. "Fuck," she yelled it. She hit his arm, his chest, slapped his cheek hard.

"Grandpa. Wake up."

She looked down at the blood on her new yellow dress, and then down at the snow, where footprints led her eyes to white fields.

She knelt once more. "We begin at the end." She took the shotgun from beside him.

She no longer felt the biting cold, no longer noticed the fullest moon. She did not see stars nor the red barns or the frozen water.

At the stable she saddled the gray and led her from her place.

She pulled herself up with one hand, the shotgun in the other. She snapped the reins and they ran after the prints.

She cursed herself, complacent, the way she had fallen into the promise of new life. She remembered the anger, the hot twisting anger.

She told herself who she was.

Duchess Day Radley.

Outlaw.

PART THREE

•

Restitution

28

He made the drive from day to night, high beams, blinking wildflower, Mojave nothing but morphing shapes.

Route 15, the lights of Las Vegas, dazzling like some grand alien craft had fallen from the sky.

Rising billboards, styled magicians with eyebrows arched and aging starlets taking their back catalog all the way to the bank.

He watched it fade in the rearview and before long it was like it had never been. He skirted the Valley of Fire, Beaver Dam, and the eternal shadow of the Canyon behind. Motel lights and gas stations and a highway that emptied as the hours drifted.

Cedar City, he stopped at an all-night diner, historic downtown in Iron County, mostly sleeping. He sat at a booth and listened to a couple guys talk about "Clarke's sendoff." He couldn't figure out if Clarke was dead or getting married.

He rubbed his eyes to signs, POCATELLO and BLACKFOOT, IDAHO FALLS.

As Caribou-Targhee came to view he saw the first blue in a thousand miles of black. He slowed on 87 and watched the sun rise by Henrys Lake, the water so many refracted colors he rubbed his eyes once more.

The first snow at Three Forks, white fields ran to white sky. He closed the window and blew the heater but did not feel the cold nor the heat.

When Iver County PD had called, Walk had been home, laid up, some kind of palsy gripping him so tight he almost could not reach the phone. But then after, when the cop hung up, he slammed the receiver down again and again until it broke apart. Then he'd heaved the contents of his desk onto the carpet, kicked his computer screen until it cracked. And then, slowly, he'd cleared it all up again.

Any illusion, the postcards, the Friday night calls with Hal, any illusion the girl and the boy might yet get their deserved life had died such a cold and final death that Walk did not speak to anyone for three days. He had taken leave, vacation time dating back a decade, got them so worried Valeria had stopped by and hammered on his door. He did not answer. Nor did he answer Martha's calls.

He spent the first day in his apartment, Darke's life mapped out on the wall behind his television set so he could never get the man from his mind. He chased leads so old the numbers did not connect or if they did he reached confused people that had not heard Darke's name in twenty years. He tried drinking, a bottle of Jim Beam, made it a quarter way through before he gave up. His meds, with the alcohol, just made him drowsy. He longed for a mistake, a reason he could carry the blame on his shoulders and sink down deep, but again he found nothing. It was a cruel hand of fate, a nothing anomaly. Darke made a choice and saw it through. And they could still not pin a thing on him. No witness. Snow buried blood. They'd put out all-points, blocked the only roads, sent a team in as deep as they could. Iver County worked the theory the killer was dead, buried in a tomb of ice somewhere among the woodland, likely torn apart by the animals once he thawed.

Walk returned to the station and got on. He wrote up routine violations, stopped by routine elementary schools and worked routine shifts, four days and one night.

Martha stopped by, uninvited, and when he told her she pressed a hand to her mouth like she wanted to scream. If Walk was broken before, what happened in Montana scattered the pieces so far and wide he gave up all hope of being whole again.

He visited Vincent, sat in the hot waiting room for three hours in case Vincent changed his mind and came out. He stood with Cuddy and watched basketball and did not flinch when men took hard falls or lost a tooth to an elbow.

The beard was long now, past his neck down to his skeletal chest. He had aged a decade in months, his skin pursed tight over hollow cheeks.

The snow thickened at Lewis and Clark, he washed up in a gas station on 89. It smelled of piss and he tried shallow breaths as he pulled off his uniform. He stood naked beneath flickering light. No bulging stomach, sagging chest, instead he saw ribs and hip bones. He dressed, shirt on, slacks, tie. His hair was cropped close now so he did not need to comb it. His hands shook. He did not fight them. They no longer cooperated, if he held the phone with one, he could not grasp a pen with the other. It was exhausting, maddening.

Canyon View Baptist.

Someone had cleared the lot, walled it off with snow piled high. He was early by an hour so he rolled his seat back and closed his eyes. A night on the road, he should've grabbed thirty minutes but his mind would not leave him. He thought of Duchess when she was small and the way she had looked at him, like he was a man who could solve her problems.

First cars rolled into the lot. He watched them, old people that wore the cold on their faces, cheeks red as they ambled into the small church.

He found a corner at the back. An organ played something serene.

At the front was the coffin. He stood when others did.

And then he turned and saw the boy, Robin, holding the hand of a lady he did not recognize. The boy looked older, suddenly, like the child had once again been robbed by the pull of a trigger.

Behind them she appeared, her dress dark and simple. She kept her eyes up and hard, challenging. She gazed around the church, people tried their best to smile sad smiles. She did not return any. She was not a child now.

When she saw him she stuttered, just one step, a reluctant memory, and then she was past.

As she sat at the front he saw the bow in her hair, tucked out of sight but it was there.

Behind her was a slight boy with glasses, and when the minister spoke and Robin began to cry the boy placed a hand on Duchess's shoulder. She did not turn, just shook his hand from her.

After, Walk followed them back to the Radley farm.

Inside were sandwiches and cake. Dolly introduced herself and handed Walk a coffee.

Robin stood with the lady and looked as lost as a child ever had. He said no thank you when Dolly offered him a donut. He said no thank you when the lady asked him if he wanted to head up and take a last look at his bedroom.

Walk slipped out and crunched the snow, following small prints. He found her at the stable, her back to him as she patted a handsome gray, her small hand on the horse's nose. The horse bowed, nuzzled against her and she kissed it gently.

"You can leave now." She did not turn. "You don't need to stay longer. I see everyone in there, watching the clock. Like Hal would've wanted them in his house anyhow."

He stepped beneath the arched roof. "I'm sorry."

She raised a hand, it's alright, fuck off; he didn't know which and it did not matter much.

"There's a kid in there, he keeps looking out for you."

"Thomas Noble. He doesn't know me, not really."

"It's important to have friends, right?"

"He's a normal kid. Two parents. Makes good grades. Six weeks at their vacation home in Myrtle Beach each summer. We breathe different air."

"Are you eating alright?"

"Are you? You look different, Walk. Where's that soft gone?"

She wore only her dress but did not shiver.

"That lady at the church with Robin—" he started.

"Mrs. Price. That's what she likes us to call her. In case we forget how temporary our place is. She came to show face."

Walk met her eye for a moment, then she looked away.

"I'm so sorry."

"Fuck, Walk. Stop saying that. Hand we get dealt, right. Fate, resignation. There's no difference."

"They don't teach that at church."

"Free will is an illusion, sooner you accept the sooner you get on."

"The farm?"

"I heard them talking. Hal had debts, it'll go at auction and they'll be cleared. Radley land. We're all just caretakers."

"And Robin?"

Sadness then, that only he could see, buried deep behind her eyes.

"He's . . . he doesn't speak now. He hasn't said much but yes or no. They'll try and place us, foster care till then. Mrs. Price, Mr. Price, they get paid to take us in. Feed us. Send us to bed at eight because they like their own time."

"Christmas." He regretted the word, like it had a place.

"Our caseworker brought gifts. Mrs. Price, she didn't leave nothing out for Robin."

He swallowed.

She turned and patted the gray again. "She'll get sold, unless someone wants her with the farm. I hope they don't run her hard. She limps a little now, after that night."

"She fell."

"I fell," she said, bitter. "It wasn't on her. She's a decent horse. She stayed with me, after, just there, beside me."

The snow began to drift once again. He looked back at the farmhouse, the boy with glasses being led out by his mother, craning his neck to get a look at Duchess. He thought of Vincent and Star.

"Will you get to stay here, same school?"

"We have a woman, she works our case. That's what we are now, Walk. A case. We are numbers and a file. A list of traits and mistakes."

"You're not a number. You're an outlaw."

"Maybe my father's blood is so fucking weak it steals away the Radley.

I'm not Star or Hal, Robin or Billy Blue. I am one night, one mistake, one reaction. I'm nothing more."

"You can't think that."

She turned from him, like she was talking to the gray. "I'll never know who I am."

He looked across frozen land, the elk in numbers at the base of the mountain. "If you need me."

"I know."

"But still."

"That old minister. He asked us the meaning of life one time, after service. The young kids, he asked us all in turn. Most talked about family and love."

"And you?"

"I said nothing, because Robin was there." She coughed. "But you know what Robin said?"

He shook his head.

"He said life means having somebody care enough to protect you."

"He's got you."

"And look where we are."

"But you know that's not—"

She held up another fuck-you hand.

"They think the man Hal shot is dead."

"I know."

"They won't search for him anymore. It was Darke. They don't believe me."

Together they walked through snow toward the cruiser.

"I think of Vincent King."

He wanted to make a link, Star to Darke. He could not.

"You know this isn't on you." He read her well.

"It is, Walk. This time it is on me."

He turned and wanted to hug her but she stuck out a hand and he shook it.

"I don't think I'll see you again."

"I'll keep in touch."

"Can you not?" The first shake in her voice, just slight but he saw her turn her head. "Just go and tell me to be good or something, like you used to. And then you get on and I'll get on. Ours is a small story, Chief Walker. Sad enough, but small. Let's not pretend different."

They stood in a silence that rode over the trees and the Radley land.

"Alright," he said.

"And?"

"Be good, Duchess."

29

Their caseworker wore purple lipstick, as close to somber as she ever got.

Shelly. Her hair was three kinds of color, none of which Duchess decided was natural. She was loving, soulful, she held their future with the kind of care warranted, and she cried openly for the man she had never met.

They sat in the back of her rusting Volvo 740. Coke cans on the floor, ashtray spilling though she never smoked when they were in the car.

Duchess turned by the water and watched the farmhouse for the last time as they dipped beneath the praying trees.

"You kids alright back there?" Shelly crunched second and the car shuddered.

Duchess reached over and took her brother's small hand. He did not fight her and did not squeeze back, just let it lie there, limp and dead to her.

Shelly smiled in the mirror. "It was a lovely service."

They drove mile on mile of white, winter reaching so long they could not recall fall, air so chill Duchess was grateful. Let the world freeze over, let all the colors drain till the canvas was blank once more.

They arrived in the town of Sadler, lines of neat, shoveled driveways.

The Price house sat on a street of identical ten-year-old homes. Theirs was painted a shade of putty so bland it was as if the developer was ashamed to blight such beautiful land with it.

"Here we are. You alright with Mr. and Mrs. Price?" Shelly asked that often.

"Yes," Robin said.

"And Henry and Mary Lou?"

The Price children, close enough in age but a world apart. Church polite in front of their parents, but Duchess heard them talking between themselves, about Hal and what happened, how they should not go near the girl because rumor had it she chased down a man and fired a shotgun at him. And what kind of girl does that.

Obviously too sheltered to know of outlaws.

"They're fine," Duchess said.

They said goodbyes and took hugs. Duchess led Robin up the Price path. Shelly waited till Mr. Price opened the door then waved again and deserted them.

Duchess went to help Robin with his smart shoes, but he moved away from her and did it himself.

Mr. Price said nothing, did not ask after the funeral, just turned his back and left them to it. Duchess could not claim they were mistreated, just left far behind. Dinner on different plates, drinks in plastic beakers instead of glass. They were left with the television set in the playroom whilst the Prices sat in the den. Here but not.

Duchess followed Robin through to the kitchen, white units and marble, Henry's report cards on the refrigerator, Mary Lou's artwork framed and hung above the dining table. Robin stood at the doors and looked out. The yard. The snowman was large, Mr. Price and Henry rolled more and more.

Mrs. Price and Mary Lou crossed snow with sticks, broke them to the right length for arms. Henry said something and they laughed.

"You want to go out?" Duchess said.

At that moment Mrs. Price looked up, saw them, then turned and went back to her own. She placed an arm around Mary Lou, protective, defining.

Their room was the converted attic. Duchess followed Robin up the stairs. They had a small bath to themselves, a basin and tub and toothbrushes in a cup. Some dog-eared books on a small shelf, Famous Five, a selection of Dr. Seuss.

"You want to change out of your smart clothes?"

He lay back on his bed and rolled away so she could not see him cry. His shoulders shook lightly and she went over and sat beside him. When she placed a hand on his arm he shrugged her away.

"You shouldn't have even come today. You hated Grandpa. Even when he was kind you said mean things to him because you're just mean all the way through."

He stared at the skylight above them, snow drifted down, borrowed shelter all that kept them from the wilds now.

"I'm sorry," she said.

"You always say that."

She poked his ribs. He did not smile.

"You want to read a book?"

"No."

"You want to throw snowballs at Mary Lou's face? I could make them out of pure ice."

Almost a smile.

"Or I could nail Mr. Price with one. Break a tooth. Spear Mrs. Price with an icicle. We could make Henry eat yellow snow."

"How do you make yellow snow?"

"Piss in it."

He laughed then. She pulled him in.

"Will we be alright?" he said.

"We will."

"How?"

"We'll—"

"You can't look after us. And I don't think Mr. Price wants us here."

"They get twelve hundred bucks each month to look after us."

"So they might keep us for all that money."

"No. This is just foster care, remember what Shelly said. She'll try and find us a decent family to stay with forever."

"With a farm and animals?"

"Maybe."

"And we can go do Grandpa's ashes soon."

"When they call Shelly."

"So we'll be alright then. Everything will be alright."

She kissed his head. She did not like lying to her brother. In the bathroom she found small scissors and cut his nails. "I should've done this before."

He watched her. "You look like Mom again. You should eat."

She rolled her eyes. He smiled.

That night they ate mashed potatoes and sausage, together in the small room, in front of the television set. They still wore their funeral clothes.

"She knows how to cook at least," Robin said as he ate. "I could eat two of these sausages."

Duchess moved to knife her sausage onto his plate but he pushed her hand away. "Not yours. You need to eat too."

"I'll go see if I can get you another."

She grabbed her plate and walked slowly down the hallway, Robin shut in, cartoons playing. On the wall were family photos, one at Disney with Henry and Mary Lou wearing mouse ears, one at Kennedy, another at the Canyon. Mr. Price and Henry wore matching ball caps.

There was a sign, BLESS THIS MESS, a caricature of Mrs. Price by the water, her smile way bigger than Duchess had ever seen it.

She stopped by the kitchen door and heard them at the dining table, Mr. Price asking Mary Lou about her test, then Henry about softball. She waited till Henry started talking then slipped into the kitchen.

"Duchess."

She turned. Silence as they looked her way.

"I just . . . Robin liked the sausage so I was looking for another."

"All gone," Mr. Price said.

"Oh."

She glanced at Mary Lou's plate and saw she had three.

Duchess turned and left them, forked her own sausage and held it out. As she got back she passed it over to Robin.

"You ate yours already?" he said.

"Yeah. They were good."

"Told you."

When the house was sleeping she moved silent down the stairs and into Mr. Price's study. All wood, neat stacks of books on finance and currency. At the computer she searched "Vincent King" and read all she could about the case. It confused her, that Vincent didn't plead it out and cop life when his guilt was clear like that. The newspapers said he still didn't speak, not at the arraignment, and still had not instructed a lawyer.

The DA was slick, she was going to bat for Star Radley and her orphans. *Those poor children.*

She spun quick when she heard someone at the door.

"You're not supposed to be in Daddy's office."

Mary Lou. Well fed, hair brushed daily by Mrs. Price, skin mottled by acne. She was fifteen and Duchess guessed she was the kind of girl that would one day wear a purity ring before losing it the first time she drank liquor.

"I had to use the computer."

"I have to tell him."

Duchess loaded her voice with childlike fear.

"Oh please don't tell Daddy on me."

"You should watch it."

"Or?"

"You think you're the first kids we had here?"

Duchess stared at her.

"I heard you talking to your brother. You think you'll get placed?" Mary Lou laughed.

"Why wouldn't we?"

"Well, Robin might. He's young enough, decent enough. But I heard Daddy talking about you, all your troubles. Who's going to want you?"

Duchess took a step forward.

Mary Lou took a step forward. "You want to hit me, don't you? Lash out. That's what kids like you do."

Duchess clenched her fist.

"Do it then." A smile, knowing.

Duchess felt the adrenaline kick, the fire burn. And then she looked back, at the computer screen. A picture of the scene that night, the small house on Ivy Ranch Road, a blur of neighbors and reporters. And the picture beside, Cape Haven PD. Walk. Smiling. Her reminder of everything good.

She slipped past Mary Lou, took a breath, and went back up the stairs.

30

Walk woke at his desk, sunlight found strewn papers.

He struggled to straighten, the pain so bad he almost cried out. He found pills in his drawer and swallowed two without water.

He'd had Leah order new pants, shirt, jacket. The scales told him he'd lost twenty-five pounds.

The knocking, he didn't know how long it had gone on for but there was something frantic in it.

He staggered to his feet, tried a stretch, and almost puked with the pain. He sucked down a breath, pushed his chest out, and stepped from his office, and then slumped a little when he saw it was just Ernie Coughlin from the hardware store.

"Morning." Walk opened the door to him but Ernie didn't cross the threshold.

"The butcher. Where is he?" Ernie barked it, hands tucked into a brown apron.

Walk shook the confusion away.

"The butcher," Ernie repeated. "It's after seven now. He gets back from vacation, same day every year. Why hasn't the shop opened up?"

"Hunting. Archery, right? Maybe he's taken another day."

"Dumb bastard, chasing turkeys all over. Twenty-two years, Walk. Since he took over from his father. Twenty-two years I've been buying breakfast sausage from him. I take it over the road and Rosie cooks it up. Three pancakes, syrup, two cups of strong coffee."

"Can't you just eat the sausage Rosie buys in?"

Ernie looked at him with something like disgust. "You see the newspaper? New homes on the edge of town. They'll ruin this place. I take it you'll vote against."

Walk nodded, yawned, and tucked his shirt into his pants. "I'll go see him."

Ernie shook his head once and then turned and left.

Back at his desk he dialed Milton but got the machine. Then he went right back to watching security tapes from Cedar Heights. Moses, on the gatehouse, had given them up without much of a fight, didn't even ask for the kind of paperwork Walk did not possess.

There was almost no movement, but the quality was so bad he had to focus hard in case anyone left on foot. He didn't know the timescales involved so he faced up to days of watching the recordings. He watched the day pass, the mailman, the neighbor with the Ford.

Another hour before he saw something. He slowed it right down and ran it three times. He knew the old truck well, the Comanche. He squinted and could just about make out the shape of the bumper sticker, the silhouette of a blacktail. Milton.

He watched with interest as the barrier lifted, then he searched real slow. Three hours later, the angle worse as he left. There was no doubting it was the same truck.

Three more hours before he found the sedan, a close enough match for the two men seeking Darke.

Ten minutes and he watched them leave.

It took nineteen minutes to get Boyd on the phone, but only a couple for him to shoot down Walk's request for a warrant to search

Darke's place. Walk mentioned the guys looking for Darke, felt like a rookie asshole when Boyd asked for the plates but Walk couldn't get a clear read.

When he hung up Walk loosened his tie, then leaned forward and banged his head on the desk, hard enough to hurt.

"I feel like I should intervene here."

He looked up, saw Martha, and managed a smile. She carried her case, laden with files.

"You got any booze in this place?" She parked herself in the seat opposite.

He reached for the bottom drawer and pulled out a bottle of Kentucky Old Reserve, a gift from one of the vacationers for checking her place during the winter months. He found a couple of coffee cups and poured them a measure each.

He watched as she drank, already waiting for the subtle flush that crept into her cheeks, the same flush she got when she was angry or excited. Martha May, he still knew everything about her.

"I got nothing," she announced with exaggerated fanfare.

"You came all the way over here to tell me that?"

"Maybe I wanted to see you."

He smiled. "Really?"

"Course not. I brought you a dish." She opened her bag and pulled out a Tupperware container.

"Dare I ask?"

"Just some leftover pasta."

"And?"

"Nothing."

He blinked, waiting.

"Cubanelle," she said, finally. "Weak-ass frying pepper. You need to eat, Walk. You're getting all skinny. I'm worried about you."

"I appreciate it."

She stood, paced, told him things he already knew, then sat again. And then he told her about Darke, and the tapes.

"Your theory is?"

He rubbed his neck. "I don't have one. Not yet. I want to look in Darke's place. And I want to know who he's paying all that money to. If I can't get him for Hal, or Star, I want him for something. I want him off the street."

"If he was the one in Montana, there's a chance he's dead."

"We put him there and we can establish a link to Star. Maybe the boy heard something, Darke wants him dead. We can use it. I just need my angle."

"The bank payment?"

"I called the manager, he won't say anything without a court order. No surprise."

"First Union. You need to aim a little lower. A teller, maybe."

He raised an eyebrow.

"What, you think I don't know how to hustle? I've got all these dead-beat fathers hiding their income, so I go straight to the source."

"And that works?"

"Not always, but I call in favors, and I lend them too. Life of a lawyer. So, you know the whole town, Walk. There must be someone you can lean on."

• • •

He walked up Main, head down, ignored greetings, stopping only when Alice Owen blocked his path, the dog in her arms. "Could you watch her for a moment, Walk. I just have to run in—"

"I have to be somewhere."

"Literally, one minute." She thrust the dog at him, the fucking snappy bastard of a dog, then headed into Brandt's Deli. He watched her inside, small talk with the girl behind the counter, no doubt ordering some kind of soybean monstrosity from the new machine while she deliberated over the twenty-dollar cheeses. He looked down at the dog and watched the teeth bare, and then back to Alice, who'd run into Bree Evans and was talking animatedly.

And then he looked at his badge, and he thought of his days, his fucking, soulless perfect days.

He set the dog down, unclipped the leash, and dropped it into the trash can beside.

The mutt looked up at him, confusion in its bulbous eyes. And then, tentatively, it took in the wild around, channeled its inner animal, and began to trot its way down Main.

Walk left, cut through a vacant lot, massaged his hands, and straightened his back. This was his act now, his side to the world. Pill-rolling, slowed down, hard to concentrate on anything at all.

He stood outside the small house and stared. He hadn't seen the men working, didn't even know the old place had been remodeled. It had come to him an hour after Martha headed home, when he was reading interviews for the hundredth time.

Dee Lane.

She'd met Darke in the bank, First Union, where she'd worked as a teller for as long as Walk could remember. He called Leah when he realized they didn't have an up-to-date address for her, felt his heart sink a little when Leah told him Dee still lived at the tired house on Fortuna Avenue, the same house Darke owned and had served notice on.

But it was tired no longer, new windows, new porch. The wood stained fresh and the paint shone, the yard, new grass and flowers planted. There was a gate, a fence, pride in place of despair.

She met him at the door before he could knock, small smile as she stood aside and he went into the house.

Inside was mostly the same, instead of the cardboard boxes he saw a life unpacked, the photos and the furniture all in their place again. She went to make coffee. He asked if he could use the bathroom then headed up the stairs. He saw the elder girl's room, Yale pennant, long time off but Walk heard both kids were smart enough. And then the younger's, painted pink, new throw on the bed. Not obscene money, but there was a new television and computer. He used to know both kids' names but found them just beyond his grasp.

Back down and Dee led him out to the yard, where they sat at a small table.

"I know what you're thinking," she said.

"I'm just glad Darke let you have your old place back. I thought it'd be pulled down by now, make way for the millions and all that."

She sipped her coffee and watched the water like it was brand-new, not just newly unveiled.

"It's a view."

"Sure is. I almost don't believe it when I wake up. Early now, maybe five. I like to watch the sunset, you seen it over the water, Walk?"

"Sure."

She lit a cigarette and breathed it like it was all that kept her from screaming out. He knew what she'd done, she knew it, yet there were still lines to run, practice for the most tiresome of plays.

"So, you were with Darke that night. Star. That night when she was shot dead."

Dee flinched at that, like it was not necessary. "We've been through this."

"We have."

"You look tired, Walk."

He steadied his hand, buried it beneath the table, pulled on his sunglasses as clouds moved in.

"He was here, that night. What were you doing? Remind me."

"Fucking." She spoke without emotion.

A while back and he might've blushed. Instead he smiled a sad smile, but he got it. There was no hatred there.

"I worked my whole . . ." She held the smoke deep. "I paid my taxes, raised my children, didn't murder my cheating husband. I never took anything from anyone."

He sipped his coffee, too hot to taste.

"You know how much money I make in a year, Walk?"

"Not enough."

"He doesn't pay child support. Is that fair? He hides it all so he doesn't have to pay for the girls he brought into the world." She looked down. "The Radley kids. Are they—"

"Their mother is dead."

"Jesus, Walk." She dragged a hand through her hair. Thin wrists, veins standing proud. "You gonna make this harder than it needs to be. You got the man already, right?"

"You didn't think to ask where Darke really was that night."

She tipped her head back, mouth a little open as she blew the smoke away.

"Did you at least get security?"

"I don't know what you mean." She met his eye with tears in hers.

"I could call you in, make you testify. You know what the penalty is for perjury?" Maybe he could prove Darke had lied, but it didn't mean shit, not really, not without so much more.

She closed her eyes. "There's no family. Just me and the girls. No one else at all."

He would not tear a mother from her children. The toll was too great. He knew that from talking to Hal and watching Duchess and Robin.

"I need something. A favor. It could come to nothing, but I need it."

She did not ask what, just nodded once.

He reached forward and touched her hand, and she grasped his tight, like she did not want to let go, like she could wring the absolution from it.

31

She slept the shallowest of sleeps each night, so was on her feet quick and pulling on a sweater and jeans when she heard the tapping. Robin slept deeply beside, curled fetal the way he used to in the family room at Vancour Hill Hospital.

At the window she held up a finger, found her sneakers and crept down the stairs and out into the cold night.

He wore a scarf and woolen hat, his bike propped by the gate.

"Shit, Thomas Noble. That was Mary Lou's window you were tossing stones at."

"Sorry."

"How far did you ride?"

"I left at dinner, told my mom I was sleeping over at a friend's."

"You don't have friends."

"I've started hanging out with Walt Gurney."

"That kid with the eye?"

"It's only contagious if you touch it."

He wore a coat so thick it was like his body was wrapped with tires.

They moved down into the long yard. Behind bare trees was a small fishpond. Robin had sat there for an hour before Mrs. Price told him it was not stocked.

They sat together on a stone bench beneath a half-moon and bright nests of starlight.

"You should really wear regular gloves. Not even Robin wears mittens."

Thomas Noble reached across and took her hand and blew on it, then braced himself but she said nothing.

"You were in the newspaper. All that stuff that happened. I kept the cuttings."

"I saw it all."

"I wish you were coming back to school."

A look toward the sleeping house, the neighbors' beside. Wake up, go to work and pay bills. Take vacations. Worry about pensions and PTA meetings, which car to buy next and where to spend Christmas.

"I liked Hal. I know he was scary and all that, but I liked him just the same. I'm real sorry for you, Duchess."

She balled snow in her hand till her bones ached. "I'm figuring out my next move. Take it back to breathing. I can't fuck up, I know that much. The girl, Mary Lou . . . I'd like to behead that motherfucker."

Thomas Noble pulled his hat low over his ears.

"I need to get back to Cape Haven. I made a promise to Robin that I'd find us a home for good this time. It's all that matters to him."

"I asked my mother if you could come live with us but—"

She waved him off, gave him an out. "The way she is with the mailman you'll likely have a sibling soon enough."

He frowned.

"I don't need anyone . . . but my brother, he's just a baby really. You think there's such a thing as a truly selfless act, Thomas Noble?"

"Sure. You coming to the winter dance with me."

She smiled.

"I like winter most. Out of all the seasons, and I think we have more than most in Montana."

"Why?"

He raised his bad hand, the mitten covering it totally.

"That's why you wear mittens."

"Yes."

"There was an outlaw, William Dangs, and he was a crack shot badass that held up three banks before they got him. He had one arm, gone at the shoulder."

"Serious?"

"Yes." Right then she was glad he did not know her tells.

She began to shiver.

He took off his coat and slipped it around her shoulders.

He began to shiver.

"They might send us someplace far. If we get anyone at all, could be anywhere in the whole country."

"I'll ride there. Doesn't matter where."

"I don't need anyone."

"I know. You're the toughest girl I ever met. And the prettiest. And I know you'll probably hit me, but I think my world is infinitely better because you're in it. Before it was just kids that laughed, pointed, whispered. But not now. And I know—"

She kissed him then. Her first kiss, and his. His lips were cold, his nose cold on her cheek. He was too startled to kiss her back. She broke it and turned back to the frozen pond.

"Shut up," she said.

"I didn't say anything."

"You were going to."

They breathed mist.

"Hal said we begin at the end."

"So where are we now?"

"I'm not sure it matters."

"Wherever it is, I hope we can stay here a little longer."

They held hands awhile, then stood and walked back down the yard, spring buried so deep. In the house was her suitcase and her brother, and she had nothing else in the world. She could not decide if that made her free or so terribly cursed.

Thomas Noble pulled his bicycle from the gate and dusted snow from the saddle.

"How did you find me?" she said as she handed his coat back.

"My mother was talking to your caseworker."

"Right."

He climbed on the bike.

"Hey. Why did you come here tonight?"

"I wanted to see you."

"And? I can read you. Tell me."

"I'm looking for him. Darke. Every day after school I ride to the Radley farm and walk the woodland."

"Could be you'll find a body."

"I sure hope so."

He freewheeled to the end of the Price driveway. She followed him out into the street. Mailboxes neatly lined, each had a family name painted on. *Cooper* and *Lewis* and *Nelson*. Robin liked to read the names, to see himself inside.

"Thomas Noble."

He stopped, leaned on one foot and looked back over his shoulder.

She raised a hand.

He raised his own.

When she got back to their room she found Robin crying, scooted back against the wall, his head in his hands.

"What is it?"

"Where were you?" he said between sobs.

"Thomas Noble came here."

"The bed."

She looked over at the balled sheet.

"The bed is wet," he said, distraught. "I had a dream about that night. I heard things. I heard voices."

She pulled him close and kissed his head. Then she helped him out of his shorts and T-shirt, put him in the bathtub and washed him.

When she was done she dressed him in clean pajamas and laid him in her bed. He was sleeping by the time she got to work stripping the mattress down.

Walk lay in his bed wrestling with facts he already knew. Dickie Darke had lied about his alibi the night Star was murdered. Milton had paid him a visit. Maybe the two had gone hunting but Walk didn't buy it. Milton was missing, Walk had stopped by his place and found it in darkness. There was no one he could check in with, no motel or anything. Milton camped, hunted, moved through the acres in the kind of solitude he couldn't bear in the Cape.

An hour from dawn he stood and dressed, drank coffee, then climbed into the car and drove to Cedar Heights.

No one worked the gatehouse during night hours, so Walk left the cruiser beneath trees that swayed against lightening sky, crossed the driveway, and stepped through the smaller gate to the side.

No life in any of the houses, not even the place across the street. He moved without care, head up, no doubt caught on the cameras. He did not know if it was the lack of sleep or the way his body tremored, but that morning he did not give a shit about the trouble he was inviting.

He moved down the side of the house, opened the gate, and stepped into the yard, and then stalled when he saw it. The back door, a single pane of glass missing, removed with great care, likely made no noise at all. He thought of the men looking for Darke as he reached in and turned the handle.

No sign of anything as he moved through the house, TV off, plastic fruit in the bowl, up the stairs and through the bedrooms, made up like a perfect family had stepped out for an hour so interested parties could get a look at their lives.

He checked beneath the bed, pulled the sheets back, and then tossed the pillow to the floor. And then he saw it, far out of place. Right there in the bed, a sweater, small and pink. A girl's sweater. He thought of bagging it, taking it, and then explaining it to Boyd. He left it, but he made a note in his pad so he'd remember.

And then the flash of lights.

He ducked low, moved to the window, then heard the car idle. He risked a look, different sedan but the same two. The bearded guy rolled the window down, lit by the glow from his cigarette. He stared at the house.

Walk counted off the beats of his heart.

Fifteen minutes till they backed up, turned, and slowly rolled away. He got the plates, for what it was worth.

Back in the kitchen he switched on the lights and searched every cupboard.

He almost missed it.

Down on his knees he checked the tiles.

No doubt it was blood.

It took three hours to get a tech van over, and that was all on favor. Tana Legros had been at the end of her shift when he called. Walk had once busted her son smoking weed at a party he broke up on Fallbrook. He'd recognized the kid's surname and driven him home instead of writing him up. Tana would be grateful till the day she died.

Once Moses arrived at the gatehouse Walk tried to liaise with the guy, but he found the easiest way to deal with his questions was to slip him a twenty.

He ventured through to the back where he found the small office. The computer was plastic, hollow, as fake as the ideal.

Tana came, one other guy with her, young and methodical and eager. The guy stood back and raised an eyebrow as Tana lowered her mask. She pointed in the direction of the kitchen, blinds pulled, luminol reagent set the floor aglow.

"Jesus," Walk said. "Blood?"

"Yes," Tana said.

"Is that a lot?"

"Yes."

"Can you run it?"

"You got a warrant to be in here?"

He said nothing.

"Guess I can't remove this tile then."

"Sorry."

"I'll take a swab and hold on to it. You give me something more and I'll work up a profile. Won't get nowhere if it's not in the system though."

He thought of the men after Darke. And then his mind ran to Milton.

He left the cruiser up on the sidewalk, ran across Milton's front yard, and hammered the door.

"Milton," he yelled, then stepped back into the street and looked at the upstairs windows. He heard a noise behind, turned and saw Brandon Rock watering his grass.

"You seen Milton?"

"Vacation." Brandon looked like shit, dark glasses, stubble, feathered hair collapsed.

"You alright?"

"Leah didn't tell you?"

"What?"

"Those two don't even talk anymore. She probably doesn't even know," Brandon slurred it.

"Know what, Brandon?"

"Ed let me go."

Walk took a step nearer and smelled the booze.

"Me and John and Michael."

"I'm sorry."

Brandon waved a hand, turned and walked unsteadily toward his house. "Falling market. Failing economy. Bullshit. Ed ran the place into the ground. Booze, the women. Used to go to The Eight more than me, and I lived in that place."

Walk dragged a trash can over, stood on it, pulled himself over Milton's side gate and dropped into the backyard, feeling his bones jar as he hit the ground.

He found the key under a false stone. Five years back Milton had taken in a stray, a skinny mongrel that he turned so fat it was put to death a year later. So much meat it went happy. Walk had agreed to feed the thing when Milton's father passed.

Inside.

He smelled blood right off, guessed Milton secreted the scent wherever he sat. He saw a calendar on the wall, two weeks marked, even had a circle on the day he'd be opening up again.

"Milton," he called it loud, in case the guy was bathing, the kind of sight that'd chase dreams with nightmare for all eternity.

Nothing in the living room.

He climbed the stairs, tried the guest room. A mattress on the floor, no sheets. And then he came to the master.

It was neat, thick blanket on the bed, despite the warmth, an old dresser with a mirror above, maybe the kind his mother had used. On the wall was the head of a deer, mounted on mahogany. The dead eyes made Walk wonder what kind of man wanted the thing watching over him like that.

There was a bookshelf, heavy with texts on hunting, traps, maps of the wild. Nothing on astronomy.

He walked over to the window, saw the telescope, the Celestron, and ran a finger along the back. The dust was thick, like he hadn't used the thing in a year.

He leaned down, peered through and took a breath when he found the telescope not angled at the sky but on the house across the street.

On a single window.

The window of Star Radley's bedroom.

He thought of Milton, always offering help, the Comanche, taking out her trash, giving Duchess cuts of meat to take home. Walk always had him down as good, misunderstood, a little off, but basically a decent man. He cursed under his breath as he began searching through drawers.

He found the suitcase beneath the bed, hauled it out and dropped it on top of the mattress.

Neighborhood Watch.

Scrawled in marker across the top. There was order inside, the photos catalogued.

They numbered in the hundreds. Some were Polaroid, some better quality. He picked one up and saw Star in a state of undress, bare chest, just underwear. And that was the theme. In some she was clothed, working the yard, some had Duchess and Robin in view, clear they were not the focus. He turned from the nudes, Star bent over, Star undressing for bed.

"Fucking Milton."

Some of the shots were old, ten years of watching. He noticed a couple with a guy she was seeing, Walk couldn't quite recall the name. He guessed Milton hoped to catch them fucking; instead he got a series of shots of Star kissing him good night then the guy retiring to the living room.

And then he stopped.

The file marked *June 14*.

The day Star was murdered.

With a shaking hand he turned the pages, then cursed again when he saw they were blank.

He took a final look around, then called it in. Leah Tallow took it and sounded shocked when he told her.

He'd bring Milton in, just as soon as he found him.

32

They settled into a fragmented life.

They trailed in silence each morning as Mary Lou and her brother collected friends on the walk to school. The group stared back and whispered and laughed. One time Duchess slipped on the ice, tore her jeans and cut her knee. They did not stop to help. She limped on in quiet, still holding her brother's bag as well as her own.

Mrs. Price added a plastic sheet to Robin's bed. It rustled so loud each night he climbed in with Duchess.

They met with two couples.

The first, Mr. and Mrs. Kolene. Duchess knew right off that Shelly had worked hard to get them to the table, the table being a play area in the park on Twin Elms Avenue. Duchess pushed Robin on the swing while the Kolenes and Shelly sat on a park bench, drank a thermos of coffee, and stared at them like they were attractions in a petting zoo.

"What the fuck are they looking at? They want us to do tricks or something?"

"Quiet, they might hear."

Duchess took a tissue from her coat and wiped his nose, then went back to pushing the swing while Shelly smiled at her.

"The dude looks like a librarian."

"Why?"

"Those glasses. He's got a sweater with no sleeves. I think they're too old to have kids naturally and now they want a second shot. Could be problems with his sperm, or maybe she's barren as the Mojave."

Robin stared over. "What's barren?"

"Her parts have died off."

"She looks alright."

"I can feel the bitter seeping from her pores. Should've frozen her eggs. She won't love us right."

"But no one else has come."

"They will. Shelly said we have to be patient, right?"

He looked down.

"Right?"

"Yeah. I guess."

"These people, they get tested. Vetted. They take classes so they know how to parent right."

She pushed him higher, till the chain began to flex and he screamed and laughed. She marveled at his ability to adapt, the way he smiled at Mr. and Mrs. Price so much, just the chance they might return it enough for him.

She worked hard to keep her temper in check now, didn't say anything when Mary Lou smirked or Henry wouldn't share his games with Robin. She buried the part of her that thought about Hal and the way he had died, and her mother and the way she had died. She watched old Westerns, read her books, knew that lives could be colored so boldly by revenge they blackened all the good a person might once have had.

It was Walk who kept her from doing something foolish, he anchored her to the good, he kept her aimed toward the future instead of the now. Walk reminded her men could be all good. He kept her from marching over to Shelly and the Kolenes and telling them to get the fuck away, that she'd cared for Robin his whole life and didn't plan on quitting anytime soon. Mrs. Kolene raised a hand and Robin grinned and waved as hard as he could, like he couldn't read what was going on. They'd barely spoken to them, a couple of questions in broad Midwestern accents, no way of placing them, just another couple looking for a way to make themselves whole but knowing right off the Radley children fell short.

"Not the right fit," Shelly said on the drive back to the Price house.

Mrs. Price had been pissed at them that evening, like they'd played it wrong, like she was tiring of them and wanted younger, fresher faces to drag to church each Sunday and show off.

The next meet was bad. Mr. and Mrs. Sandford. He was a retired army colonel and she was a homemaker with an empty home.

They sat on the same bench with Shelly, made small talk while they sized up the kids. The colonel kept laughing and slapping his wife's knee, hard enough to leave a print.

"He'll beat us," Duchess said from her spot by the swing.

Robin stared at him.

"Probably want you to shave your head and enlist."

"Could be she'll teach you to bake," Robin said.

"Motherfucker."

"You said that too loud."

They looked up at the colonel watching them. Duchess snapped off a salute. Shelly smiled nervously.

Early March, the thaw began.

Duchess sat at the window each night and watched the steady drip from windows as the color slowly began its return to Montana. Morning broke to cold sun, but sun just the same. Sidewalks melted, yards emerged from burial, shadblow shed browns to white blossom that reached skyward. She watched the change but could see no beauty at all.

Duchess moved through her small life without feeling, each motion so automatic she sometimes forgot which day of the week it was. She cared for Robin, walked him to school, and ignored Mary Lou and her sidekick Kelly when they cut her down, her shoes, her top, the brand of her jeans. Shelly came each week, sometimes she took them out for ice cream and once even to the movies. Robin talked about a new family, how the father would be like Hal, teach him to fish and play ball. He held the belief in his small hands, tighter with each passing day.

One Saturday Shelly took them to see the farm. Probate would take months, so it was still Radley land for a little longer. They swung by to collect Thomas Noble.

High spring morning. Robin took Shelly to see the coop and told her of the jobs he used to carry out. Duchess and Thomas Noble walked the wheat fields, no crops planted, just rows of weed and mounded earth. She felt a sadness so profound she could not speak for a long time. Hal in every step she took, cigar smell as they walked up to the porch and took a seat on the swing. She pushed back, the chains pulled and creaked, and she wanted to cry but did not. She visited the field where the gray once ran, she missed her almost as much as she did her grandfather.

After, they left the farm in heavy silence and Robin did cry. She held his hand in her own. When they got back to the Price house they sat idling on the street, watching the neighbor kids ride their bikes. It was warming up, summer a while off but making its intent known.

"I've got someone," Shelly said.

Duchess could hear something in her voice, a trace but it was there. Something different.

"Who?" Robin said.

"Their names are Peter and Lucy. They're from Wyoming, where I used to work. Till now they've been searching just for one child, but I told them how special you two are—"

"So you lied," Duchess said.

Shelly smiled and held up a hand. "Hear me out. They're small-town, he's a doctor and she teaches third grade."

"What kind of doctor?"

"A real doctor."

"A shrink? Because I don't want some guy messing with my—"

"A regular doctor. In a practice. Making sick people well again."

"I like them," Robin said.

Duchess sighed.

"You can meet them next weekend if you want to."

Robin looked pleadingly at Duchess till she nodded.

•••

They rode Route 5 in her Prius, Medford to Springfield.

A hundred miles from Salem they left bright lights and smooth asphalt for bumping down dark tracks that slivered through Marion and the kind of townships that existed on old maps and nowhere else.

Martha slept. When the roads smoothed and held straight Walk allowed himself to glance over, and when he did he felt the sharp pain that had stabbed at him since the day he walked back into her life. She looked calm, at peace, so beautiful he sometimes fought the overwhelming urge to kiss her.

Dawn broke over the Calasade Highway. Walk was so tired he veered over the double yellows till Martha reached over and gently tugged the wheel.

"You should've pulled over."

"I'm straight."

On the Silver Falls Highway they watched the sun creep from the hills and color farmland a dozen greens. At a diner they ate eggs and bacon and drank coffee so strong Walk felt it sharpen him right up again.

"It's not far," Martha said, looking at the map spread out across the table.

They were headed to Unity, a private healthcare facility in Silver Falls. The same place to which Dickie Darke had been making payments as far back as they could go in his bank records. Dee had come through; she'd knocked on Walk's door the night before and given him a slip of paper with the recipient's name.

Three cups of coffee and they left, caffeine coursing Walk's veins as the Silver Falls State Park came at them. Martha navigated and before long the trees towered beside. Rocks rose above steep banks of green. Walk opened his window to the rush of sound as they passed a waterfall.

Another turn and they came to the gates. Walk had called ahead, told them he wanted to look around the place. He gave his name through the speaker and watched the gates swing open.

They followed the long road till the hospital came into view, sleek and modern, dark framed glass contrasted sand bricks, the place could've been luxury condos nestled among the trees.

The woman's name was Eicher and she met them at the door with a hearty smile. She led them into a vast entrance hall, modern art, a sculpture that could've been an eagle. There was a calm to it all, doctors strolled by, nurses moved slow, no fuss, no worry. At first Walk thought it might've been a retreat, the kind of place harried execs came to for some downtime. But then Eicher was back with them, and she reeled off the kind of work they did, the complex needs of their patients and the round-the-clock care they provided.

She moved with purpose, despite the extra fifty pounds she carried. An accent, hard to place, might've been German but it was muddied by local phrases. She didn't ask who they were there for, Walk had mentioned a relative on the phone, needed help, needed specialist care. Eicher had told him to come in and take a look around, nothing formal, the fit was important and couldn't be rushed.

Beside him Martha said nothing, just noted the sprawling day rooms, a bank of elevators and carpet so thick she felt her feet sink.

Eicher detailed the history, the proximity to the state park and the calm it inspired. They were equipped for any kind of emergency, five doctors on call, thirty nurses.

She led them out into the gardens, which stretched to a stream behind a low fence. Walk saw a couple of porters catching a smoke by a set of doors. Eicher shot them a look and they stubbed out their cigarettes and moved on.

"Can I ask how you found us?" she said.

"A friend of mine. Dickie Darke."

She smiled then, white teeth, a decent gap between the front two. "Madeline's father."

Walk said nothing.

"She's an exceptional girl. And Mr. Darke is so strong, after losing his wife like that. Did you know Kate?"

Martha stepped forward. "Not well enough."

Eicher looked sad then, the only crack in a pristine façade. "She was a local girl. Grew up in Clarkes Grove. Madeline is her double."

She led them back through the building, signed off with a brochure and a promise to call. Walk did not need to press further, he had found what he had come for.

"Will you give him my regards? I hope he's healing up well," Eicher said.

Walk turned to her, she read the look.

"I'm sorry. The accident. Dickie was limping, said he'd slipped."

Walk felt the rush then. "When was this?"

"Maybe a week ago. Some people, bad luck seems to follow them around." Eicher added another smile, then turned and left them.

Fifteen miles to Clarkes Grove, and from there they took a walk along a colorful Main Street, distant from the Cape in miles alone. Walk liked the town right off. They found the old municipal library at the end of the street, quaint but tired, like the place was running on handouts alone. Empty inside, dark and cool, the smell taking Walk back to Portola and his two years of college.

An old lady at the desk didn't look up from her screen, so they headed to the back and the couple of computers. Martha got to work, sitting close to Walk, her leg pressed against his. He watched her, the way she furrowed her brow, the rise and fall of her chest as she breathed.

"Are you checking me out, Chief?"

"No. Sorry. No."

"That's too bad."

He laughed.

She typed quick, "Kate Darke," and the archives pulled up a dozen matches. They read in silence, the car accident, how Kate died at the scene and Madeline Ann suffered catastrophic brain injuries. There were photos, the ice, the Ford had left the road and headed straight down a steep bank, meeting trees and popping the windshield. The lake behind, The Eight, the only calm in that shot.

A single photo of the family before.

Martha zoomed in close and Walk was struck by Darke, that emptiness, the hollow gaze, it was all absent back then.

"So Madeline would be fourteen now," Martha said.

"Yes."

"Jesus. She's been in there nine years. Around the time Darke started making his moves. It's a lot of money."

Walk found another article, this one focused on Madeline and the work done at Unity. It said a lot and nothing at all. The girl was kept alive by a machine.

Darke was hoping for a miracle.

33

Harbor Bay.

Walk made it there in thirty, didn't flash the lights because Cabrillo was empty. The call came in an hour after he made it back from Portland.

He left the cruiser close to the gate and walked past the bobbing trawlers, a shiny Bayliner, and a line of Navigators. Gaps between boards, water slopped beneath. He saw a cluster of catfish turning as an old man tossed what was left of the day's bait.

Frenzied water, salt breeze, a sense of dread.

The trawler was a '73 Reynolds but looked newer, fresh paint and blue trim, Andrew Wheeler on the deck, his eyes on breaking waves.

Walk knew him a little. Andrew had taken Star out a few times.

In the distance was the Cape, the cliffs, land trailing down to the beach and the King house commanding all of it. Andrew still worked with Skip Douglas, so old and grizzled he barely spoke a word on dry land. Skip stepped onto the boards, nodded once at Walk, and headed back toward the lot, no doubt to grab a couple of beers to take the edge off the day they'd had.

Andrew came down and they shook hands, Andrew's arms muscled and tan, sunglasses on his head despite the dusk sky. Lights flickered on as Walk stepped onto the boat.

"What happened?" Walk said.

"We were out with city people, group from Sacramento. Three of them, childhood friends out traveling their way up to Six Rivers."

Lobster season ran October through March. There were limits, number and size and weight, but most of the customers just wanted a day out on the water.

"We were heading in slow when Skip called me over. The net was caught, happens often, always a pain in the ass. Sometimes I pull on a wetsuit and head in, cut away where needed."

Walk placed a hand on the side though the waves were gentle.

"It was heavy, though. Skip even took off his ball cap and wiped his head, and that guy never breaks a sweat. I grabbed the trawl winch and we got it moving. Then it broke the water. The guys puked, all three. Gulls circled, more than usual, that's how I knew, cries so loud Skip closed the dead man's eyes."

"You didn't touch him other than that?"

Andrew shook his head, then stepped aside.

"The guys were so sick I had to try and cover him on the ride in."

Walk pulled the towel back then fought for breath.

Milton.

Bloated, mottled, eyes swollen over.

"You alright, Walk?"

"Jesus."

"You know him?"

Walk nodded. He thought of the blood at Darke's place, they'd match it soon enough, he had little doubt. More pieces to figure, so uneven.

"Sit down for a bit, you don't look so good."

They sat on the deck and waited for the coroner. Andrew passed Walk a beer, which he sipped as the color returned to him.

"Better?"

"You don't seem all that shaken up," Walk said.

"It's my third body."

"Serious?"

"One in Jersey, and then I worked the Keys. A lot going on in Cape Haven."

"Too much."

Walk held the bottle to his head and soothed the ache forming. His hand shook as he drank, he did not even try and hide it.

"I saw you at the funeral. I'm sorry I didn't get a chance to come over." Andrew had stood at the back, head bowed, stayed a few minutes then slipped out.

Andrew waved him off. "I was . . . it was sad. The whole thing, when I heard about her. I thought about the kids, even back then, the boy was a baby but the girl used to glare at me."

Walk thought of Duchess.

"You know who did it, this guy?"

"Maybe."

Andrew asked nothing else.

They watched a boat head in, low lights over calm water.

Andrew held his bottle to the dying sun. "It'd been five years since I last saw her. But I still thought about her. It wasn't even . . . the one that got away, nothing like that. You know when you want to save someone, but you don't have the first clue how to do it?"

"You saw her awhile."

"A few months maybe. Met her at a bar, watched her sing then bought her a drink, thought she was nice-looking and funny and kind of damaged, which wasn't all that unusual in the kinds of bars I drink in."

"And then?"

"We were together but not. Almost like friends. I wanted more."

Walk watched him.

"Sex. We never did."

Walk saw a speedboat, out of place, white and garish, no doubt a vacationer bringing out their toy, the old and new colliding in a way that still pained him. FOR SALE sign. Walk hoped whoever bought it took it someplace far away.

"She was beautiful. Sex is something, right. I know we don't talk about it, but it's something. In a relationship, without it what have you got?"

Walk thought of Martha, the nature of their friendship, the undercurrent that pushed him every time he saw her, dragging his mind someplace it shouldn't go. She had closed off the parts that were his, her mind, gone to ground with the child she once lost.

"Did she give a reason?" Walk said.

"She said you get one great love. And you're lucky if you find that. Anything less might as well have been nothing."

Walk thought of Star. She didn't get her happy ending. Each night he prayed her children would.

· · ·

Robin was nervous the day of the meet.

They lay awake the night before and Robin talked of Peter and Lucy like he knew them well. He decided he might like to be a doctor too, that or a teacher. She told him to sleep, that he wanted to be fresh. He talked another hour.

She laid out his shorts and T-shirt. He exchanged them for his smart slacks and funeral shirt. He tried on his bow tie, discarded it. He shined his best shoes with spit and paper towels. She tried to untangle his hair, gave up and pressed it to a parting.

She wore jeans and a top, and he yelled till she changed into a dress. He chose a yellow bow for her hair then asked if she should wear a little makeup. He ate no breakfast, just sipped his juice at the window.

"You need to relax."

"What if they don't show?"

"They will."

The drive to the park, Robin was quiet, staring out. Duchess saw his small fingers crossed. They pulled into the lot, stepped out to sun, birdsong, a gentle breeze.

Peter was short, a little overweight but he carried it well. Lucy smiled in the kind of wholesome way that made Duchess think she was born to be a mother or a third-grade teacher. Shelly waved and they began to walk over.

Peter turned and whistled. A black Lab looked up, one paw in the air, then began to run.

"They've got a dog," Robin said it in a whisper.

"Just try and be cool."

Robin looked up at her. She waited a little, then nodded and he took off, running at the Lab and waving like a madman.

"Shit."

"Don't worry," Shelly said.

"He wanted to bring his suitcase, in case they want to take us right off."

"Shit," Shelly agreed.

It could've been awkward when they met, like the other times, careful handshakes and too much eye contact, but Peter and Lucy were warm and open right off. They introduced themselves, talked about how far they'd come, driven up with Jet, their Lab, from their small town in Wyoming. Peter set off with Robin and Jet, staying just about in sight as they crossed over long grass. Robin kept looking back and waving till Duchess waved back. Duchess did not say anything wrong, just did not really say anything at all. Lucy told her she liked her dress and Duchess told her thank you. She asked about school and Duchess said it was nice. And about living with the Price family and Duchess said that was nice too.

The whole time she watched and worried, Robin taking Peter's hand and clutching it tight, then petting Jet and smiling too wide. When Lucy mentioned they kept chickens Duchess hoped and prayed Peter didn't tell Robin the same thing.

Ten minutes later Robin turned and mouthed *chickens* to her. Duchess gave him a smile and Robin clapped his hands.

They kept to a safe limit, no talk of the past, though Lucy said she was sorry about Hal, about everything. She told how her own mother passed when she was small.

When it was time, Robin hugged Peter so long Duchess had to intervene.

Robin talked on the journey back, not stopping for air. He said Peter mentioned meeting again, how he'd let him hold Jet's leash next time. Shelly told him he did good, that Peter and Lucy said how much they liked meeting them.

"And?" Robin said.

"We'll see. But I've got that good feeling again," Shelly said. Robin clapped his hands, then he jumped from the car and ran up the path to the Price house. Mrs. Price met him at the door and smiled for Shelly.

"You shouldn't say shit like that. Not till you know."

"It's important to stay positive," Shelly said.

Duchess rubbed her eyes, the year long, the uncertainty draining.

She was not sure if she believed in God, but that night she prayed.

34

W alk found her at the church.

He stood by the door, rested a hand on the old clapboard and looked to the water, the flowers on graves.

Martha sat alone on the front bench, her eyes on the stained glass and the pulpit, the same seat she used to take each Sunday morning when her father was minister. Walk took his seat at the back, silent, not wanting to disturb her. He had spent the morning on the phone, first to Boyd, to fill him in on Milton. He told him about the link to Darke, that they went hunting together and that Milton was seen entering and leaving Darke's place. He could not mention the blood, but Boyd said he would work on it, get a warrant.

And then he'd called a trial lawyer over in Clearlake, a guy named Carter, one of Martha's contacts. Carter wanted a meet with Vincent King, Walk could not make that happen. It was looming, only weeks away, not long enough for anyone to prepare.

"I need you," he said, and the old church carried his words, causing her to stop, lift her head but not turn. She finished speaking whatever silent words she had chosen.

He walked down, and together they sat before the old cross and the sainted neighbors.

"I need you. For the trial."

"I know."

He looked down at his tie, gold clip, starred collar, he had never felt so weak, or maybe he always had but did not realize it till then. He had seen Kendrick again, upped the dose. There was no way to stop what would come.

"I'll make mistakes. And they will matter."

"I know it's unfair."

"It's more than that. It's life and death. I once wanted to stand up front and help people that way. A port of call when times were good and bad. He took that from me. My father."

"You could have still—"

She cut him off with eyes full of tears. "I didn't want to live a lie."

"Milton is dead. The butcher. I think Darke killed him. I think Darke killed Hal to get to the children."

"He's worried the boy will remember."

Walk nodded. "Darke can't come back here now. He owes money to people, bad people." He'd run the plates, this time got a hit. The sedan was registered to a construction company in Riverside, one of the directors was linked to a known crime family. Darke's problems would not go away.

She looked at him then. "Take it to Boyd. They need protecting."

"I have. He still doesn't buy it."

"Because Vincent King is in the way."

"But if he were innocent. If we can get him off . . ."

"Shit, Walk. The best trial lawyer in the country couldn't get him off."

"If Vincent is innocent then Darke is coming for Robin Radley, not Duchess." Walk closed his eyes to the tremors, rubbed his neck, the muscles so stiff it hurt to turn his head.

"You want to tell me what's wrong now, Walk? You think I haven't noticed all this time. You look tired. You've lost a lot of weight."

"It's just the stress."

"Say that enough and you'll start to believe it."

"I won't."

He watched an old lady pass the door, kneel and cross herself before she went on. Maybe she slept better after.

"You're all purpose, Walk. I used to look at you and see everything inside."

"I want to be that man again. I just . . . it's all changing. I'm losing myself. I feel it, every day. I used to think everything was changing around me. I drove past Toller land. Hard to imagine, all those homes."

"People need to live somewhere, Walk."

"Second homes. They'll push the town further away."

"You like things how they are. I've seen your house. Your office. You cling hard enough to the past."

"There was a time when things were better. When we were kids, don't you remember that? I saw my life fixed, cop in the town I grew up in, wife and kids, Little League, camping out."

"And Vincent across the street, maybe your wives are friends. You vacation together. You barbeque, watch your kids in the surf."

"I still see that moment, thirty years and it's clear. It's so . . . I can touch it. But I can't change it."

"Tell me about the Vincent you remember."

"There's nothing he wouldn't do for me. That kind of blind loyalty. He had girls, but Star was the one for him. He was quick with his fists but never started the fight. He could go quiet, sometimes for days, and I knew his father was on him. And he was funny. He was everything to me. He was my brother. He is my brother."

He could not read her eyes then. Outside the sun shone, the birds sang. "I thought I'd marry you, Martha. You know that?"

"I know that."

"You're on my mind. First thing in the morning. And when I lie in bed at night."

"Masturbation is a sin."

"Don't say masturbation in church."

"You like me because I'm safe, Walk. I'm the mirror of you. I don't change, no surprises. Simple and dependable, till our idyllic childhood was shattered."

"That's not true."

"It is. But there's nothing wrong with that. We help people, Walk. I can think of no better way to live a life."

"So you'll do it."

She did not answer.

"You think we'd have been together in another life?"

"This one ain't over yet, Chief." She reached across and calmed the shake of his hand with the warmth of hers.

• • •

Peter and Lucy picked them up from the Price house.

Shelly sat with them in the SUV, on the rear seat busying herself with paperwork as they drove.

Peter and Robin talked endlessly during the ride, about Jet and how he was afraid of birds, about a patient Peter saw who had hiccups for a full year.

"Did you try scaring him?" Robin said.

"Pete's face is enough to scare anyone." Lucy winked at Duchess in the mirror. For her part Duchess smiled back, though she could not manage a laugh. That morning Mary Lou told her there wasn't a chance some nice doctor and his wife would want a troubled girl in their house, not a girl that makes shitty grades and likes playing with guns. Duchess had taken it, eaten her cornflakes in silence, while Mary Lou walked over and yanked the power cable from the back of the television they were watching.

They pulled over short of anywhere, idling at the side of the road while Peter and Lucy turned in their seats. Peter read from a guidebook.

"Going-to-the-Sun Road. You ready?"

"Ready," Robin said.

Peter looked at Duchess and smiled.

Beside her Robin squeezed her hand tight. "Ready."

Going-to-the-Sun Road spans fifty miles of towering rock. Light met them at the east tunnel, two mountains parting like the opening of a show.

They crawled along sheer drops, the road twisting to nothing ahead, a roller-coaster ride so beautiful Duchess closed her eyes.

They traversed valleys, waterfalls loud beside, wildflowers so many colors. Cliffside trails fell to limpid lakes, tall pines leaned with the hill, like they were trying not to fall.

Lucy pulled out a Nikon and snapped off shot after shot.

Behind, Shelly leaned forward and placed a hand on Duchess's shoulder, gave it a squeeze like she knew the girl needed it.

They pulled off at Jackson Glacier. Lucy took a hamper from the trunk and laid a blanket on the grass. Robin sat with Peter and they ate sandwiches and potato chips, drank juice boxes, and watched waving shadows over the lagoon.

"Grandpa would like it here," Robin said.

Duchess ate her sandwich, thanked Lucy, and tried to smile. At times she felt so far from a place she had never been, like home was somewhere out there and calling, she just did not know how to find it. She wiped her eyes on her sleeve, felt Lucy watching her and maybe wondering, how fucked up is this kid? Do I really want her in my life for now and always?

"Are you okay, Duchess?" Lucy said.

"Yes. Thank you." She wanted it to sound sincere but didn't know how. She wanted to convey it, that she could live quietly in their life, not disrupt, not impact at all so long as they loved her brother and cared for him.

She stood and walked to the fencing, leaned over and watched shallow water and blue stone beneath, purple flowers that bled with bright, a sweep of lodgepole serried.

Lucy joined her, said nothing, and Duchess was grateful.

On the ride back they slowed for mountain goats and bighorn sheep.

"What if they fall?" Robin said.

"Don't worry," Peter said. "I'm a doctor."

Lucy rolled her eyes.

Duchess studied Peter, the way he drove so cautiously, how natural his smile was. She imagined a life ordered, where everything fit just right. There was a calm to him, unhurried. People would pass him by and he didn't notice or care. She thought he'd make a decent father for Robin.

When they got back she watched Robin hug Peter, arms locked tight around his waist. And she saw the look that passed between them, Peter and Lucy.

Duchess knew it with some certainty.

They had found their new home.

35

They worked long into the night, Martha making coffee at midnight then again at two.

They'd spent the afternoon in Fairmount County, with Vincent. Martha had recorded the session, tried to coach and prompt, but there was no way Vincent would take the stand, so he'd said nothing. It was an exercise in futility, but Walk had hoped maybe seeing that Martha believed in him would give Vincent the excuse he needed to finally unload everything that had happened that night.

It was on the way in that Cuddy had caught up with him, handed him an envelope.

"What is this?" Walk asked.

"Vincent. He got mail. Doesn't say much of anything. Thought you might want to take a look."

Walk had waited till he was alone in the waiting room before he'd unfolded the paper. A letter, typed but no doubt it was from Darke.

> Funds are hard to come by but I haven't given up. I know
> I'm letting you down, so I've found a way to make things
> right. Good luck at trial, sometimes wishes do come
> true.

He'd read it a dozen times, looked for something that was not there, something he didn't already know. Darke had a conscience, maybe. It no longer mattered.

When he handed the letter over, Vincent had shoved it straight into his pocket, turned back to Martha and changed the subject. A line was drawn, and Walk was clearly on the other side of it.

With the trial on the horizon, Martha spent her days prepping, calling in favors, even driving down to see her old professor who lived in Cameron County.

She and Walk set up an office in his basement, covered every wall with papers and photos and maps. She read trial transcripts, practiced her opening statement so many times Walk knew every word of it. Martha knew the DA by reputation, knew that she'd have been prepping for months. The facts were cogent: Vincent King knew the victim and was found in her house covered in her blood.

There was talk of subpoenaing Dickie Darke, but they could not find him. The DA already had his statement. There was nothing tying him to the scene, and trying to do so would see Dee Lane called to the stand, and Walk would not do that to her children. No doubt he would be called as a state witness.

They mapped out local lives and where they intersected. The DA would claim Vincent had dumped the gun in the water. Martha could prove that was not possible in the time he had. It was a small win. They needed it.

At nine Walk sat on a chair and felt the tremor first in his left hand, then his right leg. He closed his eyes like he could will it away. He slowed his breathing and cursed his body for such betrayal at so crucial a time.

"Are you okay, Walk?"

He went to speak but felt it in his face, his jaw and lips. A tingling, then the same tremble of his body. It would pass, but not in time. He felt tears, hot and shameful. He tried to raise a hand to wipe them back before she saw, but his hand would not move.

He closed his eyes and willed himself from that room and that town and maybe that life. He thought back to being ten years old, riding his bike with Vincent, the two of them crossing each other and smiling the open way only children can.

And then he felt hands on his, not firm but there, warm. He opened his eyes and saw Martha on her knees before him. Her beautiful eyes, even filled with tears.

"It's alright."

He shook his head, it was not alright and would not be alright again. It had been a dozen years since he had cried. But right then, when he looked around at the perfect mess his life had become, he sobbed like he was fifteen and Vincent had been sent away all over again.

"Why do you carry Vincent with you?"

"It's on me. That night, after I found Sissy, I went to his place and saw the car. I knew right off it was him."

"I know. You told me."

"But I could have woken him. He would have handed himself in. It would have looked better, to that judge and jury. The judge would've been lenient. Instead I took it to Chief Dubois. Who does that? Who the fuck does that to their friend?"

Martha took his face in her hands. "You did what was right, Walk. You always have done. The way you looked out for Star even when I know she would've pushed you away, it's something special, to do that is something special."

"We endure, right. That's what we do for those we love."

"The world would be a better place with more people like you in it." She spoke so sincerely he could've believed her. But instead he looked over her shoulder at the board and his friend. They did not have time left for any of this.

He kissed her, suddenly, without thinking.

He started to apologize but then her lips found his, and there was something frantic in the way she kissed him, like she'd been waiting thirty years. She pushed him back, and then pulled him to his feet, took his hand and led him up to the bedroom. He wanted to stop her, to tell her she was making another mistake, that she was better than him in every way. But when she kissed him, he felt it. Fifteen all over again.

The news came in late, Walk's cell dragging him from the deepest sleep he'd had in a long time. He sat up, and Martha stirred beside him.

He listened in silence, then cut the call and lay back.

"What?"

He stared at the ceiling. "The autopsy on Milton. He drowned. Nothing else, no other injuries. He just drowned."

Martha got to her feet quick, despite the dark sky. "This is it, Walk."

"What?"

"The game changer we've been waiting for."

• • •

That night Robin woke crying, the sheets wet through, the nightmare that gripped him so vivid he could not speak for the first moments Duchess held him.

"It was Mom. I was locked in my bedroom and I heard Mom and she was screaming. I want Peter and Lucy. I want Mom. And Grandpa. I want to go back and for this to be the nightmare."

She hushed him and kissed his head.

After she helped him wash, she pulled the plastic sheeting from the other bed and they settled in there. She left the drapes open and they watched a night sky of plentiful stars and the fullest moon.

"It'll be okay, you know."

"You think they'll take us to Wyoming?"

"Your future isn't written yet, Robin. You can be anything. You're a prince."

"I want to be a doctor like Peter."

"You'd make a good doctor."

After he fell asleep she sat down by the window and took out her schoolbook. She did her history paper as best she could. She was struggling again.

She looked over at her brother and knew without doubt he was the color to her shade.

The next day as they walked toward school Mary Lou took turns leaning into the other kids' ears and whispering something that made them wrinkle their noses tight and laugh.

"What is it?" Robin said to Duchess.

"Nothing. Probably something dumb she saw on TV."

It continued the whole walk, along Hickory and into Grove Street. They collected four more kids, the Wilson twins, Emma Brown and her brother Adam. Each time Mary Lou did that same thing, brought them close and whispered, watching in delight as they recoiled then laughed.

"Ewww, gross," Emma said.

Robin looked up at Duchess again. "Henry didn't want me walking with the big kids today."

"Henry's an asshole."

Duchess stared at them as they walked, at Mary Lou who kept looking back and smirking, and Kelly and Emma and fucking Henry and his cunt friends. She felt that cold lead in her veins begin to melt and turn molten as they reached the school gates and Mary Lou took her whispers to a cluster of kids from her class. They all turned. Giggles turned to open laughs, faces pulled in disgust.

Duchess moved then. Robin grabbed her hand tight and pulled her back.

"Please," he said.

She knelt in the grass. "Robin."

He went to speak and she smoothed his curls back.

"What am I?"

He met her eye. "An outlaw."

"And what do outlaws do?"

"They don't take any crap."

"No one pushes us around. No one laughs at us. I stand up for you. Our blood is the same."

Fear in his eyes.

"You head into class now."

She gave him a gentle push and he turned and walked into the building, reluctant, nervous.

She stood, dropped her bag, and stared at Mary Lou. And then she walked toward her. Girls moved, Emma and Kelly and Alison Myers, they parted for her because they'd heard the stories.

"You want to tell me what's so funny?"

Boys came over and fanned out around them.

Mary Lou did not back off, just carried that same smirk. "You stink of piss."

"What?"

"Your bed. It was you last night. I saw my mother washing the sheet from your bed. You pissed yourself like some freak."

Duchess heard the bell ring.

No one moved.

"I did."

There were murmurs, laughter and a couple of shouts she couldn't make out.

"You admit it?" Mary Lou asked.

"Sure."

"See. I told you it wasn't bullshit," she said to Kelly. Then she turned and the group began to move.

"But you know why I did it?"

They stopped, heads turned.

Mary Lou watched her, uncertain of what was coming but tensing up, ready.

"So your father wouldn't touch me."

Stone silence.

"Liar," Mary Lou said.

Kelly and Emma inched away.

"*You fucking liar,*" she screamed then ran at Duchess.

Mary Lou was used to shoving matches, maybe some hair pulling, nothing more than that. She did not count on meeting an outlaw in the schoolyard.

Duchess dropped her with one savage punch.

Mary Lou crumpled, her tooth in the grass, the other kids hollering as blood spilled from her mouth.

Duchess stood still and calm, watching her prey, kind of hoping she'd get up and they'd go again.

When it was done, when the principal and two teachers ran out and took a look at Mary Lou, beaten bloody, tooth missing, the new girl standing over her and smiling, they hauled her inside and called the Prices and Shelly.

Duchess sat alone waiting, wishing Hal would walk down the hallway and straighten out her mess. Out the window she watched the Montana sky and wondered about Walk and the Cape, what kind of sky they saw that morning when everything changed once again.

Mrs. Price arrived crying, her husband's arm around her. "No more, we're not doing this anymore," she said between breaths, glaring at Duchess like she wanted the girl dead.

Mr. Price glared too, so Duchess flipped him off.

Shelly got there and hugged her. Duchess stood still and did not hug her back.

The adults convened in the principal's office, gold plaque on a door so heavy Duchess could make out nothing more than the odd raised voice. Mrs. Price going off, *out of my house, not one more night, safety of my own children.*

Duchess was called in once the Prices stepped out, looking away as they passed her, like she did not live beneath their roof. Shelly asked her about what she'd said about Mr. Price. She told the truth. She said it to shut Mary Lou up. Shelly backed her as best she could, the losing horse but still she threw support her way.

The principal was aghast, grave allegations, no place for violence in their school, she would not be welcome back.

Duchess flipped him off for good measure.

"You alright?" Shelly said, as they walked from the school.

"I'm alive." Duchess did not like leaving Robin there.

She climbed into Shelly's car and sat silent as they drove to the Price house.

Mrs. Price stood in their kitchen, on guard. Mr. Price had run Mary Lou to the emergency room to be checked over and see about her tooth. Threats were made, legal and otherwise. Duchess was ushered up to the attic to pack their belongings. It did not take long. Her case had been ready since the day they arrived.

She left the house without saying another word to Mrs. Price, who stood on the step, dabbing at her eyes.

Shelly drove in silence, back to the office, where she worked the phone madly while Duchess sat on an old wooden chair and watched hours pass by.

At three Shelly headed out and left Duchess under the watch of a couple of older ladies who smiled her way every ten minutes.

Shelly returned with Robin. He'd been crying.

At five they got a place. Shelly spoke without emotion, tired and beaten by a hundred other files, other cases, other lives just as lost.

"It's a group home," she said.

36

The house was grand, Greek revival, Doric columns so tall Duchess felt small beside them.

An acre of tended grass ran to quaking aspen bold green against spring sky. Duchess sat on a bench with Robin while planes wrote tracks into the sky. Shelly was inside, meeting with a large black lady named Claudette, and she seemed to run whatever it was that needed running. Youth Guidance Home.

Robin was quiet, resigned as they arrived at the house but nervous enough to keep hold of his sister's hand.

"I'm sorry." She said it with such sadness in her voice that he leaned his head on her shoulder for a moment.

There were other kids and they played a game of something complex, a ball and three hoops and a bat. Duchess watched for twenty minutes and couldn't figure out the rules. She knew the look in their eyes though, kids like her, the damned. They didn't offer smiles or nods, just went about their day like it would be a miracle if they made it through. There was a lady outside on the street, holding on to a girl no bigger than Robin and staring at the house. She had the wiry strung-out look of a user.

A half hour later they ate together in a dining room that smelled of

a hundred dinners choked down by a hundred kids. Robin pushed his
food around.

There was a communal lounge, a TV in the corner running a movie.
A couple of girls sat on a brown sofa and watched, eating popcorn but
mostly ignoring each other.

In the other corner was a chest spilling with toys, ranging from stack-
ing cubes to puzzles.

"Go play."

Robin walked over, head down, and picked up a storybook far too
young for him. He sat cross-legged on the floor, turning the page now
and then, miles away from his sister and that room.

In the hallway she found Shelly.

"I know what I did. I know I fucked up too bad . . ."

Shelly went to rub her arm but Duchess stepped back. "What will
happen now?"

"I don't—"

"Just say, Shelly. Just tell me what will happen to me and my brother."

"This home is for girls."

Duchess shook her head.

Shelly raised a calming hand. "Claudette will let you stay with Robin,
on account of his age."

Duchess breathed again. "What about Peter and Lucy?"

Shelly swallowed, looked away, at Robin, at anywhere but Duchess.

"Did you tell them?"

"I had to. Peter . . . he's a doctor. And Lucy, at the school. They, what
you said about Mr. Price. They can't risk the—"

"I get it."

"We'll keep looking. We just need to find the right fit."

"I don't fit anywhere."

The look in Shelly's eyes almost broke her.

Robin came out, and together they walked along the hallway and up
the stairs.

They passed bedrooms with kids inside, a girl reading a story aloud and her sister listening intently. The walls were colored, pastel shades of pink and yellow. Pictures tacked to corkboards, family shots of fallen families.

Their room had white walls and the corkboard was bare, their time there unwritten. Two beds Duchess would later push together, the covers striped with rainbow colors. An empty closet and chest, a wicker basket for their washing. The carpet was squares that fit together like puzzle pieces, easy to lift out if they got stained.

"You want me to help you unpack?" Shelly said.

"I got it."

Robin stood in the center of the room, looked up at the window, then pulled the drapes to cut falling light. He switched on the lamp and then climbed on the bed and curled away from them.

"When will Peter come?" he said.

Shelly looked at Duchess and Duchess told her alright, she should go now. Shelly said she would be back the next day to see them settled.

Duchess went over to him and put a hand on his back. "Peter and Lucy."

He turned then, sat up and stared at her. She said nothing more, just shook her head.

He reared fast, cursed her with every word he knew. He lashed out and caught her cheek hard. She kept her hands down, just closed her eyes as he yelled and screamed the kind of truths that no longer hurt her. She knew them already. She was a bad sister. She was a bad person. He cried so much he shook, his face in the pillow, screaming for a life so close that for a few, blissful weeks, he'd had it in his grasp.

Duchess waited for him to cry himself out. It took a long time. She felt blood on her cheek where he had caught her.

When he finally slept she took his sneakers off and covered him over. Then she worried she had not brushed his teeth.

That night she heard noise, someone as new as they were, across the hall in the small room. Crying, then Claudette and calming words.

Duchess scooted over into her brother's bed and watched him. She thought of Thomas Noble and how he would not be able to find them now. She did not know his address to write him. She could ask Shelly but she knew she would not. She was nothing more than a footnote in his life, in Dolly's, in Walk's. She left no lasting impression, her impact ugly but mercifully brief.

"Duchess." Robin sat upright.

"It's alright." She stroked his hair.

"I had a dream. That dream again. I can't work out what the voice is saying."

She lay him back down.

"Sometimes I forget where I am."

She placed her hand on his heart till he calmed.

"But you're here."

"I'm here," she said.

He reached up and touched her face. "Did I do that mark there?"

"No."

"I'm sorry."

"You never need say that to me."

Spring drifted toward the promise of summer. As Walk and Martha prepared for trial, the Radley children started at yet another new school, rode the bus with the other kids from the home, and settled into the rhythms of another, fettered life. Duchess still tended to Robin, cared for him like a mother but did so without fuss, setting about her tasks like it was all she was good for. She tried her best to smile for him, to push him on the swing and play his games, run around the big yard and help him climb the oak. But she could not outrun her mistakes, feeling they were destined to sink not only her but her brother too.

Shelly still made her visits, Robin smiling when her hair changed from pink to a cobalt blue. He asked after Peter and Lucy at every visit, even asked for their address so he could write. Duchess helped him with the letter. He told them he knew he and his sister were not the right fit for their family, and that it was okay. He asked after Jet, asked how hot it got over in Wyoming and how Jet kept himself cool. He signed off with love, then drew a picture of the group home, and of him and Duchess. Stick figures with wide bubble heads and straight mouths, as if deep in contemplation of what might have been. He made Duchess sign her name too. She scrawled *Duchess Day Radley, Outlaw* before he made her cross the last word out.

She received a postcard from Walk. He'd been in touch with Shelly and she'd filled him in. He wrote her about Cape Haven, how it was all quiet without her, his writing so small she almost could not read it.

The card was a shot of Cabrillo, Bixby Creek Bridge, the arc in Big Sur, the water below breaking so hard she could hear it. She tacked it to their corkboard, along with a letter that arrived from Peter and Lucy a week later. They said everything and nothing, told Robin it was hotter than Hades and Lucy had got sunburn tending the yard. Robin had made her read it five times, peppering her with questions she could not possibly know the answers to. They signed off with a drawing of their own, Robin and Duchess, from memory. Lucy was a decent artist, but she made the smiles a little too wide. Along with the letter they enclosed a photo of Jet. That night Robin slept with it by his nightstand, waking a couple of times and checking it was still there. The next day Duchess tacked it to the corkboard and their collection grew a little.

Duchess began to tentatively think of the future, not her own, but Robin's. Her grades fell again as she drifted toward the lower end of her class. The other children left her alone, knew she was from Oak Fair so might well be gone soon enough.

And then one day a boy named Rick Tide began to seek her out. It turned out Rick's cousin was Kelly Raymond, Mary Lou's sidekick. Rick had heard the story, then he gave it a dressing and sent it on its way. By the time it made it back to Duchess she'd been responsible for Mary Lou losing an eye. For her part Duchess let it slide, even when Rick tripped her in the lunch line and sent her and her food to the floor.

A day later she popped Rick hard enough to send him to the nurse.

Shelly was called and it was smoothed over. The principal knew enough about Rick Tide to keep it from spilling further.

She was excused for the day and Shelly took her into Main Street, where they sat outside a burger joint and drank shakes while the traffic crawled past. The road was coned for an upcoming parade. Flags were strung and a banner crossed from one building over the street to the opposite side.

"Berry Parade? Sounds about the shittiest parade I ever heard of."

Shelly smiled. "You know what today is?"

"I've been following." The first day of the trial, she'd been on the computer when the house slept, and she'd read all she could.

"You alright?"

"Sure. Hal said it'd be over quick. They'll put him to death."

Shelly sighed, her head tilted a little.

"Spill it," Duchess said.

"What?"

"Whatever it is you want to say."

Shelly hid her eyes behind sunglasses. "I never split siblings. They're always better off together."

"Jesse James and his brother Frank, they robbed banks from Iowa to Texas. Cops got their gang at Northfield, only the brothers escaped. They looked out for each other."

Shelly smiled. "I've been doing this job twenty years now. Worked all over. I've seen all sorts. They pass through, on their way out, on their way back in. I've placed hundreds, each time . . . I cried. I made it my life, and it should be. But—"

"There's no such thing as a bad kid, right?" A trace of panic in her voice.

"You're not bad, Duchess."

A truck pulled up, the same color as Hal's. Duchess felt the pain in her gut.

"Robin is six. That's a good age. That's a real good age, but it doesn't last. Hard as that is to say, and to think even."

Duchess set her milkshake down and stared into it.

"Do you know what I'm saying, Duchess?"

"I know what you're saying."

Shelly fished a tissue out of her bag, lifted her glasses and dabbed at her eyes. She looked older then, like the years had run her down, the weight of such privileged, abject responsibility night and day.

"I would die before I let go of my brother."

"It's not about letting go."

"It's about trusting his care to someone I've never met. And I've not met many decent people in my life. I don't like the odds."

"I get that."

"Is it a selfless act?"

Shelly looked up at her.

"Is it?" Her eyes desperate now. "Is it a selfless act to do that? He's so sweet, you know, he's so good and sweet and he needs a better sister than me. Can you give him that, Shelly? I'm losing him, he's turning hard. I can't let that happen. He gets up in the night and he needs me. He calls out. And if I'm not there—"

Shelly pulled her in and held her tight.

"Fuck."

"It's alright."

"It's not. None of it is."

"I would never do it to you, Duchess. I wouldn't do anything without talking to you first. And I can see this isn't right. Siblings need to stay together. I'll keep looking. We'll find the right fit. I promise I'll keep looking."

37

Walk and Martha drifted through three days so torturous they drove back to Cape Haven and lay awake in Walk's bed, unable to clear the picture that was being painted, the prisoner that spent thirty years planning revenge on the girl he could not have.

Opening statements were brief, plans laid out, seven minutes for Martha, eighteen for the district attorney, Elise Deschamps. Deschamps was impressive, lengthy list of credentials, smart clothes, black hair framed a pale face. Sincerity poured from her as she applauded the jury, told them she worked for them, for the state of California, and for Star Radley and her orphaned children. She was their voice, their justice. Proof would be overwhelming, the crime premeditated, cold-blooded. Vincent King was a murderer. He took the life of a child, then the life of a fellow prisoner. Killing came easy. They would see they had no choice but to find the man guilty, and, in doing so, pass on a sentence of death. It would not be easy, but she needed them. The Radley children needed them.

Deschamps was skilled, an alumna of Yale Law, flanked by two associates who watched and scribbled and nodded at the right times.

Clerks, bailiffs, the artist, the reporters. A small collection to watch a man's fate decided.

Despite the grand theories, the expert way Deschamps lulled the jury, the facts presented were hard and incontestable. She brought in the pathologist from the state crime lab, who reeled off qualifications so towering Martha moved to call yeah, he could be considered expert. Deschamps barked, Judge Rhodes handled things well enough. Walk smiled as Martha held her ground. He saw Vincent do the same.

The pathologist took them on the kind of journey that saw photos dealt, jurors shake heads, one cried. He detailed blows, hard enough to break three of her ribs. He tracked the path of the bullet, the kill shot, into the chest, likely she was dead before she hit the ground. Charts on easels, anatomy spelled out.

A fingerprint guy took them through prints lifted from the Radley house. Vincent King had been in the kitchen, hallway, living room. They lifted one from the front door. After an hour the jury tired. That Vincent King was at the scene was never in question.

Another expert, ballistics, a hired gun to talk guns. And then of the gun itself, though it could not be found, the bullet pulled from Star Radley's body was a .357 Magnum.

And then Deschamps ran, like they knew she would. She pulled out paper and waved it round like it was lit. Vincent King's father had a gun registered in his name, a Ruger Blackhawk. She asked the jury to guess the caliber, the type of bullet it fired. Walk watched them close and saw each of them follow the ball way out of the park.

On the cross Martha tried to score minor points by getting the guy to admit the .357 Magnum, though a little less common, could still be purchased widely. The damage had been done.

Deschamps went on to detail Star's life, difficult childhood, her younger sister's tragic death, and then her mother's own death. She recounted the events. Vincent King sat there impassive, only closing his eyes when she talked of the strip of woodland where they found that little girl's body. Left to die, cold and alone. And then on to the suicide of Star's mother, how Star had found her, how that might have felt. And, finally, brighter promise, troubled though she was, she doted on her children, Duchess and Robin, now settled into a group home in a town they did not know, at a school where they had to start over, a thousand miles from home. Another photo, the three together on the beach, Walk had taken it himself on a rare day of calm.

Walk was called as a state witness, along with a handful of first responders. As the first on the scene he took his seat in the hallowed hall, cleared his throat, and told the truth in all its ugliness. Blood on Vincent, calm in his voice. He did not slant detail, just laid it out and glanced at his friend now and then. Vincent offered him a slight smile. *It's alright, you do your job, Walk.*

After eight days the state rested. Walk and Martha went to the bar across from the courtroom, where they took a booth in the back and picked at fried shrimp fresh from the freeze.

"How's Vincent doing?"

"Oh he's just swell," Martha said. "I've got half a mind to put him on the stand, let the jury see how calm he is. We call insanity, padded cell for the rest of his life. Beats the needle, right?"

Walk picked up a shrimp, studied it, placed it back on the greased paper. "How long will you take?"

"A couple of days. I'll say my piece, call my people, and then they'll get the case and they'll put him to death." She stared into her soda.

"You're doing good, Martha. Really, you look good up there."

"Try not to look at my ass so much. It's predatory."

"It's the shoes that get me. Your commitment to Chuck Taylor."

She reached into her bag and pulled out a bottle of hot sauce.

"You're kidding me with this. You actually carry it with you."

"Doubles up as mace." She poured liberally. "You notice I'm wearing a cross." She pointed to her necklace. "Jurors three, nine, and ten, they're active churchgoers." She had done the consulting herself, sat through two days of torturous selection, struck a couple that'd likely volunteer to execute the man themselves, moved for liberals only to see Deschamps repay the courtesy.

"That gun." She sighed. "The bullet. Like it wasn't bad enough."

Walk took a steadying breath. "I have faith in you."

"You're just trying to get in my pants."

Walk noticed she seemed anxious the next morning. They stood when Rhodes came in, took his seat on the grand chair, between the flags.

Vincent sat up front in a cheap suit that Walk had picked out, no tie, he flat refused.

Martha called her own doctor first, Mr. Cohen. She'd helped his daughter out of a bind once, another sorry story of a deadbeat asshole with quick fists, but Cohen was grateful enough to repay his little girl's savior.

They went through photos of Star Radley's injuries, both noted the severity. And then the photographs of Vincent King's hands. Slight swelling on the right, but likely old, and likely from an altercation Vincent had gotten into a few days prior.

On cross Deschamps got Cohen to admit he could not say for sure when the swelling occurred, and that a man of Vincent's size could inflict injury just as easily with an open hand.

Martha moved on to the issue of gunshot residue, brought in her expert, a forensic scientist hired on Walk's dime, his savings amassed from a staid life dwindling. She was young but confident, held the room as she spoke. She ran them through the science, elemental composition, the chain reaction, the plume expelled during gunshot. No residue was found on Vincent King.

Martha looked on during cross, watched her expert admit the residue could have been washed off, the faucet was running after all, sweated off, not been there in the first place if Vincent King had left the room right after firing.

Walk took the stand once again. This time he smiled, admitted he was Vincent's childhood friend but that was a long time ago. He was actually the one who had turned him in all those years back. His duty was to uphold the law, and he wouldn't let anything get in the way of that.

And then Martha stepped to the front, took a breath, and fired her own kill shot.

The butcher.

Milton.

Deschamps narrowed her eyes and straightened up a little.

Martha had Walk detail Milton's early life, how his father was a butcher in the shop he went on to run. Walk said he was an outcast, the kind of kid that others crossed the street to get away from. Deschamps objected, cited hearsay, but the point was made.

That outcast had turned into a troubled adult. He was lonely, to the point where he often got talking to vacationers and asked them to go hunting with him. Yes, Milton liked to hunt. Martha detailed the weapons registered to him, the list was long and Walk watched the jurors exchanging glances.

"Would you say you were close to Milton?" Martha stood by the jury box as she spoke.

"I liked him. I felt bad for the guy, he always seemed a little desperate, but I just figured he was shy. He didn't have friends, no one he could call on."

"So he called on you?"

"Sometimes. We went hunting together, just the once, I like the eating but not the killing."

A couple of laughs.

"So he was proficient with these weapons."

"More than that. I saw him bring down a mule deer from a thousand yards. The man could shoot." Walk aimed his answer at juror one, who hunted the Mendocino, just like Milton used to.

Martha moved it on, establishing that Milton lived across from Star, how he used to lend her his truck and take out her trash.

"I thought it was decent of him," Walk said. "She had someone looking out for her."

"Someone other than you?"

"Yeah."

Walk met her eye then. She was doing well. He was proud of her.

Martha called their attention to exhibit C.

"Can you tell me what these are, Chief Walker?"

Walk ran them through it, what he'd found in Milton's bedroom. Some of the jurors shook their heads at them, photos of Star in various states of undress.

"And how many of these were there?"

Walk blew out his cheeks. "A lot. Hundreds. They were catalogued by date, going back far."

"An obsession."

Deschamps looked like she wanted to object but held tight.

"It looks that way," Walk agreed.

"Now you said Milton had a telescope."

"He said he liked to watch the stars." Walk said it even and waited for the jurors to catch it.

"But it wasn't trained on the sky?"

Deschamps stood, said nothing and sat again.

"So what did it aim at?"

"Star Radley's bedroom."

"And the cataloguing, did it run through last year?"

"Up to the night Star was murdered."

"And the photos from that night?"

"Missing. They haven't been found yet."

Martha eyed the jurors. "And what did Milton say when you asked him about it?"

"I didn't get the chance. We pulled his body out of the water last month."

Gasps then, loud enough for Rhodes to quiet them.

"He drowned," Walk said. "No sign of foul play."

"Suicide." Martha let the word hang there as Deschamps got to her feet and screamed her objection. Martha withdrew her remark, but not before it had registered with everyone in that courtroom.

Deschamps tried hard at redirect, color in her cheeks as she got

Walk to admit they hadn't found Milton's prints at the Radley house. He could've worn gloves. Walk didn't need to say it. The guy was a butcher, he wore gloves. There was no stretch required.

The mood was better in the bar that night. Walk ordered them burgers and they ate in contented silence. Martha looked tired, the pressure so great. They talked a little about Vincent, and how he hadn't reacted to Milton, just sat there like always, eyes down, ignoring the stares.

"It was a good day."

Martha chewed the straw in her soda. "It's still too much, Walk."

He looked up.

"There's too much to ignore. I don't want you to get your hopes up. This case was never winnable, but we've done all we can. Milton was fortunate, as bad as that sounds. But it'll take more. The gun, the bullet. The history there. The blood on his hands. Shit, I'd convict him if I didn't know him."

"But you do know him, right?"

"The jury don't."

He walked her out and stalled by her car. "You want to come back?"

"Closing arguments tomorrow. Early night for me."

Her watched her leave, then climbed into the cruiser and headed back to the station. It was late, Leah done, the place in darkness, but he hadn't stopped by since the trial began. He found a stack of papers on his desk, hit the lights and slumped back. He fished through the mail, opened a couple before he came to it. Verizon Communications. Darke's cell phone record. Boyd had come through for him.

There were pages going back a year, numbers so small Walk had to squint. He'd get back on it once the trial was done. He flipped them, eyes blurring as he yawned and stretched. He didn't expect to get anything.

But then he found the date, December 19, the day Hal died. It didn't register at first, his eyes glossing over digits he knew well enough.

He focused again, expected to see something different.

And then he dropped the paper to the desk.

The call to Darke's cell.

It had come from the Cape Haven Police Department.

She cried. He watched.

They sat in the yard, the Cape slept. She had been awake, the shadow beneath her eyes told him she did not sleep anymore.

She blinked dark tears of mascara.

A full moon above highlighted the sorrow. Leah Tallow wiped her eyes, sniffed, cried some more. He had walked over to the house in silence, trying to find another answer, desperately searching for it.

"You want to tell me?"

There was no attempt at lying. She stared at the grass, calm set in, like she'd been waiting. "We've struggled for a long time."

He drew a long breath, hoping to stave it off a moment longer, knowing once it came it would change things.

"It's money, Walk."

He watched the tortured look.

"Ed. The business, it's all gone."

"Gone?"

She looked up.

"Connect the dots for me here, Leah."

She stared back at the house. "Tallow Construction, it's been in Ed's family seventy years. He took it over from his father, who took it on from his grandfather. It used to turn a decent profit. It used to employ half the town. Jesus, Ed still has fifteen men. We pay them out of our savings most months.

"And then Ed's father died, and he left us the house, on Fortuna, second line. Not much, a lot for us, but not all that much in the real world."

"You could've sold the business, cut the loss."

"Ed wouldn't. He loves this town, Walk. Like you do. But we need the change, the new homes, the new money. And you blocked it, you and the others, you voted it down whenever you could."

"Last I heard it'll go through regardless."

"But it's too late for us now. You buried us, you know that."

He let that sit awhile, wondered at his role, his need to keep Cape Haven from moving on without him, without Vincent and Star and Martha.

"Darke?" he said.

Then she took a breath. "He bought the Fortuna house from us for cheap. In return he had the contracts lined up for Ed to pull it down, and the rest of the street. Construction. Ed would get them, all those homes, condos, it would save us, Walk. And save the Cape, the real Cape, the locals that were born here."

"But it's gone now. All of it."

"Not yet."

"I don't understand."

"The King house. The insurance. Duchess Radley has the tape. If she just gives it back to Darke then the insurance will pay out and we'll get it back."

He let that settle, his mind spinning. "How much?"

Leah swallowed. "All of it. The house, second charge on the company, credit cards and loans. Shit, everything, Walk. We couldn't even afford to keep me on, that's why I pick up all the extra shifts at the station."

Walk watched the moon, then glanced back at the house. "Does Ed know what you did?"

"No. I keep the books. Ed is a fucking idiot. He thinks I don't know, the women, always perfume on him."

"You sold out a child."

She shook her head, the tears falling faster. "He wouldn't hurt her. You don't know Darke."

He wanted to take her hand, despite everything, he'd known her a lifetime. He steeled himself. "How did you find them?"

Emotion left her, she went on, callous facts laid bare. "The call. I knew it was Montana, I filed your receipts. The gas station. And then Hal said the name of the school on the phone with you. And the lake by the farm."

"You listened in?" he said, stunned. The facts took his breath away, he rubbed his eyes, the back of his neck, felt the heat in his cheeks. He stood, felt his knees weak and sat again. "Your hands are bloody, Leah. And for what? For your husband's business."

"For them," she said, loud, and pointed at the house. "For my kids. For all the families we support in this town. It's just a tape, a fucking tape, Walk. Duchess burned the club down. We all knew it, but you didn't do anything about it."

"That's not—"

"It is, Walk. You know it is. You and Star and your fucking misguided loyalty to Vincent King. Star was his girl, you promised to watch out for her. I know that. You told me you'd do anything for your friends. Same as in high school. If you did your job, if you brought the girl in and—"

"Where's Darke now?"

"I don't know."

He watched her.

"I don't. I swear it."

"Duchess. He's still looking for her?"

"It's about the money with him, it's always about the money. He wouldn't stop, with my help or without."

He thought of Martha then, at home running over her closing argument.

"He killed a man. That's on you."

She cried hard. "I can't think of that."

"Shit, Leah."

"There's people in our lives that we'd do anything for. You know that better than anyone."

That night he walked the streets of the Cape till sun breached the night sky and the day found him. He stopped by the Radley house, Milton's place, Main and Sunset. He stood by the King house and thought of it being knocked down. Even if Darke didn't come through with the money, someone else would buy it for less. He thought of shooting hoops on the driveway, of hiding out in the old attic and looking at Rich King's *Playboys*. There was a chance they had it right, that Milton had done what Martha said. Maybe Vincent was institutionalized, or maybe he just hated himself so much that he'd rather be put to death than go on living as a free man. There were still so many questions without answers. Walk knew there was a chance he'd colored it a shade it never was, but still, he felt it in his bones. Vincent King was innocent. And he wouldn't leave it to chance. Not anymore. He'd come so far, he would get to the finish, even if it cost him his soul.

38

That morning Walk stood in front of the mirror and shaved.

He watched the basin fill, his face emerged, pale, gaunt, sick. He did not dwell, just splashed his cheeks with icy water and took a long and heavy breath. And then he drove to Las Lomas, took his seat, and ignored the looks and whispers.

Leah Tallow was led in.

She looked calm, makeup hid the night before, simple dress, heels. She met Walk's eye as she passed, he did not smile.

Martha ran her background, how she'd worked admin at Cape Haven PD for fifteen years, sometimes dispatch. Part of the furniture, like Walk and Valeria. She spoke confidently, stuttered a couple times, but Walk could see the jury liked her. He'd called her early, told her everything, she'd agreed in a second. A truce of some kind, the repercussions could wait, but this could not. And then he'd called Martha and told her. And in her voice he heard the doubts, and he knew with some certainty that he was jeopardizing everything they both held dear.

"The system . . . it's a running joke. Let's just say Walk likes things how they were, not how they should be."

Martha smiled at Walk, who raised his eyebrows. Juror seven caught it and laughed.

"So I've been trying to overhaul it for years now, trying to get the file room sorted out. See, they brought in new templates four years back, new forms and coding. And the way Walk does it . . . I mean, there is an order. Organized chaos."

Deschamps stood, Rhodes moved it on, Martha apologized.

"So I've been at it three months now. I'm up to 1993, and that's when I found it."

Martha held up the paper. Deschamps objected, the judge called them over to the bench. Walk heard heat in Deschamps's voice, red face as she turned, shook her head once and returned to her seat. Rhodes allowed it into evidence.

"Can you tell me what it is?" Martha said.

"It's a break-in report from November 3, 1993. Number One Sunset Road, the residence of Gracie King."

"Vincent King's home. The house he returned to after his release."

"Yes."

"Does it say what was stolen?"

"Yes. Chief Walker was thorough, like always. He went through it with Gracie King, Vincent's mother. Turned out she forgot to lock the safe. They took two hundred dollars in cash, a gold brooch, and some diamond earrings. And a handgun."

"A handgun?"

"Yes. A Ruger Blackhawk."

Murmurs, till Rhodes quieted them. Deschamps went back to the bar, argued some more with the judge. It got heated enough for Rhodes to call a fifteen-minute break.

Walk took the stand next, did not need to introduce himself or run his credentials again. Martha ran him through the break-in. He spoke with calm. He did not meet Vincent's eye once, though he felt the stare.

And then Deschamps was up. "I feel a little blindsided here."

"Leah only found it last night. She works evenings sometimes, when her husband can be home with the kids. It bothers her more than me, the system, I know where everything is."

"So, Chief Walker, if you know where everything is, how come you didn't bring this to our attention earlier?"

"I forgot about the break-in."

"You forgot?" She looked at the jury, confusion on her face. "You grew up with Vincent King. You knew the family. You used to visit him in prison. It doesn't strike me, with all that's going on, as something you'd forget."

Walk swallowed and took a last breath. He knew it would change after. All of it.

"I'm sick."

He looked around the room, reporters at the back, a line of watchers. He felt the quiet, the eyes on him.

"I have Parkinson's disease. My memory is not what it was. I haven't told anyone yet, thought I could deal with it. I guess I . . . I guess I didn't want to lose my place."

He glanced at the jury and saw compassion. And then across at Vincent, who watched him with sad eyes.

And then he looked down at the break-in report, and he knew that if they studied it, if they looked hard enough, they'd see a slight lean to the scrawl, like it was written with a shaking hand.

• • •

Closing statements began at five. Rhodes said he'd rather give the jury the case late than move into another day. Martha was up first, and she took the floor, every eye on her. She didn't use notes. Walk could imagine she'd had a late night. She was brief, she detailed the facts. She spoke of Star and the tragedy that became of her. She talked of the Radley children, and how they deserved justice, but for the right person. And then Milton, the facts could not be denied. She painted a portrait so tragically accurate that the jurors sat mesmerized. And then on to Vincent. She asked them to imagine entering the prison system at fifteen years old, a frightened child in a prison with the darkest men. She spoke of his regret, his battle to serve the hardest time he could. Maybe he was institutionalized, maybe he did kill a man in self-defense. And maybe he did make the kind of mistake you don't ever deserve to recover from. But that didn't mean he'd killed Star Radley. And his silence did not speak of guilt, but rather of a crushing self-hatred that burned so fierce he'd rather be punished for another's crime than take his place in a world where the child he'd killed could not.

...

A thousand miles from that courthouse, Robin found the yellow flower from a rabbitbrush and brought it back. Duchess helped him flatten it, then pin it to their board, beside Jet. She placed an arm around him, her mind elsewhere. Rick Tide had begun again, trying for a rise, a kid that did not know when to quit. He'd spit on her back, told her that was from Mary Lou. She'd gone to the bathroom and washed her shirt, thought of Walk and how he'd told her to be good.

That evening after they ate Duchess took Robin out to the swing set in the big garden and pushed him before a sun that sat blazing beyond the trees. He squinted and smiled, and she told him he was a prince.

Then she helped him ready for bed, brushed his teeth and read him a chapter from a story about a pig named Wilbur and a spider named Charlotte.

"He's an emotional pig," Robin said.

"He is."

That night they said a prayer. Robin looked over to his sister and she made him close his eyes and steeple his fingers.

"Why did we pray tonight?" he asked.

"Just checking in."

After he fell asleep she crept from the room. She passed the beds, the forgotten children slept, dead to the world for those precious hours when they could forget their place and occupy another. The room in darkness, just the television glow. She flipped channels till she found the right news station, and she watched as reporters gathered outside the courthouse.

She'd called Walk, collect, he sounded beat as he told her the jury would think on it, that they could come back anytime at all. She guessed it would be soon.

Her mind ran to her mother, to the past year and all that had come with it.

She turned and saw her brother standing in the doorway, his eyes fixed on her.

"You're not in the bed."

"Sorry."

He walked over and sat beside her, and they watched scenes so distant it was hard to believe their connection.

They saw reporters fill, cut to commercials. In silence she sat and wondered what was on her brother's mind. When they returned they ran through the trial and detailed things they did and did not know about their mother and about Vincent King. When the verdict flashed red she sat up, heart beating fast.

"What does it say?"

"They said he didn't kill Mom."

She watched, mouth slightly open, as the reporter found a juror. The man looked tired but still managed a smile. He detailed the testimony of the Cape Haven chief of police. How the cop had found a break-in report that showed the suspected murder weapon, a gun once owned by the suspect's father, could not have been in the possession of Vincent King. The jury had been on the fence, it gave them the out they needed.

She got a pain in her stomach then, so bad she pressed a fist to it. "Walk. What the fuck did you do, Walk?"

Robin nestled close and she kissed his head, questioning everything she thought she knew about the world. It had tilted on her again, the concept of truth, the implausibility of fair.

And then they saw him.

And Robin stood.

On the screen, accompanied by a small woman in a smart suit and Chuck Taylors, was Vincent King.

The room lit with the flash of the city's camera. An innocent man being led to a waiting car.

"What is it?" she asked her brother.

He shook, his whole body trembled as he struggled for breath.

He began to cry as dark pooled and spread from his pants.

She dropped to her knees. "Robin. Talk to me."

He shook his head, clenched his eyes closed tight.

"It's alright. I'm here."

"It's him." Breathless. Crying. "I remember."

She cupped his face gently. "What do you remember?"

He stared past her, at the screen. "Vincent was in my bedroom. I remember what he said."

She wiped his tears as he finally met her eye. "He told me he was sorry for what he'd done to Mom. He told me to say nothing or I'd regret it." He closed his eyes and sobbed. She held him tight.

She led him back to the room, put him in the tub and showered him off, then dressed him in fresh pajamas and tucked him into the bed.

He slept.

And then she packed.

In her bag she found a photo of Star with them, one of so few, in their yard barefoot and laughing. She tacked it to the corkboard, along with a photo of Hal.

She cracked the blind to stars, and then took her seat at the foot of his bed, where she sat for night hours so long and quick as she recounted their time. She thought of his birth, first steps and words. All the ways he made her laugh. His first day of school, how she taught him to toss a football in their small yard.

She stayed till first light. He would not wake alone in the dark.

She pulled her bag to the door and propped it gently open. Then she returned once more, and she held back her tears till she could no longer breathe, cursed herself and pulled at her hair like the mad girl she was. If she'd had a knife she would have cut herself deep. She deserved it to hurt. She deserved all the pain.

She leaned, kissed her brother's head, told him to be good as she slipped from his life, like so many before.

39

Walk sat at his desk, found the bottle of Kentucky in the drawer, unscrewed the cap and took a long drink.

He closed his eyes to the burn, didn't feel all that much like celebrating. Vincent had gone right home. He did not speak on the ride, he did not smile, just shook hands with Martha May. Walk told her she did good, met her eye and knew that Martha knew. Victory was hollow. The district attorney had stormed from the courtroom.

He drank a little more, till the night softened, his shoulders dropped, his body stopped exhausting him.

He looked over at the stack of papers piled high on his tray, going back a year, mostly routine. He had ignored all but Vincent King and Darke. The one thing they hadn't lied about at trial was the state of Walk's office.

He pulled the stack and began to thumb pages, Valeria's scrawl, traffic violations, vandalism, possible trespass. He found it hard to focus, hard to recognize what used to be routine. He caught a couple of memos from state, and then, among it all, he saw a message from a Doctor David Yuto, returning his call.

Walk scanned his mind, the frustration growing before he settled on the autopsy of Baxter Logan, the man Vincent had killed in Fairmont.

He checked his watch, saw it was late but dialed the number. The man answered on the first ring, turned out Yuto was working his last week, preparing things for his successor, two decades younger, more than a lifetime less experienced. They made a little small talk. Walk ran over the Logan case. It took Yuto a minute to locate the file.

"What more do you need to know?" Yuto said.

"I don't . . . I guess the detail. I just wondered—"

"We weren't as stringent back then. No DNA to look for. I noted cause of death. Head trauma."

Walk sipped his whisky, his feet on the old desk. "So that was it. One punch and—"

"Not one punch. Not the way Logan looked."

Walk stared into the glass.

"I remember Cuddy called. Of course he was young then, he hadn't yet taken over from his father. But he told me not to waste that much time on Logan. Sex offenders aren't all that popular at Fairmont. I noted cause of death and moved on to the next."

"The beating . . . was it bad?"

Yuto sighed. "It's been a long time but some of them, you just don't forget some of them. Teeth gone, both eye sockets shattered. His nose was broken so badly it pressed flat to his face."

"But it was a fight. Vincent King was fighting for his life."

"I'm not sure what you want me to say here, Chief Walker. It was a fight, but Logan was beaten long after it was over."

Walk's mind ran to Star, three ribs snapped like that. He thanked Yuto and hung up.

He swallowed, tasted the whisky still, his throat drying up, heart beginning to race away. He stood, left the station and made the walk, night now, nothing to see but distant light riding the waves, the steady pull of boats crossing the bay.

He breathed salt wind, moved slow enough, tried collecting his thoughts, but they ran and formed pictures he did not want to see. Along Brycewood Avenue, neighbors he knew from the summers before, when the town was his.

He stopped at the end of Sunset when he saw Vincent across the street, back to him, moving fast, dark jeans and shirt. He thought of calling out, instead followed, far enough back. He wondered how the man felt, death to life.

Along the street and up, two minutes and Vincent climbed over the gray wall, dry laid stone, jagged against soft streetlight. He walked up to the wishing tree, not breaking stride, just bent quick, and then he was up, glancing back and around.

A car at the top of the street, falling headlights up and over the hill. Walk moved into the shadow, Vincent, spooked, moved on, at pace, away from the beams, into the night.

Walk watched the car pass, and then he climbed the wall and dropped to long grass. At the tree he felt around blind, then took out his cell and lit the base.

The hole, close to the dirt, small enough to miss.

He knelt, reached a hand in, and pulled out a gun.

40

"Those footprints on the moon," Thomas Noble said. "The Apollo astronauts made them and they'll stay there for at least ten million years."

She saw sky no longer endless. She knew about souls and the prophetic, about divine reunion and a world to come. She tried not to think of Robin, if he woke that morning frightened. She swallowed a lump of such bitter shame she almost cried out.

"Where will you go?"

"I have business to attend to."

"You could stay here."

"No."

"I could come with you."

"No."

"I'm brave. I took a blue eye for you."

"For that I will always be grateful."

They lay at the end of his yard, the woodland behind made shadows of them.

"What you've been through," he said. "It isn't fair."

"You sound like a child. The notion of fair." She closed her eyes.

"You know nothing good will come of any of this."

A star bled from the sky. She did not make a wish. Wishing on stars was for children, and Duchess knew she was no longer one of those. She wondered if she ever had been.

"All these people," Duchess said. "They spend a lifetime looking to the sky and asking questions. Does God intervene, and if he doesn't, why do they still pray?"

"Faith. The hope that he will."

"Because otherwise life is too small."

He spoke again quietly. "I worry you won't find a way back."

Duchess watched the moon.

"I used to ask God about my hand. Why? That kind of thing. I used to pray I'd wake up normal. You know what, those were wasted prayers."

"Maybe they're all wasted."

"Stay here with me. I'll hide you."

"I have to do something."

"I want to help you."

"You can't."

"You want me to just let you go alone. Is that brave?"

She took his good hand and they linked fingers. She wondered what it would be like to be him, his troubles so slight, his mother in the house sleeping, his future so unblemished, so wide open like that.

"They'll look for you."

"Not all that hard. Another welfare runaway."

"You deserve to be found. And what about Robin?"

"Please," she said, so close to the edge. "They might come see you. Cops. They might come ask you where I am and where I'm going. You'll think about telling, that you know what's best."

"And if I do."

"You don't."

She lay till morning. Mrs. Noble left early, dressed in workout gear, her Lexus creeping silent from the driveway as Thomas Noble opened the back door.

Duchess went into the Noble house, washed up and ate cereal.

There was a safe, Thomas Noble took fifty dollars and handed it to her. She fought to say no, he stuffed the bills into her hand.

"I'll pay you back."

She filled her bag with a couple of cans, beans and soup. She moved fast, saw Shelly was moving faster because the telephone rang and the machine picked it up.

They listened.

"She sounds worried."

"She has a thousand more like me."

At the door she saw bags ready to be packed. Thomas Noble would go on vacation in a few days. He would forget her. His life would go on. She smiled at that thought.

Outside the street woke, garbage truck at one end, mailman at the other.

Thomas Noble wheeled out his bicycle and leaned it against the gate. "Take it."

She went to say no but he placed a hand on her shoulder. "Just take it. You'll get further before they pick you up."

"I'll be a ghost. I already am."

"Will I see you?"

"Yeah." They both knew it was a lie, but he let it go, leaned forward and kissed her cheek.

She got on the bike, bag over her shoulder, all she had in the world.

"Later, Thomas Noble."

He raised his good hand as she rode down his driveway and into the street. Then she pedaled hard, not looking back, wind streaking her face as she left the light roads behind and sought out the dark.

An hour and she was on Main Street. She left the bike out front of Jackson Hollis Funeral Parlor and stepped inside, the central air hitting her so hard her skin pricked.

"Duchess," Magda said with a smile. "Nice to see you again." Magda ran the place with her husband, Kurt, a man that shared pallor with his clientele. He must have been with someone because the drape was pulled, the coffins hidden.

"I wanted to collect my grandfather's ashes."

"I wondered when you'd come. Shelly said she'd bring you one day."

"She's in the car." Duchess nodded toward a Nissan across the street, parked at an angle that blocked the view.

Magda headed out back and returned a minute later with a small urn.

Duchess took it, turned to leave as the drapes parted and Dolly came out, Kurt behind. Duchess slipped out and onto the sidewalk, made it almost to Cherry's before Dolly caught up with her.

"Duchess."

Dolly led her inside and sat her down in the corner. She went to the counter and ordered for them.

Dolly had aged, makeup not quite so perfect, hair not curled so neat. She still wore the names, Chanel bag and shoes.

"I'd say it's nice to see you back here."

"But."

Dolly smiled.

"I'm sorry about Bill. I didn't know."

"He was ready. Turned out I was not."

Duchess's bag lay open, the clothes, the cans. She pulled it closed and zipped it.

Dolly looked at her with sadness.

"What will you do now?" Duchess asked.

"Bury my husband. Beyond that I haven't given it much thought. There were trips, places we wanted to see. I don't know if I'll do it alone. But he had a good life, that's all we can ask, right?"

"Thomas Noble talks about fair."

Dolly smiled. "I get that."

"Fair means someone is in control."

"I heard about the man. It was on the news. I thought of you, and of Robin. Maybe that's what Thomas Noble meant. About how someone goes through life causing pain to others, and some people just try and get on. The two always seem to collide."

Duchess thought of Dolly, her life, her father, impression cast. "Hal said that man was the cancer of our family. His reach is far, to me and Robin. To my brother. I can't . . ."

Dolly reached over and closed a hand over hers. "Maybe you don't choose who you get to be. Maybe it's predefined. Some of us are outlaws. Maybe we find each other,"

"And maybe it's all nothing. No one in control but the person willing to go out and take what they want."

"Do you know about justice, Duchess?"

"Three-Fingered Jack. He rode five hundred miles to avenge the death of his partner, Frank Stiles."

"But what do you think it means? And I don't mean defined, I mean what do you think it means for the people that get hurt."

"An end. I could take it back to breathing. But I know that's not enough."

"And for Robin? What do you think he wants?"

"He's six. He does not know what he wants. He does not know a world beyond the immediate."

"And you?"

"I know too much."

The waitress came over with two cocoas and a small cupcake with a single candle in it. She placed them down, winked at Duchess, and then returned to the counter.

"Happy birthday, Duchess."

Duchess stared at the cake. "You didn't need to—"

"Hush, now. It's not every day a girl turns fourteen. You need to make a wish."

When she realized Dolly would not quit, she leaned forward, closed her eyes and blew.

Outside they walked the shaded side of the street. When they got to the funeral parlor Duchess picked up the bicycle and wheeled it along.

Dolly stopped beside her truck. "There's a lot I should say here."

"But nothing I don't already know."

"Will you come back to the house? There's something I'd like to show you."

"I can't. I have to get on."

"Another time."

"Sure."

Dolly took her hand. "Promise me you'll stop by one day."

"I will."

"And I know you'll make good on that. An outlaw is only as good as her word."

Dolly looked frail then, written with concern, like Duchess was even close to being her problem.

"I can check on Robin."

Duchess nodded, a slight tremble in her lower lip. She would have to get tougher for what would come.

"You stay safe, Duchess."

And then Dolly reached into her bag and took out her purse. As she began counting out bills Duchess got on the bicycle and rode.

She turned at the end of Main.

She waved and Dolly raised a hand.

Duchess made it to Radley land an hour off noon, legs burning, T-shirt damp through, hair slicked down. She buried the bike in grassland by the gates and walked slowly up the winding driveway, beneath the praying trees, beside the dead water.

She thought of Robin, if he was at school now, if Shelly was with him. It took all she had not to break from her path, return, and fall to her knees and take him in her arms. She'd kept one photograph, him smiling, a year back when his hair was longer. She took it from her bag as she climbed the old porch steps and sat on the swinging seat.

There was a board back on the gates, SULLIVAN REALTY. There would be an auction one day in the future and someone else would move in, take care of the land, run the same tired circle. In the distance Duchess watched elk, clustered like always at the foot of the hills. The fields needed tending. She thought of Hal out there, a lifetime alone.

At the red barn she opened the door and saw his tools still where they were, nothing of value to anyone. She crossed into the shade and walked to the rug and dragged it back.

She pulled up the door in the floor, it was heavy. Sweat dripped from her chin. She propped it and walked down the steps.

A low store. Guns on shelves, a rifle rack.

An old leather chair, Hal's place where he could be alone.

Beside was a small table, and on it a thick stack of letters. She thumbed them, settled on the last and opened it, and as she did, two papers fluttered to the ground. She picked them up, two halves of a check. She pressed them together, swallowed dry, a million dollars. Post-dated, a couple months after the trial was due to start. The signature was simple, more like print. Richard Darke. On the back she saw Vincent had endorsed it, signed it straight over to Hal.

She placed it all back, thought of the cost of atonement, warmed by the thought of her grandfather ripping it in two.

She stood.

Across she saw boxes.

She walked over, took a knee when she saw the colored wrapping paper. Gifts. She checked the tags, saw her own name scrawled, and then her brother's. There were dates on each, going back each of her years. She sat back on the low rung and tore one open. A doll. Then another. A puzzle. She did not open any of Robin's.

She stalled at the last one, dated that day. She opened it with care, took the lid from it, and swallowed when she saw what was inside.

She lifted the hat out and admired it. Leather studs on the band, vented crown and four-inch brim. She thumbed the tag, the intricate gold.

John B. Stetson.

And then, slowly, she placed it on her head, the fit perfect.

She took two guns, hers and one of his. She took a box of bullets, the kind he'd shown her.

When she was done she placed everything back, loaded her bag, and felt the weight.

His ashes drifted away by the water, in the spot where they sometimes sat.

She steeled herself and dipped her hat. "So long, Grandpa."

41

Walk spent a day dodging calls from above. News traveled quick, he would be summoned to Governor Hopkins's office where they'd talk over his replacement, no doubt offer him a desk job. Three calls so far that day, like they ran with the assumption he was nowhere near fit to serve.

He sat at his desk, the file spread out, Milton's bloated face staring at him. The man had no family to speak of, only a distant aunt that lived in a care facility in Jackson. He'd called, she'd claimed she did not know a Milton.

He looked up when he saw her at the door, tried a smile but it was hard.

Martha closed the door behind.

"You been dodging my calls, Chief?" She said it with a smile.

"Sorry, I've been busy here."

She sat, tilted her head and raised her eyebrows. "Truth?"

"I haven't been able to face you."

"You hustled."

"But I didn't want to hustle you."

She crossed her legs. "I'll get over it. We both went into this with our eyes open, right."

"I think me more than you."

"I've got business coming in now. Fuckers on death row want me to run their appeals. Forget it. Give me deadbeat men and broken-down women. They're my bread and butter." She ran a hand through her hair, and he watched every move.

She reached over, tried to take his hand but he drew it back.

"Talk to me," she said.

"When we started this, I only saw the end. I saw Vincent walking free and the clock rolling back. That was enough for me. That was my endgame. I'm sick, Martha. My cells, they're dying. What's happening, this is the early stage, it's just the start."

"I know that."

"Do you? I've read up, spoken to the doctor, seen others in the waiting room further down the line than me."

"So what are you saying?"

"I don't want you to be a carer. I want more for you. I always did."

She stood. "You sound like my father. Like I'm some little girl that doesn't get a say in her own life. I choose . . . you're my choice. And I thought I was yours."

"You are."

"Bullshit. You choose yourself, your fucking noble, dependable self."

He looked down.

She wiped her eyes. "I'm not sad, I'm mad. You're a coward, Walk. That's why you left it all this time."

"I didn't think you'd want to see me."

"Well, I did."

"I'm sorry."

"Don't fucking say that. All these years you could've reached out, come seen me, shit, even picked up the phone. It was Vincent that made you, like he always did."

"That's not—"

"When I asked you about the Vincent you remembered, you highlighted the good and didn't say shit about all the times he fucked Star over. All the girls, all the times she cried on my shoulder. You used to cover for him, even lied to me. You always covered for him."

"It didn't mean anything."

"I know that. I'm just saying, you've lived the past thirty years for someone else. Isn't it time you stopped?" She strode to the door, then stopped and turned and jabbed a finger toward him. "When you're done, when the pity party is over and you find your balls again, you call me."

The door opened and Martha brushed past Leah Tallow, who turned and watched her leave.

"Is she alright?"

He stood, closed the door and ushered Leah into the chair opposite. She wore no makeup, hair pulled up, face drawn.

He took his seat.

"Are you sure you want to do this, Walk?"

"Yes."

He watched as she dialed from a burner cell.

Darke did not answer. Leah waited for the mechanical voice mail.

"I know where they are. Call me." Leah's voice caught as she spoke. Tears fell as she cut the connection.

"When he calls back you give him this address. You tell him the kid is friends with Duchess and might know where to find her." Walk slipped her a piece of paper, the handwriting just about legible.

"Don't do this, Walk. I'll speak to Boyd. I'll tell him everything."

He watched her, what was left, and he tried to hate her but could not.

• • •

She knew to head south, to the bigger town, Fort Pryor, where there was a bus station. She did not know how far fifty bucks would get her, she guessed not far enough. Maybe Idaho, Nevada if she was lucky. She decided right off to look no further than the day ahead, any more and the task at hand reared up and pushed her back.

She rode single tracks, kept her pace slow. When the climbs began she got off and pushed, when they dropped she went with them, hand pulling the brake, cautious.

Montesse, Comet Park, areas of outstanding beauty all hidden by enveloping trees and shadow. Pretty houses spaced far apart, yellow signs calling for votes on Keystone Pipelines that would pump life into stalling towns, the few trucks outside a grocery store nothing more than the twitch of death.

Two miles from anywhere she got a flat. A blow that brought her close to tears. She tried to move onward, the bike slow now, each pedal double the effort.

She cursed as she dumped Thomas Noble's bicycle in the woodland beside Jackson Creek.

She sat on a fallen tree, ate bread already turning hard, drank the rest of her water, then moved off on foot, her sneakers not up to the land, the skin pulled from both heels.

She passed farmhouses and patchwork fields, every shade of green and brown, Trinity churches that still had bells and people to ring them. For a mile she trailed an old couple, rambling gear, long sticks and easy smiles. She listened to each of their steps; though she kept off the trail she at least had some sense of direction. They would be heading somewhere. She was still sure it was south.

She lost them, cursed again, feeling weak and thrown.

She came to a road so big and long and empty that she stopped beside and tilted her head toward the sky.

And then the old couple reappeared. Hank and Busy from Calgary. Retired, vacation, staying at motels and hiking trails, looking through old eyes at new sights.

She fell into step with them, gave them half a story, how her mother was sick and she was heading into the hospital in Fort Pryor to see her. They gave her water and a candy bar.

Busy spoke about her grandchildren, seven of them scattered, a banker in the Far East, a doctor in Chicago. Hank walked in front like he was scouting the land, moving branches for the ladies, his neck red from the sun.

Hank noticed her limp, soon had her on the grass while he fished through his bag and found pads that he taped to her heels.

"Poor girl."

They moved again. Hank had a map and he pointed out Lake Tethan.

"Another lake," Busy said and made eyes at Duchess.

"I used to live in a town called Cape Haven. When I was small."

"That's a pretty name," Busy said. She had powerful calves, hiking legs. A broad face, handsome not soft. "Do you remember it well?"

Duchess batted blackflies from her face as they emerged on another trail. "No."

They crossed Route 75 and took a road not wider than a truck. She did not question as Hank moved with such purpose. They were staying half a mile out of Fort Pryor and would get her there safely. She was due luck. Long due.

"Do you have any siblings?" Busy asked.

"Yes."

Duchess saw Busy wanted to ask more, saw it in the sad smile and watery eyes. She let it go and the moment drifted high above them.

An hour of walking and they came to a set of gates at the curve of a road that climbed so far its end could not be seen. Beside honeysuckle and flowers that were dying they pushed through because Hank said they should stop for a little bit.

The house emerged large and stately. They walked to the front and looked up at the stone, blocks bigger than her head, windows ornate and pretty.

Hank looked around and Duchess watched him, clutching her bag tight and checking her guns.

"The house is Attaway, Hank likes architecture."

Hank pulled out a camera and snapped off a dozen shots.

They circled to the back and saw neat, long bodies of water that stretched to woodlands.

"Smoke," Busy said and pointed.

It rose from a fire by the clearing. Another couple, same age, same look in their eyes. Like they'd found heaven a decade before they were due. Introductions were made,

Nancy and Tom from North Dakota, had an RV back at Hartson Dam but wanted to see the Attaway house.

They ate grilled hamburgers. Duchess thought of Robin, checked her watch and saw he would be eating now, alone. He would not eat without her. She got a pain in her stomach so bad she clutched it.

At sunset they made it to the motel. Fort Pryor was a ten-minute walk. Hank filled her hands with candy bars and another bottle of water. Busy hugged her tight and told her she'd pray for her mother.

Duchess walked downtown, her feet aching a little less. Dark fell on the mountain behind, a couple of lights, a diner, Stockman and Bob's Outdoor.

She found the bus station on the corner, across from a body shop, a line of shiny cars, streetlight bouncing from their hoods. Inside was a black lady at the counter, not busy enough for Duchess's liking. She guessed Shelly would have called the cops and maybe they would've taken a look at the farm, spoken to Thomas Noble, but she doubted they'd have put anything more together.

"How far can I get with fifty bucks?"

The lady peered over her glasses. "Which way you heading?"

"South. California."

"You alone? You don't look old enough to—"

"My mother is sick. I have to get home."

She watched Duchess, tracing her features for something, the lie maybe. Decided she didn't care enough so turned to her computer.

"Buffalo, it'll set you back forty."

There was a map behind Plexiglas. Duchess found Buffalo.

It looked a long way but nowhere near far enough.

"It doesn't leave till morning. You want to think on it?"

Duchess shook her head, pushed her money over the counter.

"We're closing up soon," she said, as Duchess eyed the cushioned bench. "You got somewhere to go?"

"Yes."

She handed over the ticket.

"Where do I go from there?"

"You want the quickest or the cheapest?"

"Do I look like I got more money?"

A frown, then another look at the screen. "Cheapest seats I got is Denver. Then Grand Junction, on to LA. Long way, girl. Still a lot of money."

Duchess left the bus station. She had seventeen dollars, a bag with two guns, a little food, and a change of clothes.

Outside a bar named O'Sullivan's she found a pay phone, picked up the receiver but realized she did not have anyone to call. She wanted to speak to Robin, not even speak, just listen to him while he slept. She wanted to kiss his head and pull him close, sleep with her arm around him.

She found a park, a cluster of trees and a playground. She slipped into the woodland and lay back on the grass. In her bag she found a sweater and spread it over herself.

At an hour when the town still slept she hiked the half mile, each step heavy, leaden, every muscle resisting.

The motel was quiet, not even a clerk, not anyone at all. BIG SKY sign, COLOR TVS, VACANCY. She walked along the lot, family cars in front of each door, a cluster of trees that rose high above the low roof of dark tile. Drapes over the glass, she moved to the door with the Bronco in front. Calgary plates. Hank and Busy, their window wide open, that was them, unworried.

She laid her bag down and took the gun from it. And then she said a silent prayer as she climbed through and into their room.

A shape that was Hank, sheet covering him, dead to the world, a day of hiking would do that. Just enough light to make her way to the chair, where his pants lay. She fished the pocket, found a wallet, a photo of smiling children inside. She could not swallow as she slipped the bills from inside, could not breathe because her chest ached.

And then she saw Busy, eyes open and sad. Duchess reached behind and felt the gun tucked into her jeans. The old lady said nothing.

Duchess was broken as she left.

It was her job to remind them, to let them know the world was not good.

42

Walk sat in a rental at the end of Highwood Drive.

A line of single-family houses, big, expensive, German cars on every drive. He wore his uniform but sank low in his seat. Beside him, empty coffee cups, no food. He'd made the drive, the thousand miles. He thought of flying, facing his fear, but he needed his gun so he left that fight for another time.

The Noble house was empty, Thomas and his family on their annual vacation. Duchess once told him they spent every summer in Myrtle Beach. Walk had given the address to Leah, knew Darke would show up if he thought the trail might lead to Duchess.

Walk had no newspaper, no book, nothing at all to distract him from the task at hand. An hour back he'd popped a couple of pills, the muscle pain was bad, the convulsing, the need to just lie back and let it ride over him.

This would be his last job as a cop, the last hurrah in decades of nothing. He gave no thought to Martha, to Vincent and the unfurling mess in the Cape; this was for the Radley children, he would keep them safe, he would do it for Star and for Hal. He did not know how close Darke was when he called Leah back, but guessed he was near Montana. Duchess, the tape, it was Darke's last chance to save his crumbling empire.

Walk felt the tired like a warm blanket on the coldest night, weighing on him, pulling him deeper, his eyes heavy. The pills, drowsiness was one of the blessed side-effects, he reasoned he hadn't slept well in a year so there was no danger of it finding him now. Still, he yawned once, then, slowly, he closed his eyes.

Thomas Noble was lying on his bed watching the television when the power cut.

He stood, silent, nothing but the sounds of the house, the clock in the hallway, the steady hum of the boiler. He stood, took a step and stumbled over his bag, packed, ready. His parents had dropped him at camp, same every summer; they lived it up by the beach while he made sand art and tie-dyed T-shirts eight miles from his own house. He'd snuck out after dark, hiked it back, cut through woodland into his yard and found the spare key in the garage. It would hit the fan in the morning, by then he'd be on his way to California. Trailing her. Helping her.

His heart beat fast, he placed a hand on it and tried to calm. He listened but heard nothing, felt dumb for getting freaked out by the dark. He walked to the window and saw the neighboring homes lit, the porch lights burning. He knew where the box was, what to do when the power tripped.

He'd made it to the stairs when he heard the glass break. He froze then, rooted to the spot, unable to move a muscle. He heard the lock turn, the door open.

The crunch of steps on shards.

He knew his father kept a gun and that it was locked in his office. He also knew he would not have the courage to aim it or fire it, not even with two good hands.

Steps again, hard on the kitchen floor then soft on the carpeted hall. He wanted to cry out, announce himself because half the fear was in the surprise. A nice house on a nice street, his mother had jewelry, the kind of showy pieces that might've been noticed.

He took a breath and moved fast, treading on the outer edges of the stairs, from the top floor to the middle and into his parents' bedroom. He reached for the phone on the nightstand.

No tone.

He ran to the window, thought of yelling but heard steps again, closer this time, at the foot of the stairs. His mind worked fast, he looked at the drop, reasoned he'd break a leg, at least.

He spun, looked around, saw a gap beneath the bed, knew there was space in the closet, settled for the guest bedroom and moved fast.

Shadow on the stairs. He did not look back until he made it, slipped behind the door and pressed himself flat to the wall. He wanted to cry, fought hard not to, thought maybe whoever it was would think the house empty, take what they needed and leave.

"Thomas."

He closed his eyes.

"I know you're here. I've been watching from the woods. You tell me what I need to know and I'll leave you be. I give you my word."

He wanted to call out, to ask what the man wanted and then give him whatever it was, right away, no arguing. And then the man called out again, and Thomas Noble felt his blood chill.

"Duchess Radley."

The guy with the Escalade. Darke.

Thomas Noble looked around wildly, saw nothing he could use, nothing heavy or sharp, nothing that could buy him precious seconds. Darke would find him now.

He thought of Duchess, of the first time he'd seen her and what she had been through, their first dance and the time she'd kissed him. He thought of his perfect home and loving parents, and where she was now, alone on the road, a gun in her bag and the courage to use it. He hadn't been able to help her. But now he could, he could prove himself. He could be an outlaw too.

He watched the shape step through the door, big like a fucking monster, and as it neared Thomas Noble took a deep breath and launched himself through the darkness.

***

Gunshot.

Walk woke, jumped from the car and took off at a run.

Broken glass, open door, he barreled through, gun trained out, room to room. He moved up the stairs.

The kid was on the floor, backed up to the wall, knees against his chest.

"You hurt?"

He shook his head. Above was torn drywall, half the ceiling gone, a warning shot.

"Where is he?"

"Back door."

Walk ran down the stairs. He saw the fencing at the end of the grass, jumped it, and found himself in the woodland behind. He followed a loose trail, moonlight fell in silver shards that cut their way through thick growth.

"Darke," he yelled, heard nothing so kept running.

He moved through towering trees.

And then, ahead, he caught sight of the shape, by a tree, moving slow.

Walk raised his gun.

He stood, feet apart, hands locked.

He fired once.

The big shape fell. He moved on, slow.

By the time he made it to him Darke had propped himself back against a tree. Nothing in his hands, Walk saw the gun a couple of feet from him, bent and picked it up.

Darke breathed hard. Shoulder wound, painful enough but he'd live.

Walk listened out, heard nothing. The neighbors would call the cops soon enough.

At that moment Walk did not feel the twitches in his body, just focused solely on the job. His job, his place. He was not yet ready to give either up.

"Didn't think you had it in you."

"You want to get this done, Darke?"

"Sure, Chief Walker." His voice was calm, no emotion, despite the end coming at him.

"You've been holing up all this time."

"Healing up. There's people, I owe them. They aren't going away. You ever been shot, Chief? Twice for me now."

"I've got questions."

Darke did not press a hand to the wound, just let the blood run steady down his arms and drip from his fingers.

"We found Milton. Trawler hooked him."

Darke stared up at him.

Walk continued. "What did he have on you?"

Darke looked confused, but maybe the wheels were slowly beginning to turn. "He liked to take photographs."

Walk nodded to no one but himself.

"He just wanted a friend, someone to go hunting with. So I went. We're all looking for angles, Chief. That's what we do."

Walk thought of Martha.

Darke clenched a fist and the blood ran faster. "This the part where I confess my sins?"

Distant sirens.

"I know about Madeline."

Darke swallowed then, the first trace of emotion. "She's fourteen now."

"Same age as Duchess Radley."

"I didn't want to come for the girl. I tried every other way."

"Hal."

"He didn't give me a chance to speak, just pulled a shotgun."

"You're a murderer."

"Just like your friend."

Walk took a step back, that dizzying feeling all over again. "Vincent . . ."

"Tragedy has a way of making saints out of sinners. Believe me, I know." Darke gulped air, the pain was sharp. "The boy in there. I didn't hurt him."

"I know."

"People see me. The way I look, they think certain thoughts. That's alright, it helps me get things done."

"You murdered Star Radley."

"You even believe that anymore, Chief Walker? I asked her for a favor, to talk to Vincent for me, get him to sell up. I only had to mention his name and she lost it, throwing punches. She was wild."

"You and Vincent made some kind of deal. You couldn't see it through. Couldn't raise the money."

"I'm a man of my word. Ask Vincent, he'll tell you."

"You talk like you know him."

"Maybe I do. Maybe Star told me things, she liked to drink, drugs, whatever. Confession doesn't only happen in church."

"What are you saying?"

"Vincent . . . he's not who you think he is."

Walk watched him, looking for the truth, maybe not wanting to see any of it.

Darke's breath grew short then. "I have life insurance. Enough to keep Madeline."

"It was always about the money."

"They won't pay out for suicide. Believe me, I checked."

"Suicide by cop."

"Not if you tell it right."

"She doesn't need you?"

Darke closed his eyes, then opened them to the pain of it all. "A child is always better with a parent in their life. But the place she's in. That's what she needs. That's all I can give her."

"She won't get better."

"They can't say that for sure. There's a chance, in time. Miracles happen every day."

Walk didn't know if he really believed that, but guessed it was what kept him going.

"Shoot me."

Walk shook his head slowly.

"Put my gun in my hand and then shoot me."

Walk took a step back.

The blood still dripped. Darke was too strong, too big and strong.

"Fucking shoot me. Please. Just fucking shoot me. I killed the old man. I came for the girl. Please."

Walk heard noise behind, distant but coming.

"I can't do that."

"Mercy, Chief. Your god believes in that."

Walk shook his head, nothing clear, the right thing, the fair thing. He thought of Madeline, a girl he did not know, and Duchess, a girl he did.

He took a step toward Darke.

"Give my girl a chance. You can do that. It's in you."

Walk took another step. "They'll lock you up."

"I'll get out one day. And then I'll come for Duchess again. This time it'll be revenge. Simple. I'll end her."

Walk saw through it, too easy.

"Fuck. Please, Walker. You let the cops take me and my daughter dies. I'm out of money now, I've got nothing. The club was all I had. I can't pay to keep her alive."

Walk stood there, the gun so heavy he could barely hold it.

"You need to wipe your prints off it." Darke laid his head back against the tree, tears filled his eyes. "There's a key in my pocket. A lockup outside the Cape. West Gale. There's things in there I want Madeline to have. It's important she knows us."

Walk just stared.

"We don't have time. Just do it, Chief. Give my girl a chance."

Walk wiped Darke's gun, then leaned down and handed it to him.

Darke winced as he raised it, then aimed wide and pulled the trigger.

The echo. The ringing in Walk's ears as he raised his own gun.

Darke nodded once.

Walk pulled the trigger.

43

Duchess passed the faces of towns and lonely mountains and a sky at times so blue it brought her home to the endless waters of Cape Haven.

She rode above the wheel, every bump in her bones, the road laid out like a scar across land her grandfather had once traversed, his only happiness far behind.

They stopped at towns and people came and went, old men that carried something quiet and forgotten, young men with backpacks and maps and plans, and the couples whose love spilled down the aisle and made Duchess turn her head. The driver, a black man who smiled at her when the bus slept and they were the only people to see a hitchhiker framed by a Colorado sunrise.

Trucks broken down, hood up and men bent over and in, their women watching the silver pass. Diners and cop cars, Lincolns and a stretch too far from anywhere worth going.

At Caroga Plain a man with a guitar got on and asked the few if they minded, and they all shook their heads, so he sang about golden slumbers, his voice rough but something in it stripping the roof from the old bus and letting the stars fall in.

It was only in the night, when the moon emptied into the Artaya

Canyon and the driver slowed the bus and dimmed the lights, that Duchess allowed herself to think of Robin. It hurt her, not like the kind of sweetheart hurt she read about in the glossy someone had left in the seatback, this was a raw kind of gut-your-soul pain, so fierce she doubled over and gasped for air, reached into her bag and found her water and took shallow breaths into the bottle. The driver caught her eye, his filled with wasted concern, she would not be alright, nothing about her would ever be alright again.

She ran out of money someplace outside of Dotsero, bulging hills cratered, a volcano rose, green trees parted for sterile land so red she bent to touch it.

She found a phone booth at a truck stop on 70, water rushing on ahead, fighting its way from the Rocky Mountains to the spread of Mexico and beyond. She called collect and the operator connected her to a world she felt far from. By grace alone she got Claudette and she fought off talk of coming back and the cops and the trouble. She held on just long enough for Claudette to tell her yeah, he was doing okay. And then Claudette told her to wait and she'd fetch him.

She hung up when she heard him, and then fell against the brick, a long road from anywhere, too small to be alone, the sky a gathering storm she could not outrun. Her brother saying hello, quiet like he was in on a secret, and her unable to find a word, not a single word to say to him, not even sorry for what she had done and what she would do.

She spent her last two bucks on milk and a dry bagel.

She sat there four hours, the sun crawling its arc, the hand of a clock that pushed morning to the blaze of afternoon. In the gas station a woman worked the counter, a magazine hidden behind, her head down and tired. She wore large glasses and had a stain on her shirt. She gave Duchess the key to the restroom, smiled quick as she did, like she knew the crossroads the girl lived at and had seen so many like her before.

Inside smelled bad, graffiti scrawled on every surface, romantic declarations, *Tom & Betty-Laurel Fucked Here*, numbers to call for a good time.

Duchess carefully stripped off her T-shirt and jeans, washed herself with soap she pumped from the dispenser, then dried off with paper towels. She splashed icy water onto her face, the tired creeped from her eyes.

Outside she watched truckers, trying to select the right one based on nothing more than a gut instinct that had not steered her all that well in the past.

An hour later she settled on a big guy with a plaid shirt and handlebar mustache. He drove a clean rig, the name *Annie-Beth* on the hood, a heart on either side.

She approached him and he smiled, took in her wet hair, Stetson, small bag and eighty-pound frame.

"Where do you need to get?"

"Maybe Vegas."

"Vegas, huh."

"Yeah."

"You a runaway?"

"No."

"I could get in trouble."

"I'm not a runaway. I'm eighteen."

He laughed at that.

"I'm passing Fish Lake."

"Where's that?"

"Utah."

"Alright."

As they drove she watched the world, the view high and commanding. The cab smelled of leather. The big guy was Malcolm, like his parents expected him to stop growing at five seven and work accounts. There was a plant on the dash, she took that as a good sign. And a photo of a girl not much older than her and a woman beside.

"Is that Annie-Beth?" she said.

"My girl."

"Pretty."

"Sure is. That's old now . . . nineteen. University, political science."

Pride colored every word. "I check in with her every night. She's just, she's so smart we didn't even know where it came from. A blessing."

"That your wife with her?"

"Used to be. I liked to drink." He pointed to a pin on the dash. "Eighteen months sober."

"Maybe she'll take you back."

"Not on the cards for me yet. I got a plant, cactus, I keep that healthy for six months then maybe. It's all about taking it back, right?"

She looked at the cactus on the dash, long dead. She wondered if he knew, and also just how hard it was to kill a cactus.

He tried asking her a little, she gave nothing so he quit, pushed his visor down to cut the bright, and then rode mile after mile.

She slept a little, woke with such a start he told her it was alright. She saw red rock, dried-out yellows and orange, sunset on a road so long and straight she wondered if she was dreaming.

At a truck stop he told her that was all. She thanked him and he wished her well.

"Go home," he said.

"I am."

At the edge of a town that did not have a clear name, Duchess walked beneath a silver sky, her feet so heavy it was all she could do to keep them moving. Tall buildings either side, painted colors that lightened with each step. Yellow planters and sapling trees, dying stores and floating noise, a bar across the street that fluttered neon. Sounds that told her not to go in. She stood there, her bag pulling the skin from her shoulder, eyes so tired edges blurred and streetlights smothered. Across, each step wayward and hard to point. She breathed in stammers, not knowing how to be any longer, her hands numb from the weight, the occasional memory of Robin lighting up her chest, all fire and hatred for the man that had stolen her old life and discarded it so carelessly, like litter in the wind.

She pushed the door against better judgment, fought her way to the bar, the men, and some women, parting, the light all red.

The bartender was old and she asked for a Coke before she realized she didn't have enough. As she fished in her pockets he set it down, read her well and then pushed it toward her in an act of kindness so distant she had almost forgotten that such a thing existed.

She found a corner and put her bag down, sat on a low stool and closed her eyes to the sweet drink. A man with a guitar held the other corner, and he called on regulars and together they played and sang, and the bustling crowd watched and sometimes laughed. There wasn't one that could hold a tune, but Duchess stared on like she hadn't heard music in the longest time.

For a moment she closed her eyes, wiped dirt and sweat that crossed her face and found her mother, holding Robin up to the stars like he was something blessed instead of another mistake.

And then she found herself on her feet, and she was moving, and again the people parted, the women watching her like she was a child, the men watching her with something like curiosity.

She passed the pool table, breathed smoke and beer and the breath of tired men, leaning on each other, some swaying to the guitar.

When the music died she reached the corner, and the guitar player dipped his hat and she dipped her own in reply.

"You want to sing, girl?"

She nodded.

"Alright then."

She took a seat and looked out, meeting them in turn, some smiling and some not.

She leaned, whispered because she wasn't sure of the song's name, only the words, but the man got it and smiled like she'd chosen well enough.

He played and she sat silent, he didn't seem to mind when she closed her eyes and missed her cue. There were murmurs but she blocked them out. She let those chords carry her a year back, when her mother was some-one she could reach out to, never quite grasp, but the feeling was there.

She saw her brother, and then her grandfather, the reparation in his love stealing all the air from her chest.

She opened her mouth and sang. She told them she was on their side, when times get rough. The murmurs fell silent, and the men at the table stopped lining their shots and instead moved toward the little girl that sliced heavens wide open, her soul bared and burned, the man beside so transfixed he almost could not match her with his chords.

She was down and out, on the street. Darkness had come and pain was all around.

She was under no illusion, his blood would not cleanse hers. But she would do it, she couldn't not.

When she was done she let the silence hang. The old man came from behind the bar and handed her an envelope stuffed with bills. She frowned till he pointed to the sign. Sing to win, monthly, a hundred bucks.

She did not wait for the cheers, she would hear them carry out into the lonely night as she left with her bag and found her way to the bus station.

This was her path to perdition.

A girl on her way to right a lifetime of wrongs.

44

Walk spent a night and day dealing with the fallout.

There were questions from Iver County PD, he said little. They were still trying to figure out why Darke had broken into the Noble house. Walk did not help much with that. He said he was tired, sick, that he'd write a full report in the coming days. He wouldn't speak of Duchess and the tape. He'd find a better angle.

He climbed into the rental and drove someplace he could sleep. A motel fifty miles from anywhere.

In a tired room he lay on his bed and thought of Duchess, lost out there now. He did not fight the way his body shook, just caved to it. His pants were loose, he'd punched new holes in his belt three times now. If he looked in the mirror he would see a frown where his smile had once been. They said he'd never change. He'd clung to that.

In the drawer beside he found a Bible and a pen and paper, and he wrote, resigned to resignation, he gave up his badge. There were still questions, maybe forever unanswerable, but he would try, for the girl and the boy, he would still try.

He called Martha, got her machine so left the kind of rambling message that told her he was good, knew she wouldn't buy it but signed off with a promise to call again after he got some sleep. He also told her he was sorry, sorry for more than he could possibly atone for.

His cell rang at nine.

He expected to hear Martha's voice but it was Tana Legros, from the lab. He hadn't leaned heavy this time, just asked if it could be done quietly.

"I owe you some bloodwork. I did leave messages, several over the past month."

"Sorry. I've been . . ."

"Anyway, I made the gun a priority."

"The blood in Darke's place. Milton."

"No, actually. Animal, not human."

Walk ran a hand through his hair as he thought of Milton, hunting with Darke then heading back to his place after. "Deer?"

"Could be."

"Right."

"You okay, Walk?"

"The gun. Did you get anything?"

"We pulled prints."

"Vincent King?" He held his breath, the room doing its spin, all or nothing now.

"No, actually."

Walk took it, too tired even for his pulse to quicken.

"It's small."

"Woman?"

"Child. Small child."

Walk closed his eyes. And then he dropped the phone as the pieces began to fit. He ached, so beat he could barely hold his head up.

He thanked Tana, then dialed Vincent.

Vincent answered on the second ring, a man that did not sleep anymore, one of the night people.

"I know."

He listened to Vincent draw breath.

"What do you know?" Vincent said it quiet, not a challenge, just acceptance now.

"Robin." The little boy's name hung long in the air, the last year, all that had gone before. Walk stepped to the window, saw the freeway empty of cars, the sky empty of stars. "I found the gun."

The silence was long, just the two of them, holding together, like always.

"You want to tell me?"

"I took two lives, Walk. I can live with one of those."

"Baxter Logan. He paid his price, right?"

"You think it makes that woman's family happy, what I did to the monster that ruined her? Maybe. I know what I did. I live with that. But not Sissy. Each time . . . each one of my breaths is stolen from her."

"Tell me what happened."

"You already know."

Walk swallowed. "The boy shot his mother."

Vincent breathed.

"But he was aiming at someone else," Walk said, quiet, sad.

"Darke."

"The girl burned his club. Insurance wouldn't pay. How do you fit here?"

"I saw his car, I went round back, took the cut. Darke said he was searching the place, tried the kids' bedroom door and Star lost it. The boy climbed out the window, heard his mother scream and came back."

"Brave," Walk said. "Like his sister."

"Star shoved him in the closet, got him out of the way. The kid found the gun. Maybe he thought she was getting beat. He aimed out, closed his eyes and pulled the trigger. Still had them closed when I got there."

"Darke."

"Would've killed him. He had her blood on him. Kid's the only witness. Whatever he says, Darke's at the scene. Darke goes down."

Walk rested his head against the glass as light rain began to fall.

He thought of Darke, that perception and how he used it. Maybe he would've killed the boy, Walk didn't think so. But the angle presented itself. "How'd you plead it?"

"Told him I'd take it all. I'd take the fall, no one else for the cops to look for. He was never there."

"He bought that?"

"No. The house, Walk. He wanted the house. So I gave in. He could buy it if he left the kid alone."

"Why didn't you just plead guilty?"

"Plead guilty and I spend the rest of my life in that cage. Plead innocent and the end comes at me. The case wasn't winnable. Questions would have come. The gun."

"You hid it."

"Darke took it. His insurance in case I changed my mind."

"You helped Robin back through the window. You washed your hands. Shit, Vincent."

"Thirty years inside, you learn about crime scenes."

"You plugged the holes and stayed silent."

"Your questions didn't need answering. I look more guilty if I just stay silent. Start talking and you tie me up, no gun, I couldn't explain that. Let them stick a needle in my arm. Let them do what they should have done thirty years ago."

"Sissy. It wasn't murder."

"It was, Walk. You just didn't want to see it that way. I'm ready now. I want to go. I've always wanted to go. But after I'd served my time. Hal said he was glad I was in there, that I should be punished. Death was too good."

"Darke couldn't raise the funds to buy your place. Not the down payment, the taxes. Not after what Duchess did," Walk said.

"I didn't know that. But then he wrote me."

"I saw the letter."

"Right."

"You must've been mad."

"I was. At first I was. Not for me . . . but the money. I needed that money."

"He gave the gun back because he couldn't keep his side of the deal. A man of his word, right?"

Silence for a long time.

"People are complex, Walk. Just when you think you got them figured . . . he gave me an out if I ever needed it."

"Sometimes wishes do come true . . . the wishing tree." Walk said it to himself, tired smile on his face, right there and he'd missed it.

Walk thought of Vincent on the other end. He wondered how ground down he was, if there was any of the kid left in there. "You banked on the boy not remembering."

"I saw him, gone like that, out of this world. I don't think he knows. So I told him I did it. That's enough, just that doubt. Let someone else take it away. Fuck, he deserved that. I tried to bring her back. I pumped her chest with everything I got."

Walk thought of Star, the broken ribs. And he thought of Darke and Madeline and the cruel hand of fate.

"You lied for me. You stood in court, wearing your badge, and you lied. You still know yourself, Walk?"

"No."

"You can't save someone that doesn't want to be saved."

Quiet a long time.

"How's things with Martha?"

Walk just about managed a smile. "That's why you wanted her."

"A million tragedies began that night, Walk. Most of them I can't fix."

Walk thought of Robin Radley. "I used to want to go back and do it all again. But now I'm just tired. So fucking tired. Maybe you did a good thing."

"I owe a debt to the Radleys. He might not remember. He's small. I could die giving him his life back. There's a chance it'll all stay black."

"You near gave your life for a chance."

"I couldn't let him be me."

45

Walk drove down last roads, each mile behind one he would not travel again. He had spent a life afraid of change. He had killed.

Nothing outward was different, he knew it would not be. The bay came at him in such glory, he kept his eyes locked on broken lines. Twenty miles from home he found the place, a storage facility, West Gale, tired, red lockups, no office, just a number to call if you needed service.

Walk pulled up, headed over and took the keys from his pocket. He checked the number on the tag and found one of the smaller units. He unlocked it and stepped into dark, found the switch, light flickered, strips cast dull yellow.

On one side he found a couple of plastic storage containers. He worked slow, saw everything from an old, happier life. Wedding album, Darke looked young, tall but not so imposing, his wife was beautiful. And there were photos of Madeline, brown hair and light eyes, wide smile in every shot. She looked like her mother. A christening gown, an old wedding dress, the kind of things passed down generations.

Walk would keep hold of it, pay the rental, let the people at the hospital know where it was in case miracles did happen.

He was about to turn, to kill the lights and lock up, when he saw a pile of boxes and garbage bags in the far corner. He checked them, old files, nothing of note, and then he saw a stack of junk mail. And he saw the name and address. Dee Lane.

He trained his mind back a year before it came to him. Darke's offer to store her things while she found someplace else to live. Before they made that deal she'd carry with her.

He tossed the mail back onto the pile then cursed when the whole thing toppled. As he bent down it came to view. Out of place.

A single videotape.

He drove back toward the Cape, breached the town limit, saw a new sign, hard metal and towering scaffold, light falling on the promise of new homes, new stores. The motion had passed silently, Walk distracted, just another change in a changing world. The station was dark. He left the lights off, sat in his office and loaded the tape, then frowned when he saw The Eight, Darke's club. And then he noted the date in the top corner, and his pulse began to quicken as he realized what he was watching.

It covered a day, he rolled it forward till he saw her, Star, working the bar. He watched her like the ghost she was, the way she smiled and flirted as the tips rained down. He skipped a little, stopped at a scuffle, bodies everywhere. Star fell back, clutched her eye and appeared to curse. She was stumbling, moving like the liquor had finally taken effect.

Walk couldn't see who the guy was, back to the camera.

But then the man walked out.

He recognized the limp, the pain it took to try and correct it.

Brandon Rock.

He searched again, rolled it forward till he saw her, clear as day. Small, blond hair, face tortured with hate as she worked. He watched Duchess start the fire that would burn for a year.

When he was done he stood. He took off his badge and placed it on the desk, then took the tape from the machine and stepped out into the night air. He walked a little up Main, snapped the tape from the case and pulled out the reel, then he dropped it into the trash.

. . .

The King house was empty.

Duchess stood out front, an old Taurus parked up at the curb. She'd taken the keys from a lady playing the slots in a bar in Camarillo. She'd leave it there, keys inside, too tired to feel sorry now.

She'd circled it and knocked on the door. There was doubt that lingered, that she could go through with it, despite the journey she had been on to get close to this moment.

As she'd driven down Main she had stared at streets like she expected something to have changed in the year she'd been away, nothing major, just something that told her Cape Haven was not the same without her and her small family. Instead she saw the town at rest, nothing different, not even a yard left overgrown. Just gloss, like her mother's blood had been painted over so thoroughly, like she had never been.

She went round to the back again, found a rock and broke a window, crashing waves stealing the sound.

Inside the King house she walked through the rooms, gun in hand. Photos on the wall, Vincent and Walk, their backs to the water, the kind of carefree smiles she herself had never known.

She climbed the stairs and checked each bedroom. Only moonlight to guide her. She saw a closet, Vincent's clothes, so few. Three shirts, a pair of jeans, heavy boots. She thought of the making of a murderer, if it began long before birth, cursing the parents' genes, the fatal bloodline. Or maybe it slowly crept, too many knocks, too many scars. Vincent King might have once been good, but a child's blood did not wash from your hands. And thirty years among the most flawed of men, it would take the strongest to survive intact.

There was no bed, just a mattress on the floor. No furniture in the room, no paintings or television or books.

Just a single photo, taped to the wall.

A photo that took her breath, for the girl looked just like her. Blond hair and blue eyes. Sissy Radley.

She left the house and walked the mile, climbed the trails that rose high above the town lights. She stopped halfway, every muscle ached, air pained her chest like her body did not want her to go on among the living.

As she crested the final hill she saw the light, the late service. She had been once before, sat with the half dozen for no other reason than she could not sleep.

Little Brook Episcopal.

She walked up the road, alongside the picket fence, came to the door and listened to the heavenly music. She dropped her bag for a moment, leaned against the wood, the long day almost over. With nowhere left to go she made her way to the small grave where her mother lay, beside Sissy, in the part of the cemetery reserved for the most innocent. Duchess had asked they be together again.

She stopped dead.

He stood there, tall against the precious night. Behind him the land fell away, the sheer cliffs and endless sea.

• • •

At Ivy Ranch Road Walk headed up the path and knocked.

Brandon looked like shit, said nothing, just stepped aside as Walk went into the house. It smelled bad, takeout cartons everywhere, beer cans, thick dust on every surface. A stack of fitness DVDs, *Rock Hard*, Brandon sucking in his stomach on the cover. Brandon's eyes looked glazed as he sat down at the kitchen counter. Walk thought of Star, how she'd knocked him back one too many times, and maybe that was why Brandon had let his fist go that night.

"I know what you did," Walk began. And that was all it took.

Brandon cried, the dam burst, he cried till his shoulders shook. Walk watched him, the confusion building.

"I didn't mean it. I'm sorry. You have to believe it, Walk."

Walk said nothing, just listened as the story broke between sobs.

"I reached out, like you said. I offered to take him out on the boat. Fishing or something, whatever. I wanted an end to it. But then I thought about it, how he scratched the Mustang. I knew it was him. Who else would do that? At first I was going to report it, but then everything with Star happened. It was supposed to be a joke. To get him back. We weren't even far from shore."

Walk breathed, the confusion passing, just sadness left. "You pushed him in. Milton."

Brandon cried more, coughed like he was retching up the memory. "I waited for him back at the dock. I just wanted to show him. Make him swim back. Just a joke. And then he didn't show, so I went back. But he was gone, Walk. He was gone."

Walk sat with him, called Boyd and waited, told Brandon what to say. Be honest. You'll sleep better at night.

He watched them take him, Brandon doing the walk with his head bowed low, only breaking once more when he glanced up and saw Milton's old house across the street. It might've been karma, the cosmic forces Star used to talk about. Walk didn't have long to think it over, because Dee Lane called his cell, and she told him she'd seen someone break into the King house.

"Did you get a look at them?" Walk said, breaking into a run.

"It looked like a girl."

He ran all the way to Sunset, with the weight gone he moved light and fast. He was sweating when he made it to the door and hammered it hard.

Round back he saw broken glass.

He traced her steps, her counterstroke, he knew he was too late for what would come. On the mantel he found the photo, barely recognized the boy he was, but in Vincent and Star he saw only smiles, a snapshot of time he could no longer call back, no matter how hard he tried.

And then up the stairs. And he too stopped still when he saw it.

Maybe Vincent could move on from the cell, the warden, the men and the chain-link fences. But he'd never leave the little girl behind.

• • •

She watched him a long time before she took those steps.

"I was waiting for you," Vincent said.

Duchess stepped nearer, slowly set down her bag and pulled out the gun. It was heavier than she remembered, right then she could barely hold it up.

He looked at her like she was the last child, the last good thing in his world. She saw he had laid flowers on the graves, like he had a right.

He saw the gun but did not seem alarmed, instead his shoulders dropped and he breathed out steady, like he had been waiting on the final end to a lifetime of endings.

Vincent stepped back as she stepped forward, again and again, until she planted her feet and watched the moonlight behind him.

Music from the old church carried.

"I like this song," he said. "There was a chapel . . . at Fairmont. I always liked this song. Earth's joy grows dim, its glories pass away."

"Change and decay in all around I see."

"I'm sorry."

"I don't want you to talk."

"Okay."

"I don't want you to tell me what happened, I don't want to know."

"Okay."

"People say it's not fair."

"It never is."

"That day when you gave me a gun. You said it was your father's gun."

"Yes."

"I cleaned it like you showed me. Respect it, right? But then I hid it in the closet, even though you told me to use it to protect myself."

"I shouldn't have told you—"

"So that's what I'm doing. Hal said you're a cancer. Everything you get near . . . you just kill it all dead. He said you don't deserve to live."

"He was right."

"Walk stood up in court and told a lie. Star said he was all good."

"I'm sorry, Duchess."

"Fuck." She reached up and fixed her hat, her breath left her. Her voice barely held but she steadied her hand and reached for the trigger. "I am the outlaw Duchess Day Radley. And you are the murderer Vincent King."

"You don't have to do this." He smiled gently.

"I know what I have to do. Justice. Vengeance. Whatever it is I can handle it."

"You can still be anyone you want, Duchess."

She leveled the gun.

His tears fell but still he smiled at her. "I came here to say goodbye. This isn't on you. I won't let you carry me with you."

She gasped when he stepped back, his arms out as he took flight.

She ran and screamed and stopped at the cliff edge as the darkness took him.

The gun fell by her side. She dropped with it, her knees in the dirt as she reached a hand out, over the cliff, and grasped at the air.

Behind, her mother lay, and Duchess used the last of her strength to crawl over to the grave. She pressed a cheek to the stone and closed her eyes.

•

PART FOUR

Heartbreaker

46

Blair Peak bordered the Elkton-Trinity National Forest and the Whitefoot, the kind of town where Walk could have spent the day just staring out at the sprawl of wilderness, at trees so tall it was as if they were reaching up for God's hand.

He'd made the drive, past the barren hills and dead grass of a dozen haunted communities, more than a hundred times over the past twenty years, Star beside, counting off the miles in quiet thought. And then, after, as happy as he ever saw her. What demons lived in her soul were exorcised by a man named Colten Sheen, a counselor who worked out of a room above a store that sold secondhand pianos.

In his hand was a small urn. The service had been brief.

The last will of Vincent King had been clear and vague enough. The forest spanned six counties and two million acres, Walk figured here was as good a place as any.

He crossed the street and dropped down, trod the dead leaves to towering sugar pines, and then scattered the ashes over the forest floor. He said nothing, no grand goodbyes, just allowed himself a moment to remember a time finally beginning its fade.

After, he walked up Union Street and found the door, the shop closed up but a light burned against the winter's day. He buzzed up, heard the door give and headed into the small lobby and up narrow stairs. He'd been in once before, the first time, just to make sure she didn't bolt.

"I'm Chief . . ." Walk stammered. "Sorry, I'm Walker. Just Walker. I used to be chief of Cape Haven PD."

Walk was not surprised when Sheen drew a blank. The man that stood before him had aged nicely, full head of gray hair, an inch off six feet. He extended a hand when Walk mentioned Star Radley.

"I'm sorry, it's been such a long time," Sheen said. "I have someone due in ten minutes, so I can give you those, but that's all, I'm afraid."

They sat, Walk falling into the soft chair, smiling at the serene prints on the wall. Beside was a large window, opening on a view of the Elkton-Trinity and the white-capped alps.

"I could lose a day staring out."

Sheen smiled. "I often do."

"I'm here about Star."

"You should know I can't tell you anything. I'm bound—"

"Yes," Walk cut in. "I just . . . I'm sorry, I found myself in town again, just thought I'd stop by. You see . . . she died."

Sheen smiled, compassion emanated. "I saw it. I followed the story in the news. It's tragic, really. But still, even in death . . ."

"I'm not even sure why I'm here, not really."

"You're missing your friend."

"I . . . yes. I'm missing my friend." It hit him then, out of all the feelings, all the chasing leads and battling theories, he hadn't thought about just how much he missed his friend. It was easy to see her troubles, her beauty, everything but the real, sweet person he had known a lifetime.

"I guess I just wanted to know why she stopped coming. She did well, for so long she did so well. And then it all stopped so suddenly. And she never really came back from it."

"There's a million reasons why people turn back or choose a different path. Even if I could tell you, it's been so long. And I only saw her the one time."

Walk frowned. "I'm sorry, it is Star Radley we're talking about."

"Yes. I remember you now. It's not often a patient gets brought in by a police officer."

"But I drove her every month."

"Not to me. I did see her though, often. The view, I'm always at the window."

Walk leaned forward. "Where exactly did you see her?"

Sheen stood. Walk followed him to the glass.

"Right there." Sheen pointed.

Outside the cloud swept in as Walk stood on the sidewalk. There was only one bus that ran through Blair Peak and Walk got on, same as Star had, once a month for a dozen years, the bus stop facing Colten Sheen's picture window.

He sat at the back, the bus half empty as it climbed the steep hillside and dipped into the valley. Trees rose and shadowed the road.

A while till they cleared the woodland, California opening up, the plains vast. He got up and walked to the front, stood beside the driver and looked out.

He didn't see it till they made the last turn, and then, suddenly and without warning, he realized where he was, and what he stood in front of.

The bus stopped and he got out, he looked around as it passed. There was nothing else for miles in either direction, just a long track road, the razor fence twenty feet high, and the low buildings that made up Fairmont County Correctional Facility.

He waited an hour, sat in the room alone, held his hand up and watched the tremor. He'd slipped a little, missed medication, life in the way, not his but Vincent's. It was bad now, the pain sometimes, the fear always. He set his alarm an hour earlier, allowing time for a battle that was getting harder to win. The future was a frightening thing, but then he reasoned it always had been.

There was a half smile when Cuddy came out. "Almost didn't recognize you without the stars. I'm finishing up if you want to walk with me."

Walk fell into step with the big warden, stayed close behind him at the gates as they opened and locked. A life of it, order and not, keeping the bad inside and good out. He could not imagine such a toll.

"I'm sorry I didn't make the service," Cuddy said. "Not all that into goodbyes."

They walked along the fence, towers like silos.

"There's things I don't know," Walk said.

Cuddy breathed deep, like he'd been waiting. Walk did not know what they were doing, walking the perimeter, maybe Cuddy just liked the free air after pulling ten hours.

"Star came here," Walk said.

"She did."

"But her name, I checked the visitor logs. I checked everything I could."

They passed a guard in a tower, Cuddy raised a hand.

"I like dusk," Cuddy said. "The end of astronomical twilight. The sun, degrees below the horizon. I let them out sometimes, to watch a sunset. Five hundred men, killers and rapists and pushers. They stand together and stare at the sky, it's the only time we don't have real trouble."

"Why?"

"The beauty, maybe. It makes it harder to deny higher power."

"Or easier."

"Don't lose your heart, Walk. That would be the real tragedy."

"Tell me about Star."

Cuddy stopped, the furthest point from the prison, between two towers and guards ready to end life just as quick as any jury. "I liked her. I got to know her plenty over the years. Vincent King was as decent a man as I ever met. And I got to see it, the change. Scared kid, fearless for a while, and then he got to be okay with it."

"What?"

"His own skin. Okay, but not good. And Star, she helped him. He caused her the pain, and he was the only one that could take it away. He had purpose again."

Walk watched the first stars burn, heavenly from out there.

"He needed her, to feel something again, more than who he was when he wore orange and walked in chains. It played like a marriage, over twenty-odd years she'd come. Sometimes they didn't speak, at the start, just watched each other, she was all fire, burning up, and he'd look at her like she was placed on this earth just for him."

"What about the other prisoners?"

"Oh, I didn't let those two in the common room. I mean, at first, of course, but I saw right off she was too young for it, the men were too cruel with their words, promises and threats. Vincent got it bad after, guards broke it up in time but once the others knew his weak spot they'd run with it. There's another room, an apartment we had. Conjugal, it was to be earned. Just us and three states now."

"You let them alone like that?"

"Vincent needed it . . . to feel human again. Shit, I needed to see him human again. And Star, the two of them. Cosmic forces and all that. Not a prison on earth could cut that kind of pull."

Walk smiled.

"I couldn't put it through the logs though, not strictly allowed. I watched her, the shape, nine months, that glow, you know. Twice. Two miracles born from despair." Cuddy smiled.

"But she didn't ever bring them—"

"He wouldn't have it. Not caged like that. And he didn't want them to know. Can't really blame him. He said there's not a kid out there that wants a father from Fairmont. We talked about it, it gave him resolve. Live life for someone else. That's not wasted, right."

Walk closed his eyes and thought of Duchess and Robin, their blood, that unknown.

"He asked me not to tell. I said I wouldn't volunteer it, but also that I wouldn't lie if someone came asking. I'm a man of my word."

"Right."

Cuddy laughed softly. "Not many of us left."

"I think maybe Star told Darke."

"Why?"

"Just something he said at the end. The things people do for their own, right? They saw that in each other. Vincent and Star, they couldn't keep it going."

"And then it was changed, they pulled the apartment down to make way for the new Cat-5. Vincent wouldn't have her in the common room again, not after the last time. I mean, these are men that'd make promises, that they'd go look her up when they got out. Empty, but still. Vincent didn't want that, not for her, not for his children."

"So he cut her off," Walk said, sadly.

"Just about the hardest thing I've ever done. Turning her away like that. He told her move on, find someone else. She still came, a year she waited, in case he changed his mind. And then nothing. I figured she'd found a way to move past."

"She did. Not past, just a way to feel nothing."

Cuddy said nothing but he knew. There wasn't a tragedy of any kind he had not witnessed or seen the fallout from.

"So you didn't know any of it?" Cuddy asked.

"No. Star knew what I would've said. That she needed to look out for herself. That it wasn't helping, dwelling on the past. Like I know. Like I'm one to talk. Maybe they needed something just for them. Their small family, broken, but theirs."

When they reached the gate Walk shook his hand. "Thank you, Cuddy. You did a good thing."

"Can I ask, why now? What brought you back?"

"Chance. Vincent wanted me to scatter his ashes in the Elkton-Trinity. I'm not even sure why."

Cuddy smiled, then took hold of Walk's shoulder and pointed. "That's Vincent's cell up there. Eleven-three. Thirty years looking out. You see what it faces."

Walk turned.

And there, above the ranging hills, he saw the two million acres of freedom.

47

It was a fine fall morning, bright sunlight crossed the mountain behind. Duchess rode the gray, the two heading out together each day, before Montana woke. She knew the trails well enough now, breath billowed, the gray content to go slow, she would not run well again. Duchess stroked her as they stood atop the butte and looked out over the ranch.

The house was sawn timber and beautiful, fire burned, the chimney smoked. There were barns, a river she had followed three miles through aspens before seeing wolf tracks and quickly retreating. She had a knife, her grandfather's, and on weekends she would explore alone, cut paths into the shrubland, stepping through shallow water tables crafted by the fall.

The months that had followed had been long and difficult, but she found the new surrounding helped. She took it back to breathing, like Hal had once told her, and though it did hurt, all of it, she knew time was all-powerful.

When she reached the stable she led the gray in, made sure she had water and straw, and patted her nose.

She found Dolly in the kitchen, reading a newspaper, the smell of coffee rich in the air. Duchess had gone to her, turned up at midnight and made good on her promise. At first she had agreed to stay one night, the next morning Dolly had led her to the stable and showed her the gray, which she'd taken for free after they settled Hal's estate.

One day had led to a week, which turned to a month and more. Dolly acted on the pretense of needing help with the land, though she was wealthy enough to have several men stop by each week. Duchess worked hard, stayed out from dawn till the sun fell away. They did not speak much at first, the girl so beaten Dolly knew it was only in time she could help her.

Dolly broached the subject of formal adoption one morning, as they swept chokecherry leaves from the driveway. Duchess said nothing for three days, then told Dolly if she was stupid enough to want her as a daughter then she should see a doctor. But if he gave her a clean bill then yes, she would like to stay.

Duchess kicked her boots off. "I need to earn some money."

Dolly looked up from her newspaper.

"I owe someone. I need to pay it back."

"I can give you—"

"I have to earn it myself. Outlaws settle their debts." She hadn't yet figured out how to track down Hank and Busy. She'd start at the motel, make calls. She would make things right.

Duchess went to pass her, stopped when Dolly held up a letter.

"This came for you."

Duchess took it from her. She saw the Cape Haven stamp and retreated to her bedroom, which she had painted a shade of green that matched the hills.

She closed the door behind her and settled into the big chair by the window.

She knew the writing, small enough that she imagined Walk spent a week composing it.

She read it slowly. He apologized for lying in court, for shaking her faith in him. He told her sometimes people did the wrong thing for the right reason.

For twenty pages he spoke of his life and her mother's, a young Vincent King and Martha May. He told her how he was sick, and how he used to be ashamed of it, and scared of losing his place. And of place he rambled for a page before he got to it, and told her the kind of truth that saw her drop the papers, stand and pace her room.

When she calmed she gathered them up and read on. He told her of Vincent, of the blood in her veins, and how she should not feel sad but proud. Of how her mother had always loved him, and had kept that love alive through the harshest of conditions. He mentioned Vincent's torture, of how he could not atone for the life he had stolen. She was loved though, that's what he said. She and her brother were born of the most unbreakable love.

Enclosed was a single photo, Walk on a rusting boat, the sign new, CAPE HAVEN FISHING. In the water Duchess saw the reflection, a small lady with dark hair, holding the camera, the widest smile on her face.

And along with the photograph was a legal document that was Vincent King's last will and testament.

Later, Dolly would tell her that she, along with Robin, now owned a grand house in Cape Haven. Vincent had been restoring it for them. And that they need not do anything yet, but one day she could visit, or sell it, or do whatever she pleased. In the space of a little time she had gone from having nothing, to something, the future still uncertain but it was there.

That night she lay awake and thought of all that had gone before, what she had learned and what she would forget. She had been waiting, healing, getting strong enough again.

The next morning she told Dolly she was ready.

48

The town announced itself without fuss, just a small sign that told its name.

Owl Creek.

Dolly had a friend in Rexburg, they'd made the drive overnight. From there Duchess had ridden the bus herself. Dolly had asked once if she needed her. Duchess told her no, but thank you.

The bus was long, silver with red and blue detail. When it pulled over she grabbed her bag and stood, walked her way down the aisle and stepped out into Wyoming air.

The driver called and wished her safe travel, closed the door, and moved on. She cast a last look at the windows, reflected stares, a couple of smiles. The smell of the engine, mechanical heat.

She walked with her head down now, since that day, quieter than she had been before.

She passed the Capitol Hotel. Awnings hung over the kind of stores that beguiled well-heeled visitors to shop their windows. Lacey's Pottery, Aldon Antiques, the Pressly Flower Shop.

Past the Carnegie Library, the sun low and heavy over the Bighorns, the vista of rolling plains before it. She breathed deep, her back ached from the seat. She freshened up in the restroom of a shiny gas station, wanted her hair to be just right beneath her hat.

She carried a small map, where she needed to be was circled and didn't look all that far. She walked less than a mile and came to a wide patch of grass bordered by pretty houses.

Another road and she found it.

Owl Creek Elementary.

The building was low, signs painted white, flowers broke from hanging baskets. Across was another patch of grass, and beyond that a large oak that reminded her of the wishing tree. She made her way over, stood beneath the arms then sat on a shaded patch of leaves so orange she scooped one up and held it toward the sky.

In her bag was a bottle of water and she drank a little, saving some for later. She had a candy bar but was too nervous to eat.

The first car pulled up, then another, but most, she noticed, walked their way through the town to collect their children.

She saw Peter right off, Jet tugging on his leash, Peter smiling hello to just about everyone.

She clutched her chest when the first children came out. She fussed with her hat, then retied her sneaker. She wore her best dress, yellow, his favorite color.

She gasped when she saw him.

He looked taller, his hair cut shorter, his smile unalloyed and beautiful. She knew he would one day be a heartbreaker.

Beside him was Lucy, and he gripped her hand tight as she led him to the end of the path. And then he saw Peter, and Robin ran toward him and Peter scooped him up and they hugged tight, for a long time, her brother's eyes closed.

Peter set Robin down and handed him the leash, Jet jumping up and licking his face, Robin laughing. Duchess stood rooted as Peter led them to the small park beside, pushed Robin on the swing, helped him up the steps then collected him at the bottom of the tall slide.

She watched them, felt each of his smiles as if they were her own, heard his laughter carry far. Lucy joined them, she carried a bag, papers spilling from it. When Robin saw her he ran toward her like it had been the longest time.

Duchess moved when they did, stayed a good distance behind, but they would not have noticed her. She tried to call out, several times, so quiet she could barely get out his name.

They lived in a nice home. Green clapboard, white shutters, neat yard. The kind of house she had once dreamed of finding for them.

They had a mailbox, *The Laytons*. She walked up their street as the sun dropped, Wyoming sky coming at her with such delicate beauty. She checked out the neighbors, saw kids, bikes, a bat and ball.

When dusk fell she made her way back and slipped down the side of their place, into the yard. A swing set, a barbecue, a bug motel.

For a long time she stood frozen, night replaced day with so many stars.

She made her way to the porch, took the steps and stopped by the window. The light burned from inside, the perfect scene played. Lucy with Robin, helping him with his reading, Peter at the counter, calling out dinner, a plate for each of them. They sat together, the television on but muted, Jet beside Robin, his eyes expectant.

Robin finished every bite.

She watched them till it was time, till Peter kissed Robin's head gently, and Lucy took the reading book and his hand and led him up the stairs.

She wondered if he would remember all they had been through. She knew there was a good chance he would not, not the detail. He was young enough to be anyone. The world was his. He was a prince, and, finally, she understood why.

She was not a girl that cried, but right then tears fell as she allowed the dam to break.

She cried for everything she had lost, and everything he had found.

Duchess pressed her palm to the glass and said goodbye to her brother.

49

Duchess took to her bedroom for the next few days.

Dolly knew to give her time, space, room to breathe, despite the worry. She left her meals outside the door, checked in only once, to ask if she'd like help tending the gray that morning. Inside she found Duchess at her small desk, sunlight on her as she wrote.

Monday and Duchess walked into class with Thomas Noble.

"Did you finish?" he said.

"Yeah."

It had been a free assignment, a report of their choosing. She watched kids stand at the front and speak of things as varied as Jefferson and football, summer vacation and how to track a whitetail.

When the teacher called her, Duchess walked to the front of the class, fixed her paper to the board, and swallowed down her nerves. She shoved her hands deep in her pockets and stood before her family tree.

Complete.

She felt all the eyes on her as she glanced at Thomas Noble, who smiled and motioned for her to start.

Duchess cleared her throat, turned to the front and began. She led with her father, the outlaw, Vincent King.

ACKNOWLEDGMENTS

This one took a long time to write. I was fortunate enough to have help from the very best in the business. Without them this book would not exist.

Amy Einhorn. I don't even know where to begin here. Thank you for taking a chance, and for helping to turn this into the book I dreamed of writing. You've gone above and beyond, you've worked so incredibly hard. You are the absolute best and I'm acutely aware of how lucky I am to work with you.

Conor Mintzer. The Con Man. Con Air. Thank for you glancing my way, for your sublime editorial touch, and for the mesmeric catches. There's no one I'd rather disgrace myself in Vegas with. I love you, buddy.

Maggie Richards, for everything. (I was going to say for masterminding world domination but that makes you sound a bit like a Bond villain.)

Pat Eisemann and Catryn Silbersack, publicity titans. I am eternally grateful to you for getting this book out there. Your bribe game is strong.

Caitlin O'Shaughnessy, for taking me to market and ensuring I return with more than just magic beans.

Chris Sergio and Karen Horton, thanks to you I'm very happy if people judge this one by its cover.

Jason Reigal, for turning my words into something I can force my loved ones/anyone I make eye contact with to pay for.

Kenn Russell, I bow down to your greatness (Conor referred to you as a "czar").

Maggie Carr. There's copyedits, and then there's a *Maggie Carr copyedit*. Thanks for the jaw-dropping detail and for making me smile in the margins. If they pay by the mistake then I'm pretty sure I've made you a millionaire.

Meryl Levavi, for the beautiful design. My wife caught me stroking the pages.

John Hart, for being so gracious in the stalkerish face of my email bombardment.

My fellow authors, for being so generous with your words.

Cath Summerhayes and my Curtis Brown family.

Katherine Armstrong and my Bonnier family.

Victoria Whitaker and my annoying family.

To the people reading this, it's like staying in your seat when the credits roll. I love you for it. Let's do it all again soon.

Recommend *We Begin at the End*
for your next book club!
Reading Group Guide available at:
www.readinggroupgold.com

About the Author

Chris Whitaker lives in the United Kingdom with his wife and three young children. When not writing he works part-time at a local library, where he gets to surround himself with books. Follow Chris on Twitter @WhittyAuthor.

A LETTER TO THE BARNES & NOBLE READER

It's 1 a.m. and I've just received an email from Amy, my editor, telling me that *We Begin at the End* will be the Barnes & Noble Book Club selection for March. To say this is beyond my wildest dreams is an understatement.

Things like this don't happen to people like me.

I'm lying in bed, in my house, in the small town I live in just outside of London. A world away from the setting of this book, from the lives I write about.

This feels like the culmination of a journey that began twenty years ago.

I look across at my newborn baby daughter, who sleeps in our room, since she's up so often she'd wake the other kids. She looks back, and for a moment it feels like we're the only people awake in the world. I know I have no chance at all of getting back to sleep, so I take her over to my desk and can't help but wonder if one day she'll pick up this book and read what I'm about to write. The thought is both heartwarming and terrifying.

I think a lot about what it means to be a good parent, and a good person. I'm not sure I manage either all that well.

I've been asked to consider writing, what it means to me, and how this story came to be. It's hard to explain. It's more than I can put into words. Because, in truth, writing saved my life. Twice.

I've always struggled with the concept of asking for help. To me it seemed like acknowledging a failure, raising a hand and declaring myself inadequate. Mental health is in the news every day, in theory it's never been more acceptable to talk about, yet I still find it difficult to write this.

My dad left my family when I was five. He started again, rented an apartment, but was still entirely there for me. He's a strong person, I've never seen him afraid. My mum worked in a bakery during the day and a liquor store in the evening, just to pay the bills. I never saw her admit that she was struggling, I never saw her as anything less than perfectly happy.

Like them, I work hard, but to the point where I become obsessive, writing a book can feel like life or death. I was fanatical in preparing for my university entrance exams, and then, the night before, I got so drunk I woke up in the hospital.

So, no surprise, I didn't go to university. I had no idea what I wanted to do. I bounced from job to job. I worked in supermarkets and bars, sold electrical cabling. It was when I was out dropping leaflets that I was mugged.

I was nineteen, an age when it's too easy to blur the line between fearless and foolish. It was early in the day, the street was quiet. A man approached and asked for my wallet and cell phone. We struggled. It was fairly evenly matched, for a while at least. And then he pulled out a kitchen knife. I didn't run. I wonder now why that was. I don't think it makes me brave, and I'd certainly tell my own children to run away in that situation. He stabbed me a couple of times, in the side. I still have the scars. And then he brought the knife up and aimed for the center of my chest. I grabbed his hand. He dropped the knife. I dropped my wallet. He picked up both and ran off. I stood there bleeding until he was gone, then drove myself to the hospital, where they stitched me back together again.

Reading that back now, I find I'm clutching my daughter tightly. It sounds pretty traumatic, but at the time I remember thinking it could've been much worse. Bad things happen every day, we all know that, we just hope they won't happen to us. Wrong place, wrong time. I joked about it with my dad. I think he was proud of me.

I stopped sleeping after that. I didn't eat much. I kept making jokes. Shrug it off and move on, that's what I told myself. I felt really down and couldn't work out what was happening to me. I went to see a doctor and he prescribed me antidepressants. I threw them in the garbage.

We moved houses, my brother graduated from university and we had a party, I went away for the weekend with my girlfriend. Life went on.

They all thought I was fine.

I remember trying to read a book and being stuck on the same page for hours. I'd try and watch a movie, then totally forget the plot. I tried running, but ended up running so far I had to catch a bus back home. Even now, it's hard to accurately put into words just how bad it was. I stood in front of a mirror and didn't recognize myself. I just wasn't me anymore.

I started drinking and taking drugs, often alone, because it made me feel nothing for a while. I didn't know how to cope with what had happened or how to ask for help. I didn't even want to ask for help. I just wanted to die.

Outwardly, there was no preamble to my suicidal thoughts, no cry for help, not even a whisper. And yet I don't think it would have come as a huge shock to those who really know me. I can be a bit all or nothing, I'll drown myself before remembering to breathe. This was my way out, my way to both fix and break myself. And so I began hoarding painkillers, then sat down, took out a paper and pen, and wrote. It wasn't some grand farewell, or even an apology, it was just me writing my story in the hope it might help my parents understand.

And as I was writing, I remembered a technique I'd read about in a self-help book I'd borrowed from the library. The library had always been my refuge, the place I went to shut out my world and inhabit another. The smell, the calm, the kind smile of the librarian as she noted the book I was borrowing. Back then I imagined another life, where I had my shit together, started a family, worked in the library, and found a reason to smile each day.

The technique was simple enough. You take the traumatic incident, and you write about it. Only you completely change the people involved, the setting, the outcome. A girl appeared on the page, close to fully formed. I had such a strong vision of her. Outwardly small, fragile, and vulnerable. My grandfather was a big Johnny Cash fan, so I grew up listening to "A Boy Named Sue." I named Duchess with him in mind. So, from her name, to her family, to the cowboy hat that swamped her, everything about Duchess screamed victim. Yet in her hand she carried a gun, a sign that even though she was afraid, she was choosing to fight. And as strange as it sounds, she felt real then. I needed her to feel real.

I moved the setting four thousand miles away, to a place I'd dreamed of visiting. My most treasured childhood memory was traveling to the US with my father. In line at Walt Disney World we met a family from Montana, and they told us we needed to visit. They described an expanse of beauty, crystalline air, a place I imagined clarity of thought is easier to find. *It's like switching from portrait to landscape.*

And as for the outcome, I still wasn't sure, but for the first time in a long time it didn't seem quite so dark. I wrote till the early hours. And then I slept; for the first time in close to a year I properly slept. The next morning I wrote some more. It wasn't a quick fix, magic-pill type of solution, but it got me through the night.

A week later I was involved in a car accident. I'd been drinking heavily and drove my car off the side of the road. I escaped with cuts and bruises, and was again stitched back together again. My mum was understandably disappointed in me. I really wanted to tell her what was going on with me, to help her see what was happening. Instead I turned back to writing.

The days slowly grew lighter, but when I felt the world struggling to turn, I'd sit and write a little more. Sometimes just a line, sometimes a page or two. It was more than an exercise in self-control, in self-preservation. I drew comfort from Duchess in a way I couldn't from anyone or anything in the outside world. I wrote her struggles and thoughts as if they were my own. I'd spend a month working on a single paragraph, reworking the detail until I could see what she saw, and feel what she felt. I suppose it was a way to leave myself behind, to take a vacation from problems I couldn't ever imagine overcoming. And writing this girl, who undoubtedly had it worse than me, who still managed to be so brave and fierce, turned into a reminder that no matter how lost we feel, we can still find our way back.

A long year passed before I gave some thought to the future. And then I read an article about a stockbroker, and he had this amazing life and in the photograph he looked so happy.

"I'm going to be a stockbroker," I announced to my brother.

He looked up from his breakfast and frowned. "You're shit at math and you fucked up at school."

I paid for my exams with my credit card, marched into the city with my (awful) CV, and managed to find an entry-level job. I threw myself into my new career with the kind of gusto that didn't leave time to dwell on the past, let alone write a self-help exercise about a young girl in Montana. Eighty-hour weeks. Sleeping at my desk.

My parents were proud of me. I felt like I'd turned a corner and left behind that boy who was afraid to look in the mirror.

I eventually worked my way onto a trading desk.

"You lose twenty thousand dollars and you stop trading, and we sit down and work out what went wrong. That's the only rule," my boss told me on that first morning.

The next day I lost two million dollars.

I'd broken my trading limits, then channeled my inner Nick Leeson and hidden the loss. I was young, stupid, and largely unaware of just how serious the situation was. Inevitably, I was caught. I sat down with my bosses as they contemplated going to the police. They certainly could have. Instead, and I'm eternally grateful to them for this, they agreed to let me work to pay back half of it.

That day I left the office owing them a million dollars.

I was twenty-four years old.

I stopped sleeping. I stopped eating. I didn't tell my family. I got engaged to my girlfriend and we planned a wedding. I started drinking and taking drugs again. I was unable to ride the train into work without some chemical assistance.

I still maintained that happy and successful façade, but behind closed doors I was in serious trouble again. As the wedding costs spiraled, I once again began to think of a way out. In the day we'd be viewing churches, at night I'd be checking the terms of my life insurance policy.

And so, for the first time in years, I went back to Montana, to pick up where I'd left off, to see how that fragile girl was getting on. I went back to writing each day, sometimes all night.

Duchess saved me. Writing her helped when nothing else could, giving me grounding and purpose. Even on our honeymoon I would sit up writing when my wife thought I was sleeping.

It took years to work off the debt, but I did. And again I was the person I wanted to be. I was successful. My parents were proud. But then I started slipping. I took pills because I couldn't sleep at night, and more drugs to make me feel human during the day. The hardest thing was, this time there was no reason for it. I wondered if there was something innately wrong with me. I wondered why I couldn't just be, why I couldn't just fit somewhere and stay there. I looked around at friends—they worried about jobs and mortgages, and where to go on vacation. I worried that sometimes I found breathing too difficult; that the only time I felt close to sane was when I spent time with Duchess, and now Walk and Martha and Vincent.

I didn't give serious thought to writing a book until I came across an interview with John Hart, my favorite author. I learned that he had turned his back on a successful law career in order to follow his dream and, I guess, to do something that made him happy.

My friends thought I was mad when I quit my job. Nearing thirty, I had the chance to secure our future. My wife was pregnant at the time. We lived in a nice apartment and drove a nice car. But I needed the change. I needed to stop projecting and start living. That night my wife and I talked until the early hours. I didn't feel deserving of her support and belief, but she gave me both without question. That selfless act is one of the countless reasons I love her. The next day we made a big decision.

"I'm moving to Spain to write a book," I announced to my brother.

He looked up from his beer and frowned. "You're shit at spelling and you don't speak Spanish."

In Spain I wrote every minute of every day. I felt that constant draw to return to Montana. But in truth it was too hard, the memories too raw. I wasn't close to ready.

Instead I worked on my debut novel, *Tall Oaks*. I set it in the US; I still clung to that childhood memory, the country so close to my heart. I'd grown up reading Stephen King, cherishing each trip to Castle Rock. America became more than a place to escape to. The landscape, the diversity, the sheer breathtaking size allowed my imagination to soar, giving me a sense of freedom in the stories I could tell, and the characters I could create.

On our return to the UK, *Tall Oaks* was plucked from the slush pile and I landed an agent and publishing deal. The book was shortlisted for a major prize. I went to a fancy award ceremony and was very much the long shot, very much out of my depth. I was up against big-name bestsellers but, to my eternal amazement, *Tall Oaks* won.

When we got back to our hotel room, I looked at my wife and she burst into tears. It had been a long and difficult road, not just for me.

I now write constantly. I still allow the words to drive me totally mad, and I still have trouble sleeping. If I'm honest, the fear of slipping again is my constant companion, whispering in my ear when I'm feeling low, tempering the gains when things are going well. I feel better now. Maybe I haven't exorcised my demons, but sometimes just granting acceptance to our flaws can allow us to focus on what is, rather than what was or what might be.

Another book, another few years passed. Every day I heard the call of Duchess, the story I'd begun but never had the courage to end. Nearly twenty years had passed.

I knew it would be difficult, but I also knew I had to finish what I'd started.

We Begin at the End is, by some distance, my greatest achievement (if my children are reading this, apologies). And it's not because it took many years, working three jobs to complete. Or the fact that I've had major help from Amy and the most talented team at Henry Holt.

It's because my heart is on every page. It's because I took my experiences of trying to live in the shadow of past events and poured them into this story. It's both huge in scope and intensely personal. So while it is a crime novel looking at revenge, and where that can lead, it's also so much more. It's a book about family, the evolving meaning of that word, and the joys and burdens it brings. It's a book about first love, self-sacrifice, the concept of good and bad and the shades of gray between. It's a story of a girl struggling through each day, and the policeman holding too tightly to an ideal. It's a story of mistakes, of picking ourselves up and putting one foot in front of the other.

And most of all it's a story of forgiveness, both for ourselves and for the people who have hurt us.

It's 6 a.m. and the sun is rising. I work in the library now, and I'm due there in a few short hours. I check my email and see a message from John Hart, telling me how much he enjoyed the book. I reply, resisting the urge to tell him he probably helped save my life. He'd think I was a total loon.

I look down and my baby daughter is asleep on my lap. I wish I could spend more time with her, though I know my career change was the right decision.

Because although I earn less, I smile more.

When Amy asked me to write something for Barnes & Noble, I'm not sure this is what she had in mind. But I wanted to convey just how much writing has helped me, and just how grateful I am for you taking a chance on this book. You'll never know how much it means to me. Thank you.

CHRIS WHITAKER
December 1, 2020

Welcome to the Book Club Guide for *We Begin at the End*. Please note: In order to provide reading groups with the most informed and thought-provoking questions possible, it is necessary to reveal important aspects of the plot of this novel—as well as the ending. If you have not finished reading *We Begin at the End*, you may want to wait before reviewing this guide.

1. What do you think about the character and place names in this book? Do you think the author had anything in mind when choosing them? Did you note any literary allusions? Suggested names to consider include: Duchess, Robin, Darke, King, Bitterwater, Walk, Radley, Star, Sissy, and Cape Haven.

2. Duchess says to Walk, "There's always a man. Whenever anything fucked-up happens in the world, there's always a man." (chapter 1, p. 10). Later, Duchess thinks about Darke: "She knew what men could do, all of them, capability was enough." (chapter 24, p. 199). What do you make of the portrayal of each gender in this book? Are men or women worse in this novel, or might they be equally good or bad?

3. Star tells her daughter, "Selfless acts, Duchess. They're what make you a good person" (chapter 5, p. 42), yet she seems to be entirely selfish in many of her actions. Why do you think this is? Do you agree with Star? What makes a good person good?

4. Hal asks Duchess, "If the good stand by idle, are they still good?" (chapter 25, p. 204). What do you think? Are there any ostensibly good characters in this novel who lose their goodness by standing by?

5. Hal tells Duchess: "I am a constant disappointment to myself" (chapter 25, p. 207). Why do you think he feels this way? What could he have done differently in his life? Is self-disappointment what makes people decent?

6. Considering Walk's intervention, Duchess thinks: " . . . sometimes adults thought watching out meant doing shit that'd lead to the kind of consequences that rippled far from them." (chapter 6, p. 48). In this novel, are good intentions a dangerous thing?

7. Duchess addresses Vincent: "'Freedom,' she said. 'Is it the worst thing to take? Worse than anything. Maybe it is'" (chapter 6, p. 53). Later, talking about Vincent, Hal tells Duchess: "After that night, after what he did, he knew none of us would find freedom again" (chapter 25, p. 208). Why do you think Duchess asks Vincent this? What could be worse than losing freedom? Do any of the characters reclaim it?

8. Star says to Walk: "You're like a kid. Better and worse. Bad and good. None of us are any one thing. We're just a collection of the best and worst things we've done" (chapter 8, p. 67). Later, Duchess talks about Dolly's abusive father to Hal: "Some people are all dark" (chapter 25, p. 203). But Hal, thinking about Sissy, tells Duchess, "But with children . . . there is no bad" (chapter 25, p. 206). Are any of the characters in this novel morally pure in either direction?

9. Star believes "the universe finds a way to balance the good and the bad" (chapter 8, p. 67). Thinking about the story, do you agree with her?

10. Duchess asks, "You believe in an eye for eye, Walk?" (chapter 11, p. 93). Later, we see that Duchess "knew that lives could be colored so bold by revenge they ate away all the good a person might have once had" (chapter 32, p. 257). Duchess and Dolly discuss retribution (chapter 40, p. 315):

> "Do you know about justice, Duchess?"
>
> "Three-Fingered Jack. He rode five hundred miles to avenge the death of his partner, Frank Stiles."
>
> "But what do you think it means? And I don't mean defined, I mean what do you think it means for the people that get hurt."

What does this novel say about revenge? Is it a worthy aim? Are its consequences certain? What impact does the desire for revenge have on the avenger? Is true justice possible? What does it look like for those who have been harmed? Can they ever truly be "made whole"?

11. Warden Cuddy and Walk discuss morality (chapter 13, p. 114):

> "But then maybe there aren't degrees of bad. Maybe it doesn't matter by how much you cross the line."
>
> "Most people get near. At least once in their life."
>
> "Not you, Walk."

Is there a moral line that, once crossed, cannot be retraced?

12. Cuddy tells Walk that he sees himself in Vincent: "His life and mine. They aren't all that different, save for a single mistake" (chapter 13, p. 114). Later, explaining to Duchess how Star found out that he'd sent Baxter to kill Vincent, Hal says, "All and everything. A single act on a

distant night and here we are because of it'" (chapter 25, p. 217). Is it fair for one mistake to forever change a life? What does this novel say about the possibility of forgiveness for mistakes?

13. Walk "sometimes wondered about the damage done that night, immeasurable, the spiderweb of hurt that culled so many lives, replacing the new with the old, the fresh with decay. He saw it in Star and had seen it in her father, but none more so than Duchess, who carried that night long before she was born" (chapter 4, p. 24). Vincent says to Walk, "Guilt is decided long before the act is committed. People just don't realize it. They think they have a choice. They look back, play it different, sliding doors, but they never really did" (chapter 13, pp. 116–17). Shortly after Hal is murdered, Duchess tells Walk: "Free will is an illusion, sooner you accept the sooner you get on'" (chapter 28, p. 231). Duchess wonders to Dolly: "Maybe you don't choose who you get to be. Maybe it's predefined" (chapter 40, p. 315). Toward the end of the novel, Duchess "thought of the making of a murder, if it began long before birth, cursing the parents' genes, the fatal bloodline. Or maybe it slowly crept, too many knocks, too many scars" (chapter 45, p. 347). Is free will an illusion in this novel? Do characters have control over their lives? Do they believe they do?

14. Is Duchess right to tell Robin several times that he doesn't ever need to apologize to her? Why does she tell him that?

15. At school, Duchess learns that the triangle is the strongest shape (chapter 23, p. 189). How is this fact reflected in her life? What's the strongest trio of characters in this novel?

16. Talking to Duchess about Sissy's death, Hal says, "'I know it was an accident . . . I do know that. But that doesn't really mean anything'" (chapter 25, p. 205). Explaining in a letter to Duchess about why he

lied in court, Walk writes, " . . . sometimes people did the wrong thing for the right reason" (chapter 47, p. 362). Does the fact of an act matter more than the intention—or lack thereof—behind that act?

17. "It was cold, no matter how he felt, it was a cold and cruel thing to do. When she saw him she remembered the darkest part of her life, and she always would" (chapter 27, p. 221). Is Walk selfish to try to come back into Martha's life?

18. Duchess tells Walk, "Ours is a small story, Chief Walker. Sad enough, but small. Let's not pretend different" (chapter 28, p. 233). Why do you think Duchess says this? Why does she revert to calling him "Chief Walker"?

19. Duchess derides Thomas Noble, telling him: "You sound like a child. The notion of fair" (chapter 40, p. 311). Why do you think he believes in fairness and Duchess does not? Is the world of this novel fair?

20. About Walk, Duchess thinks: "Star said he was all good, like that was a thing" (chapter 1, p. 10). Did Walk do the right thing in killing Darke?

21. About Robin, Vincent tells Walk: "I couldn't let him be me" (chapter 44, p. 344). What do you think Vincent meant?

22. Vincent says about Sissy, "' . . . each one of my breaths is stolen from her" (chapter 44, p. 342). Duchess says to Walk: "I can't decide if suicide is the most selfish or selfless act" (chapter 1, p. 11). Is Vincent too harsh on himself? Did he do the right thing in killing himself?

23. Do you think Duchess would have shot Vincent if he hadn't gone over the cliff's end (chapter 45, p. 351)?

24. To his doctor near the beginning of the story, Walk says: "I tell you, you ever see me wasting my days on some fishing boat, you just come down and shoot me" (chapter 7, p. 58), yet this seems to be the life he chooses at the end. Later Walk thinks, "The future was a frightening thing, but then he reasoned it always had been" (chapter 46, p. 357). Why has Walk changed his mind? What does this frightening future mean with regard to Walk? Is Walk better off at the beginning or the end of the novel?

25. Duchess asks Thomas Noble, "You think there's such a thing as a truly selfless act . . . ?" (chapter 31, p. 248). Does Duchess find out the answer to this question by the end of the story? Do you think there is such a thing?

26. Why do you think Duchess leaves Robin with Peter and Lucy? Did she do the right thing in letting him stay with the Laytons rather than reclaiming him (chapter 48, p. 366)? Is this her truly selfless act?

27. Is Darke a good person? Why do you think he gives the gun back to Vincent?

28. Why do you think Duchess clings to the belief that she is an outlaw? Why does she reference outlaws throughout the book?

29. Do you think each character gets the ending they deserve?

30. Why do you think the author named this book what he did? Do you think the title fits the book? Why or why not?